T0089184

Tales of Pannithor

KINGS OF WAR

Rise of the Celestians

By

C.L. Werner

ZMOK
BOOKS

Tales of Pannithor: Rise of the Celestians
By C. L. Werner
Cover from
This edition published in 2022

Zmok Books is an imprint of

Winged Hussar Publishing, LLC
1525 Hulse Rd, Unit 1
Point Pleasant, NJ 08742

Copyright © Winged Hussar Publishing
ISBN 978-1-950423-14-9
ISBN 978-1-950423-90-3
LCN 2022932311

Bibliographical References and Index
1. Fantasy. 2. Celestians. 3. Pannithor
Winged Hussar Publishing, LLC All rights reserved
For more information
visit us at www.wingedhussarpublishing.com

Twitter: WingHusPubLLC
Facebook: Winged Hussar Publishing LLC

Timeline

-1100: First contact with the Celestians

Rise of the Celestians

-170: The God War

0: Creation of the Abyss

2676: Birth of modern Basilea, and what is known as the Common Era.

3001: Free Dwarfs declare their independence

3558: Golloch comes to power

3850: The expansion of the Abyss

Tales of Pannithor: Edge of the Abyss

3854: The flooding of the Abyss, the splintering of the Brotherhood, and Lord Darvled completing part of the wall on the Ardovikian Plains.

Nature's Knight

Drowned Secrets

Claws on the Plains

Steps to Deliverance

Pious

3865: Free Dwarfs begin the campaign to free Halpi – the opening of Halpi's Rift.

3866: Halflings leave the League of Rhordia

Broken Alliance

Chapter I

-1100, *Age of Nobility*

Reiliur Ythriil gazed into the magnificent crystal, his eyes drawn down into its unending depths. There was a sense of wonder and awe as he peered into the shimmering vistas, at the spectrum of worlds within worlds that flitted at the very edge of his vision. He tried to bring these images into focus, to narrow and confine the haze into clarity, but even his tremendous will was unable to compel them into distinct images. Frustration raged within him. This sphere had taken fifty years and many spells to cultivate, to grow into its current shape. It was the most powerful and magnificent of the seer-stones ever crafted by an elven wizard. The arcane calculations that went into its creation had been checked and verified over the course of decades and hundreds of experiments.

All the same, it did not work.

Reiliur turned from the onyx pedestal on which the seer-stone rested. He glanced about the laboratory with a dull, defeated gaze. A rounded hall with tiers of benches and desks that rose in intertwined rings almost to the amber dome which served as the tower's roof. His attention lingered on the bookshelves and the precious tomes they held. Wisdom and knowledge from generations of arcane pioneers, elves who'd pushed the boundaries and by their efforts had opened new vistas of exploration and possibility. Reiliur berated himself for the pride and arrogance that made him aspire to stand among their ranks.

One of Reiliur's students hurried over to his master. "Your theory is true. Do not let this one experiment defeat you." There was a desperate look on the young elf's face, his eyes imploring Reiliur to attend his words.

"It has all gone wrong," Reiliur replied. "I have invested too much hope, too many dreams into the Scrying Star. I believed it would open new worlds to our people, let us stride across lands beyond the reach of gods or mortals. New dimensions where new ideas could thrive and the old ways would be unknown." He gave his student a halfhearted smile. "I appreciate your concern, Calisor, but it is done. There's nothing else to do."

Reiliur could see that his words cut Calisor like a knife. Of all his disciples within the Circle of Heaven, Calisor was the most brilliant. He showed enormous potential. One day, he would far surpass the accomplishments of his teacher. *He* would earn a place among the great wizards. Reiliur, however, would vanish into obscurity. If he was remembered at all, it would be as a failure.

It was difficult for Reiliur to look across the faces of his other students. All of them were sympathetic to the anguish he felt. He could see from their drawn countenances that many of them shared, at least in part, his sense of failure and defeat. They had shared his ambition. Other seer-stones had enabled wizards to glimpse realms far from the lands of Pannithor. Reiliur had aspired to go much farther. He sought more than a tantalizing view of these places. He wanted to establish a connection between worlds, a bridge across realities.

Instead, all he found were fragments and shadows. The thrill of discovery had sickened into the morbidity of despair. Reiliur could almost envy the race of men. Their lives might be brief, but they did not feel as keenly as elves. They did not suffer the true depths of an emotion, only the veneer of it. Seldom did human passion approach anything experienced by an elf. Neither in joy nor sorrow. At the moment, Reiliur felt as though his heart would crack for the magnitude of his failure.

"Clear these things away," Reiliur told his students. He poured what authority he could muster into his voice, but the effect was still heavy with emotion. "We shall set ourselves upon a new endeavor," he added, trying to reassure his disciples. None of them stirred, not until Calisor intervened and repeated their master's orders. Then they began gathering the astronomical charts, the volumes of calculations, and the assorted paraphernalia devoted to the failed experiment.

Reiliur withdrew, stepping away from the laboratory and out onto the exterior balcony. The air outside was warm for the autumn, stirred only by a soft breeze. From this vantage atop the Tower of Heaven, he could see the glittering lights of Ileureleith below. Even at so late an hour, the great city was alive and vibrant. He could hear the strains of a bard plying his lyre while the enchanting voice of a songstress related the tragic love between an elven lord and a human maiden. The sad song only added to Reiliur's own grief. Frowning, he looked away from the city below and cast his attention farther afield.

Across the benighted landscape, Reiliur could see the glow of villages and towns. He could see the silvery aura of the old forests, the sacred groves where no tree had known the threat of axe or saw. These ancient forests had a magic all their own, though it seemed only the elves could appreciate it. Even the mostly civilized men of Primovantor were blind to the majesty of the old forests, seeing only timber to harvest and earth to till. The ignorance of men darkened Reiliur's mood. He looked even further for distraction.

The great aura that shone about the Glades of Adar, a sight that usually captivated him, did nothing to stir his soul. The wizard drew upon his arcane power, filling his eyes with a mage-sight that could transcend leagues. At the limit of his enhanced vision, just a shining light on the horizon, Reiliur could see Therennia Adar, the grand capital of Elvenholme. He always felt small when he looked toward the fabulous city, remembering its unrivaled magnificence, its art and splendor. What could even a wizard accomplish that should be as enduring as Therennia Adar?

Suddenly a thought came to Reiliur. A strange, abstract thought that fumbled around inside his mind before assuming any cohesion. It was an old mantra taught to him long ago by his father. *Pride is the bane of greatness.* The wizard ruminated on this lesson, wondering what import it could have for him now. He had failed in his gambit toward greatness, so pride could work no mischief now. Or could it? Perhaps the lesson wasn't that pride would poison greatness, but that it would prevent greatness from being achieved?

Reiliur rushed back into the laboratory. He saw that two of his students, under Calisor's direction, were going to remove the Scrying Star from its pedestal. "Leave that as it is!" he shouted to them. He looked across the startled faces of his disciples. "We will try again. Just as before. Resume your places and begin your incantations."

"You've discovered why the experiment failed?" Calisor asked, his excitement rising to match that of his teacher.

"The one factor which I, in my pride, did not consider," Reiliur said. He slapped his hand against his chest. "The most fragile component of them all. Me." He smiled at Calisor's confusion. "We forget that for all our accomplishments, the elven people have limitations. We are vessels of flesh and spirit. Young by the reckoning of the cosmic vastness we would seek to penetrate."

Calisor nodded, but it was an expression of understanding, not agreement. "If the experiment is beyond the limitations of an elf, then why repeat it? Does it not follow that the ambition of this study is something outside our power?"

"Yes, and no," Reiliur answered. His eyes shone with intensity as he explained his epiphany. "We know that there are things far older than we. Earth and sea, sky and stars, all these things were before the first elf opened his eyes. The gods walked the world before us, and who can say how many other worlds they visited before that? Who can say that there are not others, in the vastness of reality, that awakened in strange eons before the birth of the elven race?"

"But how will this hypothesis help your experiment?" Calisor wanted to know. Reiliur could almost see his disciple's keen mind racing to follow these ideas to their end point.

"If my own limitations aren't enough to reach out past the veil," Reiliur said, "then I will try to entice a higher intelligence to reach past the veil to me."

The answer troubled Calisor. "It could be dangerous. We've only had the most fleeting glimpses through the seer-stones before. There's no way of knowing what world will reach back to you, if indeed any can. What if what responds is harmful? You would put yourself at great risk."

Reiliur shook his head and walked to the Scrying Star. "No. I reject that concern. Any mind that responds to my searching must, by necessity, be greater and more advanced than my own. Such could be accomplished only with the consequent moral restraint and goodness..."

Calisor raised a further objection. "Men are neither as restrained nor good as elves, yet in their crude ways, they surpass us in their magic."

"You speak of the crude and unreliable sorcery of men as a parable of caution," Reiliur laughed. "Dismiss such worries. Only a superior intelligence will be able to reach out to me. Because it is superior, it must likewise be good. Beyond the petty, base urges that govern men." He turned from Calisor and set his hands against the cold surface of the crystal.

"You will see," Reiliur told his disciple. Then he focused his entire being into the shimmering depths of the Scrying Star. Body, mind, and spirit, everything that composed Reiliur Ythriil was committed to the task. He ignored the panoply of images that flitted at the very edge of his perception, all the other sensations that tried to drain his focus away from his purpose. He concentrated upon making that connection, on drawing the notice of an awareness greater than his own.

"I am Reiliur," the wizard muttered, sending his words through the crystal. "I am Reiliur," he repeated over and over. The long hours of night were fading into morning and the first light of day began to shine down through the amber dome.

"I am Reiliur." He sent his voice out into the darkness between worlds.

From out of that darkness, there finally came a response. A voice that touched his mind and shaped its intent into meaning. Into words Reiliur could understand.

"I am Eoswain," the voice from beyond announced.

Reiliur cried out in triumph. His hands were jolted away from the Scrying Star, thrown aside by a mighty crackle of electricity. He was sent reeling across the laboratory before collapsing against one of the desks. Calisor and the other students rushed to their master's aid. With smoke still rising from his singed hands, Reiliur waved them aside.

"An answer!" the wizard cried. He looked past the students to the Scrying Star. The crystal had taken on a sapphire glow, a light that shone from deep within its facets. "Rapport has been established! We must repeat the ritual! No, we will strengthen it! Summon the entire Circle of Heaven!

"I have heard a voice from beyond," Reiliur declared. "I must speak with her again!"

***

-1095, Time of Light

Atop the Tower of Heaven, the laboratory had undergone drastic changes since that historic morning when Reiliur Ythriil first heard the voice from beyond. The layered tiers that once rose in concentric rings had been broken down and removed. The shelves of precious books had been taken away, stuffed into the many arcane libraries maintained by the wizards of Ileureleith across the great city. The amber panes of the dome had been stripped away, replaced by a wondrous glass that altered both hue and opacity to suit the demands of the experiments being conducted. Though Reiliur had supervised the mixture of rare elements that were fired to create the glass, though he had been present to invoke the enchantments that went into each pane, even he understood little of their nature. Their design and function had come from beyond, from that same voice that had spoken to him all those years ago.

For five years, the wizard regarded by many to be the wisest and greatest mind in all Elvenholme had felt himself little more than a student. The knowledge Reiliur learned from Eoswain had opened new vistas of discovery to him, fantastic possibilities beyond his wildest imaginings. Through her guidance, the Circle of Heaven made incredible advances. To peer into a seer-stone and spy upon other worlds, once a feat beyond their magic, had become as commonplace as drawing water from a well. The elves had gone much farther. By magical processes, they'd grown gateways of crystal, portals that allowed the physical or spiritual passage of an explorer into other planes, realms beyond all mortal experience. The dream of walking upon other worlds had become a reality. No longer was the Circle of Heaven divided between master and pupil, for all of them were equal in the adventure of discovery.

Only one thing weighed upon Reiliur's spirit. Though the elves had now stepped across the barriers of reality and walked upon the earth of distant worlds, the domain they most wished to see was still beyond their reach. Most of all, they wanted to see the world wherein their benefactor Eoswain and her people, the Celestians, dwelt. Though Eoswain described a land of peace and plenty, and she could push into the minds of Reiliur and his companions the images of that world, it remained beyond their powers to gaze upon it themselves. The realm of the Celestians was too distant, too remote for the elves to reach. To journey there would be to pass through temporal distortions that would wither even the long-lived elves.

But if the way was shut to the elves, it didn't follow that the Celestians couldn't endure the journey. If the elves couldn't come to them, then the Celestians would simply have to make the journey to Pannithor.

"All is in readiness," Reiliur said as he walked about the laboratory. In removing the tiers, the Circle of Heaven had erected crystal gateways, portals by which they might make the journey to other worlds. Now these too had been taken away and replaced by twenty frames built on far grander and more magnificent scale. Each stood a dozen feet tall and was eight feet wide. The frame was of silver and malachite, forged by arcane fire. Within the boundaries of that frame was a sheet of molten diamond, restrained and bound by powerful glyphs and mighty enchantments.

"It has taken most of the Circle's wealth and resources to construct these gates," Calisor reminded Reiliur as he inspected the laboratory.

Reiliur smiled at the comment. "What will money mean to us after this? Do you realize that in a little while we shall help to usher in a new era? There is so much we can learn from the Celestians. Just think what we have accomplished by utilizing what Eoswain has taught us. And now we will bring twenty of her people to our world. Think what they will be like! Think how much we can learn from them!"

"I agree with your dreams," Calisor said. "But wouldn't it have been more prudent to build only one gate? To make certain everything will work?"

"There comes a time when risks must be taken." Reiliur gave Calisor a sharp look. "Besides, the Celestians have every confidence in this ritual. It is they who risk the most. If anything should be wrong, if there should be any flaw in the design and pattern, it is they who would be lost. They'd be drawn out into the black void, scattered in the emptiness between worlds. Even if they were gods, that would be a doom to be feared."

Calisor bowed his head in defeat. Reiliur sympathized with the young wizard's concerns, even if he couldn't share them. This was a debate they'd had many times since the plan to bring the Celestians to Pannithor was first discussed. Always they came back to the same place. "Prudence and caution are the chains that shackle dreams. To achieve anything of greatness, there must always be risk."

Reiliur turned from the gateways and moved toward the center of the room. Twenty of the Circle of Heaven's wizards sat upon the floor, their blue robes drawn about them. Around each, drawn in powdered adamantine, was a different cabbalistic symbol, an emblem exactingly copied from Eoswain's instructions. Little rivulets of liquid salt connected one symbol to another, creating a spider-web pattern across the laboratory. At the very center of the room, standing upon a raised dais, was the Scrying Star. Reiliur hurried up the few steps and laid his hands upon the crystalline sphere. Calisor took his place beside the elder wizard, ready to act if it needed an outsider's help to pull his teacher away. There had been incidents before when Reiliur had been seized by a fascination he couldn't break, held in a state of paralysis by the Scrying Star. Calisor was on hand to guard against that possibility.

"I am here. All is ready," Reiliur sent his thoughts racing into the crystal. He could see the image of Eoswain within the Scrying Star. Her face wasn't quite that of an elf but had within it all that made an elf beautiful. There was strength and wisdom in her features, both compassion and determination. Most of all, there was an eagerness that Reiliur recognized in himself - the excitement of discovery, the thrill of learning something unknown by anyone before you.

Eoswain's response reverberated through Reiliur's mind. "The constellations are in their proper alignment?"

Reiliur craned his neck back and stared up at the glass dome. As he did, the enchanted panes underwent a change. They magnified the stars overhead, intensifying them so that Reiliur felt as though they'd been drawn down into the laboratory for him to inspect. He quickly noted the positions of the ones vital to the ritual. "The dragon is in the house of the sword, and the kraken is in conjunction with the laughing dog."

"This alignment will not come again for a hundred of your years," Eoswain stated. "It is only at this auspicious moment that our worlds are in sympathy and the gates may be opened."

Reiliur looked again at the stars. He studied them closely to reassure himself that they were precisely where they needed to be. "We are ready," he told Eoswain.

"Then let us begin," the Celestian replied.

In the next moments, Reiliur had the eerie sensation of translocation. He knew he was standing in the laboratory on top of the Tower of Heaven. He could hear the Circle of Heaven begin their incantation. He could feel the air growing cold as the magic they invoked began to manifest. He could see the gateways and their panels of molten diamond begin to convulse, pulsating with an elemental power. A tremor vibrated through the floor, shivering up through the wizard's bones. Strange lights, motes of visualized sorcery, danced across his vision before being sucked down into one or another of the gates. Calisor's hand closed tightly around his belt, ready to pull the elder wizard back.

Yet at the same time, Reiliur knew he wasn't within the Tower of Heaven. He was standing in a stone amphitheater, ancient and fading to rubble. Strange weeds grew among the toppled stones, barbed vines with red leaves and opalescent flowers. Above in the sky, a weird sun shone, its rays warm and comforting after the chill of the laboratory. He could see a trio of moons overhead and the first twinkling of unknown stars. A twin-tailed bird with a beak that shone like rubies flew across the ruins and uttered a melodious cry as it passed overhead. As he followed the bird's flight, he found rolling hills covered in tall, lavender-hued grass that swayed and sighed in the gentle wind.

Never had he felt a sense of such tranquility and peace. Reiliur longed to escape into that paradise, but before he could move, he heard Eoswain's voice cry out to him.

"You must go back," she commanded. "You must remember who you are. You must remember your own dreams. Do not abandon yourself to a fantasy built by another."

So forceful was Eoswain's compulsion that Reiliur at once responded. The sense of translocation vanished instantly. Gone was the beautiful paradise with its three moons and comforting sun. He was now fully within his laboratory, his mind clear and aware, focused upon the events unfolding around him.

The Circle of Heaven continued their incantation, the ritual's formula reaching its peak. Around each elf there now crackled a nimbus of energy, a white light that fended off the motes of sorcery that whipped around the room. The liquid salt that ran between the adamantine sigils erupted into flames, little streams of blue fire that undulated along the floor.

Then Reiliur's attention was drawn to the gateways themselves. Each was vibrating in its setting, the molten diamond distorted by a gray steam that bubbled outward. The wizard knew the steam was no product of the diamond, but rather something seeping out from behind the surface. Something from beyond the gate itself. As the steam expanded into the room, it rapidly cooled and became a freezing fog that left little specks of frost wherever it rolled. The expanding fog became thickest around the gateways, absolutely concealing the diamond panels, though leaving the framework itself utterly unobstructed.

"They're here," Reiliur gasped. He could feel Calisor's tension as the young wizard stared across the laboratory.

One of the gateways suddenly lost its veil of fog. The molten diamond surface spilled outward in rivulets that hardened into gemstones as they clattered across the floor. Through the now empty framework, a figure stepped forward. Reiliur marveled at the magnificence of the sight. Not merely the image of a Celestian, but a Celestian in the flesh!

The Celestian was tall and powerfully built. There was a suggestion of the elven in his features, but so too were there qualities far too handsome and fine to be reduced to mortal terms. Reiliur held his breath as he considered the authority and regality of that countenance. His face was both stern and compassionate, his pale blue eyes shone with wisdom. His blond hair was tied back in a single braid and the beard he wore was short, leaving most of his face clean. Armor encased his mighty figure, golden plate so brilliant it seemed forged from sunlight rather than metal. A great sword hung at his side, its hilt wrought in a swirling pattern that appeared to move of its own accord in an endless spiral.

Reiliur bowed to the Celestian. "I welcome you to Ileureleith." The words came forth in a fumbling greeting, his poise utterly lost before this august presence. "My name is Reiliur Ythrill, of the House Dragaren. I welcome you, Your Grace."

The Celestian returned the wizard's bow. "You may call me Mescator." His voice impressed Reiliur as being at once as loud as thunder and as soft as silk. He gestured for Reiliur to remain where he was. "We can speak better after my companions have completed their passage."

Mescator turned away and faced toward the other gates. His majestic voice joined in the incantations of the wizards. Another of the swirling masses of fog vanished and again the panel of molten diamond crashed to the floor. The Celestian who emerged from the portal now was female, her fair hair flowing in a thick mane about a face that was both enchanting and rugged. There was an excitement in her hazel eyes that couldn't be contained. She smiled as her gaze darted from one part of the laboratory to another. Unlike Mescator, she wore no suit of armor, but only a scarlet dress embroidered in gold and leggings that seemed to have been spun from silver.

Reiliur had less time to study the second Celestian before a third portal opened and another entered the laboratory. This one was another male, dressed in a long white robe, his fingers adorned with jeweled rings, fabulous necklaces hanging down across his chest. Reiliur could at once sense the arcane power of this Celestian; to one attuned to magic, he seemed like a walking firebrand of energy. As profound as his awe of Mescator, Reiliur was even more fascinated by this arrival. When he joined in the incantation, Reiliur could feel the air become charged with magic, swelling to an intensity that far surpassed anything before.

One after another, the gateways opened and the Celestians crossed into Pannithor. Nineteen of the gates opened without problem. Then came time for the twentieth to fall away and allow a final traveler to pass between worlds.

At once, Reiliur sensed something was wrong. He shifted around the edge of the dais, his hands still gripping the Scrying Star. Calisor moved with him, but like the elder wizard, he had eyes only for the disturbance unfolding about the last gateway. The fog remained thick around the portal, billowing and howling with violence uncharacteristic of the other gates. Reiliur could see flashes of energy – magical energy – roiling inside the fog. He cried out in warning when Mescator approached the anomaly.

"Stay back, Your Grace!" Reiliur shouted. "There has been a concentration of hostile magic within that cloud. I don't think even you could withstand it."

Mescator swung around and turned to a Celestian in white robes. "Valandor, we must do something! He will be lost to the void!"

A grave expression came upon the one called Valandor. He looked up at the glass dome, pointing with one of his ringed fingers at the night sky. "The stars are no longer in alignment. The transference has taken too long. You know the forces with which we must contend. I advised you that he was too weak to make the journey."

"We must save him," Mescator declared. "There must be a way."

Reiliur clasped his hands tighter about the Scrying Star. He focused his mind, finding the rapport with Eoswain. Briefly, he felt the pull of the paradise he'd fleetingly visited, but he rejected its enticing influence. Too much depended upon maintaining his concentration to be distracted now. "Eoswain!" he called out. "Something has gone wrong! The last of your people isn't able to cross into my world! You must draw him back!"

Eoswain's voice responded, her tone grim. "The stars are no longer in alignment," she said. "If I tried to draw him back, he would never make it. His essence would lose cohesion and he would be lost to the void. Speak with Valandor. Tell him he must perform the Nekanthikra rite. Only that can force the passage."

"Valandor!" the wizard shouted. "Eoswain says that your companion can't go back. He must come through to this side! She says only the Nekanthikra rite can save him."

Reiliur did not know what manner of rite Eoswain had called for, but from the expression that came upon Valandor, it was clear that he did. The Celestian's eyes took on a haunted quality. For a moment, he was silent.

"Do this for me," Mescator said. "We have to save him."

Valandor shook his head. "There is always a price to pay when the Nekanthikra rite is invoked. Misfortune will stalk those who call on such power. Nor is even my magic strong enough to bend it to our purpose. I will need help."

"You have only to ask it," Mescator replied. "Whatever you need, it is yours."

"No," Valandor declared. "It makes no sense to risk two of us to redeem only one. We are few enough already."

Calisor suddenly left the dais and rushed down to the Celestians. "Your Grace, if I can help you." He looked from Valandor to Mescator. "Please let me help, if I can. I will accept the consequences."

Reiliur's heart swelled with pride to hear the young wizard so selflessly offer himself to save the last traveler. At the same time, he felt guilt boil in his stomach. Had he been as cautious as Calisor advised, perhaps they could have avoided this crisis.

The elder wizard broke away from the Scrying Star and joined Calisor. "I too, would like to help." He gestured at the rest of the Circle of Heaven. "They are needed to maintain the incantation. We are the only elves who can be spared."

Mescator smiled sadly. "I could not ask this of you."

"The obligation of hospitality," Reiliur returned. "It was by my invitation you made this journey. I can't remain idle and allow one of your company to suffer because of me."

"There is no time to debate," Valandor interjected. "If you will risk the curse, then I will do the same." He held out his hands to the two elves. They both felt an electric shock when they touched the Celestian, as though it were lightning rather than blood that flowed through Valandor's veins.

"Join your magic to my magic," Valandor commanded. "Meld your minds with my mind. Focus upon the constellations. See them not as they are, but as they were when the first portal was opened. You must ignore the present. Envision only the past. What was, must be again. What is, must be forgotten."

A shadow stole across Reiliur's vision. The laboratory flickered for a moment. He felt something being drawn out of him, pouring into Valandor. Suddenly he was peering through the Celestian's eyes, staring up through the enchanted dome at the stars above. For what felt to him like an eternity, he was transfixed by the celestial vision. Dimly, he could perceive a kind of chanting scratching at the edge of his perception. The words were unknown and imperceptible, yet they conveyed a sense of foreboding and doom. He wanted to cry out, to tell Valandor that he was mistaken, that he didn't want to share in the consequences of this rite. Yet he knew it was already too late. Power had been summoned, and its price must be paid.

Even in his moment of dread, Reiliur was seized by awe when he saw the magnitude of the spell Valandor was casting.

The stars turned back! They shifted in reverse, resuming the alignment when Mescator first stepped out from the portal! Time itself had been thrown back, the past overwhelming the present. It was a temporal disruption that would be recorded by all the astronomers of Pannithor, retold in hushed whispers as 'the lost hours'.

Only within the Tower of Heaven did time remain unchanged. When Valandor ended his conjuration, Reiliur found that the laboratory was just as it had been before. The only difference stemmed from the last gate. The fog around it was quickly losing its angry, menacing discharge. It was becoming the same as that which had emanated from the other gateways.

"You've succeeded," Mescator said. He clapped Valandor on the arm and nodded to the two elves. "We will never forget the help you've rendered us." He turned and walked toward the last portal.

Valandor was no less grateful to Reiliur and Calisor, but his thanks were tempered by a dour warning. "From this moment, a shadow hovers over our fates. It may be that the shadow will pass without incident. It may be that a grave doom lies before one or more of us. Even I cannot say."

Reiliur looked over to the final gateway. The diamond panel crumbled away as he watched. "We've saved your companion. Whatever awaits us in the future, at least we've done that much good."

The last Celestian stepped through the gate, apparently oblivious to how close his passage had come to ending in tragedy. He had a youthful, exuberant look. He was more spryly built than Mescator, with short dark hair and a shrewdness about his features. Reiliur thought him a complete contrast to Mescator, but there was no mistaking the adoration in the Celestian's eyes when he looked over at the armored paragon.

"I did just as you told me," the young Celestian stated. "I focused all my concentration on the gateway, with no thought of home to draw me back." He turned and laughed as he looked on the other Celestians. "And here I am." His merriment faltered when he noted the worried looks his companions wore.

Mescator stepped forward and embraced the other Celestian. "The danger is over now. Whatever happened, it is behind us. You are here now."

Reiliur could see the great affection between Mescator and the youthful Celestian, a connection that reminded him of his own tutelage of Calisor. He wondered if they too were mentor and pupil. But such questions quickly faded when he heard a low whisper cross Valandor's lips.

"Yes, you are here now, Oskan," Valandor said.

Never in his seven hundred years had Reiliur heard words uttered with such a feeling of menace.

Chapter II

-1095, Time of Light

The walls within the great hall the elves called the Shining Sanctum were well-appointed to suit the name. Oskan was fascinated by the shimmering smoothness of the material that clothed walls and ceiling. It had a curious opacity about it that seemed to draw and magnify the light, yet never intensifying the effect to such a degree that it became overwhelming. Calisor had told him that the material was a thin shaving of pearl that was gathered by elves in the far north from vast beds deep beneath the northern sea. Wizards would use their magic to bind the pearl plates into a seamless whole and augment an already present reflective property.

Oskan was eager to see the place from which the pearls were farmed. He wanted to see the rolling sea described by Calisor and the elven divers plying their trade. He wanted to visit the vast forests and the rolling hills. He wanted to feel the rich soil of Elvenhome between his toes and listen to the songs of Pannithor's birds. He longed to smell the flowers in the fields and to feel the wind of a new world whispering through his hair.

All would have to wait. Oskan couldn't kill his eagerness, but he could control it. Though it was tantalizing to know that just outside the Tower of Heaven there was a whole new world to explore, he curbed his impatience to experience it for himself. Mescator would decide when the Celestians were ready for that moment, and it had been decided before any of them made the journey that he would have the final decision in such matters. Even if Mescator weren't his mentor, Oskan would have deferred to his judgment. There were many among the explorers who might have greater knowledge, but he didn't think even Valandor had the same wisdom as Mescator.

"Oskan." The name whispered through Oskan's mind, pushed into his thoughts from outside. He turned his head to see Liliana glancing at him. Seated in a lavishly carved chair crafted from some gold-colored timber, there was a hint of reprimand in her eyes. She didn't inject any further thoughts into his brain. She simply returned her gaze to the little dais at the middle of the hall.

A tinge of embarrassment tugged at Oskan's conscience. He was relieved it was Liliana who'd noticed his momentary distraction. She was always gracious and didn't see the value in belaboring a mistake. Some of the other Celestians had less sympathetic understanding. Valandor, for instance, would have announced Oskan's inattentiveness to all the rest. Oskan could shoulder the sting to his pride, but he didn't want to know he'd disappointed Mescator at the same time. There were few things he treasured more than the esteem of his mentor.

There were five Celestians gathered in the Shining Sanctum. All reposed in throne-like seats while they listened to Reiliur relate to them the nature of this new world. Oskan's group was one of four dispersed within the Tower of Heaven. Each group was receiving instruction on different facets of Pannithor. Some learned the natural order, the drift of the seasons and the material substance of the world. Others were being instructed about the diverse animals and plants that inhabited Pannithor. A third group, headed by Valandor, was learning the basics of elven magic and how its workings differed from that practiced by the Celestians.

The last group was being tutored by Reiliur himself. It was natural, Oskan supposed, that the master mage should take onto himself the instruction of Mescator and those with him. They made for a curious group. The great, powerful Mescator with his somber mien. The intense Fulgria, the flame of her red hair exceeded by the fire in her gaze. Belkon, dark and reserved, always looking as though he were measuring the importance of every word that reached his ears. Liliana, her hair cascading about her shoulders in a blonde cataract, her mouth curled in delight as she listened to the elf's words. Oskan understood that smile. There was no fooling him. Liliana was every bit as eager as he was to explore this new world. Only she had sense enough to not let her eagerness become a distraction.

"The god Ohmpek is the Steward of the Sun," Reiliur lectured. "Ever he is at strife with the goddess Lonok, Queen of Shadows."

Oskan listened while Reiliur began to discuss aspects of elven culture and society that he'd only scantily mentioned while describing the lands of Pannithor and its history. Again, the wizard related to the Celestians the gods the elves venerated. Perhaps Oskan had been distracted when the subject was briefly touched upon before, but this time, he noticed a catch in Reiliur's voice. It was a fleeting instant, but for a moment there was an up-swelling of emotion that pulled at the elf's features and put moisture in his eyes. Something, some aspect of this subject, had inflicted a grave hurt upon the wizard.

Unchallenged, Reiliur would have simply pressed on with his lecture. Indeed, he started to do so. It was Oskan who interrupted him. "There is something more. Something that has caused you great pain," he said. He knew they'd agreed to hold all questions until the end of these lectures. The interruption brought reproving looks from Fulgria and Belkon, but he persisted. This was the moment when Reiliur's emotion was at the fore. When he would be less likely to provide them a more nuanced answer. Now, in this moment, they would hear more than the facts of the subject, but also the way it made the wizard feel. "If you told us what it is, we could help," Oskan elaborated.

The wizard was quiet. He lifted his eyes to the pearl-coated ceiling. Agony flashed across his visage, but when he lowered his gaze and faced the Celestians once more, he'd again affected a composed detachment. "There is nothing that could be done. A custom to which I do not ascribe."

Mescator rose from his seat. His face was solemn as he regarded Reiliur. "You've helped us bridge the void between worlds at great cost to yourself. By your efforts, we are able to visit your world and learn about your people. It would be ungracious to pay what you've done without the respect you're due." His voice dropped into a softer, sympathetic tone. "A tragedy has afflicted you. Something from the past that yet casts its shadow across your heart. If you would, then tell us what has happened. Let us return the good you've performed on our behalf."

"My hurt is of the past," Reiliur said. "There's nothing that can be done now." He shook his head. "An old wound that refuses to close."

"A wound that doesn't heal will fester," Liliana told the wizard. "Pain unforgotten will always hurt."

Reiliur stiffened at Liliana's words. A determined, defiant mantle descended upon him. "No, I will not forget. I will never forget the happiness that was briefly allowed to me. Even if that memory must be cousin to pain."

Oskan regretted the quiver in Reiliur's voice. He'd provoked the wizard to this confrontation with his past. Now, however, the Celestian felt the only thing to do was to probe the wound and draw out the rot within. "What happened to you? Who caused you such harm?"

Again, Reiliur looked as though he wouldn't answer. "Bhanek," he said at last. It was the name of the elven god of life, a deity he'd described before to the Celestians. There was no reverence in the way he spoke the name now. Instead, there was a mixture of hate and revulsion. "Bhanek has many roles, and his temples are in every town and city. Many venerate him as the god who bestows vitality to the fields and the herds. It was he who planted the first tree, the World Tree, in Ileuthrien and thereby created all the forests of Pannithor. He is invoked when each child enters the world, and no birth chamber is ever without one of his clergy in attendance." Reiliur's hands clenched into fists at his side and a growl entered his voice. "But Bhanek is also called 'Chooser of the Born,' and it is in this role that his nurturing presence takes on a darker aspect. Elven children are not endowed with a name until they have seen their fifth summer, until then they are merely referred to by the honorific *vilidane*, which means 'uncertain blessing'. A reminder to the parents that what is most precious to them can be taken away."

"Is that what happened to you?" Oskan asked. "Was your child taken away?"

Liliana shook her head. "The elves are a noble and intelligent people. Their society couldn't tolerate such barbarity."

"We are a people of contrasts," Reiliur stated. "Our passions run deep. So deeply that not even wisdom cannot defy rites that have been respected for thousands of years."

"What does it mean to be taken before this Chooser of the Born?" Fulgria wanted to know.

"It means life or death. It is that simple." Reiliur let the words echo through the hall, whispering away into the shadows. "When it is time, the children are brought into a temple of Bhanek and the priests make a careful examination of them. They seek out any divergence from what is recorded in the sacred texts. Any difference that they interpret as impurity. They examine mind, body, and spirit. If anything if wrong..." The wizard bowed his head, his body trembling with emotion.

"If anything is wrong, the child never receives a name."

Oskan felt rage boiling through his veins when he heard the ghastly revelation. "Butchers! They would slaughter their own people's children!" Color flashed into his eyes, turning them a dark red. His facial features drew back, losing some of their elegance and becoming savagely vicious.

"Oskan. Calm yourself." Liliana's words rippled through his mind. Oskan struggled to suppress the outrage he felt. He was only partly successful, for discipline couldn't restrain the disgust evoked by Reiliur's revelation. He looked toward Mescator. His mentor might have been carved from stone for all that his expression betrayed the feelings inside him. Yet there was just a hint of emotion there in the glint of his eyes. A hint Oskan thought only someone as close to Mescator as himself would see.

"Your child was killed by the priests," Mescator said.

"Our son was deemed unworthy," Reiliur wept. He sank back against the lectern, using it to support his weakened body. "His mind, the priests said, was feeble. They told us it was a mercy, to spare him a life blighted by infirmity. I tried to accept that. His mother couldn't. I have told you that we elves feel things most deeply. On the anniversary of our son's death, she ate three petals from the death rose. One would have been enough to kill a bull, but she took three." The wizard's voice trailed off into sobbing.

"Vile beasts!" Oskan snarled. "How can such abomination be accepted?"

"It is not our place to judge," Belkon said. "We are strangers to this world. We must watch and learn. Then, only then, can we truly consider the actions of these priests."

Liliana turned to the dusky Celestian. "Can you be so cold as to deliberate upon so terrible a thing? There are things which are good, no matter the land or the people. So too, there are things which are always evil."

"But it is not our place to judge," Belkon repeated. He glanced aside to Fulgria, seeking her support. He frowned when he saw that she sympathized with Liliana's indignation more than his urge to practicality.

Oskan shook his head. "Have we come to this world simply as a novelty? To sate our own curiosity?" Though Belkon was his elder, he presumed to ridicule his stance. "If we haven't come here to help and nurture the people of Pannithor, then what do we have to offer to them?"

"Would you have us become tyrants?" Belkon retorted. He waved his finger in warning to Oskan. "The danger of power is that it can be used to dominate as easily as it can be used to protect. The elves have built a society that is their own. Would you have us reshape it in our own image? Would you take all choice from them, deny them their own destiny?"

"Evil must be challenged," Oskan argued. "Always. Wherever it is found."

"Enough," Mescator's command echoed through the hall, silencing the disagreement. Oskan bowed his head in submission. He watched his mentor walk over to the lectern. Mescator laid his hand on the crying wizard's shoulder.

"I mourn what you've lost, my friend," Mescator said. "But I must intrude upon your sorrow. I must know if this rite, this practice you've described, continues to this day."

Reiliur straightened his posture and stared up into Mescator's eyes. Oskan could sense the power his mentor was bestowing, the energy that was flowing from his hand into the wizard. Bolstered by that power, Reiliur stirred from his despair. "Yes, Your Grace," he answered. "Here in Ileureleith, the priests of Bhanek continue the traditions."

Oskan could hear the stony determination in Mescator's voice. "Then we must leave the Tower of Heaven sooner than we had planned." He looked across at the other Celestians. "We will go and see for ourselves the rites of Bhanek who judges if a child is to live or die."

"Invite Valandor to accompany us," Liliana suggested. "If the priests are making use of magic to maintain their hold over the rest of the elves, he is certain to detect it." She favored Reiliur with an apologetic smile. "Your knowledge is great, but if the priests are trying to deceive you, they will know ways to hide that fact from another elf. They will not be so accomplished when confronted by a Celestian."

"We'll set things right and end this," Oskan growled. Mescator shot him a warning look.

"No one will do anything until I decide what we will do," Mescator declared. "Belkon is right. We're strangers to Pannithor, and there may be things here which we don't understand."

"And when we understand?" Oskan asked.

"There is such a thing as evil," Mescator said. "And we'll not suffer it to prey upon those who've opened their homes to us."

***

Reiliur could feel his heart hammering inside his chest. Since that dreadful day two hundred years ago, he'd never set foot inside the temple of Bhanek. For him, it had become a place of misery, a symbol of the pain that always lurked at the edge of his awareness.

Now he was going back. Reiliur led the Celestians through the wide streets of Ileureleith, past the tall white spires of the great houses and the jeweled doorways of the artisans. Pedestrians paused on their errands, tarrying while the Celestians passed them. Even draped in heavy cloaks, the aura of might that exuded from Reiliur's companions couldn't be hidden. The elves watched and marveled wherever they went. The whispers would reach the princess herself soon enough, and she'd send her agents to investigate. He only trusted that eventuality would wait until after Mescator had seen the temple.

"Your people have an eye for elegance," Liliana said. She waved a gloved hand absently at a narrow bridge that stretched high above the street and connected two of the spindly towers.

Reiliur sighed at the sight. "It is a courtship crossing," he explained. "When two families seek to mix their bloodlines, a bridge will be built between their houses. A symbol of their unity. The genealogy of the elves is recorded to the most distant days, and there are connections betwixt almost every family within those records, so a faint relation can always be found living across from one or the other of the betrothed. They play host to one of the lovers while the other household constructs the bridge." He shook his head and sighed again. "The bridge is torn down only when the pairing is broken. Be it by death or circumstance."

Liliana nodded. She didn't press Reiliur further, for which he was grateful. He was picturing the crossing that had been built for himself and his Mirrahn. When she died, it had been taken down. Each sliver of wood laid upon her pyre, for a suicide wasn't allowed to be consigned to a crypt lest the lost soul haunt the site. Instead, the ashes were cast into the wind, scattered to the elements so there would be nothing to anchor a ghost in the land of the living.

The street widened ahead, expanding into a boulevard lined with spindly trees with white boles and amber leaves. Each trunk had been cunningly carved to depict scenes from the city's long history, exactingly crafted so that the living wood suffered no hurt from the artist's chisel. Spells kept the trees from growing back and maintained them all at a uniform height. Reiliur noticed the interest Valandor paid to the display and for a moment felt pride that the Celestian was impressed by the handiwork of his people. Then the knowledge of their errand reasserted itself, and his attitude became dour.

"Are these the palaces of your nobles?" Belkon asked, indicating the vast structures that loomed behind the file of trees at either side of the boulevard.

"The princess who governs this region and the other nobles dwell on estates outside the city," Reiliur said. "These are the scholariums where any elf is entitled to receive instruction on any subject he has the wit to learn. Here are schools devoted to every art and trade. Great libraries on any subject a student might seek."

Valandor turned to Reiliur. "Are all of your cities so endowed?"

"All," Reiliur replied. "Though Ileureleith is considered a seat of learning surpassed only by Therennia Adar itself."

"That is the capital, where your king holds court," Oskan commented. "Where the laws that govern your people are decided." His face again took on a severe expression. "We may have need to discuss policies with him."

Reiliur gaped and nodded. Until this moment, it hadn't occurred to him that the Celestians would seek to visit Therennia Adar or speak with the king. While he knew it was a momentous thing, helping these powerful beings cross into Pannithor, he hadn't thought things through to their final extent. The Princess of Ileureleith was simply the regional representative of the royal family. Of course the Celestians would need to be presented to the king!

"The building with the crowd outside it. Is that the temple?" Mescator pointed to a sprawling structure that shone like gold in the afternoon sun.

"Yes," Reiliur confirmed. "That is the temple of Bhanek." He couldn't keep a trace of hate from his voice when he spoke. Objectively, the temple was a beautiful thing, gorgeously fabricated from towering goldwoods that had been trained by magic and cultivated by arborists to give shape to the building. A canopy of greenery billowed above the walls as the branches reached up to the sun. Just like the smaller trees of the boulevard, the goldwoods had been exactingly carved with religious icons and etched with the tenants of Bhanek's faith. Wide steps climbed up to where two goldwoods bent downward to form an archway – the entrance to the temple.

The crowd outside was composed of distinct factions. All of them represented the extended families of couples who'd brought children to be judged by the priests. There were the jubilant mobs who were celebrating the worthiness of children returned to their parents. There were the grave and somber groups who waited to learn the fate of those still inside the temple. Grimmest of all were those who clustered around grieving parents and tried to console them in their sadness. Only too well did Reiliur understand the futility of such gestures.

Oskan's eyes flared when he saw the misery of the mourners. He started forward, but Mescator held him back. "Restraint," he told the younger Celestian. "Lead the way," he said, turning to Reiliur.

The wizard guided them up the steps. They marched beneath the great archway where two immense goldwoods had bent inward upon one another and entwined their branches together to serve as the temple gateway. Beyond them was a cavernous chamber. The fragrance of blooming flowers filled the air. Bees and butterflies flitted about, darting from garden-boxes suspended by long strands of vine from the ceiling. The floor was composed of rich, dark earth so fertile and robust that the very sight of it would bring a farmer to tears of envy. Enormous windows shaped from thin panes of amber let sunlight shine down upon the sanctuary.

"There is where the children are judged," Reiliur pointed to the sanctuary. The priests of Bhanek were there, distinct in their cassocks of woven leaves and fur collars. The altar was there, a rounded stump some ten feet across. Behind it, elevated upon a dais, was the font of purification, a great basin of white wood filled with water as pure and brilliant as crystal.

While others within the temple turned their heads and stared at the cloaked Celestians in that mix of awe and bewilderment they'd seen in the city streets, the priests spared only the briefest attention for Reiliur's companions. Whatever questions they had, they couldn't make them delay the demands of their ritual. Most of the clergy were busy studying the children brought to the temple. Some in white robes would lead children back to the parents kneeling on the floor, advising them that Bhanek had ruled them as fit for elven society. Two priests in black robes led another child away from the judges, a thin wisp of a girl with silvery hair and a complexion like alabaster. She cried and tried to pull away from them, but their grip was too strong, and they carried her toward the basin. There, a priest wearing an ivory mask awaited the child to administer the final test. The test that would determine life or death.

"In a moment, the fate of that poor waif will be decided," Reiliur breathed, his heart cracking from the memory of his own son's immersion in the fountain.

"Valandor, do you sense anything?" Mescator asked, keeping his eyes focused upon the masked priest.

Valandor shook his head. "There is magic here, but it is of a reclusive and vestigial nature. If there is some deity here, then its presence is too minimal to detect."

Reiliur gasped as he watched the little girl handed over to the masked priest. The touch of his hand caused her to go limp. He caught hold of her before she could fall and lifted her toward the basin. "She will be immersed in the water. If it turns black, the priest will hold her under until..."

Mescator waited for no further discussion. He strode forward, toward the altar. As he did, he threw aside his cloak. Gasps of wonder and amazement filled the temple, all eyes captivated by the awesome aspect of the Celestian. Even the priests faltered in their duties to gape at Mescator's imposing presence.

"Unhand the child," Mescator demanded, his voice reverberating like thunder across the sanctuary. "There will be an end to this obscenity."

The masked priest recovered from his shock. His eyes glared down at Mescator. "Who are you to spout blasphemy within the house of Bhanek? You, who are not of the firstborn dare to scorn the holy rites of elves? Back to whatever barbarous lands that claim your blood and profane not the sanctity of this ritual!"

Mescator glowered back at the priest and marched toward the altar. Some of the lesser priests moved to intercept him, but as they did, the other Celestians cast aside their cloaks. Sight of one of them had been imposing enough, to find themselves confronted by six of the mighty beings was more than the priests were ready to challenge.

"You have no right here!" the masked priest shouted at Mescator as he came nearer.

Reiliur ran forward, falling into step beside Mescator. "He has the right!" the wizard snarled at the priest. "The right of all who cherish good to defy evil. Wherever it lurks and whatever shape it takes!" He couldn't be certain this was the same priest who'd drowned his son, for the mask served to conceal the identity of the elf who carried out Bhanek's decision. It didn't matter. It was the practice itself that was his enemy.

"How long will we tolerate this tradition of slaughter?" Reiliur cried out, turning to the congregation inside the temple. The presence of the Celestians was like fire in his veins, emboldening him to speak words that no elf had dared to speak before. He pointed to the masked priest. "How long will we allow our children to be murdered before our very eyes? How can any of us call ourselves civilized while we permit this abomination?"

"Silence the blasphemer!" The cry rose from many of the priests. They started toward Reiliur, but before they could reach the wizard, they found the Celestians in their way. Valandor raised his hand, and a wispy barrier of shimmering blue light rose before the rushing priests. They faltered before the barrier, their outrage tempered by caution.

"You see!" The masked priest cried. "Reiliur has brought demons to profane the sanctuary of Bhanek and guard him while he spouts his blasphemies! Seize..."

The masked priest's words faltered when he saw Mescator stride through the barrier Valandor had conjured. The Celestian's golden armor seemed to blaze with a light all its own as he walked past the altar and mounted the dais.

Reiliur felt the magnitude of what he was witnessing. A moment that he knew would forever change the elves... and perhaps all of Pannithor.

***

"These atrocities will end." Mescator's voice thundered through the temple. Elven clerics came toward him from every side, but when he fixed them with his furious gaze, the priests withered before his ire. They fell back, making warding gestures with their hands and invoking the protection of Bhanek. Mescator studied them for only a moment, wondering if they would attempt some manner of magic against him. He dismissed such threat. If the priests were so brazen, they'd have already tried to stop him.

"She must be judged," the masked priest insisted as Mescator came nearer. "Bhanek must test the child for corruption."

"The only corruption here is you," Mescator declared and pointed at the priest. "You are the vein of corruption that infects the elves. You and these obscene rites!"

The eyes behind the ivory mask flashed with zealous indignation. "She *will* be judged!" Gripping the child in both hands, he swung her toward the basin.

Mescator moved with a swiftness that amazed even the other Celestians. His armored bulk sprang up the steps. One hand caught the child and ripped her from the priest's grasp. The other locked about the cleric's neck. "She *has* been judged. By me."

Limp and senseless in the priest's clutches, the child stirred in Mescator's grip. He tenderly lowered her to the floor. "Go, little one. Go back to your family," he told her. He returned the timid smile the girl showed him and gently nudged her toward her waiting parents. He let his gaze linger on the other clergy in silent warning. None moved to intercept her as she ran to her mother and father.

"Sacrilege..." the masked priest gasped as he struggled in Mescator's hold. "Bhanek will..."

"What will Bhanek do?" Mescator demanded. He reached for the priest's hand and pulled away the silver ring he wore. When the girl had been brought to the masked cleric, Mescator had seen him grab her with that hand and noted how she'd fallen senseless the next instant. "Will your god make me sleep with a poisoned ring?" He held the silver band between his fingers. All eyes were upon him as he crushed it into a shapeless mass.

"You dare..." The masked priest's hiss trailed off into a rasping cough as Mescator's hand closed tighter. Mescator swung him around so that they both faced the congregation gathered in the temple.

"What is the custom? What is the tale you've told those who come here?" Mescator swept the great hall with his eyes, projecting his will so that every elf in the temple felt as though the Celestian were looking directly into their souls. In truth, his gaze lingered upon only one elf. He watched Reiliur as he spoke. "Bhanek must judge the worthiness of all who are born. This is the cruel custom you've been forced to obey. The priests test and study, then the child is brought to the font for the final test." He turned his eyes upon the masked priest. "If they are corrupt, the water will turn black. Is that not so?"

"It is the judgment of Bhanek!" the masked priest snarled.

Mescator gave his captive a cold smile. "Let us put that judgment to the test. Let's test your worthiness." He swung the cleric toward the font. The priest yelped in terror, thinking the Celestian meant to drown him in the pool. Instead, Mescator shifted his grip and seized the elf's right hand. "I notice you wear another ring."

Before the priest knew what was happening, Mescator forced his hand down into the pool. As the Celestian had expected, the moment the ring was submerged, the waters began to blacken. Some substance or property within the metal was reacting. Not the divine intervention of a god, but rather the trickery of the priests decided the fate of those brought before them.

The temple erupted into furious shouts. The congregation rushed forward, a howling mob enraged by the deception

Mescator had exposed. Reiliur spoke truly when he said that the wisdom of the elves was exceeded by the depth of their passions. In this moment, the emotion that filled them was rage.

"No!" Mescator cried out as the crowd took hold of the clergy. His command was like an avalanche churning down the hall. The elves were stunned by the power of his voice. Hands that a moment before had been tearing at the priests now fell limp at their sides.

"Do not add to the evil done here," Mescator told them. "Rejoice that your children have been restored to you. Give thanks that these rites are finished and never again will your people need to tremble before the Chooser of the Born." He released his hold on the masked priest and let him slip to the floor. "Leave these wretches their lives. Don't befoul the good that has been done to you this day with their blood. Go back to your homes with the treasure that has been returned to you."

One of the elves stepped forward. Mescator saw that she was the mother of the girl he'd taken from the masked priest. "Please, my lord, who is it I must honor for returning my child to me?"

Before Mescator could answer, Oskan stepped through the barrier Valandor had raised. "He is Mescator the Just," Oskan announced. "Descended from the celestial sea to restore righteousness to your world."

The bold pronouncement brought awed gasps from the gathered elves. They fell to their knees in adoration and praised both Mescator and Oskan. Valandor lifted his barrier and the others stepped forward to greet the grateful elves. Even several of the clergy joined the throng, tossing aside the icons of Bhanek they wore about their necks.

"What you've done here is incredible," Reiliur told Mescator as he walked up to join him beside the font. "Never could I have imagined anyone could defy the priests."

Mescator nodded. "It was a cruel deception that needed to be exposed."

The masked priest was massaging his bruised throat when he heard Mescator's words. "Cruel, but necessary," he stated in a solemn whisper. "There was a time when plagueblight decimated the elves. Only the intervention of Bhanek allowed our people to survive. He showed us how to detect the plague before it could mature and spread. But for his holy power, our race would have gone extinct a thousand years ago."

"But this wasn't the work of Bhanek!" Reiliur snapped. "This was trickery. Murder!"

"Bhanek no longer favors us with his miracles," the priest said. "Over the centuries, his power has withdrawn from us. It became necessary to use other methods to maintain the faith and keep true to the traditions."

"Was it tradition or power that was more precious to you?" Mescator wondered. "How many children have died needlessly to satiate a god you no longer hear?" His hand closed into a fist. "I am not certain which is more despicable, one who slaughters the innocent to hold onto power that isn't rightfully his or the fanatic who does the same in the name of his faith."

"My faith is real, and the threat of plagueblight is real," the priest declared. "If we don't guard against it, it will return."

Reiliur glared at the cleric. "Lunatic! You murdered my son, killed my wife for this!"

Mescator caught hold of the wizard, clutching him by the shoulder in a grip like iron. He could sense the arcane power Reiliur was drawing into himself to send searing into the priest.

"Leave while you still can," Mescator warned the masked cleric.

The priest bowed his head. "I go, but I will report what has happened here to the theocrat in Therennia Adar. She will speak to the king about this blasphemy."

"Be about your errand then," Mescator dismissed him. "I too will speak to speak to the elf king about what has happened here." He kept his restraining hold on Reiliur while the priest hurried away.

"You should have let me kill him," Reiliur said when Mescator relaxed his grip. Mescator could hear the frustrated agony in the elf's voice.

"Enough needless death has happened here," Mescator declared. "Don't be so eager to add to it." He turned Reiliur around so that the wizard could see the elves gathering in the temple. Not to witness the rites of Bhanek, but to see those who'd broken the cruelty of the Chooser of the Born. "They're beaten. Even some of the god's priests have turned from him. Be gracious in your triumph. Noble is the victor who displays mercy to the vanquished."

"I... I will try," Reiliur said. "It is a hard thing to kill an old hate." A bitter smile squirmed onto his face. "But I will try."

Mescator left the wizard to his thoughts. He descended from the font and walked to where Valandor stood waiting beside the altar. "More direct than you'd have liked?" he asked, feeling the anxious mood of the other Celestian.

"No, but I have a confession to make," Valandor said. "I wasn't entirely truthful with you." He looked about the sanctuary, his eyes roving about the amber windows and the lofty ceiling. "There *is* a power here. Faint, unfocused, but here just the same. Something different from Reiliur's magic... and our own for that matter."

Mescator nodded, thinking of the masked priest's words. "Perhaps Bhanek was once what all his followers claimed him to be. Perhaps ages of indolence have caused his power to wane, his presence to dissipate. Steadily losing his focus until now his priests invoke a god who no longer hears them."

"We've seen before the legacies of gods forgotten by their people. Perhaps now we see a people forgotten by their god." Valandor scratched his chin as another thought came to him. "Maybe the other gods Reiliur has told us of are just as nebulous. Names left behind by faded powers."

"Let us hope that names are all they've left behind," Mescator said. His gaze turned to the elves in the temple, cheering and praising the Celestians for delivering them from the shadow of Bhanek's rites. He couldn't feel any jubilation. His mind was turned to all the other temples devoted to the god scattered across Elvenhome and all the other children even now being brought before the Chooser of the Born.

"We have a new purpose in this world," Mescator decreed. "We will liberate the people of Pannithor from the tyranny of priests beholden to vanished gods."

Chapter III

-1094, Time of Light

The Transcendent Palace of the elven king was a spectacle to make Liliana weep in appreciation of its beauty. The walls were raised from the most magnificent stone she'd ever seen, a kind of golden marble veined with sapphire. Reiliur said it was called by a name that meant 'ocean-wrought,' for it was only in the deepest parts of the sea that the stone could be found. The ceiling was shaped from wide bands of wood fifty-feet long and half-again as wide, endowed with a deep crimson color that echoed the last rays of the setting sun. The floor was a tile fresco, vibrant and afire with the thousands of gemstones of which it was composed, a thin layer of translucent resin providing visitors a surface on which to stand. The scenes depicted in the frescoes were the great deeds of the elves, exactingly drawn from the official royal histories. When some new accomplishment was deemed more worthy than one already represented on the floor, the scene was dug out and artisans set to work creating its replacement.

"Soon they will put your image in the floor." Oskan whispered the statement to Reiliur, but Liliana caught his words just the same. "You've brought us to your people, and nothing will ever be the same again."

Liliana pondered Oskan's sentiment as they walked through the grand hall flanked by elven knights in diamond-glazed armor. Change was always fraught with danger. There was ever the hazard of being so focused upon what needed to be altered that too little concern was shown for what would replace it. She shared the determination of Mescator that the foul practices of the Chooser of the Born must be ended, but that didn't mean she hadn't thought of what must come afterward.

Mescator led the little group of Celestians and their elven host. For most of a year, they'd been waiting to see the elf king. Yarinathar had delayed their reception as long as he dared. After the breaking of Bhanek's cruel worship in Ileureleith, a company of royal knights and templars of Bhanek had ridden to the city to put down what had been described to them as rebellion. What they found was a city completely united against any interference and arrayed behind the leadership and guidance of the Celestians. The knights were prudent enough not to force the issue. Bhanek's templars weren't. In the space of a few minute's battle against Mescator and his companions, all two thousand of the green-cloaked warriors were dead. The twenty Celestians fought alone, for unless the royal army should take a hand, Mescator had warned the people of Ileureleith against partaking in what would be adjudged kin-slaughter, the most abominable crime in elven law.

The spectacle had lessened the eagerness of the royal knights to force the issue. They'd turned back to Therennia Adar to explain to King Yarinathar what had happened. The result was months of tense calm. The king was reluctant to initiate a war upon his own subjects, much less a war he might not win. Mescator, for his part, was resolved to make no move until he could be certain Ileureleith was protected. The city became an armed camp, great fortification raised under the careful guidance of Fulgria and designs engineered by Belkon. Valandor instructed the Circle of Heaven in new, refined magics that would enable them to cast spells for both attack and defense without the lengthy preparations and arcane apparatus to which they were accustomed.

Into Ileureleith flowed thousands of elves each week, families who'd fled the rites of Bhanek to preserve the lives of their 'uncertain blessings'. The tide of refugees became so pronounced that Yarinathar finally was moved to suspend the Bhanek ritual, lest even more of his subjects defect to the rebel city. It was then that the king finally agreed to meet with the Celestians.

Liliana had warned the meeting might be a trap, but the very possibility only amused Mescator. "It will indeed be a trap, but it will be the ones who set it who are caught in it." He'd been prudent about the affair just the same, declaring that he would make the journey alone. It had taken the best and most persistent arguments before she and Oskan were able to prevail on him to allow them to join him. Reiliur was even more persuasive, pointing out that they'd need someone to represent the elves who'd come under the Celestians' protection.

Now they were in the Transcendent Palace and approaching the Thousand-Year Throne. Liliana could see it at the end of the great hall, resting at the top of a dais of fused sapphire. The throne itself had been exactingly carved from the heartwood of the rare iron-oak, a tree only a magic blade could cut and which only a pure heart could harvest. It was the physical representation of Yarinathar's rule, for both these feats were conducted by the king, and only his success in crafting his own throne would legitimize his rule. The chair, with its tall back and lowered arms, was a bright silver in color, and every inch of its surface had been carved with elaborate designs, abstract symbols of the glories Yarinathar would bestow upon his subjects as their sovereign.

"He has a wise face," Liliana told Mescator as she fixed her attention on the elf on the throne.

"Pragmatic," opined Mescator. "He knows that to delay meeting with me is to risk further unrest in his kingdom." He drew Liliana's attention away from Yarinathar and over to a silver-haired elf woman dressed in a mantle of golden leaves and amber jewels. There was a faint dweomer about her that Liliana at once sensed, a whisper of energy that none of the other elves possessed.

"The theocrat," Liliana said.

"Drysala," Reiliur invoked the name of Bhanek's high priestess.

"Yarinathar will force the conflict to a conclusion here and now," Mescator said. "Under his supervision, whatever happens his authority will be maintained. If we prevail, he can appear to his people as an enlightened champion of new ideas. If it is Drysala, then he will be the staunch defender of tradition and the old faith. Either way, he has made it so his rule is secure."

"Opportunistic rogue," Oskan snapped. "He'll not get away with such perfidy."

Liliana smiled at the young Celestian's idealistic ire. "It is because Yarinathar has positioned himself so that he can't lose that he can be trusted as an arbitrator. Were things otherwise, we should have to contend with the secular crown as well as Bhanek's temple."

As the Celestians walked nearer to the throne, a herald emerged from behind the ranked knights. Upon a trumpet that looked as if it had been cut from a gigantic ruby, he blew a lilting note that rippled through the great hall. He turned and bowed to the monarch before stepping aside to join the knights. A veil seemed to lift, a distortion that shivered through the hall. Now the Celestians could see that there were many more elves gathered around the throne than just the theocrat. A great crowd of elven nobility, their tunics and gowns glittering with gems, stood arrayed behind their king. More stood behind the rows of knights, the less fabulous extent of their raiment suggesting them to be favored artisans, traders, and scholars – community leaders brought into the royal presence because of their individual positions rather than the legacy of their families. Again, Liliana was impressed by the craftiness of Yarinathar. A cross-section of elven society would witness this confrontation, and so when the story was spread, it would begin from a source of the listener's own class.

Silence filled the hall when the last echo of the trumpet faded away. Mescator took one more step toward the throne and stopped. He didn't bow, but rather he locked eyes with the king. "I am Mescator," was all he said.

"We welcome you into our palace," Yarinathar said, just the faintest hint of a smile slipping through his air of regal indifference. "Therennia Adar is honored to accept your visitation. There is much we would discuss with you, who have traveled so very far to meet with us." He deigned to shift his gaze to Reiliur. The wizard bowed and dropped to his knee when the king's eyes were upon him. "We are told that your journey has brought you a distance that is not easily credited to belief. However, we are also aware of the incredible feats of which the Circle of Heaven is capable. In all Pannithor, you will find no greater practitioners of the arcane sciences."

Liliana saw through the flattery voiced by the king. Yarinathar was trying to make it clear to Reiliur and the powerful elves crowding the hall, that whatever happened, the Circle of Heaven remained valuable to the kingdom. He was curbing any expectations of reprisals if events didn't favor the Celestians.

Drysala now came forward. Her eyes were a pale green, like two leaves caught in ice. "Your forbearance is commendable, majesty," she said, her gaze roving across Reiliur and the Celestians. "Mercy should indeed be extended to those who've been led astray by ideas strange foreign to them. It is the deceivers and not the deceived who have transgressed upon the dominion of Bhanek and his sacred rites."

Mescator returned the theocrat's icy stare with a voice as cold as the void between worlds. "I have walked among your people only a short while, but in that time, I've found the elves to be a wise and gracious race. I wouldn't call decency and mercy either strange or foreign to them. Indeed, if there's anything strange and foreign to the nobility of the elven soul, it is the barbarous rites that attend the Chooser of the Born."

The ice of Drysala's gaze now melted into a fiery glower. She gestured with her hand to the throne but kept her eyes locked upon Mescator. Liliana had never seen such concentrated hatred before. "You hear, Your Majesty?" she snarled. "From the invader's own lips and in these regal halls, he dares to spout his blasphemies!"

"The only blasphemy are these murders in the name of your god!" Oskan shouted at the theocrat. A murmur of shock spread through the elves, their expressions hardening as they listened to Oskan disparage both Drysala and Bhanek.

"It is Mescator's place to challenge her," Liliana told Oskan. She tried to temper his indignation with caution. She could tell that Drysala appreciated the power of the Celestians and thought there was no chance the theocrat would risk provoking them unless she was confident she could triumph.

"Murder?" Drysala threw the word back with an audible sneer. "That is what I should expect from impious strangers who understand nothing of our history and customs." She pointed at Oskan. "Who carry the seed of evil inside their hearts as a rotten tree bears worms within its wood! Murder? Only those obsessed with transient, worldly things could fail to appreciate the grace and glory of sacrifice. To shed all for the betterment of all."

"For the betterment of Bhanek's temple and the enrichment of his priests," Mescator countered.

"Again you spout words of ignorance," Drysala snapped. "Those who serve Bhanek do not covet wealth. All must adopt a humble and selfless mien, to take nothing for themselves but devote all to Bhanek."

"Because you don't claim material wealth for yourselves doesn't make you selfless," Liliana thrust her verbal jab like a lance to pierce Drysala's haughty posture. "Those who spurn gold can covet other riches. I have seen your priests. They lust after virtue with the ferocity of a starving wolf. They judge their value, weave hierarchies of riches among themselves, by how blind their zealotry can be. The more abominable the deeds they perform in the name of Bhanek, the more they pride themselves in their commitment. They fatten upon the horror they themselves invoke, their own repugnance for what they do feeding back into their pride because they don't allow that repugnance to restrain them. To do the unspeakable to serve their god is to prove the depths of their devotion. And by doing so, they aggrandize themselves in their own minds."

Mescator took up the thread. His steely gaze turned from Drysala to Yarinathar. "Someone can be as greedy for virtue as keenly as wealth or power. To feed that hunger, there's no extreme toward which their zealotry might not one day take them." The way the king's expression changed, it was clear the warning struck home.

"You would compound your sacrilege?" Drysala shook her head. "Madness. You provoke Bhanek by your words. Would you scorn the protection of he who created all things? The fountain from which all life emerged?"

Liliana looked across the hall. Every elf was watching Mescator, their faces tense. They were eager to hear how he would respond. How he would meet the theocrat's accusations.

"I owe and ask nothing of Bhanek," Mescator replied. "I want only that his role as Chooser of the Born be ended. If he's so mighty a god, surely he can afford to show such mercy to the elves who, I am told, are his first and most favored people."

Drysala's visage dripped with outrage, all pretense of decorum and civility cast aside. The hate in her eyes, restrained before, now blazed forth at its full magnitude. Liliana could sense the energy swelling up inside the theocrat. It was a strange energy, unlike anything the Celestian had encountered before. There was the faintest hint of the power they'd sensed in Bhanek's temple, but this was aggrandized to such a degree as to be unrecognizable. Yet even this, Liliana knew, was naught but an echo. She felt there was a prodigious force behind the power that now infused Drysala, a force at once mighty and remote.

"Upon your head let the wrath of Bhanek descend!" Drysala howled. She stretched out her hands and from her palms a surge of emerald light swept forth. It wrapped itself about Mescator in a pulsating field of cascading energy. The floor under his feet bubbled and cracked, gemstones shattering as the power infused them beyond all endurance. A scream of boiling wailed through the hall, causing the elves to cover their ears as the grisly sound of disintegrating matter assailed them.

For a ghastly moment, Liliana wondered if even Mescator could withstand such unleashed fury. Withdrawn and distant as it was, perhaps the power of Bhanek was yet more than the Celestians could defy when it was harnessed by someone like Drysala.

Smoke billowed up from all around Mescator. When it dissipated, it was revealed that a hole had been melted into the floor in a radius all around him. Yet where his armored feet rested, the floor remained intact. Mescator's body was unmarked, his mail bearing no trace of scorching by Drysala's curse.

"The wrath of Bhanek appears uninterested in my head," Mescator said. His gaze hardened. "Or could it be that it is not your god's wrath, but your own which you invoke?"

Before anyone could react, Drysala lunged at Mescator. Her hands were now enveloped in a deadly glow, a bright light that stung Liliana's eyes. Mescator didn't flinch or turn away from the theocrat's charge. The instant she closed upon him, that was when he moved. He caught hold of her wrists, just behind the murderous glow, his armored fingers digging into Drysala's pale skin.

The theocrat struggled against Mescator's hold, flailing from side to side. He tried to restrain her, but though he could hold her in place, he couldn't prevent the elf's wild thrashing. In her struggle to break free of his hold, Drysala pushed herself forward. As she tried to twist aside, her neck brushed against one of her glowing hands.

A shriek of horror rang out, a cry that would haunt the nightmares of every elf who heard it. Mescator kept his hold on the theocrat's wrists, but the glow that had surrounded her left hand was gone. Instead, it now pulsated against Drysala's neck. Liliana could tell from the subdued reactions of the observing elves that they could see the light only. They couldn't see what was happening within that light. The spectacle of watching Drysala's flesh crumble away into ashes.

The grisly spectacle spread with each pulsation of the glowing light. From neck and throat, the corrosive energy swelled upward, consuming Drysala's cheek and jaw. Downward it coursed over her shoulder and chest. The theocrat tried to scream again, but this time only a burbling rattle shivered across her lips.

Mescator released his hold on her wrists when the glow dissipated from Drysala's right hand. Unable to maintain the concentration needed to harness the anathema she'd invoked, the threat to her enemy was gone. Now there was only the devouring light that was rapidly eating her body. Mescator gazed down at the dying theocrat, boldly standing his ground in the presence of this grisly destruction. After a few minutes, the glow faded away. By that time, the left side of Drysala's face and chest had disintegrated into powder, and Bhanek's high priestess was quite dead.

Stunned silence filled the hall. Yarinathar was the first elf to recover his wits and break the grim spell that filled them all with dread. "The rites of the Chooser of the Born are no longer suspended," the king decreed, looking from Drysala's wasted remains to Mescator's triumphant figure. "They are abolished. Let it be known that from this day forward, those who would perform these proscribed and antiquated rituals do so in violation of the law. Be they priest, commoner, or noble-born, all who participate invoke the displeasure of the crown from this moment forward."

The decree produced a mixture of applause and discussion from the onlooking elves. Liliana saw that there were tears in Reiliur's eyes and a joyful expression on his face. She knew that this was a day the wizard had only dared to dream about. The moment when the rites that had taken his family from him were put to an end.

"You've prevailed against Bhanek's theocrat," Reiliur said. "No more will elven children perish in his temples. You've allowed us to cast aside a grim burden we've carried far too long."

Mescator shook his head. "No burden can be lifted unless the people themselves are ready to cast it aside. In time, the elves would have risen up and freed themselves of this tyranny."

"Not without far more bloodshed," Liliana said. "Only war could've accomplished what you've done today. Perhaps several wars, and in that time, the innocents would continue to die upon Bhanek's altar. No, this day you've worked a great benefit for Elvenhome and spared its people much grief that otherwise should have been inevitable." She gestured to the throne where the king was in huddled conference with several advisors. "Yarinathar recognized that and seized on the opportunity to force the issue in a way that would at least delay the inevitable for a time."

"But now it is the priests of Bhanek who are vanquished," Oskan pointed out. "Their power humiliated and their leader dead."

"It will take time for tradition to wither away," Reiliur said, "but from this moment, the temple of Bhanek is a fading power. Another generation, perhaps two, and it will be insignificant."

Mescator watched as three priests in green robes came forward to gather up Drysala's body. The clerics bowed deferentially to Yarinathar's throne, then did the same to the Celestians. Awe, not affection, provoked their actions, and they hurried away with their grisly burden to vanish among the crowd. As they did, Mescator followed their path. Liliana did likewise, watching as the crowd cleared the way for the priests. She noted the strange figure among the watching elves at the same moment Mescator did.

"Reiliur, who is that?" Mescator asked, drawing the wizard's attention to the curious figure in the crowd.

"An envoy of Primovantor," Reiliur answered.

Liliana knew it wasn't the response Mescator was after. The stranger was utterly unlike the elves around him. He was shorter by several inches, but much more robustly built, with broad shoulders and thick limbs. His hair was cut short, but on his face was a trim brown beard, an affectation the Celestians had seen on no elf. His skin was dark, tanned by the sun and with a harshness about its texture that was again alien to the elves. The clothing he wore was the same blend of fine elegance of material and exacting craftsmanship as that of any elf in the court, but if it had been woven by an elf it had been cut to a far different style.

"No, Reiliur," Liliana said. *"What* is that?"

"He is a human," Reiliur replied. Before he could elaborate further, the herald came toward them and requested that the Celestians might indulge Yarinathar and exchange pleasantries with the king until a less public meeting could be arranged.

Liliana gave one last, lingering glance at the human envoy before following the herald so he could present them each in turn to the elf king. She wondered about this curious people, this race of which the elves had been rivals, mentors, allies, and enemies of over the ages of Pannithor. There was something fascinating about them. She'd felt it in that first glimpse.

More, she knew Mescator had felt the same impression. Perhaps even more keenly than she had.

***

-1076, Time of Light

Mescator reclined upon the long divan, his eyes shut while his mind contemplated the happenings of the day. Another consultation with Yarinathar, advising the king in matters of state. Since the breaking of Drysala's power, Mescator had been increasingly sought out by the monarch to lend his insight to decisions before they were made. The responsibility of such a role was tremendous, especially when Yarinathar preferred to heed the wisdom of Celestians over that of other elves. Such a state of affairs could have easily engendered jealousy from the court, but Mescator was careful to include the nobles in this process, seeking their own suggestions and information even when he knew his was the only voice that would sway the king. He strove to maintain a harmony of collaboration that would build confidence rather than resentment.

This too, Mescator took as a sign of Yarinathar's strategy. He entrusted the role of diplomat to the Celestian, and by doing so, allowed himself to maintain a poise of regal indifference that was far above the fray. The truth of course was that the king was enthralled by the innovations the Celestians had brought to Elvenhome. He welcomed a new era of prosperity and wonder under Mescator's guidance. To his great credit, Yarinathar wasn't concerned about the legacy of his rule so much as he was about advancing elvish culture and improving the lives of his subjects.

Much good had been accomplished in this alliance of Mescator and Yarinathar. The elves had broken away from long-held traditions in their eagerness for the new ideas the Celestians brought with them. The temples of the old gods like Bhanek were largely deserted now, maintained more as historical artifacts than places of worship. The cruel rites associated with the worst of them had been cast aside. If anything was venerated by the elves, it was the wisdom of the Celestians. Almost every aspect of their society had been enhanced by the knowledge the Celestians brought to them. New feats of engineering taught by Belkon brought ever greater structures into being across the kingdom. Wondrous alloys, fantastic meldings of metal and gemstone, emanated from Fulgria's instruction. Valandor guided the Circle of Heaven in increasingly complex and amazing feats of magic, opening the veils between worlds and realities. No corner of elven society was left untouched by the Celestians.

Mescator knew they were doing great things, yet there burned inside him a restlessness. He knew other Celestians felt the same. Liliana, wise and gracious as she was, had often confided her feelings of wanderlust. She'd traveled the length and breadth of Elvenhome, but she was anxious to go further. To see with her own eyes the lands beyond the kingdom. The places and peoples she'd heard spoken of by the elves. She was impatient to explore the whole of Pannithor, to go beyond the reaches of where even the elves had gone.

Rising from the divan, Mescator curled his fingers in a complex gesture. At once, the feylight that flickered within the crystal fixtures along the walls of the room swelled to brilliance and replaced the soft illumination with the glimmer of a noonday sun. He looked about the chamber, its walls draped in rich purple, its floor covered in thick rugs. The room, like all others within the palace Yarinathar had bestowed on Mescator, was built to a grand scale, and he recognized that the finery of its furnishings represented a fortune in the reckoning of elves. Throughout the seventy room palace, the place was exorbitant in its luxury, a factor he'd only grudgingly embraced when Yarinathar observed that the manner of someone's home was often considered a reflection of their importance. The king himself had impressed on Mescator an opulence that rivaled that of the royal residence.

At Mescator's stirring, the door at the far end of the room opened. He wasn't surprised when Oskan entered. None of the elven servants would think to enter the sanctum. However important their tidings, they'd await his emergence.

"You have visitors," Oskan said, a slightly amused look on his face.

Mescator gave his protege a resigned frown. "Another summons to the court? Yarinathar is wise enough to know what he should do, whatever the problem might be."

"Yarinathar is wise enough to know that when he has the support of the Great Mescator, then there's no opposition to his decisions," Oskan countered. "Even a king must be wary of imposing his will too freely." He smiled and shook his head. "Your guest, however, is not from the court. At least not from that of Therennia Adar."

Intrigued by Oskan's coy words, Mescator made a closer study of him. He could see an undercurrent of excitement in Oskan's manner, something that had become increasingly rare as year after year found them guiding the elves in their development. Like Liliana, he was impatient to see new things.

"Who is it that has come to see me?" Mescator asked. "I know you are taking great amusement from drawing out my curiosity, but I wonder if you anticipate how little my appetite is for mysteries at the moment."

Oskan wasn't ready to surrender so easily. "I left them in the study. If you'll allow me, I'll conduct you to them." Still wearing that amused look, Oskan turned and withdrew from the room.

Mescator chided himself as he hurried after Oskan. He'd been too indulgent with his protege. Had he been stricter, Oskan wouldn't have such a headstrong streak and impulsive manner. Of course those very qualities were also why Mescator saw such potential in him – however frustrating they might be in the current moment. He was someone who would remain steadfast to his principles and act upon them without hesitation or compromise.

The study branched off from the reception hall near the entrance of the palace. Mescator passed an elven steward carrying a tray laden with slender bottles of sapphire-colored glass. The shape of the bottles told a story all their own. They contained what was deemed a crude and unrefined vintage of wine typically employed only for cooking meals. The crystal goblets that accompanied the bottles, however, indicated that someone was imbibing it in a direct fashion. However rustic an elf's background, Mescator knew of none with so undiscriminating a palate. He guessed now the identity of the visitors, but the observation only heightened his curiosity.

Oskan opened the door to the study. Gathered within the wood-paneled room were five visitors who were most decidedly not elves. Mescator had encountered humans several times since establishing himself in Therennia Adar, but such meetings had been infrequent and always within the context of broader gatherings with many elves in attendance. This was the first time he'd met with them in a more private setting.

"Gentlemen, I present to you Lord Mescator," Oskan announced as he stepped aside and conducted his mentor into the room.

Mescator gave the humans a quick inspection. Two of them were dressed in rougher fashion than the others, their clothes woven from materials less elaborate than the silks and satin favored by the elven court. Their hair, skin, the very way they breathed and moved all had a somehow raw quality that was devoid of the casual grace of the elves. A human envoy to Therennia Adar, consciously or otherwise, took on some of the refinements of his hosts after being among the elves for any great time. Everything about this pair said they'd come from outside Elvenhome and had done so but recently. That in itself was a puzzle that intrigued Mescator greatly.

"It gladdens me to welcome you," Mescator said. Uncertain of the rank of the newcomers, he addressed himself first to the human he knew to be Primovantor's ambassador to Elvenhome, a gray-headed pudgy diplomat called Bryce Vander. Mescator was struck by how greatly the years had taken toll of the man. He recalled the robust figure from that day when the priests carried away the body of Bhanek's last theocrat. Truly Reiliur had spoken of how quickly the life-force burned within the human frame.

"We're honored by your reception," Bryce returned, bowing to Mescator and Oskan in turn. He smiled appreciatively as the elven steward entered with the tray of wine, distracted for just an instant by the arrival of the libation. He swiftly recovered and indicated one of the men who had remained seated. He was one of the strangers in the foreign clothes. The brief bloom of human youth hadn't withdrawn from him yet. His face was smooth and full, his hair was a deep black, which was only rarely seen among the elves, his eyes were clear and sharp.

"May I present to you, my lord, His Grace Prince Lyzander of Istvoor, Heir-apparent of her majesty Queen Tamira," the ambassador continued the introduction.

The prince rose from his seat and snapped a stiff salute to Mescator. "Forgive this intrusion, your lordship," Lyzander said. "I can only beg your indulgence and entreat you to spare some little time to consider the request I would put to you." The prince's tongue was ill-accustomed to the elven language, evident by the slow and cautious way he enunciated each word.

"Please, be seated," Mescator invited the prince. He took up a chair opposite Lyzander's. He could see the uneasiness working on the man's mind, an uncertainty that he judged must be rare to him for the prince to wear it so poorly. Lyzander was someone accustomed to controlling the things and people around him. To be in a situation where such wasn't the case was rare for him. Mescator wondered what could be so important that the heir to Primovantor's throne would leave his own country and place himself in such an unaccustomed position.

"Tales of your great accomplishments have spread into Primovantor," the prince explained. "Among many of our people, the name of Mescator is invoked with not only reverence, but hope. We've glimpsed from afar all that you've done for the elves. How, under the guidance of the Celestians, you've brought Elvenhome into a new age of glory and wonder. There are many of us who would dare to pray you might bestow upon us the same wisdom and enlightenment."

Mescator looked over at Oskan. "You knew the purpose of the prince's visit?"

Oskan nodded. "I did, but it wasn't my place to render him a decision. All I could do was promise to arrange this meeting." He turned to Bryce. "The original intention was to let the ambassador put this proposal to you, but Prince Lyzander felt it would be a slight against your greatness if anyone but himself were to make this request of you. We've been waiting three months for the prince to make the journey to Therennia Adar."

Mescator turned back to the prince. "You're asking that the Celestians leave Elvenhome and visit Primovantor. To help your people as we have the elves."

"If even a few of the Celestians could grace our lands with their presence, it would inspire my people," Lyzander said. "It would fill them with hope. Tell them that a new era of greatness is possible. That we can shake off the shadows of yesterday and reach for a bright tomorrow."

The prince's words, the passion behind them, made an impact upon Mescator. The elves haughtily considered humans as shallow and simple beings, incapable of the depth of feeling that formed their own character. Mescator saw things differently. The lifespan of a single elf would last centuries. In that same span, generations of humans would be born and die. The brevity of their lives forced humans to possess a determination that spoke to him more than the resigned fatalism of the elves. A human couldn't endlessly ponder a decision before it was made. A human had to act and seize the moment that was offered because there wasn't the luxury of waiting for the chance to come again. More than the wisest elf, a human had to think in terms of what was going to come afterward, in the years he would never see. What he built, he built not for himself, but for those who would follow after him.

"You understand that to build the new, it is necessary to cut away the old," Mescator cautioned Lyzander. "The elves were ready for such a change, because they could look to experiencing for themselves the future they were building. Forgive me for saying it, but the candle of life burns fast in humans. Many who set upon this path will not see the change they're working for. Those who've built upon the foundations already there will be determined to defend the traditional ways, because without them, the legacy they think to leave will be lost."

Lyzander's face was grave. "It is as you say, your lordship. Many of my people are shackled by superstition and fealty to decayed gods who no longer listen to their prayers. Even as Elvenhome was, so we are, held back by an antiquated past that refuses to step aside and allow us to advance." His gaze brightened and he nodded his head. "But now there's the example you've made here. What you've done for the elves gives all of us heart. Queen Tamira was a staunch and ardent follower of the old gods. Now she would eagerly attend the wisdom of the Celestians. She knows that in you is the way forward."

"King Yarinathar is aware of how things stand in Primovantor," Bryce said. "In private, he has conceded that while his majesty is reluctant to lose the advice of the Celestians, he also appreciates that your guidance can strengthen Primovantor and turn our kingdom into a powerful and prosperous land. A strong Primovantor means a strong friend to Elvenhome. That can only bring good to both our peoples."

Mescator was silent as he deliberated upon the proposal. Again he saw the wisdom of Yarinathar in play. The king was leaving the choice to him, but through Bryce, he was making his own position clear. The elves wanted the Celestians to stay, but necessity dictated otherwise. What was unspoken by the humans and merely suggested by Yarinathar was the possibility that jealousy of the elves might poison Primovantor's friendship and, eventually, lead the two kingdoms into conflict.

A middle course would be best for all. Some of the Celestians would journey to Primovantor while others remained with the elves. Valandor's work with the Circle of Heaven, as well as several of the other projects being guided by the Celestians, were too important and complex to be set aside. Others, however, could more easily be concluded. Mescator would meet with those he thought could be spared and see if they were willing to undertake the journey.

Besides the wisdom of extending their stewardship to Primovantor, there were other reasons Mescator was amiable to the plan. Just as much as Liliana and Oskan, he was restless and eager to see new things.

"You may return to you lands," Mescator addressed the prince, "and know that some of the Celestians will soon be among you to share our knowledge with you." He glanced aside at Oskan and smiled. "I can't say how many of us will go to Primovantor, but I know there are at least some eager to see your lands."

Chapter IV

-1075, Time of Light

Only five Celestians made the journey from Elvenhome to Primovantor. At least at this early stage, Mescator was wary of causing too much disruption to their collaboration with the elves. His own presence was something he felt could be spared, especially if he could help raise the humans into a new era of reason and enlightenment as they had the elves. Yarinathar was a wise king, and if he did need the advice of the Celestians, he still had Valandor to consult.

With him, Mescator brought Oskan and Liliana, each gripped by the wanderlust that held him in its sway. He was surprised that Fulgria was also curious enough about the humans to make the journey, but she'd finally confessed that the elven penchant to place artistry paramount against practicality had become an annoyance to her. There was much she'd have taught the elves, but they were incapable of adjusting their own preconceptions when it came to craftsmanship. She was of the hope that humans might prove more pliable to her instruction and less set in their ways. Naturally, when Fulgria decided to leave, so too did her devoted Belkon.

Prince Lyzander sent riders ahead of them, and in each town they passed through, the Celestians found a grand reception awaiting them. Or at least as grand as the humans could muster. Their efforts paled beside the magnificence they'd seen with the elves, but even so, Mescator was enchanted by the waving banners that lined the streets and the colorful costumes of the crowds. There was an energy, a vitality that the humans possessed that was simply absent from the staid, refined elves. An immediacy that the long-lived elves simply didn't have and which, Mescator suspected, they could neither understand nor appreciate.

"There is much we can teach these people," Liliana commented as they rode through one of the towns. The svelte, agile steeds gifted to them by Yarinathar were irritable for having to retard their fleetness to keep pace with the bulkier horses of Lyzander and his entourage. The humans, they'd learned, bred their animals for hardiness and endurance rather than the more specialized traits favored by the elves. "They build much like they breed their horses," Liliana said, pointing to the half-timber structures they passed. "Solid foundations, rugged materials. Performance before aesthetic quality."

"These are but the outskirts of the kingdom," Oskan reminded her. "When we reach the royal capital, we'll find things much different."

"All wealth flows back to the crown," Belkon said, a sour note in his tone. "It is a far less egalitarian system than that of Elvenhome, where the bulk of resources remains in the hands of those who produced them."

Fulgria gave him a bewildered look. "Can't you appreciate the efficiency of such a system? By gathering resources in a single concentration, they can be better dispensed where they're needed. It is a pragmatic way of administering the land's wealth."

Belkon indicated the crude buildings lining the street and the simple garb worn by the crowds of humans. "I think it is these people who don't appreciate the efficiency of such a system. Compare their raiment to the quality of Lyzander and his retinue. None of them are so finely arrayed as the elves, but there's still a wide gulf between their condition. I suspect when we see the capital, we'll find that extends to dwellings and roads and every other aspect of life."

"We've seen the excesses enjoined by the elves by their frivolity," Fulgria said. "A centralized authority with a firmer dominion than Yarinathar possesses could ensure nothing was left to waste."

Mescator listened as the debate continued between his companions. They employed the Celestian language, lest the trend of their speech disturb Lyzander's men. Liliana and Belkon took up the tack that it was better to allow independence, under which conditions discovery and creativity would thrive. Fulgria and Oskan were of the other position, that the waste of too much liberty would weaken society overall and breed within it selfishness and envy.

"You are both right and wrong," Mescator declared. "There is inevitably waste when a people are left too much to themselves without any sense of unity or obligation to their fellows. But too much control is a dangerous thing. When vested in someone unworthy of that sort of power, you encourage tyranny under which none but those useful to the holder of that authority will prosper. Think on the harm wrought upon the elves by the theocrat of Bhanek, and then consider that she did what she did not out of self-interest but from a sincerity of misplaced faith. Now endow someone whose mind is twisted with greed or hate with that measure of power."

He looked across the other Celestians. "Only someone who loves his people more than himself could be trusted with that kind of power," Mescator warned. "Otherwise, you'd create a monster."

Oskan nodded toward Prince Lyzander as he rode at the front of the procession, horse and man alike draped in purple. "What do you think of Lyzander? Is he a monster such as you describe?"

"I think his intentions are honorable and his heart is in the right place," Mescator replied. His gaze lingered on the prince, studying the warmth of his smile as he waved to the crowd, the glimmer of affection that shone in his eyes. "The great danger of power is you can never be certain what someone will do with it until after it has been given to them."

***

The great city of Primovantor might not have had the grandeur of Therennia Adar or Ileuriath, but if the capital lacked the artistic elegance of the elf king's domain, it surpassed it in sheer size. The city itself extended for miles, connecting with three rivers that coursed down from the nearby mountains and flowed away to the distant sea. Around the city were innumerable towns and villages, communities that existed solely to support the inhabitants of the capital. Seven layers of walls encompassed Primovantor, each denoting periods in its long history when it had swelled beyond previous limitations. The foundations of an eighth wall were now in progress, consuming some of the outlying communities and enfolding them into the expanding metropolis.

Lofty towers reached up from the city's sprawl, and Lyzander took pleasure in pointing out to the Celestians the banners of the kingdom's great houses. All of the prominent nobles maintained a residence within the capital so they might be near Queen Tamira and seek both her support and her favor.

In this way, the prince said, the needs of the whole kingdom were brought before the sovereign; for even if the nobles preferred to remain in the city, their fortunes were directly tied to the prosperity of their provinces and the productivity of their people.

The spires of the great temples were likewise a prominent feature of the city's skyline. Here the worship of Ohmpek was observed, and here too, there was a cruel ritual similar to that of Bhanek in his role as Chooser of the Born. It was a ritual Lyzander loathed and one that Queen Tamira tolerated only because of the power of the priesthood.

"To Ohmpek there is the soul-tithe," Lyzander explained. "During the festival of Long Night, when the hours of day are at their lowest and the might of darkness is ascendant, lots are drawn for each child born during the year. One of the tokens drawn is that of the Accursed, the vessel in which the forces of destruction seek to annihilate all that Bhanek has created and the light of Ohmpek nurtures. The Accursed is brought to the Cathedral of the Sun, which stands on the highest peak in the Dragonspine Mountains. There the child is kept until Bright Day, that day of the year when the night is shortest. When dawn breaks, the Accursed is walled alive within the temple so that the evil within can be imprisoned."

"There seems no limit to the cruel customs of your gods," Mescator said, taking no effort to hide the disapproval he felt.

Lyzander frowned. "Tradition is a difficult thing to defy, even for monarchs." He gave Mescator a studious look as they rode past the outskirts of the city where the new outer wall was being raised. "A mortal can't defy a god. Only another god can do that."

"Is that how all of your people think?" Liliana asked.

"It is how the ones who need guidance think," Lyzander replied. "It is how those who most need your help believe."

Mescator was silent as they approached the gatehouse in the seventh wall. It was built to a colossal scale with immense doors a hundred feet tall. Tiers of battlements jutted from its face and wrapped about to encompass its sides. Pennants bearing the golden eagle of Queen Tamira crackled in the wind at every level, while from the conical roof, a giant flag, a blue field with a black tower and a yellow sun, flew above the city. These details caught Mescator's notice, but his attention was drawn to a timber pillory just outside the gate and on the edge of the road. An old woman was locked in the pillory, her gray hair dripping with filth, her body caked in detritus. About her feet, the debris of spoiled fruit and vegetables was strewn along with the offal and dung that had been hurled at her by passersby.

"What was this woman's crime?" Mescator turned to Lyzander and demanded an answer.

Lyzander pointed to a glyph that had been burned into the back of the woman's hand. "That is the brand of Shobik. His priests found this woman guilty of witchcraft, of trying to commune with the spirits of the dead. Something that is prohibited to all but Shobik's priesthood. The first instance of such transgression, the offender is marked with the brand. This woman has been found guilty of a second offense and so is placed in the pillory and subjected to public scorn."

"Has this woman brought direct harm to anyone?" Mescator stopped his horse beside the pillory. His gaze fixed upon a group of children creeping forward to throw rotten vegetables. They dropped the garbage and scurried away, frightened by the Celestian's glower.

"There was a time when the priests would have burned her alive upon a pyre for such a crime," Lyzander said. "Now they agree to be restrained by the royal decree and may execute only those who can be proved to have brought death to another by means of their spells." He shook his head. "Even so, Shobik's inquisitors execute dozens each year, mostly in the frontier provinces."

"The queen permits this?" Oskan asked.

"Only a god may defy a god," Lyzander repeated.

Mescator spurred his horse to the side of the pillory. Soldiers from the gatehouse started toward him, but as with the children, a single glance made them withdraw. Mescator looked down at the abused woman, her clothes clotted with the stains of her ordeal, her skin blackened where harder objects had pelted her. She gazed up at him with weary eyes, her head restricted by the yoke around her neck. A faint flicker of hope shone in her face as she looked at Mescator.

The Celestian's armored hand reached out and tightened around the peg that held the yoke in place. Beneath his grip, the peg and the iron staples that held it crumbled into powder. A flick of his hand sent the yoke sagging against the side of the pillory. The old woman started to fall, but Mescator's fingers caught her.

"You've suffered enough," Mescator said. As he spoke, energy rippled out from his body. Some of his essence coursed over the old woman, suffusing her with a golden light that brought gasps of wonder from the humans who saw it. The light became so intense that the woman's form was lost within its glow. For an instant, there was nothing except the light.

In a moment, the light was gone, the power flowing back inside Mescator. The effect of the energy he'd briefly invested into the woman, however, remained. All traces of filth and abuse were absent now. No debris clotted her hair and clothes, no bruises marred her skin. Her hair, though still gray with age, now had a silky and vibrant sheen. Her wrinkled skin had a glow of health and vitality. Her clothes were no longer faded but instead seemed as if their threads had just come off the spindle.

Shocked gasps resounded all around from the spectators. Many fell to their knees, overcome by the wondrous sight. The old woman approached Mescator, not on hobbling legs that struggled to support her but with a firm and certain step. She gripped his hand and pressed her cheek against it, tears of gratitude streaming from her eyes.

Mescator turned to his fellow Celestians and spoke to them in their star-born language. "If it needs gods to overcome this injustice, then we shall be gods."

***

-1050, Time of Light

Oskan was still unable to believe that the withered, feeble man who had to be carried about in a special cart was the same youthful and impassioned prince who'd brought them away from Therennia Adar. He knew that even for humans, Lyzander's decline had been rapid and abrupt. It was only the second year of his reign as king, but he was already more wasted than Queen Tamira when the sun set on the sixty-third year of her rule.

Lyzander smiled when he saw the concern on Oskan's face. "Your kind are eternal, or nearly so," he said. "You'll forget me soon enough."

The king's words echoed through the confines of the royal pavilion. The tent had been raised on a little hill that overlooked Primovantor's frontier. From its shaded opening, Lyzander could see across the river plain and out toward the wooded hills in the distance. The squat, brutish mass of a border fort crouched against the peak, its parapets adorned with the impaled bodies of captured spies and scouts. Shining in the sunlight was a golden stake, a mocking promise from the garrison as to the fate that awaited the king of Primovantor.

Oskan bristled at that murderous threat. Of all the humans he'd met, Lyzander had truly been admirable and noble. For a man of his quality to be derided by the barbarous people of Chult was insufferable. He wished the Celestians were truly capable of the tremendous powers that the people of Primovantor credited them with. If so, he'd have obliterated the savages the moment they'd dared to turn their sorcery on Lyzander.

"You'll not be forgotten," Oskan said. "Neither by your people, nor by us. Not least because there is so much you've yet to do for Primovantor."

"I fear it must be left for others to accomplish," the king said, sinking back into the thick cushions of his bed. "Please, guide my son. Make of him a good and wise king. Let him finish what I must leave undone." A shiver swept through Lyzander. The physicians attending him hurried over to inspect his condition. One pulled back the thin, gauzy robe he wore and began rubbing a pungent-smelling ointment on his chest while another beckoned to the court magician to strengthen the arcane wards drawn in the earth around the king.

"Prince Juliarius will bring glory to Primovantor," Oskan assured Lyzander, "and you will be there to see his time of greatness."

The focus of all within the pavilion was drawn suddenly to the entrance. The tall, armored figure of Mescator marched in, a great sword hanging from his belt and a plumed helm held in the crook of his arm. The visage Oskan's mentor bore was one of severity and determination. Since coming among the humans, the Celestians had adjusted their appearance, taking on qualities that were similar enough to them as to bolster a sense of familiarity and kinship just as they'd done when dwelling with the elves. A human face, however, was more raw and emotive than the practiced refinement seen with the elves, less prone to that degree of subtlety and nuance. Oskan was still trying to become acquainted with the precise blend of exhibition and reserve Mescator had already come to master.

Following a respectful three steps behind Mescator was a youthful human wearing a cuirass of plate upon which was engraved the symbols of tower and sun. The cloak that billowed from the man's shoulders was of richest purple, and the scabbard of his sword was covered in jewels and golden filigree. The weapon itself, to judge by its simple steel hilt and pommel, was designed less ostentatiously and more for utility than grandeur. Like the Celestian, the human carried a plumed helm under his arm. The expression on his face, however, faltered when he saw Lyzander on his bed, and all the confidence was smothered under a display of the most intense concern.

Oskan was still struck by the remarkable resemblance between Juliarius and his father. If not for the deep red of the prince's hair, he might be the same man who'd met with them in Therennia Adar.

"Your legions are ready," Mescator told the king. "The generals have put them into position. A company of light horse has been set to the rear, dragging rakes behind them to create clouds of dust. Unless the enemy's sorcerers see through the deception, they will believe more troops are coming to bolster the army."

"Primovantor's wizards have been tasked with thwarting such spells," Oskan said. "A natural precaution in any event. No army wants the enemy spying on them. Chult will not guess there is direct purpose behind such methods."

Lyzander waved away the healers administering to him. "Enough of my subjects have betrayed me that the enemy knows how large Primovantor's armies are." His eyes clouded with sorrow. "I thought only to better my people. I did not intend it to come to this. I didn't think it would come to war. Perhaps I should have listened to those who advised executing Shobik's priests."

"To do so would have done even greater harm," Mescator said. "It would have been seen as the act of a tyrant, callous of the traditions of his subjects. You would have fractured Primovantor into rival camps. War would have come just the same, but it would have been an even more bitter kin-strife that should have left scars which might never heal."

"The most zealous of Shobik's priests have sought to use the kings of other lands to restore the dominance of their power in Primovantor." Oskan expressed the cause of the war in the baldest terms. "They collude with foreign temples they condemned as heretical only a few decades ago in order to prevent reform. Your people see all of this, and they understand who the real enemy is." He looked about the pavilion and saw the resolve in the faces of Lyzander's attendants. "When the war is over, your people will welcome the abolition of Shobik's priesthood and the casting down of his temples. They'll be ready to follow a new path."

"There's an old adage," Lyzander said, "something that ironically comes from *The Book of Shobik*. It warns that the sons of your enemies must be destroyed or they will become the enemies of your sons." He looked to Juliarius and frowned. "I fear I've brought that curse against you even sooner than I appreciated."

The prince stepped forward and took his father's hand. Kneeling beside the bed, he gave Lyzander a kiss upon his brow. "You've only brought forth a conflict that was inevitable. It is better that it be fought now, with you here to inspire your soldiers and lead us into victory." He looked up at Mescator and then to Oskan. "You've shown us gods who are more than distant whispers in a darkened temple. The Celestians bring us hope, the promise of a paradise that we can share in this world, not the shadows of an underworld and empty prayers learned by rote until even the priests no longer believe in them. Primovantor is set upon the road to greatness, and it is you who made that possible."

"The priests in these other lands wouldn't be content to see Shobik's hold on Primovantor slip away," Oskan stated. "Chult has ever been a hostile neighbor to your kingdom, but with the Ahmunites to your south, there has long been peace. Now, at the instigation of the priests, conflict brews there as well as here. The old gods have faded until they are naught but whispers and shadows, but their priests are very real, and they will not allow their dominion to be toppled without a war."

"Here is the place to fight King Borri," Mescator said. "The terrain forces Chult to come against us along a narrow front. The hills are too rugged for cavalry or blocks of infantry. He must come against us through the pass. And he will. We've convinced him that the whole of Primovantor's army is here, that at best only a token force remains to oppose his Ahmunite allies. Borri has only to keep us here long enough for the south to be invaded, then he expects your legions to fragment in panic as they rush to counter the invasion."

Lyzander shifted painfully on his cushions. "The danger in the plan is that Chult *is* bringing its entire army against us while our own forces are much smaller than they think. I am confident Fulgria and Belkon will stop the Ahmunites in the south, because the invaders won't be expecting such a force to be ready to meet them, but here..." He shook his head and made a helpless gesture with his hands. "It will go hard for my soldiers. They will each need to do the fighting of ten men." He banged his fist in frustration against the side of the bed. "If only I could help instead of lying here like a helpless hulk."

"I'll be there with our soldiers," Juliarius said. "Through me they'll know their king is with them." He indicated the Celestians with a bow. "Too, they know that we have Mescator and Oskan with us. Our gods fight beside us. Chult has only the lies and trickery of its degenerate priests."

"Don't be too quick to dismiss their sorcery," Lyzander cautioned. "I'm proof there's still some power to be drawn from the old gods."

Oskan scowled at the reminder. "We'll bring justice upon them for what they've done. They'll not prosper from their infamies."

Mescator nodded in agreement. "There's a weakness in Borri's strategy. He thinks in terms of how many warriors he can bring onto the field. He forgets that he rules over his people through fear." He made a chopping motion with his hand. "However vast the serpent, strike off its head and the dying body writhes in aimless confusion. To defeat Primovantor, Borri must vanquish your army. To defeat Chult, all we need to do is kill one man."

***

The clamor of trumpets sounded from the ranked infantry of Primovantor while the roar of kettle drums boomed from the gathering hosts of Chult. In every aspect, the gulf between the two cultures created a marked contrast. Though both peoples were human, Mescator considered that those of Primovantor had more in common with the elves than they did these brutish enemies. Orderly and disciplined, each soldier equipped in the same manner as the rest of his company, the legions of King Lyzander exhibited all the refinement of an advanced culture. Their breastplates of bronze and iron gleamed in the sun, the colored tunics that denoted their regiment were bright and vivid. Swordsmen were grouped with swordsmen, spears with other spears. Troops of knights kept their armored steeds behind the blocks of infantry, ready to respond to any breaks in the line and to ride down the first foes who broke through.

The horde of King Borri was far different. His warriors presented a disordered appearance. Some wore chain shirts while others were arrayed in layers of animal hide. They grouped together in rude packs, each bound to one of the dragon-bone totems carried by their priests. Each totem was carved into the semblance of some beast and represented the aspect to which the individual warriors swore brotherhood. Within each pack there was a wide array of weaponry. Swords and axes, mauls and flails, all were in evidence as the barbarians brandished them defiantly in the air. Only the archers had been divided from their companions and broken off into groups to guard the flanks. These and the huscarls of Borri's elite were the only specialized troops among the horde. The huscarls, their totem cut into the savage countenance of a fanged giant and gilded in gold, carried both pole-axe and broadsword, and they were uniformly armored in mail. Each of Borri's elite had a young woman with him, her role to carry a long shield as tall as herself and protect the warrior from enemy blows.

"There is where you'll find the head of the snake," Oskan commented, waving his hand at the huscarls. The two Celestians walked their horses between the companies of Priomvantor's infantry as Prince Juliarius gave his soldiers some final words of encouragement.

Mescator studied Chult's elite infantry and nodded. "King Borri will be with them. To do less would expose weakness – weakness another chieftain would quickly seize upon to take the crown for himself. Yes, that is where he will be. That is where we must strike."

Oskan frowned. "It won't be easy. He'll hold them back until he's sure of victory. Lyzander might have qualms about spending the lives of his people. Borri doesn't. He'll let the rabble die and keep his elite in reserve."

Mescator gave his protege a reproving look. "Never do what the enemy expects. Borri can read the terrain as well as we can. He knows the safest thing for Primovantor to do is stand fast and hold their ground. What he won't expect is for us to take the battle directly to him."

"It's a risk," Oskan said.

"Not when two Celestians will be riding with Juliarius and his knights," Mescator stated. "The only risk would arise if Chult decided to fight on without their king. They won't. Tyranny dies with the tyrant. At least until another monster can replace the one that's died."

From the hordes of Chult, jeering howls rang out. The barbarians smashed weapons against shields, creating a thunderous din that swelled ever louder as more and more warriors joined in. The gilded standard of King Borri dipped slightly. It was the final signal to his chieftains. The brotherhoods chosen to lead the attack lunged forward now and charged the waiting legions of Primovantor.

Arrows arced upward from Primovantor's archers and scythed down into the oncoming barbarians. Many of Chult's warriors ignored the missiles even as they pierced their flesh, so lost were they in the crazed lust of battle. Those who did succumb were trampled underfoot, their comrades indifferent whether the stricken were dead or merely wounded. All that counted for them now was to close upon the enemy.

Mescator climbed into the saddle of the huge white destrier gifted to him by King Lyzander. Half a head taller than any other steed in Primovantor, the war horse was suited to the imposing frame of a Celestian. From the vantage of its saddle, Mescator could peer over the heads of the infantry and observe the impetus of Borri's attack.

"They take small notice of your archers," Mescator informed Juliarius as the prince mounted his own steed.

"They drink a mixture of wolf's blood and mead before entering battle," Juliarus said. "Over this, the priests of Shobik weave spells and add special herbs that will make the men of Chult fight like wild animals. They become impervious to pain. Only the most grievous injury will make them relent."

Oskan donned the plumed helm he'd been carrying, the feathers of a black eagle standing out in a crest that ran from the edge of his visor to the back of his neck. "We'll make short work of them if they fight so recklessly."

"Don't be quick to underestimate a foe who attacks without thought for his own safety," Mescator cautioned. He was silent as he watched the first barbarians hit the front line. A roar like that of an avalanche boomed across the battlefield when the howling warriors met the shields of Primovantor's legion. The earth itself shuddered from the impact. Despite their resolve, some of the soldiers were pushed back by the barbarians' charge. Others were pulled out of formation, overwhelmed by the brawn and savagery of the enemy, cut down by axes and swords.

The foremost rank of the legion crumbled, shattered by the initial assault. Those soldiers who held their ground were struck from the flanks as the barbarians lapped around them. Dozens of Primovantor's troops were hacked apart by the cleaving axes of Chult.

The second rank, however, held fast. Mescator watched with grim approval as soldiers stepped back to allow survivors from the doomed front rank to slip in and take their place. The first line was shattered and decimated, but the barbarians now found another layer of opposition ready to defy them. The impetus of their crazed charge was spent, the shock of their onslaught exhausted. Now it was discipline and resolve that would show their quality. With each soldier guarded by the shield of the man beside him, the warriors of Primovantor now brought their stabbing swords into play. Again and again they thrust at the barbarians. The very eagerness of their own comrades pushing from behind forced Chult's fighters onto the blades that ripped into them. In that press of bodies, there was no room for maneuver, only space enough to kill or be killed.

The tenacity of the barbarians remained tremendous. Mescator saw soldiers bodily ripped from the line by an enraged warrior and flung back to be hacked apart by the axes of those behind. Yet each time a gap was created, another man of Primovantor stepped forward to take the position. The enemy remained faced by an unbroken line, and however furiously he raged against it, the formation refused to falter. Now the legion's archers loosed more volleys into the horde, whittling away at their strength. The army of Chult tried to return the favor, but their arrows only clattered harmlessly against the upraised shields of the swordsmen in the rear ranks. Of the hundreds of arrows the barbarians loosed, the casualties they inflicted could be reckoned upon one hand.

Howls of frustration rose from the hordes Chult had yet to commit to the fray. Again the gilded standard of King Borri gave the signal and brotherhoods of barbarians rushed into the fight. Juliarius had no need to give direction to his own forces. The generals had their orders and knew the battle plan. Archers whittled away at the charging warriors while more swordsmen advanced to hold the line. Mescator kept watching the disposition of Chult's reserves and particularly where their horsemen waited, ready to ride down the soldiers of Primovantor once they broke. The repositioning of the warrior brotherhoods as they advanced created an obstacle to Borri's cavalry. More, they formed a corridor, a gap that led directly to the huscarls.

"Juliarius," Mescator pointed and drew the prince's attention to the channel that had developed behind the vanguard of Chult's horde. There was no need to explain further. Juliarius sent his adjutants to relay commands to the captains of his infantry.

"We ride when they make their push," Mescator told Oskan. The knights around them steadied themselves for the coming effort. The horses, sensing the tension, stamped their hooves and champed at their bits.

Three sharp blasts from a lone trumpet initiated the thrust. Through the rear ranks of the swordsmen, spearmen had quietly drawn close to the front. Now they struck, surging forward in a sudden tide of piercing steel. Concentrated along a narrow wedge, they forced the surprised barbarians back. A hole opened in the line.

"For Primovantor! For the Celestians! For King Lyzander!" The cry started with Juliarius as he spurred his steed forward, but it was swiftly taken up by the rest of his knights. A thundering crash of armored cavalry plowed into the opening. The few barbarians who'd hurried to exploit the breach now found themselves crushed under the charge.

Over and through the barbarous warriors Juliarius led his followers. Whatever savage rites had been performed to embolden them for battle, the men of Chult were stunned by the sudden assault. Scores were flattened by the charge. The warrior brotherhoods who'd been moving forward to confront Primovantor's infantry were too far away now to rush back and close the corridor they'd left open. The barbarians' cavalry was caught behind a screen of their own infantry and incapable of reacting with any manner of speed. Only the bowmen were able to present any sort of defense, and their barbed arrows were incapable of bringing down the armored steeds or their riders.

The knights didn't waver as they rushed past the hordes of Chult and plunged deep into the enemy ranks. Poised near the fore of the cavalry lance, Mescator lashed out with his gleaming sword whenever the barbarians tried to impede the attack. At each stroke of his blade, enemy warriors were sent flying through the air, their armor rent asunder and their bones crushed by the force of his blows. To the other side of the formation, Oskan's sword wrought equal havoc on those unfortunate enough to oppose him.

"King Borri!" Juliarius shouted as the knights smashed into the elite huscarls. Shieldmaidens did their best to defend the veteran warriors while the barbarians used their pole-axes to cut men from their saddles. If not for the presence of the Celestians, the huscarls might have resisted the impact of the charge through sheer tenacity, but none of them could defy the awesome might of Mescator and Oskan.

"Repent your infamies!" Mescator shouted at his foemen even as his flashing sword smashed through their shields and crumpled their helmets. "Cast aside the blight of darkness and seek the ways of justice!" The force of his blows sent dozens of the huscarls tumbling away, maimed and crippled by his incredible strength. From the corner of his eye, he could see Oskan exacting an equally severe toll from their enemy.

Suddenly, the huscarls fell back. The knights didn't press them, however, for out from the midst of the barbarians the gilded standard appeared. Advancing with the standard bearer were two men. One was roughly-built, his face scarred from an old wound that caused a long white streak to course through his beard. He was clad in heavy plates of dark iron, and about his head was a horned helm. In his hands he carried a double-bladed axe; from the heft of which a number of scalps dangled.

The other man was, if anything, even larger than the armored axeman. He wore a wolfskin robe, and around his brow he wore a circlet made from the claws of bears. His face was inked with whorls and glyphs of primitive design, so completely covered that even his lips and throat bore tattoos. The eyes that gleamed from amid the images were a pale blue that was at once both intense and distant. This man bore no weapon in his hands, only a crooked staff topped with a grinning human skull.

The axeman glared up at Juliarius, and his scarred face pulled back in a sneer. "You dare yap for King Borri, dog? Well, here he stands! Are you Lyzander, or did the coward send some thrall to fight his battles for him?"

The huscarls and other barbarians had drawn back, forming a circle around the knights of Primovantor and the Celestians. Every face was turned to Juliarius, waiting to see how he would react to Borri's challenge.

Every face except two. Mescator was looking at the tattooed figure with the pale eyes. He was a stranger, the snowy color of his skin and stark white hair marking him as from some people distinct from the men of Chult. He was young and powerful in his physique, more so than either Borri or the huscarls. Mescator could sense an energy about the man, an impression of menace he hadn't felt since emerging into the world of Pannithor.

The tattooed man returned Mescator's gaze. There was enmity in that look, the impression of a landholder regarding a trespasser. Mescator couldn't shake the feeling that the stranger was fully cognizant of the power of the Celestian. Rather than be awed or intimidated, the robed man seemed to resent his presence as an intrusive annoyance.

Mescator glanced aside as Juliarius dismounted to confront Borri on equal terms. "I am Juliarius, Prince of Primovantor," he snarled at the barbarous chief. "My father, King Lyzander lies infirm. Struck down by the foul sorceries of your warlocks." He cast a withering gaze at the tattooed man.

Borri laughed at the prince's hate. "I've no need for witches, boy," he sneered. "Angbold is a priest, a servant of the great god Korgaan of the Nine Winds." He turned and swept his gaze across Mescator and Oskan. "A stronger gods than the ones you've turned to." His voice faltered when he made the claim, but confidence boiled up inside him once more. "If they're so mighty, they'd have healed Lyzander, and I would be adding a king's scalp to my trophies instead of his whelp's!"

With alarming abruptness, Borri lunged at Juliarius. The double-axe flashed down in a cleaving arc, narrowly missing the prince as he darted aside. Borri's boot smashed into his knee and sent him sprawling, but as he dove for the prone noble, he was struck in turn by Juliarius's sword. A wide gash opened up along the barbarian's forearm and made him recoil in surprise. He hadn't expected such speed from his foe.

"No, damn you!" Oskan shouted. Mescator was surprised when his protege spurred his horse forward. His goal, however, wasn't the dueling leaders, but the tattooed man. Only when Oskan plunged toward him did Angbold's eyes break away from Mescator's. He swung around to meet the charging steed. His hand balled into a fist, and he brought it smashing down into the animal's head. A loud crack echoed through the air and the horse crumpled, its skull shattered by the priest's bare hand. It slammed to the ground, bearing Oskan down with it.

Mescator saw two things unfold at the same time. First, there was Oskan, his slaughtered horse lying atop him. The huscarls, a moment before content to observe the duel, now rushed forward with their axes to hew the Celestian's body with their blades.

Second, there was Juliarius. Though the prince had regained his feet, he had suffered much for the effort. Blood masked his face, streaming from four deep furrows in his forehead. Not the cut of an axe, but the mark of bestial claws. Mescator knew why Oskan had acted as he did. Angbold had worked some ghastly magic against the prince while holding the Celestian enraptured by his gaze.

Juliarius was blinded by the blood streaming into his eyes. He staggered back as Borri came rushing in. Now it was Mescator who intervened. Snatching off his helm, he hurled it at the barbarian king's feet. The crude missile cracked against his ankle and sent the enemy stumbling away, his attack thwarted.

Mescator swung back around to help Oskan, but now it was he who was under attack. Exhibiting a speed he'd have believed impossible for an elf much less a human, Angbold rushed at him. The priest's staff lashed across the white destrier's neck and opened it down to the bone. Mescator leaped clear of the dying animal and confronted his attacker.

"These lands, these people, all belong to Korgaan," Angbold growled. He sprang at Mescator, whipping his murderous staff at the Celestian's face.

Mescator's sword tore through the staff, bisecting it across its length. Before he could capitalize on the advantage, Angbold closed upon him and struck at his wrist. His armor crumpled under the blow, and the sword tumbled from his stunned fingers. He brought his other hand up to protect his throat as the maddened priest tried to get his fingers around his neck.

"You and your kind think to reshape the world," Angbold snarled, his voice deepening until it seemed to issue not from him but from some place deep underground. "Your meddling ends here. It ends now."

Mescator had never felt such power as he now felt coursing through Angbold's body. This was far more than the theocrat of Bhanek drawing energy from a fading god. This was a manifestation of something far more intense, a god who wasn't indolent and lethargic. Not a mortal using a god, but a god using a mortal. Angbold wasn't a priest of Korgaan, he was some manner of avatar. And if before there had been only a mere spark of the war god within him, now that spark had risen into a roaring flame!

As Mescator struggled to break free, to keep the clawing fingers away from his throat, the body of Angbold was at once both expanding and diminishing. He was growing mightier in size and strength, but at the same time, his skin was crumbling away in flakes of dust. The pale hair drifted off in wisps. Teeth dropped free from his jaws. There was only so much of the god that Angbold's flesh could sustain, and that limit was now being exceeded. But as the clutching fingers slipped around Mescator's neck, he feared the priest's body would last long enough for Korgaan's purpose.

"Mescator!" The shout rose from Oskan. The young Celestian lurched up from the ground, lifting his dead horse in both arms. He hurled the carrion into the terrified huscarls, who a moment before, had been trying to attack him. The elite warriors were bowled over by the heavy carcass, several crushed under its weight. Oskan spared them no further attention but instead raced to aid his mentor. His sword crashed down into Angbold's distorted skull, chopping down until it bisected the nose.

For an instant, it seemed the avatar would defy the ghastly wound. Angbold's elongated fingers started to tighten around Mescator's throat. Then they fell slack and dropped away. The pale eyes rolled back in their sockets and the priest slumped down on his knees like a puppet whose strings had been cut. Mescator recognized that such was the limit of his victory. The destruction of a puppet. The master, an ancient force calling itself Korgaan, remained.

"Timely," Mescator told Oskan, rubbing at his throat. Later, there would be time for gratitude. For now, there was the threat of a barbarian horde all around them. A horde whose high priest they'd just killed.

A horde that now set up a terrific wail of horror. The masses of barbarians, only a moment before ready to hurl themselves at the soldiers of Primovantor and the Celestians with a vengeance, now were turning to flee into the hills. Cries of alarm and panic rang out across the battlefield as the horde disintegrated into a general rout.

The cause of the sudden panic stood with blood streaming down his face and seeping from his rent armor. Juliarius held a mangled arm pressed against his chest, but the other he held high for all to see. Gripped by its long beard, the severed head of King Borri dangled for all to see.

Prince Juliarius held the pose only long enough to inspire the rout of Chult's army. Even as Mescator and Oskan rushed to tend him, he dropped to the ground. The light of life was already fading away when Mescator would have used his powers to restore it. He was too late to rekindle the spirit that now withdrew from the prince's body. Debilitated by Angbold's magic, Juliarius had been able to overcome Borri only at the cost of his own life.

"Lyzander must be told," Oskan said. "Told of what he's won and what he's lost."

Mescator looked up at the hill where the king's pavilion stood. From that vantage, Lyzander could gaze across the entire battlefield. As he watched, the flaps at the front of the tent were drawn closed. "He knows," Mescator said.

A black pennant was raised above the pavilion. The cheers that had a moment before risen from the legions of Primovantor now fell silent. Each soldier knew the meaning of that banner.

"Lyzander knows what was won and what it cost," Mescator said, sorrow filling his heart. "The cost was too much to bear.

"The king is dead."

Chapter V

-995, Time of Light

Reiliur stood upon the exterior balcony that opened from the Tower of Heaven's highest level. Below, he could see Ileureleith, the lights of the city glittering like a million diamonds. Only in the areas around the temples was there darkness. The elves had set aside worship of Bhanek and the old gods. Largely, the ancient rites were no longer observed. Only a few of the priests and the most traditional of their followers still participated in the ancient ceremonies. For the rest, it was a new age. An age guided by the light of reason and the wisdom of the Celestians.

A century had passed since the Celestians crossed the bridge between worlds. Though Mescator and several others had gone abroad to lend their aid to the humans of Primovantor, Valandor and other Celestians remained in Elvenholme to guide and instruct the kingdom's people. Valandor made the Tower of Heaven his home, and with his help, the Circle of Heaven made their preparations. No expense was spared. The great crystals that had served as gateways a century before were replaced with even more magnificent portals. The whole of the king's treasury had been put at Reiliur's disposal. Every elf in the land waited in excitement for what this night would bring. The night when the constellations would align and once more the Celestians could cross between worlds.

Valandor stood beside Reiliur. "It will soon be time," he informed the great wizard. "The stars will be in the proper conjunction here. I have spoken with Eoswain through the Star, and she confirms that all is in readiness there."

Reiliur gestured at the gleaming city below. The sounds of music and celebration reached their ears. "Only twenty of you have brought so much change, led my people to new heights of knowledge and wisdom, that we hardly dare dream how much greater it will be when another twenty Celestians are brought to Pannithor."

"Yet I note a tremor in your voice," Valandor stated. "You're uneasy. Something weighs on your mind."

"I was thinking of Oskan," Reiliur confessed. He felt ashamed by his worry when Valandor had none. Everything had been prepared far more exactingly than that first conjunction. The small details that Eoswain had struggled to convey to the elves through the Scrying Star and which had failed to be executed properly by the Circle of Heaven had been remedied by Valandor's direction. He thought back to the first great experiment. Then it had been him arguing with Calisor about the need for prudence. Now he was the one urging caution.

"There will be no such mishap this night," Valandor said. He nodded his head as he read the self-recrimination on Reiliur's face. "Do not think you alone were at fault. There is enough blame to be shared. Eoswain felt Oskan's mind lacked the discipline to maintain focus, but Mescator desired his pupil to accompany him." Valandor nodded and looked out across Ileureleith. "This time there will be no such risk. Eoswain will send the best of our people. Those with skills and talents best suited to nurture the lands of Pannithor."

Reiliur was reassured by the conviction in Valandor's voice. Still, there was one worry that persisted in gnawing at his mind. "When we saved Oskan, you said the power you invoked would demand a price. What if it decides that price should be paid now?" He regretted posing the question. For just a brief moment, he saw an expression of concern on Valandor's face.

"Even the Celestians can't cheat the dictates of destiny," Valandor said. "All we can do is hope that the doom that hangs over our heads maintains its distance this night." He pointed his finger at the sky. "Come. It is time we withdrew. The hour is now upon us."

Celestian and elf stepped back into the great laboratory. It was vastly changed from how it had appeared a century before. The whole of the dome above had been transformed by the alchemical knowledge of Fulgria and the engineering mastery of Belkon so that now it was formed by a single translucent ovoid. The will of an observer could magnify the distant stars into a clarity undreamed, yet this magic was for the observer alone, others in the laboratory saw only what they themselves desired to see. It was a harmony of mind and magic that created, in its way, a separate view of reality. A distillation of individual experience.

"The dragon is in the house of the sword," Calisor reported. Anticipation gleamed from every pore, his eyes fairly glowed with excitement. Reiliur could only shake his head at the role reversal the two elves had undergone. But, then, he supposed Calisor's youthful exuberance had served him well. He was less reluctant to toss aside old notions and concepts under the tutelage of the Celestians than his former teacher was. An idea once set into the brain was difficult to dislodge. Stubbornly, it clung on in defiance of all contrary evidence, seeking to twist and distort facts so that it might still claw out a place for itself.

Reiliur shook his head, irritated by his gloomy thoughts. He looked to Valandor. "Will you establish the contact with Eoswain?"

Valandor smiled. Reiliur could tell the Celestian had read the motive behind the question. "That is your place," he said, his voice loud enough so that it carried to the other elves and Celestians in the laboratory. "It is by your determination and conviction that all of this has been possible. Yours was the will that guided us across the tides of space and time to reach Pannithor. Should we tempt things now by changing our guiding beacon?"

Though Reiliur knew the truth, that any sufficiently powerful will could act in his stead, he felt pride when he heard Valandor's words. His own confidence was bolstered when he saw the admiration in the eyes of the other elves and the respect that was on the faces of the Celestians.

Reiliur took his place at the center of the laboratory, mounting the raised dais where the Scrying Star rested. With Calisor beside him, he began the ritual. Around them, the elven wizards began to chant and weave the magic within the Tower of Heaven toward the grand purpose of the night's ritual. Valandor took a position among the elves, standing within one of the adamantine circles. The other Celestians hung back, ranged about the periphery of the chamber. Valandor had warned that the gateways were attuned to the particular harmonies of the elven mind and spirit. Of all their number, only he'd been able to simulate the condition of the mortal soul enough to put his own into sympathy with the Circle of Heaven. Without that cohesion, the Celestians would prove a hindrance rather than an asset to the ritual.

"I am here. All is ready." Reiliur sent his thoughts streaming into the Scrying Star. Instantly, he felt the connection with Eoswain far across the gulf of space and time.

As it had a century before, Eoswain's reply flowed into Reiliur's very being. "Then let us begin."

Reiliur wasn't tempted by the sense of translocation this time. Valandor had instructed him in precautions both mental and magical that would anchor him to the reality of the Tower of Heaven. It wasn't that he was unaware of these other existences adjacent to the arcane bridge, but their fascination had dwindled almost to nothingness. After meeting the Celestians in the flesh and seeing for himself the wonders they'd brought to Pannithor, he doubted if anything could have distracted him from the monumental importance of what was now unfolding in the Tower of Heaven. The second arrival of the Celestians.

Fog rippled within the gateways. To the accompaniment of the wizards' incantations, a weird and eerie melody now filtered through the laboratory. Reiliur smiled at the sound. It was the keening Eoswain had devised to strengthen the bridge from her side and prevent any repeat of what had happened before. With the melody to bear them along, the journeying Celestians hastened across the immense gulf at such speed that there was no threat of losing the essential conjunction of constellations.

The first of the Celestians to emerge from the gateways was a tall woman, willowy in her build, strong in her features, an excited light in her eyes. She wore an elegant gown, its material possessed of a metallic shine. When she moved, it shifted through colors so that Reiliur couldn't decide if it was a deep blue or a brilliant gold, or a vibrant green. Her hair, too, seemed of variegated hues, rippling from a pale blonde to a deep chestnut when she turned her head. Even her skin had a chameleon-like aspect to it that altered her complexion at every heartbeat.

It was with difficulty that Reiliur took his gaze from the changeling woman. Other Celestians now emerged from the gateways. He saw a lean man of a powerful and pantherish build step forth, his dusky skin and dark hair contrasting with the silvery tunic he wore and the ivory spear he carried. An exuberant laugh of unabashed joy rang out as he surveyed the laboratory, and Reiliur was minded of the excitement Liliana had shown when she first started to explore Pannithor.

Reiliur tried to watch each Celestian as they entered the laboratory, but so swift was their journey that the task became impossible. To show any one of them more than the merest attention was to lose sight of another's arrival. The process, as Eoswain had improved upon it, made the trip far swifter and devoid of the hazards of before. Almost before he was aware of it, the last of the twenty stepped through the gateway safely. She was a dark-haired, round-faced Celestian, with gold-flecked eyes and bright red hair. Her robes were arrayed with fantastical designs that depicted strange beasts and incredible landscapes. She smiled when she looked across the elven wizards, but her smile broadened even more when she saw one of the other Celestians hurry toward her. He too was crimson-haired and golden-eyed. Such was the similarity between them that Reiliur judged them more than merely related. Had they been elves or humans, he'd be confident in calling them twins.

Reiliur forced his attention away from the magnificence of the newly arrived Celestians and looked across the gateways. The fog that had swirled about them was gone. The bridge was again closed and the keening melody was now only a memory. He felt a sense of satisfaction when he saw that this time the portals had endured the strain of the ritual, rather than being consumed by the power. They would each need to be examined carefully, but at first glance, he thought they would be able to be used when the time came to again invite more Celestians to Pannithor.

For just a heartbeat, a profound sorrow gripped Reiliur. It would be another century before the ritual could be conducted again. Until that time, the way was shut between Elvenholme and the realm of the Celestians.

"Has something gone wrong?" Eoswain's concern reached into Reiliur's mind.

"No," he replied. "Everyone has made the passage safely." As he said the words, Reiliur's sadness evaporated. When he said it, he appreciated the magnitude of what he'd accomplished. All the glories and advances just twenty Celestians had brought to the world, and now their numbers had doubled. The century ahead would be remarkable enough for anyone to experience, there would be work enough for him without obsessing over something he couldn't hasten. The gates would open again, in their time.

The Circle of Heaven rose from their places, the incantation slipping away to its conclusion. Valandor left the adamantine sigil and approached the dais. The spectating Celestians hastened to greet the newcomers. Reiliur could see from their expressions that old friendships were being reaffirmed after their long separation.

"Your accomplishment today will be long remembered," Valandor told Reiliur.

The wizard bowed his head. "It isn't my accomplishment alone. What we've done today was the work of all of us. You, Eoswain, the Circle of Heaven. All of us came together to ensure this success. I was but part of the process."

"Your humility is misplaced," Calisor said. "Without your vision, without your conviction to keep going no matter the obstacles in your way, we would never have persevered." He glanced aside at the Scrying Star. "But for you, we'd never have even heard the voice of Eoswain."

Reiliur's attention strayed back to the Celestian wearing the chameleon gown. She was standing apart from the rest, gazing about the laboratory with searching eyes. It was clear to him that she was looking for something. Before long, she swept toward the dais and addressed Valandor.

"I am pleased to find you are well," she said. The warmth of her gaze briefly took in Reiliur and Calisor. "And in such fine company. However, I'd expected to meet with Mescator when I crossed. Is he not here?"

Valandor's expression turned regretful. "Don't take insult, Karinna, but Mescator was unable to be here. He felt my magic would be of greater use if anything went wrong with the portals."

Karinna was silent a moment, digesting what he'd said. She seemed to Reiliur more puzzled than offended by the absence of the Celestian leader. "It must have been a matter of great importance to keep him away," she ventured.

"Mescator has been away with the humans in Primovantor," Valandor said. He nodded to Reiliur. "The humans are a people much different from our elven friends. Rougher and less advanced, but Mescator saw great promise in their potential and led an embassy to Primovantor to guide and help them as we've guided and helped the elves here."

"It must be a demanding labor if it has kept him from being here," Karinna said.

Reiliur explained the situation. "Even more than my people, the humans have long worshiped pantheons of old gods, some of them grim and forbidding. Mescator has shown the kingdom of Primovantor a more enlightened way. By this very act, he has drawn the enmity of the neighboring lands where the hold of the old gods remains strong. He could not leave while Primovantor is beset by war."

The last word appeared strange to Karinna. "War," she repeated. "What does this mean?"

"Conflict," Valandor said. "Struggle between beings."

Karinna still had an uncertain look in her eyes. "You mean predation? When the needs of one creature can be satisfied only to the detriment of another?"

"No," Reiliur said, a feeling of shame welling up inside him. So pure was Karinna that the very concept of war was foreign to her understanding. Now it was his hideous role to introduce the ugliness of its meaning to her. "This isn't the kind of conflict when the vine sinks its roots into the tree and steals the sap of its host, or the hunting lion devouring prey to sate its hunger. War is conflict between thinking peoples. For power, or territory, or simply ideas, entire nations take up arms and fight one another. That is the conflict which demands Mescator's presence. The humans of Primovantor are beset by the humans of Ahmun. Without the Celestians to help them, they might fall to the Ahmunites."

Karinna's beautiful visage contorted with disgust. "Hunting for sustenance I can understand, but not this. Peoples who are of the same kind killing each other when they should be talking to one another. Discussion is the measure of ideas, this 'war' you describe is simply a measure of force and brutality."

"Such, I fear, has been the history of Pannithor," Reiliur said.

"You must remember, these are mortal races," Valandor said. "The elves have a longevity far in excess of the humans, yet even they have engaged in wars and lesser conflicts. For the humans, with their shortened lifespan, there is the need for swift resolution to any conflict that arises. They simply don't have the time to do otherwise. If peaceful means cannot be found, then they will take up the sword."

Karinna's gaze shifted between Reiliur and Valandor. "If this is the root of conflict in this world, then I have brought its resolution." She extended her hand so that both of them could see. Between her cupped fingers, a golden seed appeared. Reiliur was stunned by its exotic beauty, the intricate pattern of whorls that circled it and glowed with an azure light. Valandor was even more amazed.

"Karinna, can this be?" Valandor asked.

She smiled. "I have brought a seed from the Sahlirian Tree."

Though he was ignorant of what this tree might be, Reiliur knew the enormity of its importance from how Valandor reacted. He'd never expected to see such awe and excitement in the Celestian's face.

"This is why I wished to confer with Mescator," Karinna said. "And why I am so disappointed to find him drawn away by something so sordid as this... *war*."

"What was your intention, my lady?" Reiliur asked. "What purpose moved you to bring this wondrous seed through the portal?"

Karinna was silent for a moment. She looked around the laboratory. "Hope is a fragile thing. I would not have it raised needlessly. Therefore I think we should discuss my intentions somewhere more private."

Of all the tributes paid to his capabilities by elves and Celestians alike that night, it was being deemed worthy of Karinna's confidence that filled Reiliur with pride. "I know just the place," he said. "A place where even the greatest divination couldn't discern the merest whisper. Whatever you would discuss, its secrets will be safe there."

***

Reiliur led his companions deep within the vaults below the Tower of Heaven. Down winding stairs that burrowed far under the earth. This was the oldest part of the structure, constructed over a thousand years before by Thaieweil Avasharr, branded in the histories as the Mad Mage. Thaieweil's conclave of wizards preceded the Circle of Heaven by centuries, devoting themselves to harnessing arcane energies buried in the earth. Thaieweil's divinations had revealed to her a great source of magical power, and she set her followers to uncovering it. In their delving, they came into conflict with squat, brutish creatures and for many generations made war against them until at last the Mad Mage was killed and the elves abandoned what had been a costly quest.

A lesser treasure, however, had been discovered in those far off days. The wizards' digging revealed a gigantic red gemstone of enormous eldritch power. Too large to remove, resistant to even the mightiest spells, it was left where it was found. Later, the most skilled craftsmen in Elvenholme were brought into the subterranean darkness to hollow out the great stone. So it was that the Scarlet Sanctum was created.

The multi-faceted wall of the Sanctum shone with a crimson luminance when Reiliur's light revealed it at the end of the winding passage. When he saw that ruddy glow, he drew a tinderwork lantern from his belt and ignited it. Then he banished the hovering orb of magic light that had guided them thus far. "Within this place, no spell can endure," he explained to the Celestians.

Calisor stepped forward. In his hand he bore a glove fashioned from living crystal. When he stood beside the wall, he slipped the glove over his hand. It slithered around his fingers, fusing with his body. In doing so, the crystals shaped themselves into jagged flanges of spiky growth. Each finger took on a dramatic and unique shape. Calisor waited until the process was complete, only the strain in his eyes betrayed the pain the glove was causing him. The crystals finally stopped moving, and Calisor set his hand against the red gemstone. His fingers probed its surface for the cunningly concealed locks, each flange of spikes trained to match the internal mechanisms. Under his efforts, the hidden door opened, spreading outward like the petals of a flower to expose the chamber within.

"I must remain out here," Calisor said, retreating away from the Sanctum. "If something were to happen and the key were locked inside, there would be no escape." He quickly removed the crystal glove from his hand. As it lost contact with his flesh, the flanges subsided and withdrew back into the shimmering gauntlet. The elf's hand was dark with blood, every pore pierced by a crystal filament. He whispered a spell and the intrusive shards evaporated into smoke.

"Calisor will keep watch," Reiliur assured the Celestians. He stared into the Sanctum, at the menacing glow of its walls. It was many centuries since he'd come here, but never had he been able to shake the atmosphere of menace that exuded from inside it. There wasn't a quality of immediate threat in that sensation, but rather the dread evoked by some distant and indomitable calamity. The specter of a terrible tomorrow.

Reiliur entered the Sanctum. The place was expensively appointed and well-stocked. In more tumultuous times, it had been prepared as a final refuge for the Tower of Heaven's master.

Three Celestians accompanied the elf wizard into the red room. Karinna and Valandor, and the dusky man who'd been introduced to Reiliur as Kyron.

Karinna seated herself. The others gathered around her. She lifted her cupped hand and once more the fantastic seed appeared. Reiliur was entranced by its wonder and beauty, but when he looked at the Celestians, he saw an expression in their eyes that was almost worshipful.

"A seed from the Sahlirian Tree," Karinna said. There was both sadness and amusement in her expression when she saw that her words had no meaning for Reiliur. "You gaze upon something that can change Pannithor forever, but you don't recognize what it represents. I don't know if such ignorance is to be admired or despaired."

Valandor shook his head. "It is only when ignorance is willful that it becomes a thing of contempt. Think, Karinna, of all the worlds we've seen, all the places we've walked. Yet only in one did the Sahlirian Tree grow freely. You shouldn't wonder that its power is unknown here."

Reiliur bowed to the lady Celestian. "I would try to understand whatever you deem fit to teach me." He felt like an apprentice again, struggling to wrap his mind around the most basic and fundamental concepts of magic. Things so familiar to his instructor that he could often see the frustration born by trying to explain such mundane ideas.

Karinna's face softened with sympathy, touched by Reiliur's humility and eagerness. "The Sahlirian Tree was native to the world the first Celestians left many aeons ago. Through all the domains which we've made our home, it has been brought with us. The light of a hundred suns has warmed its leaves, and the soil of a thousand lands has nourished its roots. Somewhere, without our knowing it, the Sahlirian Tree adapted properties unmatched by anything else we've met in our travels."

"The fruit this tree bears," Valandor told the elf, "has the most wondrous magic of all. Those who eat the fruit achieve immortality."

Immortality. The word lingered in the air. Reiliur felt his heart freeze in awe at the awesome potential in that single word.

"Any creature with a soul that consumes the juice from the fruit will never suffer the pangs of age, but they will persist always in their prime," Karinna elaborated. She held her graceful arms out toward Reiliur, letting him study their robust health and youthful delicacy. "The Celestians have eaten of the Sahlirian Tree, and we've existed as you see us far longer than you would comprehend."

"Now we would share that boon with the peoples of Pannithor," Valandor said. "Our intention is to find a place where we may plant this seed and share this gift with your people. Yes, and with the humans too. When the promise of eternal life is brought before them, only the completely mad will have any thought for war."

"Death will no longer be an inevitability," Karinna said. "The spirits of the mortal races can be strengthened by this gift."

"The limitations imposed on your magic by the fragility of your essence would be overcome as well," Valandor pointed out. "Elves would be able to explore even more distant worlds. Places beyond the reach of your current mortality."

Reiliur gasped at the prospect, his mind afire with all the possibilities. It was a noble pursuit to gather knowledge and pass it down to posterity, but to actually see and be there to watch how future generations would build upon his discoveries... More than that, to help them achieve these undreamed heights of accomplishment was a glory he'd never dared to dream of. There was something else, as well. He thought of the ritual to bring the Celestians across the void between worlds. "If elves had spirits of such endurance, we could open far more gates to your home. We could bring more Celestians to Pannithor than the handful we can now."

Valandor nodded. "Such might be possible, though these plans would be in the distant future."

"More immediately, we need to find a place where the Sahlirian Tree can be grown," Kyron spoke for the first time in the meeting. "Before making glorious plans, first we must know if there is a foundation for such plans." He fixed his attention on Reiliur. "I will need to study your maps of this world and then try to find the place that will suit our needs."

"In Ileuthrien there grows the World Tree," Reiliur suggested. "Surely there can be no soil more fertile than that which nourishes the first of all trees."

Valandor frowned at the idea. "The World Tree was planted by Bhanek, and though we don't know how much of the Primogenitor's awareness lingers, it would be tempting fate to place our hopes in a site sacred to an entity we've had conflict with."

"The resources of the Tower of Heaven, nay, of all Elvenholme are at your disposal," Reiliur assured him. "All the kingdoms of Pannithor will be eager to help you..."

"That, sadly, is exactly what we must avoid," Karinna said. She held the seed aloft between her fingers. "The Sahlirian Tree is too great a treasure to put at risk, its promise too monumental to be none beyond a few. The place where we would cultivate the grove must be a secluded place. A place that can be hidden from the world. If I am to grow the trees, then I must have solitude in which to work."

Reiliur was bewildered for a moment by the gravity with which Karinna spoke on the need for secrecy. "Surely this boon would inspire hope. As you say, it would end war. Even the conflict that occupies Mescator right now would soon end."

"You're wrong," Valandor said. "If we were to tell more mortals of this gift, it would cause despair. Your world would be racked by the most obscene war it has ever seen."

"To bring your people this gift, I must grow a great grove of trees," Karinna explained. "For generations, the fruit of the Sahlirian Tree can't be harvested but must be set back within the ground so that more trees could be grown. The gift must be set aside unopened so that it could be shared with many more once the grove was large enough."

"Think what knowledge of the Sahlirian Tree would do," Valandor pressed. "Especially to the short-lived humans. They would age and die knowing that the promise of immortality was just beyond their reach."

Reiliur bowed his head in agreement. "It would drive the humans to madness. They would do anything to claim the fruit, even at the expense of their own descendants. Nor can they be entirely blamed for such desperation. To be the last of your people to grow feeble with age, to know that a glorious future is just ahead but that you will never see it for yourself. Yes, only the wisest of the humans would remain stalwart against such things."

"Then we're agreed," Kyron said. "The secret must be kept. I will study your maps and learn all I can of your world." He nodded to Karinna. "I know what is needed both to grow the trees and to keep the secret."

"Kyron is reckoned one of our greatest explorers," Karinna said. "His affinity for wild places and wild things is remarkable among our people. He is the best of us for such a task."

Valandor laid his hand on Kyron's shoulder. "Pannithor is a large place, and there are regions of it that our elven hosts have only dimly written about in their records." He smiled at Reiliur. "It is to be wondered that a people so eager to explore the mysteries of beyond do so while leaving so much of their own world unknown to them."

"I will succeed," Kyron vowed. His confidence became somber when he looked to Reiliur. "I will make all haste in my task."

Reiliur felt a chill rush through him when Karinna expressed the reason for haste.

"The sooner I plant the seed," she said, "the sooner the grip of death can be lifted from Pannithor."

Chapter VI

-990, Time of Light

Kyron journeyed far from the settled lands of Primovantor. The task entrusted to him by Karinna depended on him scouting the wild places for a location suitable for growing the Sahlirian Tree. In truth, it was a duty much to his liking. Kyron didn't share the passion of the other Celestians for the elves and humans of Pannithor. His interest was drawn to the wide variety of beasts that inhabited the world. His delight was discovering new species, learning their habits and methods. He found that Pannithor had a vast variety to offer, and as he made his way through the land, he was never at a loss for some new source of fascination, some new creature to study.

His only regret was failure to find an ideal place for Karinna to establish her grove. She'd entrusted to Kyron the precious Sahlirian fruit from which to draw seeds to make his determination. He knew the kind of ground the trees needed, so it was seldom he found any that looked suitable. Even then, when he extracted a seed and set it into the ground, it would fail to flourish. So the search continued, year upon year.

Kyron wasn't lonely, even as he strayed to the frontiers of Pannithor and past the domains of humans. Among the Celestians, when the connection between two of them was strong enough, there would develop a special bond that resisted the separation of time and space. A parent sometimes had such great affection for their offspring that they could sense each other's thoughts and feelings across thousands of miles. So too, might the bond be between mentor and protege, as Kyron sometimes suspected with Oskan and Mescator. Then too, there was the link between lovers. Many times, this connection was only one-way, inevitably resting with the one possessed of the greater devotion toward the other. But in rare instances, the link was mutual. So it was between himself and Liliana. Though she'd remained behind in Esk, a part of her was still with Kyron. She shared in his happiness when he discovered a new hawk or gazed upon an unknown breed of deer. Across the leagues, she consoled him when the seeds failed to take root and encouraged him not to lose heart.

Now Kyron had entered the great range of mountains that served as the northern border of Primovantor. Both men and elves designated these peaks as the Dragontooth Mountains, naming them for the awesome beasts seen there. Of all the creatures described to the Celestians by the mortals, it was the dragons that were the most magnificent. Kyron had seen the drawn representations of these flying reptiles, but he longed to see one for himself. The elves of old had woven spells to protect their lands from prowling wyrms, and some of the mightiest lords in their history had even been able to tame them after a fashion, though whatever secrets had allowed them to do so had been lost. Humans, however, lived in dread of dragons. Many times, the creatures had descended upon farms and villages to ravage the inhabitants. Only seldom had the beasts been successfully driven off. Accounts varied for where the dragons came from, but all agreed that they were seen most frequently in the Dragontooth Mountains.

Kyron climbed the rocky slopes for many days, listening to the eerie howls of wolves at night, watching the soaring eagles by day. Up into the snow his wanderings took him, to the very peaks of the range, then to plunge back down the opposite grade into the dense forests. Always pressing onward to the next height.

It was here, between the snow-capped peaks, that Kyron found the valley. Utterly hidden, cut-off from the world beyond the mountains, the valley exuded a feeling of melancholy the moment he saw it. Unlike the slopes around it, no trees grew in the valley. It was like a great, lifeless scar, knifing its way between the mountains, a rocky waste littered with weird boulders as far as the eye could see. Kyron was much intrigued by the stones, for in all his travels he'd never seen their like before.

When he descended into the valley and walked nearer to one of the curious formations, Kyron discovered why he'd never seen such rocks. They weren't rocks at all but enormous bones. The whole valley was one vast bonefield, strewn with the remnants of huge beasts. Kyron was impressed by the size of the skeletons he observed. His mind tried to picture the creatures in the flesh, clothing the remains in skin, filling out the denuded limbs and colossal tails as they'd appeared in life. He marveled at the gigantic wings as they must have been with membrane stretched between their fingers. He shook his head in grim acknowledgment of the vicious claws that tipped each foot, talons as big as a human body. The sharp fangs in the horned skull were as big as swords. Truly, this could only have been a dragon.

Kyron lifted his gaze from the beast he studied and saw dozens more on the ground around it. As far as the eye could see, the valley floor was covered in skeletons – *dragon* skeletons! The place was a wyrms' graveyard.

The Celestian wondered about how such a place had come to be. The condition of the bones impressed on Kyron that not all the beasts had died at the same time. To some of the skeletons, strips of desiccated flesh yet clung. Others were so deteriorated that they'd crumbled into dust. It was clear to him that whatever force was at work in the valley, it had been at work for many centuries. He wondered if there might be some poison here, some noxious plant or foul vapor of such lethal potency that even mighty dragons were unable to withstand it. Kyron displayed more caution as he continued to explore, wary of some hidden menace. He could feel Liliana's concern across the miles that separated them, urging him to take no risks.

Then there appeared before Kyron a sight that made him forget all else. Before his eyes there rose a vision to inspire awe even in a Celestian. Stretched along the valley floor was a dragon. Not a thing of bones and tatters, but whole and intact. Liliana shared his wonder as he approached the beast, the thrill of this discovery blotting out all other concerns.

The dragon was enormous. Fifty feet long from the tip of its snout to the end of its scaly tail. It resembled a lizard in general shape, but to say such was to liken a shark to a minnow. Four powerful legs ended in broad feet, each toe tipped with a curved claw. The body was covered in thick red scales that faded into white along its belly, a spiny ridge running down the creature's back. The wings were folded against its sides, but even in such state they were twenty feet long. Kyron could only speculate at the tremendous wingspan when those pinions were unfurled. The head, sleek and tapered in shape, was surmounted by a pair of sharp horns that protruded from the skull at a backward angle to afford protection to the reptile's long neck. The jaws at the front of the head were wide enough to devour a hog in one bite, and the fangs were like rows of daggers.

Kyron drew back in shock when he glanced at the dragon's eye. The orb was a dull yellow in color with a slitted pupil almost black in hue. The cause of his surprise was when that pupil suddenly dilated and focused upon him. The dragon he'd thought to be dead was still alive!

Something at the edge of fear pulled at Kyron, but it was unable to counter the fascination this discovery held. His connection with Liliana echoed his own thoughts, that admixture of fright mingled with irresistible curiosity.

"What was it that happened to you?" Kyron asked as he circled the great beast. Aware that life yet clung to the dragon, he was careful to keep out of reach of its jaws and fangs, well away from the enormous tail. "I wonder if you still have the strength to blast me with your fire," he speculated. He regretted the thought, for it provoked alarm in Liliana far away in Esk. "No," he concluded, shaking his head sadly. "I think you're well past such exertion."

Kyron came closer to the dragon. The beast barely moved its head as he approached, though its eyes continued to focus on him. "You're all done in, aren't you?" He stepped closer and laid his hand on the reptile's snout. The scaly flesh was cold under his palm. He could feel the gnarled, weathered surface. "You're old. So very old."

His voice was soothing as he spoke to the dragon. Kyron understood now. This valley was in truth a graveyard of dragons, but it wasn't from some hidden poison. When the reptiles felt their end was coming, they flew here so that they might expire in this hidden place among the bones of their own kind. This was what the creature before him was doing. With the last of its strength, it had come here to die.

Kyron was struck by a sense of melancholy as he contemplated the strange nobility of this instinct that brought the dragons back here. Or was it more than only instinct? As he stared into the reptile's eyes, he saw an awareness there that went beyond that of an animal. "More than a beast," Kyron observed. "The mark of a higher intelligence is the knowledge of death. That one day your own life must fail."

It was clear from the very existence of this boneyard that the dragons were aware of their own mortality. Kyron wouldn't say that their minds were like those of men or elves, but it was obvious they were more than the brutes the people of Pannithor thought them to be.

Awareness of mortality. The Celestians had surpassed mortality long ago with the Sahlirian Tree, but always there remained the understanding of death and the appreciation of life. Accident and misadventure, though remote, persisted as reminders to them that even their own existence might end.

As his thoughts took this turn, Kyron reached into the bag he carried and withdrew the Sahlirian fruit Karinna had given him. He gazed again at the dying dragon. The juice of the fruit might restore the reptile. The Celestians were certain it would do so for humans and elves, but these were beings much closer in form to themselves. Would something as different as a dragon respond?

Kyron could feel Liliana's mind reaching out to him. He sensed her awe of the dragon and her sorrow that so magnificent a beast should die. When he thought of the Sahlirian fruit, a flash of intense hope radiated from Liliana. Yes, most assuredly Kyron should try! The precious fruit was the only thing that might bring the dragon back from the verge of death.

Kyron removed the fruit from the woolen pouch it was kept in. He considered it carefully. There was no other in all Pannithor. He felt the entreaty from Liliana. Another could be brought the next time Celestians crossed into this world, nearly a century hence. It would mean a delay of the establishment of Karinna's grove. Yet such was the appeal from Liliana, such was his own fascination for the great dragon lying before him, that Kyron's resistance was broken. Karinna could wait, but the dying wyrm couldn't. It was death or life, and he held that fate in his hand.

The Celestian reached to the dragon's scaly mouth. The reptile barely stirred when Kyron held the fruit against its jaws and began to squeeze. Thick red juice and pulp dripped down into the dragon's mouth, slipping past its teeth to the gums. He watched as the liquid was absorbed by the beast's body. The nostrils atop the muzzle flared loudly, exhaling a burst of smoke and cinders. Kyron glance back at the slitted eyes. There was no mistaking the shine that now filled them, a vibrancy far different from the weary resignation of before.

Backing away, Kyron watched as an incredible transformation occurred. The dragon's hide, dull and faded, swiftly assumed a bright gleam. The cracked and weathered scales were now smooth and polished to an almost reflective sheen. The dried leather of the folded wings became rich and supple, glistening as though they'd been anointed in oil.

The dragon lifted itself off the ground and seemed to flex its entire body in one great stretch. The long tail flicked from side to side, slapping the ground with a blow that sent earth blossoming into the sky. It extended its wings, first one and then the other, letting each in turn project to its full limit. The reptile fanned the air, creating a warm wind that washed across Kyron and set his hair streaming behind him. Finally, the great beast reared back and raised its head to the heavens. From its jaws, a blast of orange flame shot over the valley for hundreds of yards.

Kyron stood in wonder at the restoration bestowed by the Sahlirian fruit. He knew he should be afraid, for this was a creature to shock even a Celestian, but he was still caught in the grip of his fascination. Of all the beasts he'd seen in all the worlds he'd trod, none could match a dragon at the very height of its prowess.

The reptile swung its head around and its eyes fixed upon Kyron. There was no menace in the reptile's attention, though the gulf between their vastly different physicality left Kyron unable to judge what thoughts might be stirring in the brain within the scaled head. Was it curiosity? Confusion? Or did the dragon possess enough understanding to feel gratitude?

For a time, they looked at one another in silence, then the dragon lifted one claw to its mouth. It nipped the digit with its long fangs, biting through the thick hide and drawing a trickle of blood. Still staring at Kyron, it licked some of the blood with its forked tongue, then extended its leg and held the claw toward him.

"You want me to drink," Kyron said. The dragon didn't react to his voice but maintained the same pose. "I don't know what you intend by this, but I've already acted rashly on your behalf. I'll trust to foolishness a little farther." He could feel

Liliana's pleasure over the dragon's revitalization turn to dread when he stepped to the claw and pressed his finger to the blood. Her concern for him intensified when he lifted the finger to his mouth. He hesitated for only a moment, then licked the dragon's blood.

At once it felt as though a roaring flame swept through his body. An intensity of pain such as he'd never imagined seized Kyron. He slumped to his knees and hugged himself as wave upon wave of torment seared his senses. Though it felt like an eternity to him, he knew it could only have been a moment before the pain subsided. As it did, Kyron knew that he'd been changed. His mind whirled with a new awareness. A bridge had been formed between Celestian and dragon.

It wasn't the same sort of telepathic link that was so easily shaped between Celestians and the elves and humans. The strange, reptilian mind of a dragon was too alien for such commonality. Yet there was communication of a sort. More primal, in its way, and less sophisticated than speech, but a convergence of mentality just the same.

"Your name is Draumdraak," Kyron said, trying to shape the individuality of the dragon into words. There was a hint of bewilderment in the wyrm's eyes when he spoke, but after a moment there came a sense of approval. "You came here to die, knowing your time was finished. But I have given you new life."

Draumdraak fanned his wings, and a hiss rumbled up from his throat. Kyron could feel the sound vibrate through his bones. The dragon exulted in the new vigor that filled him, the strength of youth restored to a being that only moments before had been venerable and decrepit.

"A dragon grows in strength and power until it has reached the end of its span," Kyron observed, his strange connection with Draumdraak giving him insight to the biology that governed the reptile. "You've been given a new lifetime to add to that which you've already possessed. There's no saying how strong you'll grow." Worry filled Kyron now, for if he'd been mistaken, if Draumdraak proved the marauding fiend mortal accounts held all dragons to be, then he'd just unleashed upon Pannithor a monster the likes of which it had never seen. Draumdraak would continue to grow in size and power...

Sadness gripped Kyron when he realized something else. The Sahlirian fruit gave immortality to the Celestians. It would do the same for humans and elves. But it hadn't done the same for Draumdraak. The draconic biology was simply too different. He'd restored the dragon's youth and reinvigorated his vitality, but these things were slowly ebbing away even now. Doubled, perhaps tripled what would have been Draumdraak's normal lifespan, but the great reptile remained mortal.

The communication between Kyron and Draumdraak wasn't one-sided. As the Celestian realized this flaw, so too did the dragon. The reptile's reaction banished fears he would be a rampaging monster, for it was simply quiet acceptance. Draumdraak's life had been restored, this was enough.

"Would that the other mortals could be so noble," Kyron mused, thinking of the worries that had attended discussion of the Sahlirian Tree with Reiliur. Far away, he could sense Liliana's mournful agreement with him. But the sadness was only a part of her mind. Mostly she was filled with admiration, proud of what Kyron had accomplished. Though he'd acted against Karinna's instructions, he'd proven his decision was for a good purpose. Mescator would certainly agree.

Kyron thought of the Celestian leader. He looked to Draumdraak and the dragon's mighty wings. "There is a favor I would ask of you," he said. As he conversed with the dragon, he sent his thoughts to Liliana, advising her of his intentions.

Kyron was going to return to Esk, and when he did, he would bring to the city a sight to awe both men and Celestians.

*** *

-987, *Time of Light*

Long had the pharaohs of Ahmun and the sinister death-priests who advised them plotted to avenge their nation upon Primovantor and the Celestians. Like a wounded jackal, they picked at their hurt, never allowing it to heal. Hate festered in the southern land. Every overture of friendship was rejected out of hand, for the servants of the old gods had seen how the ancient religions had been undone in Elvenholme and Primovantor. To retain their own grip on power, there could never be peace.

Mescator wore once again the shining armor of war as he looked across the river plain. Smoke rose from burning villages and towns. These were lands that had gained independence from Nehkesharr, becoming the kingdom of Ophidia. Under the guidance of the Celestians, Ophidia had prospered, growing into a thriving agricultural center and trading hub. Both the original Ahmunite inhabitants who'd broken away from the pharaohs and the Primovantorian settlers who came with the Celestians had worked to turn the region into a rich land.

The invaders from Ahmun, however, cared nothing for wealth. Though much of their nation was arid desert with little ground that could be cultivated now that the lands along the River Ophid had slipped from their grip, the armies of the pharaohs spitefully put everything they captured to the torch. No plunder was seized, no captives taken. All was consigned to the flames. The denizens of Ophidia, whether dusky Ahmunite or fair Primovantorian, were slaughtered by the warriors. The death-priests had decried all the territory unclean and everything within it, living or dead, profane. Whipped into a religious frenzy by the servants of Shobik, the army left only devastation in its wake. Wherever the legions of Nehkesharr marched, only death was left in their wake.

Gazing at the destruction from the top of a hill, Mescator felt disgust boiling inside him. "They're more savage than any beast you discovered in your travels," he commented, looking aside to Kyron. Of the four Celestians gathered on the hill, Mescator, Oskan, and Liliana had seen war before. Only to Kyron was this butchering madness a new experience.

"It was one thing to see such acts from the barbarians of Chult," Oskan snarled. "Their society was crude and unsophisticated, but Ahmun is a civilization older even than Primovantor. They were building cities of stone when Esk was nothing but a collection of mud-walled hovels. When the first elves made contact with the Ahmunites, already they'd created their own writing and knew the fundamentals of metallurgy and alchemy." He shook his head and scowled. "A people like that should... shouldn't be reduced to this."

"They are what their priests have made them." Liliana pointed to where the Ahmunites marched. The arms and armor of the soldiers gleamed in the sunlight, but it was the gleam of bronze. Where the bright glimmer of gold was found, it shone not from a soldier's helm but from a tremendous idol. Neither cart nor wagon was allowed to convey the golden statue, no animal was allowed to pull it after the invading army. Its immense weight was borne by men alone, Ahmunite fanatics who found the greatest expression of their devotion by sweating and straining to carry the image of their god into Primovantor. "Shobik marches with them. Watching their progress. Seeing with his painted eyes their valor. None of them will falter, for to do so would be to lose more than their lives. If they disgrace Shobik, the Ahmunites believe he won't take their souls when they die. Their spirits will be cast out, left to wander Pannithor as ghosts and wraiths."

Mescator nodded. "The death-priests have gambled much on this war." He sighed, realizing that by striving for peace, the Celestians had forced this conflict. "Their hold upon the pharaohs is weakening. Another generation, perhaps two, and the tyranny of the temples might have been broken not only in Ophidia but through all Ahmun. Nehkesharr might have accepted a different path."

"The old must ever resent the new," Kyron said. "No animal welcomes a new species into its domain, for it doesn't know if the stranger will displace its own kind once it is established. It is not so unique that humans should think the same way." Sadness showed on his face as he gazed upon the burning land. "Though it is to be regretted that thinking creatures would be incapable of understanding when it is time to accept change."

"We ride out to meet the legions of Ahmun," Mescator told Kyron. He clapped his armored hand on the hunter's shoulder. "I want you to remain here. You're new to war, so wait for my signal. I'll let you know when the time has come." He glanced aside at Liliana and saw the emotion gleaming in her eyes. "Come, Oskan!" he called to his protege. "We must confer with the High Consul and the Ophidian king and ensure their generals understand the battle plans."

Leaving Kyron and Liliana to make their own farewells, Mescator and Oskan descended the hill to where the army was encamped. The Grand Republic of Primovantor had assembled a force many times the size of that which King Lyzander brought against Chult. Pennants denoted companies recruited from across the nation, every province had answered the muster.

There were even small numbers of elves who had volunteered as scouts and a few blue-robed acolytes from the Tower of Heaven who'd arrived to lend their mighty magics to the battle. Templars from the many cults that had grown around the Celestians made prayers at the shrines scattered about the camp. The more secular knights of Ophidia visited the stables to check the condition of their war horses. At the edge of the encampment, archers tested their bows, hardening themselves to the ordeal ahead. Sergeants drilled spearmen, putting them through their paces one last time before the fight. Distant from the rest of the forces were the grisly troops conjured by Ophidia's necromancers. The withered dead, arrayed in ancient armor, called up from their graves by the terrible magic of the desert realm. Rank after rank of the undead silently awaited the call to battle. Through their morbid ranks, boys with brooms chased away the vultures that swooped down to pick at the sinister warriors.

Mescator shook his head when he looked at the skeletal fighters. It was known that the pharaohs of Ahmun would use fell magic to raise favored servants into a grim mockery of life after they died, but even they had balked at drafting such graveyard battalions. "I fear that King Tothmenes will stoop to anything to maintain his independence. A man of such ruthlessness is a distasteful ally."

"The death-priests are determined to destroy Ophidia," Oskan pointed out as the two Celestians walked toward the High Consul's pavilion. "Even if it means squandering the strength of Ahmun in a hopeless battle. They were beaten before, and with a much smaller army than they face now."

"The Ahmunites are more committed than they were in the last war," Mescator cautioned, setting aside for now the questionable measures King Tothmenes had undertaken. "Don't discount the ferocity of a soldier who is willing to die for his cause." A troubled look came into his eyes. He'd met prisoners taken by the elf scouts. To a man, the Ahmunites were convinced of Shobik's divine supremacy. A strange plague had beset the lands of Ahmun, a plague they blamed on Ophidia's sorcerers and priests. Even now, there were many in the Ahmunite army who bore a withered and sickly aspect. It was only by the dread magic of Shobik's servants that the Ahmunites found any manner of hope at all. "The death-priests have performed terrible miracles to inspire their countrymen."

"Magic," Oskan scoffed. "The same sort of trickery the temple of Bhanek used. We routed the priests of Shobik from Primovantor easily enough. Their god is decayed and powerless." A flicker of uneasiness crossed his features. It was clear that Oskan was reflecting that Ophidia too persisted in the worship of Shobik and had its own deathly priesthood.

Mescator was less certain. "It would be prudent to be wary. The Ahmunites considered the temple of Shobik in Primovantor to be heretical. Perhaps, in their way, the death-priests are yet in communion with their god." He nodded as he considered another point. "Don't be quick to think all the old gods are empty names. Korgaan was real enough when we fought his priest." Mescator felt a chill rush through his flesh as he remembered how nearly the barbaric war god had overwhelmed him. "Never discount an enemy, Oskan, for to do so is to put another weapon in his arsenal."

Oskan smiled and gestured at the vast camp through which they now walked, at the soldiers who bowed and took to their knee as the Celestians passed them. "With the might of Primovantor arrayed against them, to pose any kind of challenge Ahmun will need every weapon they can get."

***

Royal war chariots smashed into the lines of spearmen, crushing them beneath brazen wheels. Scythe-like blades fitted to the spokes chopped the legs from soldiers and threw them into the air like rag dolls. The bowman standing beside each charioteer sent arrows pelting into any warrior who lowered his shield, sending shafts stabbing into faces with murderous precision.

Terrible as they were, these were sights Liliana had seen before. Not so the huge animals that pulled the chariots. Warlions of Ahmun, each the size of an ox and with a pelt as black as midnight and a mane the color of blood. The already formidable cats had been made even more potent by girding them with spiked armor and applying poison to their claws. When the animals rushed into the lines of infantry, their great weight smashed men flat and their lashing claws ripped through flesh, even the least scratch leaving the victim a dying man. Gone were the fast, nimble stallions that sped archers around the battlefield, the pharaohs now deployed these savage felines to rend and destroy.

Liliana knew only her presence among them kept the formation of archers she'd joined in position. It didn't need the telepathy of a Celestian to sense the terror that rose from the soldiers as they watched their comrades being annihilated only a few hundred yards away.

"Soldiers of the Grand Republic!" Liliana shouted to the archers. She lifted the bow she carried into the air, its jeweled grip gleaming in the sun. "On my mark... loose!"

A flight of arrows soared into the air as Liliana brought her arm chopping down. The volley arced overhead and showered the Ahmunite chariots plowing into the spearmen. Many of them failed to pierce the bronze armor of the warlions and crew, but enough slammed home to cripple some of the chariots. Liliana raised her own bow, a weapon of such power that only a Celestian could draw its string. She took aim at the onrushing foe, shooting between the combatants with a precision to balk the most daring elf. The steel-capped shaft whistled past the ears of friendly soldiers and struck a warlion's head. The arrow penetrated the bronze armor the cat wore and crunched through the skull inside. Its power barely spent, it erupted from the back of the lion's head and embedded itself in the body of the chariot it pulled. The Ahmunite bowman screamed as the point stabbed through the bronze shield to transfix his leg.

The enemy's howl was quickly silenced. The warlion fell dead in its harness, and the sudden arrest of the chariot's motion was too much for the surviving cat to negotiate. The chariot whipped upward, spinning through the air before smashing down on its top and crushing the crewmen. Debris pelted the other chariots in the squadron, throwing Ahmunites from the carriages and slashing the bodies of lions.

The brutal destruction sent cheers rising from the spearmen, rallying them when a moment before their courage had hung by a thread. They pitched into the other chariots, swarming the Ahmunites. When the press of bodies was enough to stop the drive and pin the chariots in place, they were soon overwhelmed. The ferocity of the lions couldn't stop a score of spears, nor could the bowmen loose shafts quickly enough to fell the soldiers charging into them.

"Keep those axemen back," Liliana ordered her archers, directing their attention to a company of lightly-armored auxiliaries who hastened to aid the beleaguered chariots. While her soldiers sent devastating volleys into the enemy, she turned her attention to the greater battle around them.

The Ahmunites had brought heavy mangonels with their army. The wheeled catapults sent jars of pitch spinning through the air, coating the ground with incendiary tar. Bowmen sent fire arrows into the saturated areas to ignite them and create walls of flame. By this means, the pharaohs sought to protect their flanks, but they'd neglected to consider the bravery of Primovantor's templars. The holy knights spurred their steeds through the blazing curtains. Their tabbards smoldering, they charged into the Ahmunite ranks, smashing them under the hooves of their horses and smiting them with their lances.

Oskan led the knights of Ophidia against the most imposing of the Ahmunite troops. Mighty elephants draped in scales of bronze and with armored howdahs lashed to their backs, it was among these mighty beasts that the standard of Khephren, one of the five elemental pharaohs of Ahmun, was flown. In each howdah, giant weapons launched huge spears into the Ophidians with such force that when they struck they impaled a half dozen men on them. The young Celestian plunged fearlessly among the tusked animals, riding close to slash their vulnerable bellies. The knights strove to support Oskan, but the toll on their numbers was great, and many a hero of the republic lay smashed under an elephant's foot.

The heaviest fighting found Mescator and the Gold Blades, the elite guard of Esk, engaged against a savage horde. Ahmun too had brought allies to the battle, a mass of barbarians whose pale hair and snowy skin marked them as no people of the desert but drawn from the brutal nomads of the icy north. Var'Kyr they were called and they fought with rabid fury, hacking away at soldiers already dead. Mescator was pressed by the champion of this vicious people, a monster nine feet tall and rippling with a power beyond the merely physical. Liliana thought of Korgaan and the avatar he'd sent to fight beside Chult and wondered if here, once more, was a manifestation of the grim god.

Korgaan wasn't the only divinity called to fight against the Celestians. Liliana had a clear view of the idol of Shobik, its gilded face set in an expression of merciless judgment, its arms folded across its breast as it held the rod and crook of authority in its hands. While half-naked fanatics, their bodies wracked by the plague that cursed Ahmun, toiled to carry the heavy idol, ahead of it marched several of the death-priests and their acolytes. As they advanced, the priests gestured at the Primovantorians with their fists. Liliana could see the power they invoked, wisps of energy that surged through their withered bodies. It seemed incredible that any mortal could manifest such arcane force as she saw unleashed. Scores of soldiers were obliterated, their bodies shriveled inside their mail.

The death-priests paid a price for their gruesome magic. Liliana saw their very essence being sucked out of them as they wrenched power from Shobik. Swiftly, however, they deferred that cost upon their acolytes. Streams of spiritual energy rushed out of the tonsured servitors to replenish their masters. When too much was taken from them, an acolyte would fall to the ground, a dead husk, the soul utterly consumed.

"Wretches," Liliana cursed under her breath at the callousness of the death-priests who cared nothing for the sacrifice of their own students. She took aim at one of the withered sorcerers and sent her arrow speeding into him. The man was hurled backward by the impact, his corpse glancing off Shobik's idol. The shaft had completely transfixed him.

Any satisfaction Liliana might have felt was extinguished a moment later. The stricken priest-king staggered back onto his feet while a dozen acolytes writhed in agony. As his students died, their lives ripped out of them, the sorcerer turned and locked eyes with her. A cold smile crawled onto his withered face.

The other death-priests likewise turned to focus on Liliana. Fear fluttered inside of her as she saw them draw on their terrible powers. Most of the acolytes collapsed now, drained utterly by the demands of their masters. A dark force emerged from the sorcerers, a miasma of death that boiled away from them in a rolling mass. The deathly energy of Shobik wrested from the fading god and unleashed upon the battlefield.

The black fog spilled toward Liliana's position. As it sped toward her, those caught in its path gasped and fell to the ground. Man or animal, Primovantorian, Ophidian, or Ahmunite, whatever lived died when the miasma reached them. Liliana loosed another arrow at the death-priests, shattering the skull of one of them and nearly decapitating him. The dead sorcerer remained standing, locked into the ritual evoked by his fellows. More, the spirits of those killed by the spell were drawn up into it, merging their energies into the foul conjuration.

Liliana focused her energies on defense. "Run!" she ordered the archers around her. Some took her advice, but most hesitated, unwilling to abandon a Celestian. The pause was their doom. After searing a path through the chariots and spearmen, the miasma washed across the archers. Soldiers collapsed, their flesh cold and cadaverous before they hit the ground.

The might and vitality of a Celestian allowed Liliana to endure, but even her protections weren't impenetrable. By degrees, she felt the spell closing around her, tightening about her lifeforce. Seeing how the souls of mortals had magnified the awful conjuration, she wondered what would happen if it consumed her undying essence.

A surge of panic filled Liliana's mind. Not her own, but that of Kyron watching from the hill. She urged him to stop, but she knew it was already too late. He wasn't going to wait for Mescator's signal.

***

Mescator brought his blade slashing down and opened the barbarian from shoulder to gut. He ripped the sword clear and glared at the hulking abomination who towered over the other Var'Kyr. "Face me, puppet of Korgaan. Your slaves are unequal to the task."

The Var'Kyr spread his scarred face in a savage grin, exposing wolflike fangs. In one hand, he gripped a club fashioned from the bone of some massive beast and studded with rings of bear-claws. He waved this grotesque weapon at Mescator, then with his other hand he seized a nearby barbarian. In the blink of an eye, the warlord hurled his own fighter at the Celestian. The man slammed into him with bone-crushing force. Mescator staggered back, the shattered body of the enemy plastered against his shield.

Before Mescator could recover from the ruthless ploy, the Var'Kyr was upon him. He'd just slipped his arm free of the overburdened shield when Korgaan's avatar lunged at him. He caught the downward sweep of the clawed mace with the edge of his sword and pushed it aside before it could smash into his helm.

"You should have run when you had the chance, wanderer," the avatar jeered. The eyes that glowered from the scarred face were identical to those that had glared at him the day King Lyzander fell. It was the only thing that was the same, for the mortal vessel Korgaan had possessed this time was far more imposing than the priest Angbold had been. This was the biggest human Mescator had ever seen, half again as tall as any of the other barbarians and with a physique that made the brawny marauders seem sickly by comparison. He shunned armor, clad only in a wolfskin, but his arms and legs were pierced by pieces of carved bone. Mescator couldn't decipher the runes cut into them any more than he could the strange designs tattooed on the brute's skin.

"Only a coward runs from evil," Mescator retorted. He thrust at the avatar, but the Var'Kyr caught the blow with his club. Several bear claws snapped under the impact, but the brute was unharmed.

"A liar and usurper is unfit to judge what is evil," Korgaan growled. A kick of his huge foot crashed against Mescator's armor. The Celestian staggered back but didn't fall. "You come like a thief to steal what belongs to the true gods. You would set yourself up in my place."

Mescator struck back, feinting to the left and jabbing to the right. He had the satisfaction of seeing his blade rake across the avatar's ribs. "Those who abuse power have no just claim to retain it." His eyes narrowed as he watched liquid trickle from the brute's wound. What was leaking from the avatar wasn't human blood but some pale fluid that sizzled when it struck the ground. What manner of being was it that Korgaan had chosen for his puppet this time?

The avatar laughed as he sensed Mescator's dismay. "No mere man this time, wanderer, but a thing sired by my power."

He bared his fangs in contempt. "Power is there to be used, fool, and only those strong enough to possess it can judge when it is abused."

The club slashed downward, raking Mescator's armor and slashing deep furrows in the plate. Almost as much as the physical blow, he reeled from Korgaan's words. This thing was some manner of demigod, the spawn of Korgaan and a mortal?

"What is a child," Korgaan sneered as he plucked the thought from Mescator's mind, "if not an extension of the parent? It exists only to further the design for which it was created." He struck again with the club, but this time Mescator was able to parry the blow. "This one will last a few days yet, but when he is used up, I can simply move to another." Korgaan's eyes flashed with wicked amusement. "I have others, wanderer. Many others."

The blare of the Gold Blades' trumpet rang out over the combat. Now it was Mescator's turn to smile. While the elite guard held the barbarians, a trap had been closing in around them. At the signal, two companies of Ophidian undead closed in from either flank. The Var'Kyr were surrounded as the skeletal warriors folded around them.

"I have others too," Mescator taunted the avatar. The withered husks of the undead were insensate to the axes and swords of the Var'Kyr, blows that would have left a man writhing in his own blood tore into the creatures without drawing so much as a grunt of pain. Only the fiercest strikes were sufficient to bring down one of the skeletons; and the moment it fell, another advanced to chop at the enemy with bronze khopeshes. The barbarians began to die in droves, their ferocity no match for the unwavering assault of the undead.

The avatar renewed his assault against Mescator. The scarred face split in a smile as a strike from the club knocked the Celestian's helmet away and gashed his scalp. "This battle counts for nothing," he snarled. "Whichever rabble of mortals wins is of no consequence. All that matters is you."

Another sweep of the club, but this time Mescator was able to retaliate. His sword slipped behind the brutal weapon to hack the hand that held it. The avatar lurched back as frost-hot liquid spilled from the stumpy wrist.

The Var'Kyr was unfazed by his hurt, instead lunging forward and driving his shoulder into Mescator. The Celestian was knocked back by the impact. "I need no weapon to destroy a pretender like you," Korgaan roared and clenched his remaining hand into a fist.

At that moment, screams erupted all across the battlefield. Mescator turned his head and saw a mighty conflagration inundate the Ahmunite center. The death-priests, their acolytes, and the fanatics bearing the idol of Shobik all disintegrated as a sheet of flame engulfed them. The golden idol crashed to the ground, melted into a shapeless mass by the intense heat.

Over the battlefield, soaring on leathery wings, was the dragon Draumdraak. At every turn, the reptile opened his jaws and sent another blast of fire down upon the enemies of Primovantor and Ophidia.

Kyron! He'd acted too soon! Mescator's mind raced with the realization, and with it came unbidden the plan he'd devised and until now kept from Korgaan's awareness. The elf mages were ready with their spells, to cast against the magic strong enough to bind the old god to the avatar he'd possessed. To keep him from escaping once more.

Korgaan howled in rage as he realized what was happening. The eyes flickered. For just an instant, the ancient malice of the god was supplanted by the dull, idiot gaze of the demigod he'd sired. Then the divine intelligence returned, unable to slip free as he'd intended. He gave Mescator a look of unbridled fury.

Then the avatar turned and fled back through the ranks of barbarians, pushing aside his warriors as he sought escape. Bound into the avatar by elvish magic, suddenly the outcome of the battle mattered very much to Korgaan; and with the dragon ravaging the invaders unopposed, there was little question what that outcome would be.

Mescator strove to pursue the avatar, but the other Var'Kyr impeded him. Trying to cut a path through the barbarians, he could only watch as the hulking brute hit the ranks of the undead. The unwavering commitment of the animated corpses counted for nothing against the might of Korgaan. Armored skeletons were sent flying when the avatar struck them. It was only a matter of moments before he was through and racing away from the battlefield.

Kyron must have realized his mistake at that moment, for Draumdraak suddenly diverted away from the stricken Ahmunite army and dove down upon the fleeing avatar. Korgaan's host evaporated in a gout of fire, only a blackened husk left behind.

Mescator watched the dragon's attack with misgivings. The plan had been to trap Korgaan in his host body and then imprison that body. He didn't know what would happen now that the mortal essence of the avatar had been extinguished, but he doubted the malignant spirit of Korgaan would be so easily vanquished. Capturing the host would have allowed the Celestians to imprison him, at least for a time. Destroying the host might have only set him free. How long it would take the god to regather his power was something they could only wait and see.

Horns blared over the battlefield. The banners of the Ahmunites had been cast down. From the armored howdah where the standard of Khephren had flown, there now rose a crimson pennant. Draumdraak's assault had been too much for the invaders. The pharaohs were sounding the retreat. In pathetic disarray, the legions broke and ran. Many were cut down as they fled, pursued by the vengeful Ophidians. Little of the broken army would escape back into the desert. Fewer still would survive to return to the city of Nehkesharr.

Mescator watched the miserable rout. Truly had Oskan spoken when he said this would be the end of Ahmun. The pharaohs had spent the last strength of their wasted land trying to wage a mad crusade upon Ophidia. Never again would they be able to rally a force powerful enough to threaten either Primovantor or Ophidia. This was the last gasp of a dead empire.

He would advise King Tothmenes and High Consul Vartherion to show restraint and allow the Ahmunites to withdraw back into their southern cities. Victory belonged to Primovantor and Ophidia, they could afford to be merciful. By showing restraint, Mescator was certain a people who had once been enemies could become friends. The power of Shobik's priests was all but finished. Ahmun would never again pose a threat.

There was no need to drive Ahmun to complete annihilation.

Chapter VII

-980, Time of Light

The Hills of Mordru presented a somber image. Jumbles of rock piled atop one another, gray and lifeless in the mist of morning. Beyond them towered the Mountains of Abkhazla. The legends of Primovantor claimed the hills were created when the mountains rose in rebellion against the old gods. The Abkhazla shook and trembled in the titanic duel, but in the end, it was the gods who prevailed. The wounded mountains cast their injuries down upon the land, great slabs of stone that fell into the heaps that would later be known as Mordru.

Belkon gave scant credence to the old fables. Many of the stories that were told in Primovantor were naught but imagination lent the respectability of tradition. It was an aspect of humans he'd found as frustrating as the artistic excesses of the elves, though perhaps even more pernicious. Elves sought to discover the truth of the world around them. Humans, when that truth proved too elusive, would invent their own explanations; and if such invention went unchallenged for too long, it became unquestioned fact in their minds.

Still, to every fable there was some truth, some observable fact that inspired the imaginations of those who wove fantasies to explain them. Belkon was now in search of the reality behind a story he'd heard. The people of Primovantor regarded Mordru as a strange and eerie realm, a place to be shunned and avoided. They spoke of great pillars of stone raised by ancient titans, markers that jabbed from the hills like fingers of rock to point accusingly at the sky. The humans also spoke of a strange, diminutive people who dwelt in Mordru and worshiped the primordial megaliths. A reclusive and sinister race who suffered no trespassers in their lands and punished those brazen enough to enter their domain. Many tales were told of men who vanished after setting out for the hills, slipping beyond the ken of oracles and magicians.

The other Celestians regarded these stories as naught but folklore. Primovantor was a great nation and within its boundaries were many peoples and customs. The land abounded with many such tales. Yet this one had stirred Belkon's curiosity. Perhaps it was the persistence with which the humans spoke of Mordru and its weird inhabitants. Perhaps it was the reputed magnificence of the megaliths, constructions that intrigued his knowledge of engineering. Perhaps it was simply that Belkon craved diversion.

Since the deaths of King Lyzander and Prince Juliarius, much had changed in Primovantor. Mescator and the other Celestians had been busy guiding that change. An alliance had been forged between Primovantor and the kingdom of Ophidia, cemented in the bonds of combat following the defeat of Ahmun's legions at the Battle of Hepshet. The once mighty empire of the Ahmunites had crumbled after that battle, struck by devastating plagues and calamities that further hastened their retreat into the desert and their southernmost cities. There were dark rumors about the manifold afflictions that ravaged Ahmun, whispers about the magi who served Tothmenes, now claiming the title of God-King. It was said that the sorcerers of Ophidia had called up the dread djinn of the wastelands to lay curses upon the defeated Ahmunites, to scourge their lands with magic as the Ahmunites had tried to raze Ophidia with torch and spear.

Whatever the truth of such claims, the fall of Ahmun brought with it peace. While there was peace, Mescator was using the influence of the Celestians to complete the reshaping of Primovantor. The royal line had been broken with the death of Juliarius, and a new system of leadership created. The kingdom was now a republic, governed by a house of consuls elected by the provinces they represented. Above the consuls was a High Consul, appointed by a consensus of the elected leaders. Gone was the old system of rule by birth and inheritance. Now it would be capability and merit that would raise leaders in Primovantor. Leaders – not rulers – for Mescator thought it would create greater stability for the short-lived humans if each felt he had agency, the choice to follow or not.

Belkon disagreed with Mescator on that point. The vagaries of differing interests made the republic system one that would inevitably be weighted down with inefficiency. Elected leaders would be obligated to the interests of those who gave them power – and who could strip it from them. They would be moved to safeguard the interests of their province over other and larger concerns. The needs of Primovantor as a nation would be secondary to those of their own constituents. Even if the rot of selfish ambition could be kept from the house of consuls, Belkon felt it was unavoidable that the leaders would be hampered by pettiness and a kind of tribalism. Those who had to earn their authority would take great pains to keep it, whether for their own pride or from a sincere belief in the good they were accomplishing by holding that power.

Far better, Belkon felt, to maintain a system where rule was bestowed rather than earned. Time among the humans had turned his mind away from his old attitudes. The mortals were simply too self-absorbed to be trusted to do what was right for the many and not simply for themselves. Such wisdom had to be taught. A royal heir could be built from the very beginning, fashioned to become a just and worthy monarch. There wouldn't be the scrabble for power, the promises and compromises to assume the mantle of leader. Secure in the authority of inheritance, the monarch could fixate on the obligations of a ruler, what was best for the whole of the dominion, not simply how a single region might increase its prosperity. From the moment of birth, the heir could be instructed and groomed, made into the ruler the nation would need. The difference between kingdom and republic was like that between a carefully plotted design and something swiftly improvised from the materials at hand. Both systems could work, but Belkon knew which was to be desired and which was only to be called upon by necessity.

Belkon was in the minority when it came to this outlook, however. The other Celestians lent their abilities to helping Mescator steer Primovantor into becoming a republic even as they finished weaning the people of their old gods. An infusion of new Celestians had helped bring about the later. From the Tower of Heaven, the newcomers spread out across not just Elvenholme, but Primovantor. Wherever the Celestians went, they bore with them the glory and wisdom of their kind, and they swiftly converted the humans they met to their cause.

Many of the Celestians who left Elvenholme remained with Mescator in the new city of Primantor, now the capital of the Grand Republic of Primovantor. A few diverted to other parts of the nation, but it was the example of Kyron that inspired Belkon's decision to journey to the hinterlands of Primovantor. Always brave and inquisitive, Kyron had been disappointed not to be among the first Celestians to cross over to Pannithor. He'd accepted Mescator's decision, of course, but it stung him to wait for the second conjunction before making his own trip. Belkon could well sympathize. In addition to Kyron's nature, that of a tireless explorer, there was his affection for Liliana. To be parted from her for so long had been painful. They shared a love for wild places and seeking out new things, never content to let the new sun set on the same horizon. At least so it had been, but Liliana had remained behind in Primovantor when Kyron searched for a place that would support the Sahlirian Tree. Instead, he'd returned with the dragon Draumdraak, an accomplishment that had delighted Liliana even as it vexed Karinna.

Fulgria, the object of Belkon's own affection, had expressed the hope when Kyron left on his mission that he might discover something so fabulous that Liliana would forget all else and rush to his side – as had indeed happened when he established contact with the dragons. Fulgria's words stirred Belkon's flagging hopes. Like himself, Fulgria had changed her opinion of power and authority, but in her instance, it caused her to embrace Mescator's reforms and help guide Primovantor into this new era of republicanism. She was busy tutoring the humans in the secrets of metallurgy and the art of the forge. After the armies of Primovantor defeated Ahmun, she revealed to them a potent invention that would give them a supreme advantage in any future war. A tough, resilient alloy of iron previously unknown to the humans called steel. Excited to show her eager pupils new ways to use steel, Fulgria became ever more distant and showed little interest in Belkon's misgivings about the republic.

It was in this situation that Belkon embarked on the long journey across Primovantor to the Hills of Mordru and the Abkhazla Mountains, the very edge of the world as far as the humans were concerned. He hoped to see for himself the colossal megaliths described by the humans. It would be interesting to see if they were truly constructions or merely freaks of nature the mortals had saddled with superstitions. If they had been built, then he was curious to know who had raised them and how they'd done so.

Across the great expanse of Primovantor, a great number of humans had accompanied Belkon. He was still uncomfortable with the role of god, and all that came with that role. Shrines and temples had been built in his honor across the land. While he was happy to see those dedicated to the old gods cast down, he was still uneasy when his own priests doted on him and worshipers presented him with offerings. What had started as a simple journey with only a few attendants took on the aspect of a pilgrimage by the time they were within sight of the Abkhazla Mountains. Yet the nearer they drew to their destination, the more Belkon saw the humans grow anxious.

On the other side of the mountains, according to Primovantor's cartographers, were the frontiers of Ophidia, but it wasn't fear of the sorceries of that strange land that sent a discordant note through the entourage. Along the trek across the republic, as people joined the procession, more and more tales were related about the Hills of Mordru. The sinister race that dwelt there was quantified. For the first time, Belkon heard a name bestowed on this hidden people. "Dwarf," the men of these eastern lands called them.

Fantastic were the stories told of the dwarfs. They were reputed to have skin of stone that would deflect any arrow shot at them and turn any blade raised against them. The weapons they bore could cut through stone as though it were cheese. The dwarfs could vanish into the earth and emerge from solid rock at will. Their eyes glowed in the night, and they could see in the dark as easily as a man could in daylight. If they caught anyone looking at them, they would take them away with them to the strange nether realm where the dwarfs lived, and the captive would never be heard from again.

This, then, was the legend. The magical guardians who protected the Hills of Mordru from all intruders. This was the tale Belkon had come so far to challenge when he emerged from his pavilion one misty morning and stared up at the heights. He felt a sense of anticipation course through him.

Whatever might happen, this was where he needed to be. Belkon waved aside the priests and attendants who hurried to go with him. "No," he told them. "This task is mine, and mine alone." He peered into the mist and thought of the dread with which the humans regarded this place. For all their fear, he knew they would follow unless he forbade them, such was the measure of their devotion. "If I haven't returned to you in three days, you will decamp and leave this place. Return to Esk and tell Mescator what has happened."

Belkon marched up into the hills. He would learn the mysteries of this place, or he would join its many legends.

As the god who vanished.

***

The hillsides proved to be the most treacherous ground Belkon had yet encountered in Pannithor. The slopes crumbled under his step, fragmenting into shards of rock under his tread. For someone less agile or with a mind absent the clarity of a Celestian, there was no chance of maintaining a firm footing. The sound of debris clattering and crashing to the plain below was sharp and distinct in the misty air. Belkon paid close attention as he progressed, studying the unforgiving terrain.

A smile slowly pulled at his face. The ground hadn't come by its fractious nature by accident. He could see the betraying marks of chisel and hammer, pick and shovel. Cunningly disguised, it was true, but there just the same. Belkon thought it a clever way to alert any sentinels that someone was climbing into the hills. He doubted if even the keen senses of the elves would have spotted the trick.

Belkon was certain the dwarfs were more than legend now, and they knew he was coming. Prudence would have him turn back, but he'd come this far already. He wouldn't go back to Esk without at least seeing the megaliths for himself. If he should encounter the dwarfs as well, so much the better.

Even for the tireless Celestian, it took a long time to ascend the hillside and reach the summit. The mist closed around him, coloring everything a dingy gray. A human would have been utterly blinded by the fog, barely able to see a hand held before his face, but Belkon could still perceive his surroundings well enough. When he reached the top of the hill, he found the footing more secure than it had been on the climb up. He studied the ground and could see signs that someone had swept it clean of tracks. What kind of tracks, he could find no hint, but when he lifted his gaze, he soon found something much more extravagant to occupy his attention.

One of the megaliths reared skyward from the summit he stood upon, only a few hundred yards away. Truly it was impressive in its scale, a great slab of granite at least eighty feet high and twenty feet thick. Belkon could see at once that its contours, though weathered by the elements, were too regular for any natural formation. Moreover, there was some sort of writing cut into the stone, lining each face in regular columns. It was a harsh, geometric kind of lettering, unlike the elvish and human scripts with which Belkon was familiar. There was one bit of information that needed no translation. While the megaliths themselves were worn by the elements, the writing was clear and precise. That meant, however ancient the stones might be, what was written on them was more recent or else regularly maintained by someone acting as custodian over the hills.

Belkon approached the megalith. He could now see others beyond it looming out of the mist like the teeth of some gargantuan beast. There was a pattern to their arrangement, but he didn't think it was so obvious as the circles the humans claimed in their stories about Mordru. He thought they were laid out in a manner that evoked the lettering cut into them. Some kind of glyph repeated at a colossal scale. A marker, perhaps, denoting ownership of the land.

A furtive motion near one of the megaliths caught Belkon's notice. He didn't turn his head, only his eyes, aware that more pronounced activity might provoke a reaction and spoil his observation of the lurker. There was someone watching him from around the corner of the giant slab of granite. A sentinel set here to watch for intruders.

Feigning interest only in the megaliths, Belkon was able to get the sentinel to expose himself more fully. He found that the lurker was a short, stocky person with broad shoulders and a powerful build. His face was dominated by a thick black beard above which there was a bulbous nose and a thick brow. The dominant expression in his amber-colored eyes wasn't curiosity but suspicion. Belkon could see that the sentinel was neither human nor elf, but of a different race entirely. Here, then, was a dwarf.

The dwarf was arrayed in a heavy, apron-like garment fashioned from metal scales, dull and almost black in hue. A tight-fitting cap of the same material covered his head, and in his thick hands he gripped an axe with a crescent-shaped blade. Belkon was intrigued by the dwarf's arms and armor, for they were much different than those he'd seen employed by men and elves.

"I know you're watching me," Belkon said, suddenly turning and looking directly at the dwarf. His words were spoken in the trade tongue of Primovantor, a language he thought these reclusive people might have at least some knowledge of.

Whether he understood or not, the dwarf made no reply. Spinning around, he dashed off toward the next megalith. Belkon shook his head as he watched the sentinel run before setting off in pursuit. The dwarfs might be many things, but fast on their feet wasn't one of them.

Cunning was, however, as Belkon soon learned. In chasing after the dwarf, he was drawn into a masterfully concealed trap. A pit opened up beneath his feet, exposing a dark shaft that plunged deep into the ground. Belkon twisted at the very lip of the hole, throwing himself forward with his momentum. The Celestian landed well past the gaping pit. The dwarf, pausing to watch his pursuer fall, now turned and began to run again.

Belkon was wary of more tricks. His keen gaze spotted three more expertly concealed triggers that he was drawn toward by the sentinel. These he avoided without breaking stride. He was closing the distance and would soon catch his quarry.

At least that was the conclusion Belkon expected, but when he was only a few yards from the dwarf, the sentinel suddenly vanished. It was just as the fables claimed. The ground had swallowed him up! This, however, Belkon judged impossible. It would have needed a considerable expenditure of magic to manage such a feat, and the Celestian would have sensed such power being brought to bear. No, this was another device of the dwarfs, a masterfully constructed trick.

Belkon trained his senses on the spot where the dwarf disappeared. He could hear a dull rumbling in the earth, the sound of some mechanism in action. Studying the ground, he saw the edges of a trapdoor, and closer scrutiny revealed the mossy stone that served as its trigger.

Belkon stepped onto the door and pressed his toe against the stone. Instantly he was plunged downward as the ground on which he stood flipped back. The drop was a brief one, but he could imagine it would be jarring for anyone not expecting it. He could see a flywheel quickly shift another stone panel into place, a rotating series of secret doors that instantly replaced its predecessor when a dwarf had need of a quick escape.

The chamber in which the Celestian had dropped was wide, but with a low ceiling. The walls were stone, but expertly hewn. A narrow tunnel opened at one end, and it was in this direction Belkon could hear the dwarf's retreating footfalls.

Any idea that the dwarf was unaware Belkon had followed him down inside the hill was soon abandoned. The trigger of still another trap lay in the Celestian's path. Belkon studied the thin wire, impressed at the workmanship that connected it to a section of the wall. A human dropping down here would be blind unless he'd brought his own light, and even then Belkon didn't think they'd spy the trap or its potential. He, however, did. He knew the trap would send a block toppling out from the wall to crush an intruder. He calculated the mass involved, how large a block the dwarfs could employ and still force back into its place when they came to clear the trap.

His calculations made, Belkon stepped forward and kicked the tripwire. As he'd predicted, a section of the wall lurched outward and crashed down onto him.

The rumble of the trap echoed through the tunnel. The sound of footfalls followed close upon the echoes. A great company was hurrying down the passage to where Belkon lay beneath the stone block. He could hear the gruff voices of several dwarfs discussing the vanquished intruder. The minds of the dwarfs weren't so easy to penetrate as those of elves and humans, but after a few moments, Belkon was able to read their thoughts and make sense of their speech.

"Not in my father's time nor in his father's father's time has anyone trespassed into our halls," one of the dwarfs grumbled. "You bring shame onto the Ironsmite clan, Grimgar!"

By his words, Belkon realized Grimgar was the sentinel who'd tried to lure him into so many traps. "This was a trespasser like no other," the dwarf protested. "I have never seen or heard of his like before. Though he had some semblance to a man, I'd wager my beard he wasn't a human. If you could have seen the way he leaped the first pit I drew him to, or the way he spotted the others! By my grandmother's bones, he had eyes like a dwarf!

He found the door into the sentry post so fast he nearly beat me getting down into the tunnel."

"Well, he's crushed to pulp now," a third dwarf quipped. "Whoever or whatever he was. None may trespass in Abercarr."

Belkon chose that moment to heave the huge block of stone aside. The deadfall should have crushed any ordinary intruder, but he'd determined it wasn't such a weight as to confound the strength of a Celestian. Triggering a trap that couldn't harm him, he bid his time until the dwarfs came to investigate and he could introduce himself to them in a suitably impressive manner.

"I come as visitor, not trespasser," Belkon announced as he thrust the stone block aside. It crashed against the floor and sent a deafening rumble rolling through the tunnel. Though he spoke in the language of the Celestians, in their minds, the dwarfs heard him speak in their own language. He wasn't sure which awed them more, to see him throw aside the stone or to hear an outsider using their tongue.

Belkon could sense the fear that gripped the dwarfs, but their resolve held them firm. They stood their ground, weapons at the ready, determined to protect their people from any threat, no matter how insurmountable. He'd already seen how ruthless the dwarfs could be in defending their homeland, and now he had some insight into how selflessly they were committed to that cause.

"Upon the legacy of my ancestors, I swear I intend no harm to Abercarr," Belkon invoked an oath he sensed the dwarfs would respect. "I have come to you to benefit your people. I am one of the Celestians who have come to mentor and guide the nations of Pannithor."

Grimgar edged forward, his eyes like daggers. "You teach the humans?" he asked. "The elves?"

Belkon gauged the hostility in Grimgar's tone. Isolated, reclusive, the dwarfs appeared to want nothing to do with the other races. There were long traditions of enmity and distrust, if not outright hostility, between the dwarfs and the other peoples of Pannithor. Belkon could read that from even a cursory glance at their minds. Co-operation, the brotherhood of civilizations, these were appeals that would carry little weight with the insular dwarfs. There was, however, another approach that Belkon knew would sway them.

"The Celestians guide the humans and the elves," Belkon said. "That is why I have come to you. We would bring our gifts to Abercarr so that the dwarfs will also prosper." His eyes held each of the dwarfs in turn. "So that your people aren't left behind."

Grimgar scratched his beard as he considered Belkon's words. The Celestian had indeed divined the way to pierce the dwarfs' reserve. The threat that the other races would grow powerful and become a menace to their kingdom. "We must send a messenger to the chief of our clan. If he deems it wise, he will send word to our king. If the king is impressed, then the High King of Abercarr will be told." Grimgar nodded to Belkon. "It's the High King who will decide."

Belkon smiled. He thought of the levels of bureaucracy in the republic Mescator was building and how inefficient it was. Here, the dwarfs had a direct line of authority culminating in a High King responsible for their entire nation. A pragmatic system for a pragmatic people.

"Do I wait for his decision here?" Belkon asked.

"Unless the High King decrees otherwise, this is as far as you step into our realm," Grimgar told the Celestian, though it seemed the dwarfs were uncertain if they could actually stop him.

Belkon let them cling to their doubts. Diplomacy was always the more efficient way of accomplishing things, but if he were determined to delve straight on to the High King's court, the dwarfs wouldn't keep him away.

***

-977, Time of Light

The Celestial Court was the great hall raised in Primantor for Mescator and his companions. Part holy temple, part palace, it exceeded in every aspect of size and grandeur any other structure in Primovantor. Though it had been designed by the Celestians, the construction had been entrusted to humans so that when they looked upon the building they should know a sense of pride.

Fulgria knew Belkon would disagree, but she thought the humans had reason to feel proud. Except when he pointed out the flaws in the execution of his plan by the builders, she found the Celestial Court magnificent. The opulence with which the humans had lavished the structure was without rival, in its way exceeding the artistry of the elves, for in every carving and each mural there was the hand of a devoted craftsman striving to impress in his work the devotion in his heart. There was none of the magical enhancement with which the elves augmented the limitations of their labor. That lent the wonder of the Celestial Court a kind of sincerity lost upon the sensibilities of Elvenholme.

A ring of thrones rested at one end of the great hall, each chair bathed in sunlight that streamed down from glass panes set into the roof above. Each of the windows was richly adorned, the panes fashioned from carefully arranged colored glass. Though the varied colors created gripping scenes from the history of Pannithor when viewed individually, such was the inventiveness of their construction that when the sunlight shone down through them they sent a beam of color down upon one of the thrones below. Each of the twenty chairs was bathed in a different light. That in which Mescator now reposed was illuminated in gold, while Oskan's seat was tinged a royal purple. Fulgria's chair was highlighted a fiery orange to evoke her mastery of the forge.

Many of the chairs were vacant, for not all of the Celestians were present in Primantor; yet that worked in their favor, as the builders of the Celestial Court hadn't reckoned upon the advent of more of the star-gods upon Pannithor. In the days of King Lyzander, when the foundations were laid, the arrival of more Celestians seemed a hope too dear to anticipate.

The leaders of Pannithor had their own seats brought into the great hall, arrayed along the flanks of the Celestians in long lines. Nearest to the Celestians was the chair of Rubir, the hierophant of Mescator's cult, a wise and kindly man who'd striven to blot out the remnants of Shobik's harsh faith and spread the compassionate wisdom of the new religion. Opposite him was that of the High Consul Vartherion, a man of vision and grand ideals who had done much to reshape the civic systems within the new republic. After these two notables were other ranking members of the Celestial cults and the house of consuls, masters of the various trade guilds and mercantile combines, even a few of Primovantor's generals and admirals. Off to one side was Ingthwe, the ambassador of Elvenholme, her silk gown shining with the pearlescent enchantments woven into it. Beside her was the dour Nehkbet-ka, emissary of the Ophidian God-King Tothmenes, his shaved head and gaunt face framed by a golden cowl.

This great assembly had been called to receive Belkon on his return. For two years he'd been absent from Primantor. Fulgria felt a twinge of guilt that she hadn't missed him as much as she felt she should have. Belkon had journeyed to the very edge of Primovantor, off toward what the humans reckoned was the very edge of the world, to lands even the elves knew little about. It was a long and difficult journey, but now he was back. Back to present his discoveries before his fellow Celestians.

A hush fell across the gathered dignitaries when the great doors at the end of the hall were opened by the armored warders posted there. Belkon had kept himself in seclusion upon his return to the city, and this was the first time Fulgria had seen him. He looked much changed by his travels. His step was firmer than it had been before, filled not just with purpose but energy and ambition. His eyes had an intensity about them that hadn't been there before, a kind of confidence Fulgria couldn't remember ever seeing there. These were the details she noticed, but she knew the mortals were focused on the veneer Belkon had assumed. Just as they'd adjusted their appearance to assume a familiarity comfortable to first the elves and then the humans, so had Belkon's visage undergone a metamorphosis. His features had a harsher and more rugged character. A blond beard, so rich in color it might have been spun from gold, fell to his chest and was weighted down with jeweled ornaments. The clothes he wore were of a curious style unlike any of the fashions of either men or elves — earthen tones and simple cuts that yet conspired toward a kind of understated strength, which was a far cry from the ostentation Fulgria had become accustomed to seeing in Primantor.

The quiet that gripped the hall when Belkon entered was broken when anxious murmurs shifted through the mortals. Fingers pointed in alarm at the half dozen figures who followed the Celestian into the room. Fulgria leaned forward in her seat. Belkon's companions were squat, powerfully built creatures unlike any she'd seen before. More, her gaze was drawn to the armor that clothed each of them. It wasn't the iron and bronze of Primovantor or Ophidia, nor the ensorcelled alloys created by the elves. It was steel. Had these creatures made that discovery for themselves, or was this Belkon's doing? No, she couldn't be mistaken by the used look the armor had, the air of age that clung to each suit of mail. This had been forged long before Eoswain first made contact with Reiliur.

"Mescator," Belkon greeted their leader with a deep bow. "I have returned from the Mountains of Abkhazla. There, I have found a most remarkable people."

"Abkhazla!" High Consul Vartherion exclaimed. His eyes gaped as he stared at the bearded creatures who stood behind Belkon. "You don't mean... the legends are true? These... these are dwarfs?"

The murmur of a moment before grew louder as the crowd discussed among themselves this remarkable development. Some, familiar with the dark stories told about the dwarfs, went pale and clutched at the holy talismans of their favored Celestian. Others, less credulous or less acquainted with the legends, peered at the dwarfs with sharp interest, wondering what this contact with a new people would mean for Primovantor.

It was the elven ambassador who spoke out, her voice augmented by some minor spell so that it lost none of its clarity as it swept into every corner of the great hall. "It would have been best to leave these dwarfs an undiscovered legend," Ingthwe declared. Her eyes were like daggers when she stared at the dwarfs. "My people know them of old. They are a savage and belligerent breed. It is best to leave them where they are. Only sorrow is harvested from any dealings with their kind."

A black-bearded dwarf stepped forward and glared back at the elf. "Better to trust the bite of a viper than the word of an elf," he snapped. He thrust an accusing finger at Ingthwe. "Once, there was a compact between our races. The elves would have all that their gods had entrusted to them. The seas and forests, all that rose above the earth." He slapped his chest with a dull thump. "We are the children of Dianek, Mistress of the Underworld. The treasures within the earth belong to us. The elves agreed to our claim, but they broke their word and delved down into our realm to plunder what belonged to us."

Ingthwe gave the dwarf a contemptuous smile. "I've never heard of such a compact. Nor would I say any elf remembers such an agreement between our people, however long ago it was."

"It doesn't matter if the elves remember," the dwarf returned, repeating himself when he lapsed from the Primovantorian taught to him by Belkon into his native tongue. "It only matters that we do. That we know how faithless your kind is."

"Grimgar, I didn't bring you here to rekindle old grudges," Belkon told the dwarf. Grimgar bowed in apology to the Celestian but didn't extend the gesture to Ingthwe. Belkon had his own words for the ambassador. "It seems there might be cause for a new one to lay upon the elves." He raised his gaze to Mescator. "Why is it that after so many years since our arrival in Pannithor that we should learn of the dwarfs only through vague rumors when their existence was well known to the elves? The most we've heard of them from Elvenholme have been veiled references to troglodytes in the deep places." He set his hand on Grimgar's shoulder. "I stand here to tell you that the dwarfs aren't the sinister savages of folklore, but as fine a people as any we've yet met in this world."

"They're a greedy and spiteful race," Ingthwe objected.

Mescator made a chopping motion of his hand. "It strikes me that the quality of the dwarfs should be left to us to determine," he said. "It could be argued that by not telling us of their existence, the elves are the ones who've been greedy and spiteful. Keen to keep the guidance of the Celestians to themselves and their allies. Letting old prejudices color their attitude toward the dwarfs." He looked across the mortal audience. "The Celestians are new to Pannithor, our hearts and minds unburdened by old animosities." He fixed his gaze on Grimgar. "We will make fair judgment of the dwarfs, whether their association can be reckoned boon or menace to other peoples, be they elf or human."

Vartherion glanced at the consuls around him. "We will assemble the house to vote, but I can safely say that the Grand Republic of Pannithor will defer to whatever decision the Celestians deem wise." His words brought nods of agreement from most of the humans. Ingthwe scowled but offered no further comment.

"Trust our decision," Oskan addressed the crowd. "We'll find the course that serves to best help everyone. As we've helped guide Primovantor, Ophidia, and Elvenholme into a new understanding and friendship, so we'll strive to bring the dwarfs into the fold of civilized peoples."

Not long after Oskan's speech, the mortals were ushered from the Celestial Court. Only the dwarfs remained behind to answer the questions posed to them by Mescator and the others, Belkon assuming a role as both adjudicator and moderator.

"I can believe what they say of Abercarr's size," Belkon confirmed Grimgar's account of dwarfish architecture. "They build on a mighty scale. The Hills of Mordru are filled with their tunnels and halls. I have seen their capital of Dolgarth where High King Thrayne has his throne. It's a city almost as big as Esk, but more remarkable because it extends entirely inside the Abkhazla Mountains. The dwarfs use angled mirrors to bring light down into their streets and a smokeless oil to illuminate their homes." His eyes gleamed as he described the engineering wonders of the dwarf city. Fulgria was infected by Belkon's excitement.

"They knew the secret of steel before we came to Pannithor?" Flugria asked, gesturing to the dwarfs.

Belkon's face beamed on her. "No one we've met since coming here is more skilled with the art of metallurgy." He made a gesture to the dwarfs with Grimgar. These came forward and laid before Mescator's throne a pair of golden coffers. When they opened the boxes, the dazzling sparkle of fabulous jewels greeted the Celestians.

Fulgria rose and retrieved a necklace from one of the boxes. Her fascination was less in the value of the rubies and opals that hung from the chain, but in the artistry of the settings themselves. The metal itself was neither gold nor silver but an incredible alloy that combined the glamour of both. She sat back in her chair and studied the necklace with the eye of an artist who respects the technique of a craftsman.

"Do you believe the dwarfs would benefit by our guidance?" Mescator put the question to Belkon, switching to the language of the Celestians so that the dwarfs wouldn't understand their words. "They have been reclusive and territorial, distrustful of outsiders. These are things that could be dangerous. In helping the dwarfs, we must not put others in jeopardy."

"The dwarfs are a proud people," Belkon said. "Stubborn to a fault but also rigidly honorable. They distrust because they think other people don't keep their word. I think if they're treated with fairness and dignity, the dwarfs would be valuable friends." He pointed at the walls of the temple-palace around them. "They respect only the goddess Dianek, and even she has no priests among them. The dwarfs do not ask anything of gods. They expect to work for what they have and what they would have."

Fulgria set the necklace down. "In many ways, the dwarfs are more advanced than the other cultures we've discovered. No predatory temples exploiting their people and committing outrages to honor fading gods. I think that we should help them. Foster their development and bring out the best of their qualities."

Belkon smiled at her, then turned to Mescator. "Such was my purpose in bringing this delegation here. I did not presume to act without consulting you first, but it is my desire to leave Primantor and join the dwarfs in Dolgarth. With the guidance of the Celestians, I am certain Abercarr will become a great nation and a strong ally to those we've already helped."

"Will you need help?" Fulgria asked, perhaps just a bit too much eagerness in her voice.

"If anyone were willing to descend into the mountains with me, the help would be much appreciated," Belkon said. "A companion would make the work much less lonely," he added with just a trace of appeal in his tone.

Mescator gave each of them a sharp look, then rose from his chair, a grin pulling at his face. "Then it is decided. The two of you will journey back to Abercarr and begin your work as advisors and guides to the dwarfs."

Fulgria looked again at the steel armor Grimgar wore and at the cunningly wrought necklace from the coffer. "I am certain there is much I can teach people who already have such an affinity for the forge."

Chapter VIII

-950, Time of Light

"**I**t is an unjust accusation, and we resent its implications!" Spoken by the usually cautious and unemotional King Tothmenes, the outburst had the effect of a thunderbolt within his court, turning faces an ashen gray and putting hands to lips to stifle startled gasps. The King of Ophidia reposed in a throne of gold and lapis lazuli, set between pillars of marble. At his feet, chained to the steps of the dais, was a gigantic Ahmunite warlion with a jeweled collar. Beside him, nude but for the shackles they wore, were two slaves who fanned their royal master with perfumed fronds from exotic trees. The fetters that bound both cat and men were merely for ostentation. One look at their deathly shapes was enough to tell an observer that they were caught in a bondage far more complete than that of the stoutest chains. These were the undead, conjured up from their graves by necromancy to serve the Ophidians.

King Tothmenes was a contrast to his servitors, for he was vibrant with life. Only a gilded skirt and a collar of lapis lazuli covered his robust frame. His dark skin was oiled to a glistening sheen to better show off the corded muscles beneath. His face had the bloom of youth, vivacious and eager as only those on the cusp of life can show. A hawklike nose poised above a narrow mouth and a squared chin. The cheeks were smooth, the head shorn, even the eyebrows had been plucked so that the king was as hairless as a newborn babe. Only in his eyes was there any hint of his true age, for these were filled with a cynical and jaded light bestowed by too many bitter lessons and frustrated dreams.

Oskan didn't know the secret of how King Tothmenes had maintained his youth while other humans withered and perished. The monarch was into his second century of life, yet he looked as though he were in his early twenties. The Celestians thought perhaps the Ophidians had discovered something similar to the Sahlirian Tree, but the elves dissuaded them of that idea. Spies of Elvenholme had uncovered obscene blood rites performed by the necromancers to maintain the vitality of Ophidia's royalty. Out of the young, blood was drawn to sustain the old. Remembering their fears of the chaos that would unfold should the promise of the Sahlirian fruit be made known to mortals, Oskan could only imagine the carnage should such vile magic be exposed. Far better to maintain the stability of the world to allow the myth that Tothmenes wasn't simply a king, but a God-King, to be maintained. Let dark rumors remain just that, lest they explode into an even more horrible truth.

The Ophidian courtiers gathered in the summer palace of King Tothmenes looked away from their monarch and fixed their eyes on the Celestian who'd made the journey from Primovantor to confer with one of the seven God-Kings who ruled over them. All of them had a mix of fear and expectancy in their attitudes. If Oskan let himself concentrate on any one of them, he could read their agitation despite the sorcerous wards arrayed about the palace intended to baffle his powers. All of them worried that their kings had pushed too far in their ambitions and that war was coming.

Still, there was a glimmer of hope for the Ophidians. Oskan could sense that as well. Some among the Celestians, especially Valandor, had become steadily more antagonistic toward Ophidia over the years. The dark magics they employed were a source of suspicion and worry to Valandor and the Circle of Heaven. Karinna, with her expertise in the gestation of life, was especially disgusted by the art of necromancy. It was Oskan who argued the most on behalf of Ophidia, reminding Mescator and the others that they'd been valuable allies in the final war with Ahmun.

That it was the final war with Ahmun was the point of contention that had soured relations with Ophidia. The land of the pharaohs from which Ophidia had wrested independence was collapsing back into the desert sands, its people withering away as the fertility of their realm was ravaged by plague, blight, and famine. It was this subject that had provoked Tothmenes to break from his accustomed pose of emotional indifference.

"The elves are even more learned in the ways of magic than the sorcerers of Ophidia," Oskan advised Tothmenes. "They don't make such accusations lightly. They say it is impossible that the miseries that have cursed Ahmun are natural." He looked aside to where a cowled necromancer stood, his staff topped by a golden vulture, one of the many aspects of Shobik. "Nor is it likely that the fading old gods have pooled such energies as they have left to smite the land."

"So naturally it is to be assumed that we are responsible?" Tothmenes shook his head, the jeweled crown sparkling as it moved from side to side.

"Who else would have the knowledge and the desire to devastate Ahmun in such a manner?" Oskan countered.

"The elves, as you say, are past masters of magic. Though the Ahmunites have never been so brazen as to strike at Elvenholme, the desert frontier does border on their nation. Perhaps the elves divined that the death-priests intended a new campaign, not against Primovantor or Ophidia, but against them. Such a battery of curses as have rained down upon the pharaohs and their slaves would be easy enough for the elves to conjure, but it would demand vast resources for our sorcerers to manage." Tothmenes pointed his ruby-capped scepter at the necromancer. "Is that not so, Arhotep? Remind our revered visitor of what it cost just to raise this lion from the carnage of Hepshet."

Arhotep bowed to his king, then bowed to Oskan as he turned away from the throne. "In order to revitalize the warlion, spices and ointments to the value of seven hundred shekels of gold had to be gathered, and five adepts were called upon to expend of their own vitality an energy equivalent to twenty years." The necromancer's cadaverous face pulled back in a sad smile. "No, our magic doesn't come as cheaply as it does to the elves. A ritual such as they describe would have demanded far more than Ophidia could spare."

Oskan fixed a stern look on Arhotep. "They say that Ophidia has learned to summon the djinn. Where the limitations of mortal flesh might fail, couldn't the powers of the desert demons be made to serve?" It was a stab in the dark, one which Oskan was uncertain would strike. The elves knew little about the djinn beyond the fact that they existed, and the Celestians had learned only one thing more about the beings. A sufficiently powerful sorcerer *could* bend them to his will.

Tothmenes gave Arhotep no chance to answer. A wave of the king's hand sent him retreating back among the crowd. "The djinn have ever been a threat to our people. Preying on caravans as they crossed the deserts. Stealing upon Bedouin camps in the dead of night and leaving none alive to see the dawn. Yes, those who practice magic in Ophidia and in Ahmun have researched the djinn extensively, but with the ambition of protecting ourselves. Suggesting that we would treat with such beings is like suggesting the sheep would seek fellowship with the leopard."

The king slapped his scepter against the palm of his hand. "Yet in their desperation, perhaps that is just what the magi of Ahmun did. Fearing reprisals and annihilation by Mescator and the nations who've accepted the guidance of the Celestians, it is possible they were so reckless in their conjurations." Tothmenes looked across his court. "Imagine them in Nehkesharr, so enamored of the shackles they wear that in their desperation, to keep their chains, they would try to draw the djinn into their service. So resentful of we who have won our freedom that they would summon demons to destroy us." He turned his eyes on Oskan. "Whatever knowledge the magi of Ophidia know was taught to them by the magi of Ahmun. What magic our necromancers command was first devised in Ahmunite temples."

The king's mind was closed to Oskan, so he couldn't be certain whether Tothmenes was being deceitful. He had to weigh the monarch's words and the idea that the Ahmunites had brought doom down upon themselves. Everything he'd seen of Ahmun, the example from the Battle of Hepshet, made it sound plausible to him. Yet there was something more. A sense of wariness about Tothmenes. Something the king was trying to keep Oskan from learning.

Tothmenes went further with his argument. "Elvenholme has stirred these rumors until they've reached even the Celestians." The king's expression turned bitter. "The elves are jealous of all you've done to help other races. Because they're so long-lived, they're slow to discard old ideas; while with each generation, men receive your guidance with fresh eyes." He waved his scepter through the air. "The elves have prided themselves as masters of the sea. They're envious of the great Pass of Khoem which joins the River Ophid with the mighty oceans."

"Belkon designed the channel for the betterment of all peoples," Oskan reminded Tothmenes. "Not just Ophidia."

"The burden of construction was borne by my kingdom,"

Tothmenes said. "It was we who excavated the channels. We who supplied the labor to dig the tunnels under the mountains. It is to be conceded that the dwarfs supervised the construction, but it was we who cut away the rock and hauled away the earth. Nor have the dwarfs failed to profit, for now the goods of Abercarr reach markets they could never before have dreamed to find." He raised one finger to emphasize a point. "The dwarfs have even begun to construct their own ships to move their wares. If the tolls we exact for use of the Pass of Khoem were so onerous and unreasonable, would the dwarfs pay them?"

Oskan gave the king a wary look. "The elves say that Ophidia charges the dwarfs far less than is levied upon the ships of Primovantor and Elvenholme."

"Of course they would," Tothmenes said. "The elves despise dwarfs and would do anything to hurt Abercarr." The king muttered a bitter laugh. "I suppose they also accuse Ophidia of trying to monopolize the trade in dwarfish goods? I will tell you a thing about elves. They care only for themselves. They've sought to exploit the Celestians since you first arrived in Pannithor." He laughed again, making the sound even uglier than before. "They were so gracious to allow Mescator to leave their lands and reshape Primovantor into a stronger nation. To what purpose? I shall tell you! They wanted a buffer state between their own lands and those hostile to them! A proxy they could use to fight their wars for them. Consider for a moment the 'aid' the elves rendered at the Battle of Hepshet. A few magicians and some archers? Bah, what is that beside the toll inflicted upon the human soldiers who did most of the fighting? Even the Celestians were sorely pressed that day. I understand both Mescator and Liliana were in jeopardy during the battle."

"The elves had to guard their own borders," Oskan replied, though the seed of doubt was growing inside his mind. "As you yourself pointed out, Elvenholme also edges upon the deserts of Ahmun."

Tothmenes shook his head. "No, my friend," he said, his tone softening. "It is the pattern we've noticed when it comes to the elves. They use others. Those who they cannot manipulate and dominate, they seek to destroy. They did not divulge to the Celestians the very existence of the dwarfs. Tell me, have they spoken to you of the salamanders? I can see by the furrowing of your brow that they haven't. The salamanders are a strange, scaly people from far to the east. A few Ophidian explorers have had peaceful commerce with them, but otherwise, we are careful about trafficking with them for their minds are far different from our own, and it can be challenging to predict what will cause them offense. We advised the elves to be careful when they contacted the salamanders, but they ignored us. As a result, few ships from that exploratory armada returned to the Pass of Khoem. The salamanders proved capable of defying the elves, so it is only to be expected that they wouldn't want the Celestians learning of the reptiles and visiting their lands. The last thing they want is for you to help them as you have so many others."

"There are those who would argue that it is Ophidia that seeks to manipulate and use others," Oskan told the king. "You ask why the elves have never made mention of these salamanders to us, but I would reverse the question and ask why Ophidia has never spoken of them before. There are some who say that you have befriended the dwarfs simply to exploit their enmity with the elves, finding in them a foil by which to weaken Elvenholme and bolster your own trade deals." He paused and focused upon a mural painted upon the palace walls that depicted the Battle of Hepshet. "Indeed, some go so far as to say it was Ophidia that sought to use Primovantor as a proxy to secure independence from Ahmun."

Tothmenes bowed his head, sadness on his face. "I too have heard these unjust murmurs. I had dared to hope they'd not defiled the ears of the Celestians with such vile lies." He looked up and fixed Oskan with his gaze. "My only hope is that these lies haven't turned you against my country."

Oskan was quick to reply. "I cannot speak for the other Celestians. Not even my mentor, Mescator. But I will say that I don't believe these claims laid against Ophidia, and I promise that I will take your arguments to the others when I return to Primantor."

"You have been a true friend to Ophidia," Tothmenes said. He tapped his scepter against his palm, a look of contemplation on his visage. "We know that Oskan the Generous will champion the cause of our people before the Celestians. However, it is too grave a matter to be undertaken with my blessing alone."

The speech surprised Oskan. Always Tothmenes had assumed a regal and imperious pose. Now, however, he acted with deference, even hesitance lest he overstep some boundary he dared not cross. Oskan had, of course, heard of other God-Kings in Ophidia, but until this moment he'd assumed them to be subservient to Tothmenes. He wondered if that had been a mistake, if in truth these other God-Kings held power commensurate with Tothmenes. Or perhaps, some of them might hold still greater authority.

"I must dare to impose upon your indulgence," Tothmenes continued. "There are those whom I must consult." His mouth twitched with uncertainty. "It may be that your presence will be requested."

Oskan smiled at the turn of phrase. "It has been a long time since a Celestian was summoned to an audience with a mortal," he commented. "Even so long-lived mortals as the god-kings of Ophidia."

There was no mistaking the anxiety Tothmenes now exhibited, and Oskan had to wonder at a fear so great it could penetrate the monarch's habitual mask of royal authority. "If you meet with them... some will not be mortal as you reckon such things."

***

-949, Time of Light

For several months, Oskan had waited in the court of Tothmenes while the Ophidians arranged a thing that hadn't occurred in centuries – a gathering of the God-Kings. From what he knew of the fiercely independent people, they were too cautious to allow their leadership to concentrate in any one place. Tradition and custom dictated that only in the most extreme circumstances would more than two of their rulers meet, both to avoid the disaster of assassination and the equally dire prospect of collusion among the God-Kings. By keeping them separated, it was thought that their authority could be limited within what the merchant houses considered reasonable.

In practice, the complex system resulted in the God-Kings simply carving out spheres of influence over which each exerted almost complete control. One, Oskan understood, held dominion over magic and wizards in Ophidia. Another, unsurprisingly in a nation that yet revered the primogenitor Shobik, was concerned with tombs and funerary practices, as well as governing the use of necromancy. Tothmenes, to an outsider, appeared to be the most important of the God-Kings because his special authority was over relations with foreign kingdoms, whether those took the form of peaceful trade or armed warfare – or all the many subtle layers Ophidians considered to exist between the two extremes.

Now, Oskan found himself in company with Tothmenes and a shockingly small retinue crossing the southern desert. Flatland of brown shrubs and gray cacti that marched away in every direction, a limitless vista of barren harshness. Oskan knew that the creatures of Pannithor could scratch an existence even from these brutal conditions, but he recalled an observation Reiliur imparted to the Celestians, namely that the more unforgiving the environment, the more cruel the things that called it home. None more so than the thinking races like humans and elves.

Abruptly, the procession came upon a disruption of the vicious plain. Hidden from afar, they discovered a jagged gorge many miles wide. It plunged downward to a depth of thousands of feet, a great valley concealed within the empty desert. Oskan was amazed by the scene, as were the Ophidian soldiers and servants. Only Tothmenes was unfazed. The God-King goaded his camel to draw nearer to Oskan.

"There is no danger here for you," Tothmenes whispered. "You have been summoned." Oskan could sense the tension in the monarch's voice. "As have I."

Oskan continued to study the valley below. It was fertile, though hardly what he'd consider lush. Ugly shrubs and cacti were replaced by thin, gnarled trees with thorns instead of leaves. Stretches of dull yellow grass were spattered about the land and a narrow stream snaked its way through the gorge, feeding several ponds.

All of this was forgotten when Oskan noticed the structures that were built into the cliff-like face of the valley's far wall. Their scale was at a level which surpassed any of the megalithic structures he'd seen in Ahmun and Ophidia, rivaling the soaring towers of the elves. Yet there was a creeping sensation they evoked that was far different from the impression of grandeur the palaces of Therennia Adar or the pyramids of Khom-ret. It was the wonder conjured by a spider's web, craftsmanship incapable of being divorced from the menace it served.

Yet where was this menace? Oskan could offer no explanation for that feeling, but as he looked upon the curving columns and arched doorways, the bas-relief sculptures and circular windows, he became more and more certain that whoever had built this place, they weren't elf, human, or dwarf. Someone – something – else had cut this city from the cliff. He thought back to stories so ancient that even the elves considered them legends. Tales of their first explorations of the world beyond Elvenholme... and of the enemies they'd found.

"What is this place?" Oskan asked Tothmenes.

"The meeting place of kings and gods," Tothmenes answered, bowing his head in reverence. Suddenly, his entire attitude changed. He spun around in the saddle and tightened his grip on the camel's reins.

Oskan was taken by surprise when his own animal suddenly shifted about wildly, bellowing in fear. For an instant, he had to focus on getting the camel back under control. Around him, he could hear cries of horror from the Ophidians. Looking up, he saw a strange and terrible sight.

A hideous swarm of creatures scrambled up from below the edge of the gorge. They were gray, hairless things, taller and broader than a human but with a lean and gangly aspect. Their hands ended in long claws and their heads were those of beasts with pointed ears and doglike muzzle. A charnel-house stink wafted off the monsters as they charged straight toward the Ophidians.

"There is no danger... for us," Tothmenes advised Oskan. The God-King laid a restraining hand on the Celestian's arm when he would have drawn his sword. "These are the guardians, and we are expected."

The soldiers of the retinue formed ranks to defend their monarch and his exalted guest. They presented a fence of spears and shields to the monsters, but the creatures were undaunted by the threat. Exhibiting a feral savagery Oskan had never witnessed before, the hyena-like beasts threw themselves on the bodyguards. Spears pierced gray flesh, but there was an infernal vitality to the monsters that made them defy even the most mortal wound. Even stabbed in the heart, the creatures retained enough life to tear out the throats of their killers and howl in triumph over their sprawled bodies.

The defense became a shambles in a matter of moments. Even with their ranks shattered and all hope lost, the soldiers refused to retreat and abandon their God-King. To a man, they were slaughtered by the beasts. Then the monsters turned to the servants who cowered near Tothmenes. Even after witnessing the destruction of the warriors, their loyalty was greater than their fear, and they refused to flee from the monarch's side.

"There is no danger for *us*," Tothmenes repeated, still holding fast to Oskan's arm. There was an awful power in his grip, a strength even the Celestian struggled to defy.

"Let me fight!" Oskan snarled back. "They'll be killed!"

Tothmenes turned his head and gave a weary look at his servants. "Theirs is a necessary sacrifice. They cannot be allowed to know of this place. The kaftars will see that they tell no one."

The hyena-headed beasts now fell upon the servants, tearing them to shreds. Fear finally overwhelmed a few and they tried to run away. The kaftars were after them in an instant, chasing them down with long, loping strides. When the last of the retinue was borne to the earth, the slavering monsters turned back to the fallen. Human or kaftar, it mattered not to the creatures, wherever they found a corpse, they began to feed, lapping the blood from torn veins before glutting themselves on the mangled flesh.

True to the God-King's insistence, the kaftars left Tothmenes and Oskan alone. The two might have been invisible for all the attention they paid to them.

"Monstrous!" Oskan spat as Tothmenes released his arm. Immediately he drew his sword, his ire roused by the treacherous slaughter of the Ophidians. He hesitated a moment, wondering where to direct his anger. On the kaftars who'd ambushed them or the God-King who'd led them into the ambush.

"Yes," Tothmenes agreed. "Do you think it is a simple thing for me to squander so many brave and loyal lives?" The regret in his voice was genuine. "I am a God-King and must think not of individuals, but the whole of Ophidia. I told you, this was necessary." He waved his arm to indicate the feasting kaftars. "It is a sorry truth that even the most loyal may possess an injudicious tongue. Ophidia has many enemies who would delight in learning the meeting place of the God-Kings. What friends don't know, enemies won't know."

"And what of me?" Oskan demanded. He wagged his sword at the ghoulish beasts. "Am I not a liability to your secret now?"

Tothmenes bowed his head. "You, Mighty Oskan, represent a new hope for Ophidia. Whatever comes of your meeting with the God-Kings, I do not believe you'd betray this confidence. The trust and faith that has been bestowed on you. An honor that has been extended to no one in the long history of this land."

Still smoldering with indignation over the massacre, Oskan's attitude was softened by Tothmenes's tone. The God-King was all but grovelling before him, all regal power and divine authority peeled away to expose an anxious and uncertain mortal. A mortal who, Oskan felt, truly did want what was best for his nation.

Oskan knew, in that moment, whatever might happen, he would keep the secret of this place and his meeting with Ophidia's God-Kings.

Chapter IX

-949, Time of Light

A long and eerie track led through the hidden valley. Oskan was surprised that none of the kaftars followed them down into the gorge, but the hyena-like monsters continued to pay them no notice, intent only on their morbid feast. The atmosphere within the depression was notably cooler than it had been above, though still sweltering by the standards of more verdant lands.

What struck Oskan most about the place wasn't the terrain or temperature, but rather that it was uncannily quiet. Even the wind seemed to shun the valley, no breeze sighed through the needle-leaf branches of the trees or the thorny stalks of shrub and bush. It came as no surprise to him when Tothmenes named the land the Valley of Silence.

Soon, the towering cliffs at the far side of the valley came into view again, with their brooding, megalithic structures. Their unsettling aspect became ever more pronounced as the two rode nearer. The camels grew disquiet with each plodding step until finally the ministrations of Celestian and God-King failed to stir them at all and the animals had to be abandoned.

Afoot, Oskan followed Tothmenes to the grim city cut into the cliff. Distinctly he could make out the intricate carvings that framed every archway and slithered about each sculpture. They were a writing of some sort, but with a repulsive, crawling quality to them. The sculptures weren't those of men, but of serpent-like figures playing at the activities of men. Spindly arms and legs projected from the bodies of the robed snakes. In some sculptures they held spears and halberds of strange design, in others they labored over alembics and pestles and other accouterments of the alchemist. There was, Oskan thought, a character to them that evoked in some way the style of both Ophidia and Ahmun. Here, with this strange snake-obsessed people, might lay the fountainhead of both civilizations.

But there was another disturbing thought, and Oskan recalled again the legends of the elves as related by Reiliur. Stories of the 'ancient enemy' the elves had fought in the dim mist of their prehistory. Serpents called the uraeus.

"The legends of the Ahmunites too speak of the uraeus," Tothmenes said after listening to Oskan speak of the elven myths. The God-King looked up at the cliff and pointed at the serpentine sculptures. "Of course those stories were brought into Ophidia when the reckless madness of the pharaohs became too much to endure. The elves speak of them as evil things, but to my people, they were seen as teachers and mentors, much like the Celestians. The legends say they taught the tribes who would one day build Ahmun to forge bronze and to cut stone. Magic, too, stemmed from their tutelage, raising the primitive Ahmunites from crude witchcraft to more refined arcane sciences."

"The elves speak of manipulators and deceivers who worked only to their own benefit," Oskan pointed out.

Tothmenes smiled. "Perhaps that is merely because the elves wanted more from the uraeus than the uraeus were prepared to give. Certainly the example of the dwarfs should display that not everything is as one-sided as the elves might like them to be." It was a point that Oskan had to concede, though not without reluctance. The repulsive feeling evoked by the ruins was impossible to deny.

"It is a moot argument," Tothmenes said, noticing Oskan's unease. "The uraeus vanished long ago, withering before the rise of Ahmun's pharaohs. Their cities were cast down and used as the foundations of newer and greater ones. Cities raised by humans. There are few reminders the uraeus existed at all. This lonely fastness is Sha-Seth, the last of their cities. The place to which their civilization retreated. The final redoubt as they faded from history." The God-King stirred from his reverie and motioned for Oskan to follow him into one of the shadowy archways.

"A strange place for the rulers of Ophidia to gather," Oskan observed as they climbed a spiral stair and passed beneath the forty-foot doorway.

"Sha-Seth has remained hidden for thousands of years," Tothmenes said. "Concealed from the eyes of spies and the magical divination. Could one ask for a better secret than one that has endured for so long?"

The two walked down a colossal hallway, their steps echoing through the vastness. Oskan saw now the first evidence that they weren't alone in the cliff city. Torches blazed from sconces bolted to the great pillars that supported the roof overhead. The light revealed their path through the maze of corridors, guiding them onward until they reached an immense chamber deep within the cyclopean complex.

The chamber was lit by great braziers from which orange flames crackled dozens of feet into the air. The burning wood gave off a sharp, almost overwhelming scent Oskan could liken only to cinnamon mixed with pitch. The fragrant smoke wafted to every corner of the room, saturating even its deepest recesses and blotting out all other smells.

Between the braziers, upon a circular dais, seven thrones were set. Each was of an identical height and all were carved in identical style, their tall backs patterned after the same crown Tothmenes wore. Each chair, however, was fashioned from a different material. One was gold, another silver, a third was shaped from dusky onyx, a fourth from lustrous lapis lazuli. It was to this bright blue throne that Tothmenes climbed and took his place.

The throne Tothmenes assumed was the fifth to bear an occupant. They'd been preceded by four others, and Oskan now gave these other God-Kings a wary scrutiny.

The onyx throne was occupied by a lean man wearing a green robe and a crown almost identical to that worn by Tothmenes. His skin had a bizarre appearance, so devoid of wrinkle or blemish that Oskan could compare it only to that of a newborn baby. The lean man was completely hairless, bald and clean-shaven, without even an eyebrow or eyelash showing on his wide, contemplative face. His eyes had a peculiar gleam to them and, though Oskan's attention was often drawn back to this God-King, never did he observe Khusru-Seti to blink.

Upon the golden throne sat the most physically imposing of the God-Kings, so tall that his crowned head stood about the carved backing of his chair. Standing, Oskan estimated that Rahmat would have been over seven feet tall. The monarch's build was equal to his height, with a broad chest and muscular limbs his black robes struggled to contain. His complexion was a dusky gray, reminding Oskan of the ashes left by a bonfire. The full beard that stabbed out from his chin was blue-black and curled into ringlets that fell across his breast. Rahmat had a stern, self-assured expression, the face of one accustomed to rule and secure in his authority. Here, too, Oskan found something disturbing about the eyes, for there was a brilliance to them, an impression of living flame blazing just behind the pupils. The Celestian wasn't such a stranger to the lands of Ophidia as to have failed to hear stories of the djinn, the capricious desert spirits, and he wondered if in Rahmat he wasn't in the presence of a member of that fearsome breed.

The silver throne was taken by a middle-aged man, his robes lavish with golden thread, his hands dripping with jeweled rings and his neck festooned with many wondrous gemstones. Makalani was the God-King who oversaw the economy of Ophidia, governor of its many merchant-guilds and trading houses. From his appearance, it was clear he took his own share of the nation's prosperity. His long, iron-gray hair framed a visage that had a smug arrogance in its character, an unspoken conviction that whatever obstacle arose, Makalani could pay it to go away.

Oskan was certain Tothmenes and Makalani were human, less certain that Rahmat and Khusru-Seti weren't something else wearing a guise of humanity. The last king sat upon a great seat of marble, and it was anything but human. At least, it was something that could no longer claim to be a *living* human. Amenenmhet-kau was a ghastly thing to gaze upon, a cadaverous horror wrapped in silken bindings covered in the hieroglyphs of Shobik's priests. The bindings clung tight to the body, holding fast the desiccated frame within while the sacred writings fended away the worst efforts of decay. A resurrected mummy, the God-King wore a white robe and a torc of lapis across its chest. The crown of rule rose above a face that pressed against the bindings that swaddled it, displaying each line of its shriveled countenance. The effect wasn't quite that of a leering skull, for there was still the semblance of nose and lips, but it was clear the thing beneath the wrappings had achieved a far different immortality than its fellow rulers. It was one of the undead, but unlike any Oskan had seen before. Amenenmhet-kau was no mindless puppet called up from its tomb, but a being with its own will and its own mastery. That, to Oskan's thinking, made the mummy's existence even more disturbing.

"God-Kings of Ophidia," Tothmenes announced as he sat upon the blue throne. "In answer to your request, I have brought before you the great Celestian Oskan. A dear and true friend of

Ophidia."

Oskan bowed at the introduction and listened patiently while Tothmenes named the other God-Kings and some of the titles associated with them. By degrees, he came to understand something of their spheres of influence, though it appeared their domains sometimes overlapped and there might be other responsibilities which went unmentioned. Tothmenes was charged with foreign relations and maintaining Ophidia's military, but at the same time it appeared Khusru-Seti commanded the constabulary that preserved order within Ophidia and (if Oskan intimated correctly) the spies who gathered information outside the nation's borders. Khusru-Seti also acted as High Priest of Shobik and was the ultimate authority of the god's worship within Ophidia. Makalani, in addition to overseeing the guilds, also maintained the treasury of both the kingdom and the Temple of Shobik. Rahmat held dominion over the interior of Ophidia, the many wild places throughout the kingdom, and also with the security of this wilderness. Perhaps it was connected to his role as Hierophant of all wizards and magic that Rahmat was also tasked with controlling the djinn who haunted the desert and minimizing their depredations. In all things, there was deference made to Amenenmhet-kau. Wherever matters of death and the dead were concerned, it was the mummy who governed. Funerary rites were not the province of Khusru-Seti, the undead legions that lay within tomb-garrisons across Ophidia weren't Tothmenes's to muster, the black art of necromancy was not Rahmat's to teach and control. All of these things were left to the God-King who understood the grave better than any of them.

Tothmenes was evasive when asked about the empty thrones. Whether they were unoccupied or if their occupants were simply absent, Oskan soon understood he would be meeting only the five God-Kings who sat above him on the dais.

"We have watched with the keenest interest the activities of the Celestians," Khusru-Seti stated. His hand moved with a sinuous ease as he gestured at Oskan. "It was the beneficence you extended to the people of Primovantor that inspired us to make overtures to Mescator for your aid against the Ahmunites."

"A shared enemy can be the foundation of friendship," Oskan replied. He'd found Tothmenes difficult to read, but the smooth, rigid features of Khusru-Seti were impossible to gauge.

A slab of stone would show more emotion.

"Yet now we must wonder how selfless the fellowship of the Celestians is," Khusru-Seti continued. "In every land your influence has extended, you've adopted a policy of sweeping away the faith of the primogenitors." He looked aside at his fellow God-Kings. "As you know, Ophidia maintains the worship of Shobik."

Oskan nodded. "I will not deny that has been a concern to us. In every land, we've found the priesthood of these old gods to be a grasping and tyrannical breed." He watched Khusru-Seti carefully to see if he took umbrage from such brusque talk. The monarch's face remained stoic, his unblinking eyes fixed upon Oskan.

"Ophidia is not like other lands," Makalani explained. "We split from the Ahmunites because of the excesses of the priests and pharaohs, the madness that was changing a fertile land into a realm of the walking dead. The homage we pay to Shobik is far different from that of our cursed cousins who have sacrificed their future in their pursuit of power."

Oskan paced before the dais, stopping when he was opposite the marble throne. "Yet doesn't Ophidia also employ the black art of necromancy? The most dangerous of all magic?"

Amenenmhet-kau regarded Oskan with its deathly gaze. "All magic is dangerous when used without restraint. Ahmun has doomed itself by drawing too deeply from the well. The people of Ophidia will not be so reckless." The mummy clenched one of its bandaged fists. "I will not allow it."

"You must understand, Oskan," Tothmenes interrupted. "Ophidia was founded to escape the mistakes of Ahmun. We are not such fools as to repeat the deeds that have damned our ancient homeland."

"We may revere the same god," Khusru-Seti said, "but the nature of that worship, the philosophy of our faith, is fundamentally different." The monarch's head oscillated from side to side as he elaborated on a subject it was strange to hear a High Priest admit. "The Ahmunites refuse to accept things as they are. They worship Shobik as he once was, not as he is now. The primogenitors are dead, only the echoes of their power remains."

That was a subject on which Oskan would have argued with the God-King. Twice now he'd seen manifestations of the wind-god Korgaan that indicated he was anything but diminished. Certainly not to the degree of the other primogenitors. Not an insensate remnant, but an active and purposeful force in Pannithor. Instead, Oskan chose to wait and hear out the kings of Ophidia.

"These were the lands where Shobik's influence was greatest," Rahmat spoke, his voice a brass rumble that seemed too deep to rise from even his mighty frame. "It was in these deserts that the God of Death held dominion and shaped the earth itself to suit his designs." The light in the dusky king's eyes blazed even brighter. "Shobik cut slivers from his own divine essence to become his servants and to help reshape these places, steering the rivers and raising the mountains. The djinn, these splinters of Shobik were called, and when their master's hold over them weakened, they slipped away into the desolation, jealous and fearful of their freedom." He stroked his curly beard and nodded. "The people of Ahmun long sought to bind the djinn once more, as Shobik had. The people of Ophidia, themselves seeking freedom, adopted a better understanding of the spirits of the desert and found a better way."

Khusru-Seti waved his lean hands, his fingers curling and entwining in complex patterns. "The power of Shobik endures, as the djinn amply show, but the god's presence, his will, has been extinguished." He turned and looked across the other God-Kings. "One day, perhaps, it will be restored, for what permanency is there about a god's death. For now, however, it is practical to call upon the memory of Shobik and to harness the divine energy that remains."

"We tell you this so you might understand that, even if Ophidia worships Shobik, we are not like Ahmun," Tothmenes said. "We do not resent the arrival of the Celestians. Ophidia does not oppose the knowledge and wisdom you have brought to Pannithor."

"You speak as one who believes the Celestians will have cause to doubt your friendship," Oskan stated. He could detect enough in the God-Kings' speech to discern the appeal that lay behind their discourse. "I am aware of the disagreements that have erupted between Ophidia and Elvenholme..."

Makalani rose from his silver throne and pointed down at Oskan. "There, indeed, is our worry! The elves make use of the great waterways constructed by Ophidia that they might send their ships to trade in the distant east. They haughtily make use of the Pass of Khoem without deigning to pay fair recompense to Ophidia for the expenses our kingdom has incurred."

"We are also aware of the friendship that exists between the Celestians and the elves," Khusru-Seti said, the least trace of a hiss clinging to the word 'elves'. "It is our fear that if no compromise can be reached, that the Celestians will unjustly take up the elven cause and move against Ophidia."

Tothmenes shook his head. "I well know the wisdom and benevolence of Oskan," he said. "Do not think for a moment that I doubt you. It is Mescator and the other Celestians about whom we are concerned. We fear they may be deceived by the elves and that our reverence for Shobik may prejudice them against us." He leaned forward, staring directly at Oskan. "All we ask is that a true and just arbitration be made. With your help, Oskan, Ophidia has avoided the tyranny of Ahmun. Now we ask you to defend us from the tyranny of Elvenholme."

Oskan gazed across the God-Kings, as strange an assemblage of monarchs as he'd ever seen. From his time in Ophidia, however, he knew one thing. The land's rulers genuinely sought to bring prosperity to their people. If they were in conflict with the elves, then it was more than simply the size of the royal treasury that disturbed them. He couldn't easily believe malevolence from the elves, but he knew they were a people who could let pride blind them to prudence.

"This is a decision that is beyond my authority to decide," Oskan told the God-Kings. "I must return to Primantor and relate what I've been told to Mescator and the other Celestians. The choice must be discussed and decided in council."

Tothmenes sank back in his throne. "And if Mescator should decide to side with the elves? If the Celestians rule to strike against Ophidia, must we number Oskan among our enemies?"

The possibility of defying Mescator had never occurred to Oskan before. Yet when he heard the appeal in Tothmenes's voice, an ember of doubt stirred within him. "I cannot say," Oskan replied. "Not until I have heard Mescator reach a decision and determine for myself whether there is justice in his choice."

***

-948, Time of Light

Karinna looked on with disgust as she watched the Ophidians creep across the battlefield. Never in all her long life had she imagined anything as savagely mindless as the incidence of war. Wholesale slaughter of thinking beings, people who should be able to find a way – any way – to resolve their disagreements in a less wasteful and vicious manner. It was supposed to be the mark of intelligence that creatures ceased to behave like less developed life, yet for two years she'd watched humans fight one another, butchering one another by the thousands. Nor just humans, for the soldiers of Primovantor fought beside the elves while those of Ophidia could boast dwarf mercenaries and reptilian fighters recruited from the mysterious salamanders.

So too, as the mortal races were divided were the Celestians. A great sadness welled up inside her when Karinna thought back to that day when Oskan returned to Primantor and pleaded Ophidia's case before Mescator and the others. So firmly did he believe an injustice was being done to Ophidia by the elves that even when the Celestians agreed to support King Yarinathar in the argument, he'd remained obstinate. For the first time she could remember, he'd defied Mescator. The young Celestian left Primantor and returned to Khe-Luxarn and the court of King Tothmenes. Emboldened by Oskan's siding with them, the Ophidians grew more belligerent in their demands until finally outright war erupted. Elven ships plying the Pass of Khoem were seized, their crews imprisoned and their cargoes confiscated. Thus had war returned to the peoples the Celestians had termed the 'noble races'.

Karinna knew how gravely Oskan's defection had wounded Mescator. The once proactive and uncompromising leader of the Celestians became hesitant and uncertain. He advised King Yarinathar and High Consul Timorian to be restrained in their responses to Ophidian aggression, desperate to find a way to mediate by diplomacy a war that was steadily escalating. As senseless as she found war, Karinna couldn't praise Mescator's strive to peace at any cost, for she knew it was founded upon his own inner turmoil than any true strategy. The devotion and trust that the Celestians had worked so long to build among the people of Elvenholme and Primovantor began to fracture. While Oskan marched openly with the warriors of Ophidia, the other Celestians sat idle and waited for Mescator to send them into the fight. Only Fulgria and Belkon, remaining among the holdfasts of Abercarr, managed some good by their position, keeping High King Thrayne from allying with Ophidia. Only those dwarfs whose hatred of elves outweighed their love of their homeland sided with King Tothmenes, forming themselves into merciless mercenary companies that marched under the serpent banners of Khe-Luxarn.

At last, Karinna had taken it on herself to see with her own eyes the devastation of war. Now she saw it in its most hideous shape. Leagues into lands that had belonged to Primovantor, at a place known as Five Hills, the defenders of the republic met the invading legions. Thousands lay dead, and the beaten Primovantorian army limped away from the triumphant Ophidians. Instead of pursuing the routed enemy, however, the Ophidians paused. Like swooping vultures, black-robed magi prowled among the dead. Karinna sickened when she saw what they were doing.

She'd heard of the undead before. During the Battle of Hepshet, Karinna knew that both Ophidia, then an ally of the Celestians, and Ahmun had sent the unnatural horrors into the fight. Never, however, had she seen these hideous creatures for herself or observed the profane magic that brought them back from the netherworld. The Ophidian necromancers indicated to their assistants the corpses they desired. It mattered nothing to them if the body belonged to a soldier of Primovantor or a warrior who'd fought for Ophidia. Human, elf, dwarf, or salamander, all the necromancers cared about was how intact the remains might be. Those missing a limb or without a head, crushed or mangled too extensively in the fighting, were rejected. The others, heedless of rank or caste, were laid out in long lines. There the necromancers called on their black art.

Karinna winced as elven captives were brought forward. At the end of each line, an elf had their throat slashed with a bronze knife. A necromancer dabbed a bone stylus into the wound and on the forehead of each corpse drew a hieroglyph of obscene power. When the last drop of blood was drawn out of a captive, the body was added to the line, and another prisoner was slaughtered to fuel the perverse ritual. At last, when each body had been attended, the necromancers performed their ritual. Karinna could see the fell energies that poured into the corpses. It was the very antithesis of life, oppressive rather than nurturing, stagnant instead of fecund. Not a vital force, but only a hollow mockery of it.

Yet it was enough. The corpses stirred. Clumsily they regained their feet and stood awaiting the commands of those who'd called them back from death. Now it was Ophidian officers who moved among the undead, handing them spears and swords looted from the battlefield. Rank upon rank of animated carrion now bolstered the legions of Tothmenes. Some that Karinna gazed on were so mutilated by old wounds that she wondered how often they'd been revitalized by the necromancers. How many times they'd been sent to fight for Ophidia.

Here was the awesome strength of King Tothmenes. While the armies of Primovantor and Elvenholme diminished after every fight, those of Ophidia only grew stronger. Each enemy they killed was more than one enemy less, but another warrior to fight on their own side. Mescator needed to be warned of this, for Karinna was certain that he failed to appreciate the monstrous threat Ophidia's necromancy posed. By means of this dark magic, they could eventually enslave all of Pannithor.

"The Ophidians have no desire to rule anyone." Oskan's voice echoed through Karinna's mind. She looked away from the battlefield to where the army of Ophidia was camped. Above the largest of the tents, there fluttered a standard she knew well enough, the dragon and stallion on a purple field, the symbol Oskan had adopted for his own. He sensed the nearness of her presence even across this distance and was sending his thoughts to her.

"King Tothmenes seeks only what is just for his people," Oskan explained. "He doesn't want this war. It is the elves who have forced this conflict. Ophidia desires only peace."

Karinna sent her words back to Oskan, even as she watched the necromancers separating their animated corpses into new regiments. "Ophidia's greed will not be sated. They are like a parasite vine that continues to feed off the tree it has bound itself to until the tree withers and dies."

"You're wrong," Oskan argued. "They cast off the chains of Ahmun's pharaohs and now seek only..."

"Whatever they've told you, Oskan, it is by their deeds you must judge them," Karinna said. "If you can't do that, then we've nothing left to discuss." Whatever response Oskan might have made, she closed her mind to it. She couldn't afford to have him glimpse her intentions and reveal them to the Ophidians.

The necromancers were finished recovering bodies from the battlefield and raising them into new undead. This force they now set after the routed Primovantorians. Though the republican army had many hours lead on their pursuers, they were mortal and with all the frailties that came with it. They were slowed by their wounded, tired from the battle, fatigued by the panic that set upon them with their defeat. The undead suffered none of these things. Slower than the living, their endurance was inexhaustible. They would march until the magic that kept decay from their husks wore away or those who controlled them told them to stop. There was no question of outrunning the undead, it was only a matter of when they would catch their prey.

Unless an insurmountable obstacle were set in their path. Karinna reached into the bag she carried. From it, she removed fistfuls of acorns and threw them down from the hill. Sped along by her magic, they scattered across the land and burrowed deep into the earth. As the seeds planted themselves, she poured her energies into them, infusing them with supernormal vitality. Against the deathless hosts of Ophidia, she would pit the force of life itself.

Up from the ground, mighty oaks rapidly grew. Beneath the very feet of the animated corpses, a forest sprang into being. Dozens of the undead were torn apart as their bodies were caught in the expanding branches that erupted from below. The regiments broke apart, shattered by the fecundity of the forest. Hundreds of zombies were crushed as the trees expanded. Hundreds more were trapped under the boughs of the newborn forest, unable to find a path to the other side.

Karinna sagged against the earth, wearied by the power she'd invoked. She was pleased, however, for with the forest blocking their path and their undead cohort annihilated, there was no chance for the Ophidians to chase after the Primovantorians.

Then she saw Oskan emerge from his tent. He was arrayed in golden armor patterned after the style of Ophidia, and in his fist he clenched a copper khopesh. With her mind closed to him, Karinna could only guess at the commands he shouted to the mortals around him, but soon there was a stir amid the camp. The living soldiers of Ophidia were quickly roused into action. Foremost among them were the reptilian salamanders from across the sea. These advanced upon the still-expanded forest, their red scales shining with an inner fire. None, however, shone as brilliantly as the one that marched at their head. Arrayed in obsidian armor, the horned salamander waved his arms in cabalistic gestures. Karinna could only watch helplessly as the reptilian wizard conjured a mighty spell.

Again the earth trembled as mighty forces surged up from below. This time, however, it wasn't the green vitality of life that rose up from the ground, but the molten roar of destruction. The salamander mystic had drawn up the lava that bubbled far beneath the land. Now it exploded over the forest in massive columns of liquid fire. Wherever drops from the blazing pillars were thrown, the trees began to burn. In a matter of minutes, the green forest became an inferno.

The Ophidians cheered as the trees burned, indifferent to the destruction of the undead caught within. Oskan's ploy had worked. The magic of the salamanders had overwhelmed Karinna's evocation. When the ground cooled again, the path would be clear for them to pursue the Primovantorians. Already she could see Ophidian cavalry readying themselves for the hunt. What mercy, she wondered, would the knights of King Tothmenes show without Oskan to restrain them.

"Judge them by their deeds," Karinna whispered. But now it was Oskan's mind that was shut to her thoughts.

***

-942, Time of Light

The war with Ophidia was now in its eighth year. Mescator found it difficult to appreciate the toll exacted against the embattled nations. Ophidian armies had ranged into both Primovantor and Elvenholme, wrecking great damage on the regions they invaded. Republican and elven forces had retaliated, staging punitive strikes deep into Ophidia, but for six years there had only been stalemate. Neither side could deal a decisive blow against the other. The Ophidians had twice laid siege to the walls of Esk, but so too had Khe-Luxarn come near to capture.

Attempts to broker a lasting peace between the combatants by the Celestians had come to nothing. Any concession made to Ophidia only emboldened their ambitions further. Among the most fiercely contested issues was the Pass of Khoem. King Tothmenes was no longer content simply for reimbursement for the expenses Ophidia claimed to have incurred for their part of the construction. Now he wanted absolute control of the waterway and to dictate the terms by which other nations would be able to make use of it. The engineering marvel, intended as a boon to all the noble races, had instead become a thing of jealousy and greed.

Thus far, the dwarfs of Abercarr had maintained their neutrality for the most part, but doing so meant the absence of Fulgria and Belkon from Mescator's side. Were the two Celestians to leave Dolgarth, their influence over High King Thrayne might lessen and bring the dwarfs into the war on the side of Ophidia. By the same token, Kyron had been unable to induce the dragons into action against Ophidia, though he had persuaded Draumdraak to take him into the distant regions the salamanders inhabited. As a result of his contact with the reptiles, they'd withdrawn their forces from the war. So while Kyron hadn't convinced them to switch sides, at least he had persuaded them to stop fighting Ophidia's battles.

Even without the salamanders, however, Ophidia's armies remained vast. Tothmenes had expanded the practice of necromancy beyond anything dared by Shobik's death-priests in Ahmun. No longer a mere component of Ophidia's forces, now entire armies of the undead strove against Elvenholme and Primovantor. The necromancers had begun to experiment with refinements to their black art, crafting ever more horrible abominations from corpses. Magi no longer clung to the pretense that they merely strove to protect their lands from the djinn, but actively summoned the fiery desert demons to the battlefield.

Somehow, the armies of Primovantor prevailed, and the battlements of Khe-Luxarn were once more within sight. As he stared at the sand-colored walls, Mescator could sense Oskan somewhere behind them. His rebellious pupil remained steadfast in his support of Ophidia, and several times he'd crossed paths with other Celestians during the war. Always Oskan had shown restraint, reluctant to hurt his friends. Continuously he sent emissaries to Mescator, all but begging him to see how unjust the war was and how it was Ophidia's cause that was right. Karinna was right about Oskan, Mescator reflected. He'd let himself be seduced by the honeyed words of Tothmenes and blinded himself to the atrocities perpetrated by the God-King's legions.

"There will be an end to it today," Mescator vowed. The great warhorse he sat upon was the finest of its kind to ever walk Pannithor, specially bred from stock Kyron had selected from the best stables and further augmented by the Celestian's power. The steeds of the templars around him were from a similar lineage, the strongest destriers in Primovantor. They needed to be, for the barding that encased them was of the toughest steel, and the armor of their riders was still more formidable. The templars belonged to Mescator's temple and had been christened justicars. In times of peace, they roved the republic, mediating disputes and dispensing justice to those who appealed their cases before Mescator's priests. Now, however, they were united in a fearsome warrior brotherhood, riding under the banner of the god they served.

"Justice for all the war dead," Grandmaster Savar declared. His face bore the scars of past conflict, one eye white from where an Ophidian sword had cut him. In his fervor, Savar had denied himself any healing magic until the war was over. He didn't want Mescator to expend the least mote of power on him while there were more important matters that demanded his god's attention.

"Justice will be done," Mescator said, "but beware lest you confuse justice and vengeance." He turned and gazed across the enormous host that Primovantor and Elvenholme had mustered for the final push against Ophidia. Tens of thousands of soldiers. Scores of mages and wizards. Hundreds of siege engines that even now were brought lumbering into position to batter the ancient walls. A dozen Celestians were here as well. Even Valandor had departed the Tower of Heaven to lend his powers against Ophidia to finally bring an end to the war.

Against this force, Ophidia had their undead slaves, their djinn, their black magic, their paid mercenaries. And Oskan.

Mescator could sense his protege inside the walls, but his mind was closed to him. The gulf that had grown between them was a wound that sapped his strength even before battle was joined. If this was, indeed, the final fight, what extremes would Oskan go to in order to win victory for Ophidia?

Trumpets blared from the battlements of Khe-Luxarn. The great tower at the center of the city released a black vulture into the sky. It was a gesture Ophidia had brought with them from Ahmun. A signal that the enemy should expect no mercy.

Signals flashed among the armies of Primovantor and Elvenholme. The siege engines would begin the assault and seek to batter the city into submission. If the Ophidians sallied forth, then the knights and templars would charge forward to intercept their advance. If the magi and necromancers tried to work their dark arts, then Valandor and the wizards with him would employ counter spells to disrupt their magic.

Everything was prepared, but none among them was ready for the awful surprise Tothmenes had waiting for them. Before the catapults were in position, a tremendous howl rose from the middle of Khe-Luxarn. Plumes of dust erupted into the sky, and with them arose a shape that sent dread into the hearts of even the justicars. It was a dragon, a beast so immense that it made Draumdraak look like a lowly lizard, but likewise a creature unlike anything seen in the skies of Pannithor before. No scales covered its enormous frame, for it was a thing of bleached bones and tattered sinews. It sported three sets of mighty wings and six pairs of clawed legs. A cluster of sharp tails slashed the air behind it as it rose, and from its torso there jutted three fanged skulls on fleshless necks.

Mescator understood now the treacherous deceit Tothmenes had employed. The hard-won victories of the past campaign had been only a ruse to draw them here, deep into the lands of Ophidia. The God-Kings' agents must have spent years stealing bones from the dragons' graveyard and bearing them back to Khe-Luxarn, where the necromancers bound them together into this undead leviathan. A weapon designed to annihilate the armies of Ophidia's enemies and the Celestians who supported them.

Mescator felt bitterness well up inside him as he watched the skeletal dragon soar away from the city and toward the army.

What part had Oskan played in unleashing this horror against them? Was this in truth how far he was willing to go? To see the other Celestians destroyed? To kill Mescator himself?

Bolts of arcane energy rose from Valandor and the wizards, but their concentrated powers only blackened a few bones, for the dragon's skeleton was carved with protective wards across the whole of its mighty frame. Flights of arrows rose only to glance uselessly from the fleshless body, clattering down around Khe-Luxarn in a shower of broken shafts. The dragon turned toward the siege engines. A gibbous light began to gather in the hollows of each skull. The bony jaws dropped open, and from each head, a blast of spectral power engulfed the catapults. Wood corroded on the instant while metal flaked away into rust. The crewmen too slow in running were stripped bare, reduced to mere piles of dust.

The dragon shifted and came directly toward Mescator and the justicars. "We have to draw it away from the rest of the army!" Mescator shouted to the templars. Such was the bravery in their hearts that not a single rider balked at the command, but they followed Mescator as he led them galloping toward the city walls. He hoped the necromancers commanding the undead dragon would hesitate to have it exude its terrible breath so near their own people, perhaps even bringing it to land and come to grips with them where at least the justicars might have a chance at retaliating.

Such restraint was absent from the villains who controlled the beast. Mescator was sickened to see Ophidian soldiers, living men defending their capital, annihilated by the dragon's spectral flame. The necromancers cared nothing for their countrymen, only for the destruction of their enemy and the fulfillment of Tothmenes's commands.

Another blast from the dragon's maws and dozens of the justicars were obliterated. Mescator was only inches from the extent of the ghostly flames. Grandmaster Savar wasn't so fortunate, his whole being consumed in an instant. Looking away from the brave templar's destruction, Mescator saw the dragon readying itself for another exhalation.

Mescator jerked back on his steed's reins and spurred the destrier back at the dragon. He extended his sword and swung his arm in a wide arc. On the third rotation, he let the blade fly straight for the hovering dragon. The shining sword slammed unerringly in one of the eye sockets. The undead reptile reeled back, spewing its ghostly flames upward. The earth trembled as the stricken beast slammed to the ground, dust enveloping it as the sands of Ophidia exploded into the sky.

"Back to our lines," Mescator ordered the justicars who turned to rejoin him. He spurred toward a young knight and plucked the sword from the man's grasp. "I seem to have lost my blade," he told the warrior before galloping off into the cloud of dust.

Grit clawed at Mescator's eyes as he charged into the cloud. He deafened his mind to the entreaties of the other Celestians, urging him to come away. The Ophidian monster was vulnerable for the moment. He had no idea how soon the dragon might recover from its fall.

Through the dust, the dark, skeletal shape of the dragon hove into view. Mescator urged his warhorse to greater effort and hurtled toward the undead horror. The beast moved awkwardly as it clawed itself free from the crater its own mass had gouged into the ground. As he drew nearer, he could see the jagged cracks that snaked across many of its bones. The impact had done more than merely rattle the skeletal titan.

"You kill no more valiant mortals," Mescator snarled as he rushed the dragon. The blade he'd borrowed slammed into one of the legs, ringing as it sheered away a section of bone and expanded the fracture already in the limb. The dragon whipped about, striking at him with its claw. Expertly, Mescator wheeled his horse away from the reptile's slash. The blow instead struck the unyielding ground. The connection sent the force vibrating back into the cracked limb. The already present fissures expanded and the leg shattered.

The dragon slammed down onto its side. Mescator turned his steed back around and whipped his borrowed sword at one of the reptile's jaws. Teeth crumbled under the Celestian's strike, and he left the blade buried in the corner of the dragon's mouth. Standing in the saddle, he reached up and tore his own sword from the eye socket in which it was embedded, raking it downward and opening the fleshless cheek.

Sand billowed upward as the dragon struck at Mescator with its cluster of tails. Like javelins hurled from ballistae, the spiked tails stabbed the earth, narrowly missing their galloping foe. Mescator retaliated, twisting about and slashing the tips from two of the skeletal appendages as they drew back for another strike.

A dry, rasping shriek rose from the monster. The dragon lurched upward on its remaining legs. The enormous wings fanned out. Mescator struggled to keep in the saddle as he was buffeted by a cyclonic wind. Sand swirled around him in a blinding tempest.

When he could see again, Mescator found that the cloud of dust had been dispersed by the dragon's wings. The gigantic reptile had climbed into the sky once more. The necromancers controlling it had learned their lesson, for their monster ascended to a height beyond the reach of even Mescator's arm. The dragon's skulls stared down at the Celestian, spectral fire gathering in each of its maws. There was no doubt who would be the target of the beast's concentrated ire.

The attack never came. With shocking abruptness, the dragon's assault ended. The flame gathering in its skulls evaporated. A moment later, and the huge beast fell out of the sky. It crashed to earth in an explosion of bony shards that scattered it across the plain. Mescator and the surviving justicars turned away from the city and rode back to their army. All of them were amazed to still be alive.

For almost an hour, an eerie silence held over the scene. The armies of Elvenholme and Primovantor were wary of another trick, while the forces of Ophidia appeared gripped by shock.

Then the great gates of Khe-Luxarn swung wide, and a lone figure emerged. Mescator rode out to meet him, for the emissary was no less than Oskan. His protege was contrite when his mentor drew near.

"I have come to offer you the crown of Ophidia," Oskan said, dropping to one knee and holding up to Mescator the severed halves of Tothmenes's jeweled crown. "And also to make whatever amends you deem fitting for my foolishness."

Mescator dropped down from his steed and pulled Oskan back to his feet. Try as he might, he couldn't hide the joy that swept through him. "The battle was far from decided," he told Oskan. "Why does Tothmenes surrender now?"

Oskan waved his hand and indicated the shattered remains of the dragon. "He begs terms, whatever terms Ophidia can gain and yet remain free. The beast carried upon it all his ambitions. With it gone, he has nothing that can withstand the Celestians... or Kyron's dragons," he added with a smile.

"Kyron has been unable to convince the dragons to fight with us," Mescator reminded Oskan.

"When they discover that Ophidia has plundered their graveyard, they'll need little convincing," Oskan said. "Fear of their retaliation will keep them worried for a long time."

Mescator nodded. He felt Oskan's mind open back to him and read in his thoughts the intentions that had been hidden from him for so long. "I really thought you'd turned against me."

"I regret whatever pain I caused you," Oskan confessed. "For a time, I was deceived by Tothmenes's words. It was when I met Karinna at the Battle of Five Hills that I began to see the truth. She advised I stop listening and start watching. So I did. Then I discovered Tothmenes's true intentions. He feared we would one day do to Ophidia what we did to Ahmun, so when war broke out it was his plan to destroy the Celestians." An embarrassed smile flashed across Oskan's face. "At least those he didn't feel he could control."

"But you outsmarted him and learned his plans," Mescator said, pride in his voice.

Oskan nodded. "It was necessary to wait until the trap was sprung. I had to pose as utterly deceived until then. To break his power, I had to wait until he revealed his hand. Until the moment he set the undead dragon against you, I didn't know the secret of its control." He stared down at the broken crown. "When I learned the secret, I acted."

"You killed Tothmenes?" Mescator asked.

"No," Oskan shook his head. "Someone must lead Ophidia going forward. Another king might believe he can do better than Tothmenes and try again. Tothmenes won't have such delusions. He'll be content just to save his neck and his throne."

Mescator was impressed with his pupil's reasoning. He clapped his hand on Oskan's shoulder. "Come along," he said, pointing back at his army. "There's a lot of people back there who will be eager to hear that the war is over and that Oskan has returned to us."

Chapter X

-902, Time of Light

The Tower of Heaven resonated with the mighty magics evoked by the Circle of Heaven. The conjunction of constellations had come again, and once more, twenty Celestians were making the passage from their own distant world to the lands of Pannithor. All that could be done to enhance and improve the process had been done. The materials of the gateways had been rendered to the utmost purity by Valandor's spells. Calisor had tirelessly instructed the elven mages in every facet of concentration demanded of them during the ritual. The whole of the process had been exactingly tested by the wizards who employed the gates to cross over into other worlds.

Yet still there was a tension in Reiliur, an excess of worry that coursed through every corner of his being. So much depended upon this night. This was much more than just another group of Celestians – if thinking in such manner weren't profane in itself. This time, among those making the journey, was the mighty Eoswain, the brilliant arch-sorceress without whose wisdom none of her people would ever have reached Pannithor.

Reiliur was so anxious that he feared his mind would descend into distraction. There was a terrible irony that the rest of the Circle of Heaven had been drilled and trained until they were almost a machine, yet it was his concentration that must be doubted. To be sure, Calisor could fulfill his role; his apprentice was just as capable as himself in that regard, but there was concern that his absence from the ritual could sow doubt among the other mages and thereby create dozens of potential flaws in the mystic convergence.

No, Reiliur would have to take his place before the Scrying Star. It was expected of him, not only by the Circle of Heaven, but by Eoswain herself. She desired his spirit to be the one that guided her across the gulf just as they had communed so often before. To allow another to take his place, she said, would disrupt the harmony of things. The cosmic circle wouldn't close but instead be left forever unfinished. Whatever misgivings Reiliur had, Eoswain had none. She placed all her trust and confidence in him.

Indeed, she was gambling her immortal spirit on his capability.

He cast his gaze upward, watching through the opaque dome as the stars of the dragon crossed those of the sword. The time was here. There could be no delay. Whatever else happened, Reiliur was committed now. Only by focusing his total energy on the transference could disaster be averted.

Many elves from not only Ileureleith but Therennia Adar as well were observing the ritual, representatives of royalty and the great wizards. Witnesses from the Grand Republic of Primovantor were here too, ready to carry word back to the High Consul of their land. Most of the Celestians in Pannithor were here too. No war kept Mescator away this time. Together with his protege Oskan, the leader of the Celestians stood with the others and watched as the Circle of Heaven performed the ritual. Only Fulgria and Belkon, engaged in their stewardship of the dwarfs, were absent; though they had sent a delegation of the gruff bearded people to report back to them in Abercarr.

Of the Celestians, only Valandor assisted in the ritual as he had a century before. He remained the only one among them who could so completely adapt his thoughts to those of an elvish mind as to remain in harmony with the Circle of Heaven. It was hoped that when Eoswain arrived that her greater knowledge would devise a way to adapt the ritual so other Celestians could contribute their energies. Then even more Celestians could be brought across during the next conjunction. This great ambition was the goal that had driven Reiliur for a hundred years. A way for him to exceed his already magnificent contribution to Pannithor.

"I am here. All is ready." Reiliur sent his thoughts speeding through the Scrying Star. This time, the Celestian who received his message wasn't Eoswain, but her surrogate, Carnesus. The elf knew little of him beyond his name, but he was certain Eoswain wouldn't have entrusted such a role to him unless he was a mighty wizard in his own right. She'd mentioned before that Carnesus was to her as Calisor was to him. A student wise enough to replace the teacher.

"They reach across the void," Carnesus replied. There was a nigh emotionless quality to his mental relay. Reiliur wondered if that was simply a facet of the Celestian's character, or if he'd sensed the elf's anxiety and was trying not to contribute any stimulus to further upset him. The keening that he sent through the void was different from that conjured by Eoswain, cold and purposeful where hers had been hopeful and enticing. Reiliur suspected it was the strength that mattered more than the character of the resonance. As long as it served to guide the travelers, then it accomplished its task.

Fog billowed about the gates. Reiliur watched in rapt fascination as figures began to emerge from the portals. As they stepped into the great laboratory, Mescator and his company hailed the arrivals. "Welcome, Shakara!" Liliana exclaimed as a tall woman with snowy skin and silver hair walked out from the mists. Her face was severe in its character and her eyes were like chips of ice, but there was warmth in her smile when she saw the other Celestians.

Oskan dashed forward to embrace a rakish man with close-cropped hair and florid features. "Hermanas, you truth-twister! What stories did you spin Eoswain to let you make the crossing?"

Hermanas grinned and drew back from Oskan. An impish smile curled the corners of his mouth. "We thought it best if someone helped Mescator in keeping an eye on you." The jest didn't appeal to the younger Celestian, but before his mood could sour, Hermanas made a self-deprecating remark that was more to Oskan's liking. "I might've stayed behind if I knew I'd be the shortest one here though. You've grown."

"I've matured," Oskan corrected him. He glanced aside at Mescator. "See, he doesn't think I need anyone looking out for me. Much has changed, Hermanas. Things that weren't so easy to report to Eoswain."

Mention of Eoswain diverted Reiliur's attention away from the other Celestians. He could see that Mescator was showing only the most cursory notice of the new arrivals. He was watching with great interest the gates that had yet to send forth their voyagers. Like Reiliur, he was anxious for Eoswain's safe arrival.

Reiliur looked to the oval dome, seeing there the stars as they continued to slowly drift out of sequence. He thought of the disaster that had nearly happened with Oskan and the doom-ridden rite Valandor had performed to save him.

There was no need for such measures this time. Reiliur almost shouted for joy when he saw a shape appear in the last gateway. The indistinct figure stepped forward, sweeping into the laboratory with the grandeur of royalty appearing at a ball. The billowing robe was of a lustrous blue that gleamed like sapphires, and into its folds were woven intricate patterns of silvery thread. A golden belt circled the waist, adorned with enormous gemstones that he could liken only to diamonds that had imprisoned moonlight within their facets. Similar gems graced the rings that encircled the slender hands which emerged from the robe's tapered sleeves, and about the creamy throat there clung a necklace seemingly spun from the same shimmering substance.

Reiliur's breath caught when he looked upon Eoswain's face. He knew the Celestians adapted their appearance to suit the mortals they met with, and so it was no surprise to find that she'd taken on an elvish aspect. But never had he seen such grace in one of his own people. There was charm and beauty, but so too there was strength and confidence. Above all, there was wisdom, an intellect that seemed to leap from her jade-colored eyes. Long tresses of rich black fell down about her shoulders, and within the dark cascade were hairpins adorned with stones that echoed the color of her eyes.

The elf wizard was without words, struck dumb by the mere presence of Eoswain. Though she looked toward him, Reiliur hesitated to step down from his place beside the Scrying Star. The moment was lost, and Mescator stepped into the gap left by his hesitance, becoming the first to welcome her to Pannithor.

Reiliur looked up at the ceiling, angered at himself for his unfounded anxiety and fear. As his eyes looked up at the dome, he froze in horror. He could see the laboratory, as though the ceiling were reflecting the scene below. But there was a terrible difference. The woman being greeted by Mescator wasn't Eoswain, but some diabolical witch! Her robes were black, laced with threads that smoldered like embers. The gems she wore were of a leprous character, shedding a gibbous light. Instead of creamy, her skin had a coppery, burnt appearance. The hair was dull and flaxen, set with combs fashioned from finger bones.

It was in the face that the horror was made complete, for the features were Eoswain's but grotesquely distorted. There was beauty, but it was a cruel and mocking beauty. No hint of charm but instead an imperious disdain. Strength of the most ruthless degree. Confidence blotted out by arrogance. Still more terrible was the intelligence that gleamed in the blood-hued eyes. Where Eoswain's had a nurturing character, this dark reflection showed only withering condescension.

Forcing his eyes away from the image on the dome, Reiliur saw no echo of the nightmare when he looked across the laboratory. He knew the strange materials Belkon had used to make the dome were reactive to psychic emanations, constructing things visible only to the individual. But what could possibly have provoked him to evoke such a vision?

Reiliur nerved himself to look back at the ceiling. On the dome, Eoswain remained a fiendish witch, but now he saw that another figure was changed. The wizard who stood beside the Scrying Star. He was a ragged, horrible thing, dressed in filthy rags, his hair thrown about in matted tangles. The starved frame was little more than skin and bones. Yet there was a ghastly familiarity about those wizened features despite the crazed eyes that stared back at him.

When Reiliur realized why that face was so familiar, when he understood it was his own distorted visage, a scream echoed through the chamber. He was dimly aware of people rushing toward him, but before they could reach him he'd collapsed to the floor, his mind retreating into the security of unconsciousness.

***

"How is he?" Eoswain asked as Valandor entered the room. After Reiliur's collapse, the Tower of Heaven was thrown into chaos. The elves were panicked over the distress of the ranking wizard, more so because they didn't know what had caused the fit. To the Celestians, it was also a mystery. Everything had been done to minimize the dangers of the ritual. Eoswain herself had made sure of that. Carnesus had been trained to the smallest detail, so she had no fear there'd been an error on his part. Reiliur had performed as he'd done twice before. She'd sensed no trouble there, yet something had struck him down.

"Calisor is staying with him," Valandor said. He turned and nodded to Mescator. "Shakara is tending his infirmity. He's had some kind of shock, but not something directly related to the transference. Of that I'm sure. Shakara is confident he'll recover in a few days."

In the wake of Reiliur's affliction, after the master wizard had been taken to his rooms and rendered such aid as the elves and Celestians could offer, Mescator had summoned a select group of them down to the Shining Sanctum to discuss what had happened. His concern was that there was a flaw in the ritual, a repetition of what had happened during Oskan's crossing. While Eoswain had convinced him such wasn't the case, she was relieved to hear Valandor reaffirm her case. For a moment, it had seemed Mescator would forbid any future rituals.

"We all hope for his swift recovery," Mescator said. He scratched his beard as he paced the room. At last he turned to Eoswain. "Do you think the strain was too much for him? Reiliur is, after all, a mortal. Perhaps the toll of focusing the Scrying Star has become too much for him. The elves have much greater vitality than humans and dwarfs, but they still suffer gradations of decay."

Eoswain shook her head. "I cannot speak with certainty until I've been able to examine Reiliur more completely and compare his condition to that of other elves of his generation. I don't believe the flaw lies with his own endurance and capabilities."

"If Reiliur can no longer perform his duties, then you could take his place," Oskan suggested.

"Calisor would be a more diplomatic choice," Valandor declared. "The elves must be left in a commanding position, otherwise they'll feel they've lost their agency. I'd not want to put such a strain on our friendship with them."

Liliana rose and took Oskan's position. "Simply replacing Reiliur with Calisor would only be ignoring the problem if the flaw lies with the limitations of mortal vitality."

"Had my instructions been followed, other options would be available to us." Karinna sat in a chair carved from alabaster and padded with silken cushions. "Instead, we must start from the beginning." In her hands she cradled a golden orb, a second fruit from the Sahlirian Tree brought across by Eoswain.

Kyron bowed his head in apology. "I accept the blame, my lady. I betrayed the trust you placed in me."

"Your initiative opened new avenues to us," Mescator told Kyron. "Through your restoration of Draumdraak and your communication with him, we've been able to access a facet of Pannithor we might otherwise have remained ignorant of." He laid his hand on the downcast Celestian's shoulder. "The peoples of this world have already benefited by what you've done. You've provided them a new understanding of dragons and how they can coexist with them."

"At least those of Draumdraak's line," Kyron muttered. "There are many breeds of dragon that remain unknown to us and have no reason to treat the mortal races any differently than they have before."

"All in time," Eoswain assured Kyron. "Nothing of importance is built in a single day." She looked over at Karinna. "Though Kyron's decision to give the dragon the Sahlirian fruit has delayed the planting of your grove, you have gained some benefit. He *has* explored many places where the trees won't grow. That must, by consequence, make it easier to find suitable land."

Karinna's fingers continued to stroke the golden fruit. "I will look beyond the mountains where Kyron was led to distraction."

"There's only unexplored wilderness there," Liliana objected. "Even the elves have seldom wandered those lands."

"What I require is a place where no mortals will disturb my crop," Karinna said. "I must find a place where I can be alone to plant the seeds and tend the trees."

Eoswain appreciated the necessity of Karinna's work. The energies of the Sahlirian fruit were too intense to bring more than a single one through during the transference. If Pannithor's mortal races were going to benefit from the fruit, then it was essential to find a place here where the trees would grow. Still, she knew how long that process might be, how many decades would pass before there were enough to spread to the many peoples who would be desperate for the boon of immortality, and her thoughts turned back to Reiliur.

"When you find what you need and the first trees grow, we must make sure the fruit is as potent here as those from our own world," Eoswain said. She turned from Karinna and regarded the other Celestians in the Sanctum. "If he is agreeable, then I propose that one fruit from the first crop be brought here to the

Tower of Heaven, and that Reiliur Ythriil should be the first elf to taste of its juices."

The suggestion brought unanimous approval from the other Celestians. "No mortal has been a greater benefactor to us," Oskan agreed, then bowed in apology to Kyron. "Not to ignore the great help Draumdraak offered us at the Battle of Hepshet."

Mention of the conflict changed Mescator's expression. Eoswain could see his attitude darken as troubled thoughts rose up inside him. He turned to Karinna. "There may be danger where you're going. You should take an escort. Oskan and Liliana at least, perhaps Hermanas and some of the others who've newly arrived."

Karinna shook her head. "What I need to do, I need to do alone."

Kyron crouched down beside her chair, staring up into her piercing eyes. "What Mescator fears is also my doing. There was a chance to imprison the god Korgaan during the battle, but because I acted in haste, that opportunity was squandered."

"Korgaan's avatar was destroyed," Liliana objected. "Draumdraak purged his evil in flame. By acting when you did, you saved many lives from Shobik's death-priests. Maybe even my own."

"It would be dangerous to assume so," Eoswain cautioned Liliana. "We know that the old gods of Pannithor have power, even if it is faded. I've heard enough about the magic employed by the servants of Bhanek and Shobik to appreciate that there's a force there different from our own. This Korgaan isn't a faded entity like the others, but a god that is active and demonstrates his power directly to his own purposes, not the whims of priests and sorcerers. We cannot say with certainty what it would take to destroy a being like this." Her voice grew grave as she added a disturbing thought. "If such a being *can* be destroyed."

Mescator nodded. "The tribes that worship Korgaan are most numerous in the north, beyond the Dragonstooth Mountains," he told Karinna. "The very lands you would explore to plant your grove."

Karinna was unmoved by the threat. "It may be that Korgaan is so powerful because his followers are so numerous. To weaken the god is not to confront him directly, but to strip from him the faith of his worshipers." She held up the Sahlirian fruit. "Here is the promise of a gift every mortal covets, the promise of eternity. If we can offer this to all the peoples of Pannithor, how many do you think will continue to follow Korgaan? Only the most fanatical will choose to cling to their god to shun the boon of immortality."

"It is a dangerous gambit," Eoswain advised. "Korgaan dominates his followers through fear. Not simply fear of his priests, but fear of the god's own wrath. There's no saying how far a people dominated by fear can be driven."

"All the more reason why I must go alone," Karinna said. "By myself, I can avoid the attention of those who would seek me." She pointed at the floor. Eoswain saw the emerald energy that exuded from her as she focused her magic, defying the wards that guarded the room. Up from the ground, a green tendril arose. It thickened and lengthened with every heartbeat, curling up to Karinna. It wrapped about her leg, and as it did so, the Celestian's limb was transformed, taking on the appearance and quality of the little vine.

Karinna dispersed her spell, and the transformation reversed. The tendril receded back into the floor and soon vanished entirely. "Wherever green things grow, I will be safe. The land itself will guard me."

"Then seek what you must find," Mescator said. "Know that our blessings go with you."

Eoswain echoed Mescator's words. "With the help of the elves, we've brought enlightenment to Pannithor, but it is you, Karinna, who can bestow something even more vital to the people of this world." She gestured to the golden fruit Karinna held. "In your hands you carry the dream of peace and an end to wars."

***

It was some weeks before Reiliur was recovered enough to hold any meaningful converse with anyone. When he was capable, the first person he asked to see was Eoswain.

Eoswain was dismayed when she entered the wizard's chamber. She distinctly remembered the joyous look Reiliur had regarded her with when she stepped out from the gateway. Now his face when he lifted up from the pillow and watched her was pale and haunted. His lip quivered with some unspoken dread.

His eyes darkened with a nameless fear.

To learn the cause of these emotions would have been an easy thing for Eoswain, but she resisted the temptation. Employing telepathy on Reiliur in his condition and without his agreement would be a grievous violation. She had too much respect for the wizard to treat him in such a sorry fashion. If she wanted to know what had so affected him, he would have to tell her of his own volition.

"You did come," Reiliur said. "I was afraid that you wouldn't."

Eoswain could see that the elf's words weren't entirely true. There was a hint of regret in his voice. Some part of him had *hoped* she wouldn't visit him. Perhaps his request had simply been from a sense of propriety or obligation rather than any genuine desire to speak with her. Whatever the truth, she decided the best policy was to act as though he was sincere.

"After so many centuries, how could I keep away?" Eoswain smiled at him. "We've spoken many times, but never face to face." She looked about the luxuriously appointed room he was convalescing in. "This is much more pleasant than the vagaries of the Scrying Star. Such communication is too direct. Nuance is lost in the conveyance. It is much better that two friends should speak this way."

Reiliur brightened somewhat at her warm tones. Some of the fear withdrew from his face. Not all, but it was at least something. "Are we friends?" he mused, more to himself than in expectation of a reply.

"Need you ask?" Eoswain had no need to feign the hurt in her voice. "Only through friendship and collaboration have we been able to accomplish all that we've done."

"I... I don't know," Reiliur said, sinking back into his pillows.

Eoswain drew a chair up beside the bed. Calisor had advised her that Reiliur was occupied by strange doubts and morbid fancies. During his infirmity, while being treated by Shakara, the wizard had mumbled in his delirium strange and awful things. Disordered fears that those looking after him dismissed as the ravings of nightmare.

Eoswain wasn't so ready to dismiss whatever strange fears had infected Reiliur. The wizard's mind was strong enough to project his consciousness across the void between worlds. Such an intelligence wasn't easily distracted by mere imaginings.

"What don't you know?" she prodded Reiliur.

The elf licked his lips and hesitated before replying. "So many things." He fixed an imploring look on her. "Eoswain, tell me if you've been truthful with me. Tell me if everything has happened for the reasons we agreed upon."

Eoswain laid her hand on Reiliur's. His flesh felt hot under her touch, flush with lingering fever. "What is it that worries you? What can I do to ease your doubts?"

Again, Reiliur hesitated. Eoswain had the sense he was afraid to pose the question that was on his tongue. Afraid to hear the answer. Finally, he forced himself to speak. "Your coming here, the reason the Celestians came to Pannithor, it was to help us. To benefit and guide the races of this world." He paused again, closing his eyes. "You didn't come here to conquer, to rule over us?"

"By what we've accomplished, you must know your worry is needless," Eoswain said, hiding her shock that such a concern could ever have occurred to Reiliur. There had never been any clue he harbored these kinds of doubts in the centuries since they'd first spoken. Something had happened. Something terrible had put these fears in his head. Whatever it was, she knew it had happened during the ritual.

"Mescator hasn't made himself a despot over Primovantor," Eoswain pointed out. "Fulgria and Belkon haven't turned Abercarr into a conquering horde. Kyron has done his utmost to steer the dragons away from civilized lands, not harnessed their might to conquer and rule." She waved to the window through which the lights of Ileureleith glimmered. "Valandor has stayed with you as a colleague. King Yarinathar yet rules in Therennia Adar. Nothing has been done to usurp his throne. Even Ophidia, for all their treachery, is allowed to remain free. Are these the acts of oppressors?"

Reiliur shook his head. "I know the good the Celestians have brought to this world. Not long ago I celebrated all you've given to us. But now, a terrible shadow rests upon me."

"What happened to put this darkness in your mind?" Eoswain coaxed the elf.

"After the ritual, when you stepped through the gate," Reiliur said, his voice dropping to a strained whisper. "I gazed up at Belkon's dome. There, I had a hideous vision." He rose from the pillows and his fingers tightened about Eoswain's hand. "I saw you, but horribly distorted. Everything good and decent was gone, twisted into something sinister and malignant. There was no compassion, only the arrogance of power."

Eoswain patted his hand. "You see me now. See me as I am. As I have always been." She smiled down at the elf. "Do I resemble this horror you beheld in the dome?"

Far from being reassured, Reiliur shuddered. "I doubted what I had seen and so I looked again. And this time I saw myself, wasted and ruined, madness shining in my eyes." Now, the fear he showed wasn't for himself, but for Eoswain. "The dome Belkon crafted, it shows many things to those who evoke its magic. Many among the Circle of Heaven have had glimpses into the future, revelations of things to come."

"And you think these awful sights were omens of tomorrow?" Eoswain asked.

Reiliur nodded. "It is that terror that fills me with such dread. If, somehow, the Celestians - if you, Eoswain, were to change. No longer benevolent, but bent upon conquest. Instead of the great boon I've tried to bring to Pannithor, I should have unleashed the greatest curse in history." He trembled and closed his eyes again. "If I'd dared to look again, what else would have changed? Would I have seen some horrible transformation consume Valandor or Karinna? Would I have seen some monstrous image of Mescator or Oskan?"

Eoswain was quiet for a time, weighing what Reiliur had told to her. "Visions are always enigmatic, and most especially those that flirt with prophecy," she said. "The future is ever in motion. Taking shape with each passing hour. If this was a warning of the future, then it falls upon us to be vigilant. To watch for the signs that would usher in such darkness."

"But can we stop it?" Reiliur asked, almost pleading to her.

"Forewarned is forearmed," Eoswain answered. "Mescator has ever guided the Celestians by that mantra. It is a sound piece of wisdom and one that we can follow too." She nodded to the stricken elf. "If there is a threat, we'll watch for it. Both of us. We'll keep what you've seen from happening."

Even as she spoke the words, Eoswain felt a chill run through her. Any assurances about tomorrow were always hollow. The promise of the future was that it wasn't set and could always change. Therein lay the menace it posed, for there was no certainty of what shape danger would assume when it appeared. The very steps taken to prevent catastrophe could, instead, bring it into being.

Such was the shadow that now fell upon Eoswain's spirit. How to guard against a calamity unknown.

Chapter XI

-880, Time of Light

The little village of Ander might once have been called picturesque, nestled between the green forest and the blue river. Liliana could imagine the fields of golden grain swaying in a warm breeze, the bleating of sheep grazing on the grassy hills. There would have been the strains of a lute sounding from the tavern and some song of great heroes, perhaps even one about the Celestians. The smell of incense would have clung heavy to the stone shrine of Mescator as a cleric paid tribute to Primovantor's god of justice. By late afternoon, the aroma of cooking food would have surpassed that of piety as Ander's households prepared for the farmers and shepherds to return from their labors. Down at the little pier, a barge had stopped to take on a cargo of wool and grain to transport to markets downriver.

All of this Liliana could envision, but it was only a shade of what had been. Ander now was in ruins. No sheep grazed on the hills. The fields had been trampled. The barge lay half-sunk beside the pier. The houses were absolute wreckage, flattened as though caught by an avalanche. The front wall of the tavern had been pushed in, smashed to expose the rooms within. Mescator's little stone shrine had been obliterated, pulverized into rubble.

The streets of Ander had been churned into mud by heavy and violent traffic. Wreckage and bodies lay strewn everywhere. Not a single villager had been spared in the assault. Old and young, men and women, all had been cut down with the utmost brutality, their blood splashed across the ruins. Half-eaten livestock festered beside the corpses. Tuns of beer, casks of wine, barrels of ale, these too lay strewn about the carnage – looted from the tavern. Each vessel had its top smashed in and contents drained down to the last dregs. Strangely, other objects of worth had been left behind by the pillagers. Liliana was shocked to see a bolt of elfin silk cast into the road and a masterfully carved ebony lion still clutched in the cold fingers of a corpse. The raiders who'd attacked Ander had displayed an especially unsophisticated attitude toward plunder.

It took only a little while for Liliana to discover the nature of the attackers. Stomped into the mud were enormous tracks, footprints many times the size of a human's, broad at the heel but with stumpy toes. Liliana had been shown such tracks before in wild, isolated corners of Primovantor. They were the marks of primitive creatures the men called ogres. Though far less imposing than the towering giants who sometimes strayed into civilized lands, the ogres were still twice as large as any human or elf and far more powerfully built. Like the giants, however, they had no society of their own, living in small familial groups and casting out their young as soon as they matured. While they did prey on the unwary traveler and were a menace to the lone hunter, ogres had never represented any great threat to Primovantor.

Something had changed that. Liliana was in Ander because of the frantic reports flowing into Primantor from the republic's eastern frontier. High Consul Pallandas had appealed to the Celestians to investigate what was escalating into a full crisis. Liliana was selected as the most capable for the task by Mescator. So it was that she was the first of them to discover a situation far worse than the government in Primantor feared.

The tracks in the mud showed no less than twenty ogres had partaken in the raid on Ander – a group far larger than anything seen in Primovantor before. Liliana wasn't certain what had caused such a gathering of the creatures or driven them to ransack villages, but she wasn't going to return until she found out. And the quickest way to do that would be to trace the tracks back to those who'd made them.

The trail was easy enough to follow. The ogres made no effort to conceal their activity. Indeed, from the reports that had reached Primantor, it might be that they welcomed pursuit, for every party sent by the frontiersmen to hunt the monsters never returned. Though she'd seen no evidence of it in Ander, Liliana knew that folklore claimed ogres to be man-eaters.

The tracks led off into the forest. Liliana saw branches snapped up to a height of twelve feet by the passing ogres. Several times an entire tree had been uprooted and pushed over, the size and age of them giving mute evidence of the prodigious strength of their destroyers. Scraps of loot lay discarded along the path, cast aside by the changing whims of the marauders.

Gruff voices reached Liliana's ears, rumbling booms that rose from mighty chests. She stopped and focused her mind, reaching out with her thoughts to the creatures ahead. Like some psychic spy, her awareness peered into the brains of the ogres. These raiders were simple in their thoughts, with no depth to their planning, only the immediacy of need and desire. At the moment, it was the subjects of food and conflict that had their attention. The ogres wondered how long the supplies they'd stolen from Ander would last them. They regretted the lack of worthwhile enemies in the village and the opportunity for a fight worthy of telling to their tribe.

Tribe? As Liliana lingered over the thoughts of the ogres, she realized that these were a different breed from the small families that haunted the wilds of Primovantor. These ogres belonged to tribes that numbered in the hundreds, and the tribes in turn were banded loosely in a massive confederation that swelled into the tens of thousands! The raiders who'd struck Ander and other places along the frontier were simply scouts of a vast and ravening horde. A horde that was marching every day nearer to civilized lands.

"What's that?" one of the ogres suddenly grumbled. "Funny smell on the wind," he added for the benefit of his less observant comrades. The raider's sharp olfactory senses had picked out Liliana's scent. He knew she was nearby.

Liliana cut her telepathic observation of the ogres short. Boldly she advanced upon the alerted monsters, striding out from the trees into a wide clearing.

The ogres were enormous in their dimensions. It was more accurate to compare them to upright oxen than humans in terms of size. Their hands were as big as a man's chest, their legs were as thick as barrels. They wore rough tunics stitched together from hides, both those of beasts and reptiles, and adorned their savage raiment with strings of bones and necklaces of fangs. Their garb did little to conceal the muscles that bulged across their hulking frames. Their heads jutted from between their broad shoulders on thick, stumpy necks. Square jaws protruded from vicious faces, massive fangs pushing out from leathery lips. The deep-set eyes were like those of lions, dominated by a brutal confidence in their power to overcome whatever they gazed upon.

There were seven of the monsters, a mixture of males and females. Liliana had become accustomed to the grace and delicacy of elfin and human women. Among ogres, there was no such physical variation. The ogresses were as colossal in size and brawn as the ogres with them.

The bravado of her entry into the clearing caught the ogres by surprise; clearly they hadn't expected her to come to them.

"If it is a fight you've been wanting," Liliana told the ogres, thrusting her words into their minds so they would understand, "then you've found one." She drew the blade of elfin steel she'd been gifted by King Yarinathar. The slim, silvery sword glistened in the sunlight as she flourished it before her.

Low grunts of amusement rose from several of the ogres, but a few regarded her with superstitious suspicion, wondering if she were some forest spirit made manifest. Beefy fists closed around wooden clubs and stone axes. "A fight?" one of the ogres laughed, lumbering forward. "A marmot's bite would hurt more than that silly knife."

The boastful ogre struck at Liliana with his stone axe. She whirled away from the attack and slashed with her sword. In missing his blow, the raider had leaned down, putting his thick neck within easy reach. The elfin blade whipped across his throat. Syrupy blood gushed forth. The ogre dropped his weapon and clamped his hands to his wound, vainly trying to staunch the bleeding. A glottal burble escaped his mouth, and he dropped to his knees. The next moment, he pitched face-first into the earth.

Liliana looked away from the dead braggart and smiled at the shocked ogres. "Who's next?" she challenged them, slapping her bloody blade against her open palm.

A tremendous bellow rose from the ogres. Strangely, it had more of excitement in it than rage. The six remaining monsters rushed at Liliana, shoving aside their fellows in their eagerness to confront her. A huge ogress with a split nose charged at her with a gigantic club of petrified wood. Liliana darted aside as the bludgeon swung at her. In missing, it shattered the trunk of an oak and sent splinters flying across the clearing. Scarce had she dodged the club then an ogre swung at her with an axe of sharpened stone. It ripped through the air inches above her head, the wind of its passing wafting through her hair.

Liliana struck back. The ogre with the axe howled as her blade ripped open his belly and sent his entrails spilling into the grass. She spun and struck as another tried to flank her, the fury of her slash crunching down through the powerful arm to leave the raider staring at a gory stump. The ogress with the club rounded on her, but Liliana darted in before she could lunge. The elfin blade chewed deep into her leg, breaking the bone within and causing her to crash to the ground as the limb buckled beneath her tremendous mass.

"Knife Borgrug called it!" exclaimed a surviving ogress. "I should have such a knife!"

"Whoever kills her will," a one-eyed ogre snarled. There was enough resemblance to humans in his visage that Liliana recognized the sly expression that flashed across his face. She saw him make a furtive motion with the massive stone hammer he carried. A circular gesture that was understood by those raiders still able to fight. Liliana didn't need to peer into his mind to know it was a signal, and it was easy enough to guess what the signal meant.

"You can't win," Liliana warned the ogres. "If you value your lives, go back to where you came from and leave these lands."

The ogres laughed as they circled around her. "I don't know where you learned our speech, human," the one-eyed raider said, "but if you know anything, then you know we won't go back." His face split in an ugly leer. "Soon all these lands will be claimed by the tribes! Your people will leave, or you'll be destroyed."

Liliana sensed the attack before it came. The one-eyed ogre had no interest in conversation but was only trying to distract her so his fellows could take her unawares. The first to fall to her was the raider whose hand she'd cut off. He tried to seize her behind in his brawny arms and render her helpless for the others. She spun and met his rush, skewering his heart with a thrust of her blade. She continued her spin, whipping around behind the dying ogre and using his body as cover as the others came at her. In a display of strength far beyond that of a human, the Celestian held the huge creature upright, then shoved his inert hulk full into one-eye's face. The two ogres, living and dead, crashed to the ground in a tangled heap.

From Liliana's right came the ogress, whipping a spear carved from the tusk of a mammoth at her. On her left, a raider wielding a club edged with pieces of jagged quartz charged at her. She shocked her foe with the club by parrying the blow, her incredible strength almost pulling the huge weapon from his hands. A twist and she used her momentum to jump at him and bring the elfin sword crunching down through his shoulder. Corded muscles and thick bones tore under her assault, and her enemy stumbled back, gore spraying from where she'd cut away his arm.

The ogress with the spear stabbed at her while she was busy with the other raider. Liliana caught the attack with the edge of her blade, shearing through the tough ivory and severing several feet from its length. Her foe pressed on, shifting her grip and swatting at the Celestian with the other end of the weapon. Liliana avoided the desperate blows and sprang at the ogress. Like the fang of a serpent, her sword jabbed up through the bottom of the raider's jaw, piercing into the skull and the brain within. The enemy dropped like a poleaxed ox, instantly felled by the stroke.

A bellow of anger rose from one-eye as he shoved aside his dead comrade. He lurched up onto his feet and waved his hand imploringly to Liliana. "Wait a moment, human. Let me at least recover my hammer before we fight."

Liliana took a step back and glowered at the sneaky raider. "You could still run," she advised.

One-eye's face curled with amusement. "My children would laugh at me if I ran from a human," he said.

"You're mistaken," Liliana told him. "I'm no human. Today you've fought Liliana. A Celestian." She could see that the ogre had never heard of the new gods who had been mentoring so many of Pannithor's people. "Be sensible. I've killed six of your warriors. What chance do you have alone?"

The sound of great crashings amid the trees brought a triumphant grin to the one-eyed ogre. "It's you who are mistaken, *Cel-es-tian*," he fumbled over the unfamiliar word. His hand closed on the hammer lying in the grass as more ogres burst into the clearing. "I'm not alone."

Liliana looked across the hulking raiders and her fingers tightened around the grip of her sword. She'd underestimated when she thought only twenty ogres had attacked Ander. There were thirty of the brutes, not counting those lying dead around her.

"You still have time to run," Liliana said, waving her sword at the bodies around her. The ogres laughed at her threat.

Liliana's eyes blazed with energy as she drew upon the full might of a Celestian. "Don't say I didn't warn you," she said as she readied herself to meet the ogres' charge.

***

-879, Time of Light

Dying screams and bestial roars filled the air, the trumpeting of colossal mammoths thundered over the valley. Swarms of vultures circled in the sky, drawn by the smells of blood and death, their raucous cries raining down on the battlefield, impatient for the carnage to be over so they might feed. The ground pulsed from the tramp of charging hooves and the crash of falling bodies. A nondescript speck of land, it would soon be known throughout Pannithor as Massacre Reach.

Oskan plunged his sword into the chest of an ogre and wrenched the blade free, bursting his enemy's organs and shattering his ribs. The hulking creature dragged him close and clamped his jaws on the Celestian's shoulder, using the last of his strength to try to bite through the shining armor. The yellowed fangs snapped against the unyielding pauldron. Forged by the dwarfs of Abercarr, it was proof against even an ogre's brawn.

"To me, men of Mistfell!" Oskan shouted, waving his sword high. There had been two hundred knights riding with him when they'd charged into the ogres. Now, he wondered if there were even a quarter of that number still alive. Surely he'd seen Count Ferndo cut down by an ogre's axe. Unlike Oskan's, the count's armor was only Eskian steel from Primovantor's old capital, and when the brute's axe struck, it had plowed through not only the man but the horse he rode. Many of the knights had been killed in similar ways, chopped down along with their steeds. In a macabre way, the stacked bodies had given cover to dismounted survivors and gave them a chance to strike back at their hulking enemies without being slaughtered out of hand.

Oskan could see one such knight nearby, crouched against the flank of a dead horse. The man had a spear beside him, and when an ogre started to step over the animal carcass, he sprang into motion. The spear stabbed upward, piercing the monster's groin and thrusting up through his gut. The ogre stumbled back, stunned by the sudden attack. The knight drew his sword and lunged after the reeling brute, his blade chopping down into the thick skull. A froth of blood and brains oozed from the wound, but the mortally injured ogre still had strength enough to crack the man with his club. The sound of crumpled metal and shattered bone rang out as the knight was hurled back, his breastplate driven into his broken breast.

"To me, men of Mistfell!" Oskan cried once more. Now he could see handfuls of men working their way toward him through the carnage. A few were still mounted, but most had been unhorsed in the fighting and harbored terrible injuries from the struggle against the ogres. Not a one of them gave any thought to retreat. They'd come here to die, and though they would stave off that doom for as long as they could serve the people of Primovantor, not one of them expected to see their homes again.

The Knights of the Skull, the company from Mistfell was called, their black shields adorned only with a leering death's head. The people of Mistfell were stricken by a horrible curse laid against them by the priests of Shobik when the Celestians were driving their cult from Primovantor. A magic affliction that set a slow rot into every household from the region, be they noble or common. Few from Mistfell ever saw their thirtieth year, none endured to their fortieth. The Celestians had been unable to undo the curse, and generations of living under its shadow had rendered the people grim and fatalistic. But they retained the pride that of old had caused them to rise up against Shobik's priests and burn their temples. Rather than quietly wither away, many became soldiers, fighting with a fearlessness usually seen only in the undead. So had the Knights of the Skull come into being.

Oskan admired the selflessness and determination of these men, so when they were chosen to lead the vanguard of the western forces against the invading ogres, he determined that his place was with them. He'd kept his intentions secret from Mescator. He was certain his mentor wouldn't approve. The

Knights of the Skull had been sent to certain death. By riding with them, Oskan wanted to assure them that their sacrifice wasn't going to be forgotten. That they wouldn't be forgotten.

"To Oskan, Prince of Celestians!" a knight yelled as he staggered to the small rise Oskan stood upon. One of the man's arms had been wrenched from its socket, dangling limp and useless at his side, but he took as little notice of his hurt as he did of the dark blood that stained his gray lips, the mark of the wasting curse of his people. It was in the soldier's eyes that his strength could be seen, for they burned with fanatical determination when he looked up at Oskan.

While what remained of his troops rallied to his position, Oskan stared across the battlefield. The ogre horde was as tremendous as the monsters themselves. Thousands of the brutes marched through the valley in bands of fifty and more. Huge chariots drawn by grotesque boar-like animals churned the earth as they rushed toward the western forces. Beyond them were the gigantic mammoths, shaggy beasts that made the war elephants of Ahmun look like whelps. Slavering hounds the size of ponies raced ahead, driven by the whips of the ogres who jogged behind them. Towering over even the ogres were several genuine giants, humanoids forty and fifty feet tall who carried uprooted trees for clubs.

Against this horde was ranged the alliance the Celestians had gathered to defend the civilized lands of Primovantor. Bowmasters from Elvenholme showered the ogres with volley upon volley, peppering the brutes at range as the nimble elves drifted between blocks of human infantry. Though their aim was precise, it took a lot to bring down an ogre. Several of the monsters were riddled with arrows, the shafts sticking out of them like the quills of a porcupine.

More telling were the spells elven mages and human wizards sent into the ogre ranks, yet even here, the robust stamina and incredible endurance of the foe made them difficult to kill. Oskan saw spheres of fire descend into bands of ogres, only for them to continue marching even with their skin burned black and their hide armor scorched off their bodies.

The dwarfs of Abercarr protected the flanks of the allied host. Hundreds of dour axemen arrayed in coats of steel cemented each side of the army. When the ogres came against them, it was like an angry wave smashing against the shore. The dwarfs didn't drive back the enemy, instead they did something even more vital: they held the line and kept the ogres from expanding their front.

Soldiers of Primovantor held the center - four thousand strong, stolid blocks of heavy infantry supported by skirmishers and lightly-armored auxiliaries. High Consul Cassira sent the republic's best generals to command her forces. With them were Mescator and a half dozen other Celestians. A great company of cavalry was held back as a reserve to charge should the ogres break through the front lines. Arrayed above the cavalry on the slopes of a hill were hundreds of archers and scores of onagers and scorpions. While the spear-throwers held their shots until the enemy got nearer, the archers and catapults maintained a persistent barrage that punished the ogre ranks.

For the moment, the ogres were more interested in closing with the main body of the allied army than bothering about the little island of defiance represented by Oskan and the Knights of the Skull. A few stragglers separated from their warbands trotted over to harass them, but the larger groups considered them beneath their notice. Oskan bristled at the insult. The enemy who ignored him would have cause to regret it.

"Raise the flag of Primovantor," Oskan told one of the surviving knights. "Remind everyone that we're still here. That we're still in this fight." When the flag rose, cheers erupted from the western forces. Soldiers locked in mortal combat with the advancing ogres had their courage bolstered by the sight, throwing themselves against the brutes with renewed vigor.

A few ogre hunters came charging toward Oskan's position. They cast javelins at the men, the missiles bursting their armor when they struck. Those knights who still had horses spurred their steeds full into the oncoming brutes. One ogre was impaled on a rider's lance but still had enough strength to drag the man from his saddle. He crashed in a broken heap even as the stricken hunter collapsed from his wound. The other ogre claimed two knights before a third was able to crack his skull with a mace.

The brief flurry of action and the flag snapping in the wind caused one of the warbands to divert from their advance into Primovantor's army. Oskan was stunned to see that the ogres were being led by one of their chieftains. Liliana and Kyron had both spied upon the tribes during their long trek into the provinces of Primovantor and had noted the deference the horde paid to their leaders. These could be spotted by the banners they tied to their backs, glyphs that boasted of the chieftain's prowess and accomplishments, a reminder to his followers why he was their leader. The more powerful the ogre, the more back-banners he bore.

The brute now advancing with his mob toward the Knights of the Skull had seven banners fluttering behind him. Each hide was filled with painted glyphs, indicating the many things the chief felt need to boast about. Liliana and Kyron had related many things about ogres, but never had they indicated that the tribes would suffer liars among them.

"Now we will earn death," a knight said as the ogres marched nearer. He looked up at Oskan. "Leave us, eminence. Primovantor can spare the loss of men from Mistfell, but not the Prince of Celestians."

Oskan gave the men around him a stern look. "Any man of Mistfell who hurries to death disgraces his gods. When death comes for you, you fight. You fight and make it earn your final breath." He waved to one of the men who yet had a horse. "I need your mount, and let none say that Oskan hurried to safety while brave warriors died."

He swung up into the saddle as the horse was brought to him. He exerted a measure of his power, restoring the animal's stamina and calming its fear. Oskan waved his sword at the ogre chief. "I ride forth to challenge their leader," he said. "Stay here and protect the flag. Let our army know all of us fought to the last."

Oskan galloped through the piles of corpses, intent upon the foe he'd chosen for himself. He smiled as he thought how Mescator would applaud his courage, then frowned when he considered how he would likewise decry his recklessness. But if he could defeat this chieftain, remove one of the horde's leaders, then perhaps it would be worth the risk.

"Hai! Lugbrug! Warchief of the Marrowmaws! Cross blades with me, if you dare!" Oskan plucked the enemy's name and title from his mind and hurled it back at him in the surprisingly nuanced ogre language. The Marrowmaws were Lugbrug's tribe, but while he was warchief, all the other tribes were temporarily made a part of the Marrowmaws. If another chieftain took his place, then so too would another tribe take prominence.

Lugbrug raised his arm, preventing more hunters from casting javelins at Oskan. "A human is no fit challenge for a chieftain," his voice rumbled.

Oskan sneered at the rebuke. "I am Oskan," he told the warchief. "Prince of Celestians," he added the honorific his worshipers had bestowed on him. He felt the mental tremor that rushed through Lugbrug. The ogres were no longer so ignorant of the Celestians as they had been when they first marched into civilized lands. They knew to respect the new gods, that wherever the Celestians fought, their horde was balked.

"Fight me, Prince Oskan," Lugbrug growled. He gestured to the banners on his back. "I promise you a place of honor." The warchief waved to the ogres of his band, motioning for them to rush the rise while he remained and confronted Oskan.

"I promise you will regret despoiling the lands of Primovantor," Oskan told the warchief. He urged his horse onward and charged at Lugbrug, the other ogres ignoring him entirely as they advanced on the Knights of the Skull.

Lugbrug carried an unusual weapon for an ogre, a gigantic iron sword with a blade as tall as a man and as thick as a man's leg. Where he'd gotten such a vicious tool, who had forged such a thing for him, these were questions that flashed through Oskan's brain as the warchief struck. He was too crafty to strike directly at the Celestian. Instead, he attacked the impetus of the charge. Dropping low, he chopped at the galloping horse's legs.

The animal careened across the terrain, mangled by the ogre's sword. Oskan rolled away from the mutilated steed, his bones throbbing from the violent impact. Lugbrug stormed after him, unwilling to give him the slightest respite in which to recover. He loomed above Oskan and brought his foot stamping down at the Celestian's head.

Oskan turned as the ogre's boot came down. His hands caught the foot, holding it back even as Lugbrug brought his full weight to bear and tried to crush his head like an egg. Surprise filled the warchief's eyes when he found his effort resisted. His face contorted with strain as he leaned into the attack, trying to overwhelm the impossible strength that held him back. Oskan tightened his hold on the foot, and with a twist, sent the huge ogre slamming into the ground.

Both combatants were quick to regain their feet. Oskan readied himself for Lugrbug's retaliation. The warchief clenched his gigantic sword in both fists and came roaring for the Celestian's head. Oskan blocked the cleaving sweep of the butchering blade with his sword of curved Ophidian copper. The sorcery infused into the weapon by desert mystics flared into hideous power. Electricity pulsed through the weapon and down through Lugbrug's iron one. The ogre lurched back, howling in pain, blue sparks flashing from his fangs.

Oskan had seen many enemies cooked in their own armor by the Ophidian magic, but somehow the warchief remained standing, smoke steaming from his scorched hulk. Bellowing with rage, he swung his huge sword once more for the Celestian.

Oskan avoided the ogre's drive. Lugbrug had withstood the electric shock, but he'd still suffered from it. The blow was clumsy and misdirected, crunching down into the earth a few feet from his foe. Oskan could read the confused jumble being fed into the warchief's brain by his disrupted senses. His ears were ringing, his vision was blurred, and every pore on his skin felt as though a tiny fire were burning against it.

There was more, however. Beyond the torment of his senses, thoughts were swirling in the ogre's mind. Oskan was surprised by what he read there. Lugbrug wasn't thinking about worthy fights and winning battles. He was thinking about his people. Not simply his tribe, but the whole of his race. He'd been voted warchief, to lead the vast horde into new lands. Not for the sake of conquest, but because they couldn't survive in those they'd left. In their homelands, there was only death for them now.

The killing stroke Oskan had intended for Lugbrug's neck turned into a stunning blow that cracked against the side of his head. The ogre stumbled, then dropped to his knees.

Oskan reflected on what he'd learned of subterfuge and treachery from the Ophidians. They'd been harsh lessons for the young Celestian, but now he saw a way such a callous ploy could be turned to good. He was certain Mescator would approve. The ogres weren't just marauding brutes who had to be fought. They were a thinking people just doing what they thought necessary to survive.

Oskan's face glowed with power. Still gripping his sword in one hand, he reached out with the other and touched Lugbrug's bleeding head. The resistance he encountered as he stirred the ogre's mind made him question if he'd be able to do what he intended if the warchief weren't already dazed.

"Call back the Marrowmaws," Oskan whispered, setting the idea firmly in Lugbrug's mind. "End the battle. Seek a truce. Seek a conference with Mescator."

Lugbrug's eyes struggled to focus on Oskan. He could see the ogre struggle for a moment, trying to drive out the alien ideas. Oskan battered down that defiance. "We don't need to be enemies," he told him. "If you would let us, the Celestians could help the tribes."

The promise broke through the ogre's resistance. Lugbrug stood and turned to the rise where his warband was still fighting the Knights of the Skull. "Pull back!" he bellowed at them. "Disengage!" For all their savage appearance, the ogres understood enough of tactics to obey their leader and trust his commands.

Lugbrug gave a last glance to Oskan, then lumbered off to carry his order to the rest of the army.

"The ogres will fall back," Oskan sent the thoughts racing to Mescator. "Keep the mortals from pursuing them. There's a chance for peace, but it hangs by the merest thread."

Oskan sheathed his copper sword and walked back to the surviving knights of the rise. Together, they would watch the ogres retire from the battlefield and observe the amazement of the western forces as the fierce fray abruptly came to an end. The valley was littered with dead and there would be much mourning, but Oskan had the hope now that the war was over.

What kind of peace they could broker with the ogres was a question Oskan couldn't answer. He would leave that to the wisdom of Mescator.

Chapter XII

-879, Time of Light

Mescator watched as the ogre emissary walked through the army's camp. There was no hesitation in his lumbering gait, no timidity in the way his eyes swept across the thousands of soldiers around him, warriors who only hours before had been locked in mortal combat with his people. No guards accompanied the ogre, and it was with a start that Mescator realized this was no mere messenger, but the warchief Lugbrug himself. Except for a poultice tied to the side of his head and a covering of wet mud across his skin, he looked just the way Oskan had described him.

Whether from audacity or bravery, Lugbrug's confidence impressed the watching humans and dwarfs. They appreciated courage, even in an enemy. The elves showed more wariness, vigilant for the first sign of trickery.

And the Celestians? Mescator had heard both arguments from his companions. Liliana pointed out the havoc the ogres had wrought on Primovantor's frontier, an attitude that had much support from the republic's generals. Oskan argued that the tribes had been chased out of their homelands with no choice but to migrate into civilized lands.

Mescator wanted to wait until he'd spoken with Lugbrug and heard the ogre explain for himself the reasons for the invasion. Until then, he didn't favor one faction over the other. To mete justice, it was necessary to evaluate both sides of the argument.

"I greet Lugbrug, Warchief of the Marrowmaws," Mescator said when the ogre reached the shaded pavilion where the Celestians waited to receive the horde's representative.

The ogre nodded and jabbed a thumb to where Oskan was sitting. "We had a good fight going, but he thought I should see you with my head still attached." Lugbrug looked over Mescator, approval in his eyes. "So you're the boss, eh? Have to say I can see how you'd be able to keep even Oskan in line."

"Impertinent lout," Liliana snapped. "Show respect to your betters!"

Mescator motioned her to hold her peace. "In his gruff way, I think Lugbrug is."

The warchief turned and studied Liliana for a moment. "You're the one they've called Lady Long-knife," he decided, a smile working onto his face. "You've killed more of my warriors than the Black Pox." His eyes fixated on the elf blade sheathed at her side. Mescator could see that the ogre was considering the lethal toll it had taken. Then Lugbrug looked up and glanced across the other Celestians. His brow furrowed in confusion. "I don't see the one we call Shadow Wolf. He's killed almost as many as you have."

"Kyron Huntmaster has been detained by other obligations," Mescator informed Lugbrug, aware of whom the ogre spoke. It would be imprudent to tell the warchief that Kyron was away trying – thus far unsuccessfully – to draw Draumdraak and the dragons into the defense of Primovantor.

"A shame," Lugbrug commented, genuine regret in his tone. "He's a good fighter too." The ogre slapped his hand against the enormous sword strapped to his side. "I guess you must be too. A coward would've taken this away from me the moment I reached your camp." He stared into Mescator's eyes. "You aren't afraid of me, are you?"

"No," Mescator replied. "I only fear the harm you and your people might do to those who look to me for protection." Just as the ogre was direct in his manner, so did Mescator decide that there was no utility in courtly language and intricacies. He put the matter bluntly to Lugbrug. "Your tribes have caused much pain crossing into Primovantor and many deaths. That will stop. Peacefully if possible, but it will end."

Lugbrug scratched at the poultice tied to his head. "My people are hunters," he said. He waved his huge hand in a sweeping gesture. "We come from the Mammoth Steppes, where there is as much game as we can catch. The pickings here are much poorer, and there are so many mouths to feed. When your children are starving, you grow deaf to the weeping of strangers."

"Why didn't you stay in your homelands?" Liliana challenged the ogre.

Oskan turned to her. "They were forced to leave."

Lugbrug nodded. "To stay on the Mammoth Steppes would have been the destruction of the tribes. My people would've been exterminated. If we were to survive, we had to migrate." He sighed, the sound grumbling through his mighty frame. "It is to be regretted that the lands we found were already claimed, but such is the way of things."

"What drove you off the Mammoth Steppes?" Mescator asked. "Was it famine? Perhaps plague? I can imagine no invader mighty enough to drive the ogres from their lands."

Lugbrug's expression grew solemn. There was a suggestion of shame in his gaze. "One has. Gorgroth." He invoked the name with both loathing and awe.

"Gorgroth," Oskan repeated. "What is Gorgroth? Some conquering nation?"

The ogre shook his head. "A beast," he said. He looked back at Mescator. "The mightiest beast ever seen on the steppes. As big as a mountain, with scales of granite and claws of malachite. I've seen it devour a whole herd of mammoths, swat an ice-rhino as though it were a fly. Hundreds of ogres have ended in Gorgroth's belly. Where the stone lizard crawls, nothing is able to stand against it. No amount of prey is enough to sate its hunger." Lugbrug paused and regarded Liliana. "That is why we left and why we can't go back. Why we must fight. If we don't, our race will perish."

Mescator could tell there was no duplicity in Lugbrug's story. A monster too powerful for the ogres to overcome had driven them from the Mammoth Steppes. The question now was what could be done about it. "Lugbrug, if the threat of Gorgroth was gone, would your tribes return to their homeland?"

"There's good hunting on the Mammoth Steppes," Lugbrug answered. He nodded at the valley around them, uncaring that beyond the boundaries were rich farmlands and rivers teeming with fish. "These lands are not so good to us." He shook his head. "But against Gorgroth, there's nothing that can be done. Those who do not flee before it die under the stone lizard's claws."

"If the ogres will swear to return to the steppes, if your horde will push no farther into Primovantor, then I will destroy Gorgroth," Mescator vowed.

"You've seen what Celestians can do in battle against ogres," Oskan told Lugbrug, trying to curb the warchief's skepticism. "Mescator is the greatest of us all. He's not afraid to fight the monster."

Lugbrug digested what he'd heard. Finally, he spoke. "I will tell the tribes what you've said. If you can do what you've promised to do, we will return to the steppes." He locked eyes with Mescator. There was no threat in his next words, only a statement of brutal fact so far as the warchief was concerned. "If you can't, then the ogres will push on into Primovantor and crush everyone who stands in our way."

***

-878, Time of Light

For months, Mescator and his companions trekked far beyond the borders of Primovantor. They journeyed into lands that were little more than fables to even the elves, places long unseen by civilized mortals.

Only six Celestians made the arduous passage through dense forests and barren hills. With him, Mescator brought the mystical Valandor, the imperturbable Shakara, and the cunning Hermanas. Liliana, with her explorer's eye and knowledge of the wilds, was a crucial asset. Among the Celestians, only Kyron was more versed in the arts of woodcraft and tracking, and he was yet seeking the aid of Draumdraak's dragons. Even as a truce was brokered with the ogres, a new threat to the western realms exploded down upon both Primovantor and Elvenholme from out of the northern wastelands - hosts of barbaric humans and other creatures in numbers such as no one had ever seen before. Many Celestians had to remain behind to lead mortal armies to the borders to try and contain this new enemy. An enemy Mescator knew was anything but new. In everything, he now suspected the hand of Korgaan once more.

That suspicion was all but confirmed by Oskan, the sixth Celestian to set out with Mescator. To guide them to the Mammoth Steppes and observe the destruction of Gorgroth, over a hundred ogres had broken away from the horde. Among them was Lugbrug, abdicating his position as warchief in order to see for himself how Mescator would kill the stone lizard. Of all the Celestians, it was the bold Oskan who was the most respected by the ogres. While they were standoffish toward the others, they would accept Oskan at their campfires. The young Celestian learned much about the hulking hunters from their stories. The ogres had little interest in ancient tales and the deeds of ancestors, but they overflowed with accounts of their own accomplishments and those of their contemporaries.

Some of those stories dealt with the iron weapons that some of the ogres carried, such as the gigantic sword that served Lugbrug. These, Oskan told Mescator, had been gifts to the ogres from the Var'Kyr, and the mortals who bore them down to the tribes sounded very much like avatars of Korgaan, or at least demigods spawned by him. The gift-bringers had only appeared in the years before Gorgroth's awakening, and many ogres had wandered away from the steppes and up into the icy north in hopes of winning such weapons for themselves.

"I think," Valandor mused when he heard Oskan's report, "that Korgaan sought to do more than just draw ogres into his armies. I don't think it could be coincidence that Gorgroth remained dormant deep within the earth until after his gift-bringers went down into the steppes. Somehow, Korgaan stirred up the beast, set it loose against the tribes to drive them against Primovantor."

As they held council about their own campfire, the other Celestians agreed. "That the Var'Kyr waited until the ogres stopped their advance before attacking is proof of some trickery," Hermanas said.

"We've seen Korgaan use proxies before," Mescator reminded the others. "How much of the fanaticism of Shobik's death-priests was stirred by Korgaan's manipulation? When we fought at the Battle of Hepshet, his avatar boasted to me of how he'd used the armies of Ahmun to draw us out." He stared into the fire as though gazing back across the years to the harsh Ophidian desert. "No, it stands to reason that Korgaan would use the ogres the same way."

"Then perhaps we can outfox him," Hermanas said. "If we're able to kill Gorgroth, we could turn the ogres against the barbarians." He smiled as he warmed to the irony of such a tact. "It would be a fine jest to play, using his own pawns against him."

"First, we must kill Gorgroth," Valandor warned. "A beast mighty enough to put fear in the ogres."

Oskan bristled at the admonition. "If we find it, Mescator will kill it," he declared. Mescator appreciated his protege's confidence in him, but with only the ogres' stories to go by, he thought it was premature to be so certain.

"If Gorgroth is even half the size the ogres claim it is, we can't fail to find it," Liliana said. She darted a suspicious look over where Lugbrug and his hunters were camped. "I'm more worried about these brutes keeping their word once the beast is dead."

"You're the one best suited to judge that," Mescator told Liliana. "In a day or so, we'll be on the Mammoth Steppes. Study the land. See if it has the markings of the bounteous hunting ground the ogres say it is. See if this looks like a land they'd willingly return to."

Mescator let his words linger over the campfire. "It is a mistake to think of the ogres as brutes simply because their thoughts aren't as complex as those of the other races we've encountered. All of us have been around them long enough to learn their language. A tongue so filled with nuance and subtlety isn't the creation of mere brutes."

Oskan stood, annoyance in his eyes. "I'd stake my life that Lugbrug and his people aren't dealing false with us."

"It isn't your life you're staking," Liliana reproved him, "but that of Primovantor."

"That's why each of us must be vigilant," Mescator said. "Watch for anything that would put the lie to what the ogres have told us. If we're being deceived, soon we'll have proof of it."

***

The Mammoth Steppes appeared to go on forever. League upon league of grassland broken only by the occasional river or swamp. It was a land built to the scale of ogres. It took Liliana little time to find evidence of the great herds that roamed these lands and on which the tribes depended for sustenance. Bison and mastodon tracks churned great swathes of ground, indicating herds of unbelievable size. There were also the marks of the giant wolves and tigers that also preyed on the herds, animals of such size to dwarf the wolves of Primovantor and the lions of Ahmun.

A week on the steppes brought the first signs of Gorgroth. Mescator was amazed when Liliana showed him the stone lizard's gargantuan tracks. "An ogre could lie down in one of those prints and not feel cramped," he commented as he stared down on one of the clawed tracks. It was stamped into the earth to a depth of several feet, further indication of its colossal mass. "It must weigh a thousand tons."

Lugbrug came up while the Celestians were speaking. He gave Mescator an appraising look. "Now you've seen. We'll lead you back. The battle can resume. One side or the other will win." He pointed to the trail Gorgroth had left. "Here, there is only death. No one wins here."

Mescator shook his head. They'd come too far and risked too much to turn back. The combined armies of Elvenholme, Abercarr, and Primovantor might not be enough to fight both the Var'Kyr and the ogre horde. If there was even the remotest chance of gaining peace with the ogres, they had to take it.

"No, Lugbrug, I'm not turning back. We've journeyed for months to get here. I will see Gorgroth for myself." Mescator kicked a stone into the clawed print. "The beast's trail will be easy enough to follow."

Lugbrug nodded, admiration in his eyes. "The humans call you a god, Mescator. If you can really kill Gorgroth, I'll think so too."

The expedition pressed on, following the destructive path left by the monster. The dragging tail had churned the soil into mud, and rain had collected in the deep pits left by its feet. At one point, what seemed to be a boulder was lying beside the trail, an unusual sight on the rolling steppes. Closer inspection revealed it to be a castoff scale. Once, the group startled a pack of wolves gnawing at blackened bones strewn about the landscape. Lugbrug explained that was the remains of Gorgroth's meal, a herd of bison that had been gobbled by the lizard. Fires in the beast's throat burned the flesh off the bones, and it would spit out the skeletons when it was done.

Two days after finding the first pile of bones, they came upon another. This time, no animals were scavenging the remains, and a greasy smoke hovered over them.

"Gorgroth is very near now," Lugbrug cautioned. "These bones are only a few hours old."

Mescator turned to Valandor. "If the monster is that close, you should be able to spot it with your spells."

Valandor closed his eyes and focused his powers. Mescator could see the energy being drawn into him. The same energy was drawn up from him, sent streaming away across the steppe, following the trail left by the monster. It was only a few minutes later when Valandor told Mescator that Gorgroth had been found.

"We can see the beast from here, without the need for magic," Valandor said. He pointed at a long gray plateau, just visible on the horizon.

"You must be mistaken," Oskan protested. "That's some hill or mesa. That can't be anything alive! It would have to be..."

"Four-hundred feet from the tip of its snout to the end of its tail." Valandor had a note of awe in his voice. "I've never seen such a monster, it dwarfs Kyron's dragons by an order of magnitude." He laid his hand on Mescator's shoulder. "This is something you can't face alone. You'll need all of our help."

Mescator looked aside at the ogres. "If I can kill Gorgroth by myself, I can do more than bring peace. I can make an alliance between them and Primovantor. With that horde marching beside them instead of against them, we can cleanse the north of Korgaan's hosts."

"Your ambition might be too much," Shakara warned. "Listen to Valandor. Let the rest of us help."

"I have to try," Mescator said. He gazed across the other Celestians. "There's too much to gain. If I fail, *then* you can try another way." He focused on Valandor. "Is Gorgroth likely to stay where it is?"

Valandor's expression was thoughtful. "It appeared to be sunning itself while it digested its meal, just like any other lizard. I can't say how long it will be before it emerges from its stupor. When it does, it'll start moving to burn off excess energy from the heat it has drawn into itself."

"Then we must make haste," Mescator declared. "When we get near Gorgroth, you'll all stay back with the ogres. I'll be the one to challenge the beast."

Mescator saw that his command was unpopular with the others, but they had too much respect for him to defy his order. Even Oskan, for all his visible reluctance, offered no protest.

The air grew appreciably hotter as they drew nearer to the gray mass on the horizon. With every step, the basking Gorgroth became more distinct. The rocky texture and rugged irregularity of its scales lent it the semblance of a hill, but before long, the reptilian outlines of its body were clear. Aptly had the ogres described the beast as a stone lizard, for it was in truth shaped like the animals Mescator had seen so frequently in the deserts of Ophidia and the skittering bug-eaters that prowled gardens in Elvenholme. Gorgroth had a long, broad body with a lengthy tail that tapered to a sharp point stretched out behind it. The head was both wide and short, with a blunt snout and a massive jaw. The eyes, stony lids half-covering them, were placed at either side of its head and had an umber color to them. The legs, thick and powerful, jutted out from the reptile's sides rather than being positioned directly beneath its body. Each toe ended in a massive claw that glistened in the sunlight like chips of obsidian.

Solemn silence gripped the Celestians. No words were exchanged when Mescator left them with the ogres half a mile from where Gorgroth was sprawled across the steppe. With him, he carried the weapons he'd brought to combat the beast. An elfin lance, a relic from Therennia Adar that had been constructed for fighting dragons and endowed with such dire enchantments that their study had been forbidden to generations of elven wizards. A steel mattock forged by the dwarfs, combining the new processes taught to them by Fulgria and the ancient rune-magic of their race. A sword from the treasure vaults of Esk, once employed by the semi-legendary King Bransk to slay giants. To these he could add the massive javelins impressed on him by Lugbrug. The ogre had little confidence the shafts could pierce Gorgroth's scales, but if they did, he confided that each had been treated with the poison of the Torak Cliff Spider, the deadliest creature in the lands east of the steppes.

A formidable arsenal to bear into battle, and to them, Mescator could add his own strength and power. Yet he had to confess himself doubtful of his chances as he approached the immense lizard. Gorgroth's eyelid flicked down as he advanced, and the monster regarded him with a cold indifference. Indeed, after a moment, the eyelid rose again, and the beast returned to its idle lassitude.

This contemptuous dismissal by the monster inflamed Mescator's indignation. He was prepared for the beast's malice, but not for its scorn. "Gorgroth!" He shouted at the lizard and raised one of the javelins. "I am Mescator, and I've come here to kill you!"

Gorgroth lowered one eyelid again and regarded Mescator with the same aloof disinterest. Soon the eye was closed again. Mescator bristled with anger. Drawing back his arm, he cast the javelin at the beast. It clattered off the stony scales, even the strength of a Celestian incapable of forcing it past the lizard's armor. Gorgroth didn't even deign to open its eye as the missile went spinning away into the grass.

"You'll not ignore me, damn you!" Mescator growled. Taking up the mattock, he charged at the beast. Runes blazed as he brought the weapon cracking down on Gorgroth's snout. The stony scales chipped under the blow, flaking away in a spray of shards. Dark blood bubbled up from the wound.

Now the lizard opened both eyes and reared back on its powerful legs. Gone was its sated indolence. An angry hiss boiled up from its massive frame. The stink of its hot breath washed across Mescator. Gorgroth's mouth gaped wide, exhibiting triple rows of savage fangs. At the back of its throat, a fiery glow, like that of molten lava, shone.

"That got your attention," Mescator jeered and brought the mattock sweeping around once more. This time, he slammed against the lizard's jaw and knocked several teeth loose.

Gorgroth snapped at the Celestian, its fangs flashing only inches from his face. The head of the mattock was caught in the closing jaws. Mescator was lifted into the air as the beast pulled back. He released his grip on the weapon an instant before the lizard, with a lurch of its body, sucked the mattock down into its molten gullet.

Mescator's fall brought him just beneath the monster's throat. Quickly he drew the giant-slayer's sword and brought it slashing upward. He had the satisfaction of feeling chips of Gorgroth's scales bounce off his own armor and a spray of blood erupt from the wound.

The Celestian dashed back as Gorgroth roared in pain. Its huge foot came smashing down, narrowly missing him as he darted to the side. The lizard hissed angrily and made another snap at him with its jaws. This time, Mescator leaped to one side. He struck at the reptile's snout, the sword biting deep before Gorgroth twisted away.

"Come after me, you murdering beast!" Mescator shouted at the monster. He sheathed his sword and pulled the elfin lance from where it was lashed across his back. Gorgroth charged toward him, its footfalls causing the ground to quake. Setting his foot behind the lance, Mescator let the lizard's own momentum drive it onto the weapon. Blood gushed as the beast's shoulder was pierced.

Gorgroth scurried back, ripping the lance from Mescator's grip. It contorted its body so that it could bring one of its claws up and pull the weapon out. The ancient elven enchantments took their toll, the scales around the wound sloughing away and leaving the flesh beneath exposed.

Mescator waited until the lance was torn free before he attacked. His arm drew back and cast the other javelin at the dripping injury. Here, there were no scales to deflect the throw. He had the satisfaction of watching it sink deep into Gorgroth's flesh, bearing with it the deadly spider venom.

The lizard lashed its head from side to side and flailed at the earth with its long tail. Pained hisses seethed past its jaws. There was confusion in the sound. Gorgroth couldn't understand its hurts. Perhaps nothing had even been capable of injuring it before. But if the beast was confused about the tortured sensations rolling through it, there was no confusion about who was responsible for its agony.

The monster's eyes glared at Mescator. It reared back, and from the depths of its throat it spat a blob of molten stone. The Celestian tried to dodge the attack, but the spread of the spittle was too great to avoid. His own senses reeled as the burning filth splashed over him. He screamed as it chewed into his flesh and corroded his armor. The pain was so intense that he fell to his knees.

Gorgroth brought its clawed foot smashing down on the stunned Mescator, pounding his body into the ground. Vengefully it lifted its foot and brought it down again and again. Mescator felt his body breaking under the colossal weight of the monster.

Then he heard Gorgroth shriek in pain once more. The foot was whipped away, and he could feel the ground tremble as the monster shifted to a new position.

Other sounds reached Mescator now. He heard the shouts of Liliana and Oskan as they attacked the gargantuan lizard. He felt the chill of Shakara's magic as she set spells crackling into the monster. The sizzle of Valandor's enchantments followed close upon those of Shakara. Seeing his plight, the other Celestians had thrown aside his orders.

Mescator was lifted out of the crater by Hermanas. The usually jovial Celestian was grim as he carried Mescator away from the pit. More than his own senses, he could tell by Hermanas's expression how grave his injuries were.

When he was clear of the pit, Mescator told Hermanas to raise him up so that he could see what was happening. With the other Celestian propping up his shattered body, he gazed on a scene of absolute chaos. Gorgroth was beset of all sides. Liliana attacked the beast's flanks, striking deep into its scaly flesh with her blade. Oskan struck closer to its head, electric shocks sizzling into the monster whenever he chopped at it with his Ophidian sword. Shakara too kept near the front of the lizard, moving with it as it turned and twisted, directing her magic against its face. Sheets of ice covered the reptile's eyes, and whenever it tried to claw them away, she would freeze the air and coat them over again.

Valandor used his magic to more indirectly hamper the beast. Gorgroth's claws had churned the earth, ripping deep into its soil. The Celestian's enchantments further weakened the ground, changing it into a tarry mire that sucked and dragged at the huge reptile. It took ever more effort for the lizard to lift its legs or turn its body to meet the many threats that attacked it at every turn.

For a time, it seemed Gorgroth was helpless, but if it couldn't raise its claws, it was still capable of attack. A flick of its powerful tail finally connected with Liliana and threw her hundreds of yards across the plain. A second gout of magma forced Shakara to refocus her energies to defense as the molten rock flew at her. Chilling the air around her, she was spared the lizard's fiery wrath, but the magical cold caused the magma to instantly harden, and she was locked inside a stony shell.

Absent for the moment the blinding sheets of ice, Gorgroth's gaze fixated on the Celestian who continued to send shocks pulsing through its body with his enchanted sword. A sidewise twist of its head struck Oskan with the force of a battering ram. He was thrown from his feet and smashed against the lizard's stone-covered leg. The sound of armor being scraped to shreds rang out as Gorgroth began grinding his enemy against its scaly body.

The sight enraged Mescator. He felt this was all due to his own hubris, his insistence that he fight the beast alone. Had he been thinking clearer, he would have known the others wouldn't sit idle. He'd been too focused on what there was to gain, not on what could be lost. Oskan had become more to him than just a protege over the centuries. He was like a son to Mescator, a son who was now paying the price for his father's folly.

Mescator focused all of his energies. The healing power he'd used on mortals now surged through him. He abused that magic, pushing it beyond any limitations he'd been taught. Pain flared through him as broken bones welded themselves back together, as ruptured organs were made whole. His blackened skin became whole once more. His muscles surged with reborn strength. He pushed free from the supporting arms of Hermanas and drew the giant-killing sword. Whatever enchantments it possessed, it had endured Gorgroth's assault. Now, he would use it to bring the beast's final ruin.

"Oskan!" Mescator roared as he charged the reptile. The lizard ignored his cry and continued to grind Oskan against its leg. But it couldn't ignore the bite of Mescator's sword when he brought it chopping down into the exposed flesh of the wound the lance had opened. The beast reared back, shrieking in pain as gore cascaded from a severed vein.

The beast's agonies had little interest for Mescator. Ignoring any reprisal from the monster, he ran in the very shadow of its jaws to where Oskan had fallen. He picked up the battered Celestian and dragged him away from Gorgroth's reach.

"He's bigger than he looks," Oskan quipped, but the levity of his words was spoiled by the agony on his face.

"I'll make the beast pay," Mescator vowed. He waved to Hermanas and gave the wounded Oskan over to him. His own healing energies were exhausted and would be so for a long time.

"Not as bad as the thing did you," Hermanas said when he looked over Oskan. Considering how gravely Mescator had been savaged by the monster, the speech offered little comfort. Oskan's armor had been almost completely stripped from him. Wherever his skin was exposed, it had been scraped into a bloody ruin. In several spots, Mescator could see the white of exposed bone.

"Help him," Mescator said. He spun around, ready to return to the fight and punish the beast.

Gorgroth, however, had lost its appetite for battle. Assaulted from all sides, its body wracked with pain, poison, and magic, the gargantuan lizard sought only escape. Its huge claws tore at the ground already weakened by Valandor's magic. Great plumes of earth and rock flew through the air as the monster burrowed downward like an enormous mole. Mescator was stunned by the rapidity of its retreat. In less than a minute, the reptile created a hole big enough to swallow its gigantic bulk.

"Stay," Valandor's voice echoed through Mescator's mind when he would have pursued the retreating beast. "We've won."

The Celestian wizard emphasized that fact by turning the debris thrown up by Gorgroth's digging into tarry sludge that rushed back down into the pit. When the pit was nearly filled, Valandor altered the enchantment, and the sludge took on a steely hardness.

"It won't be back," Valandor stated. He marched about the edge of the depression, making cabalistic gestures that scored the slab-like surface with arcane wards to doubly ensure the beast couldn't claw its way out.

Mescator watched Liliana limp over toward him, bruised and weakened by her part in the fight. The stone shell that encased Shakara split open, and the pallid Celestian took a deep breath of the open air. Mescator turned back and gave Hermanas an inquiring look.

"Oskan will recover," Hermanas assured Mescator. "He's as tough to kill as you are."

Mescator started to ask more questions about his protege's condition, but then he noted that the ogres were advancing toward them. Lugbrug and his followers were somber, displaying none of the joy he'd expected them to show in the face of their victory.

"Gorgroth has been driven from your lands," Mescator told them. "Crawled back into the dark to wither from its wounds."

Lugbrug nodded, but the ogre's expression didn't change. "You've defeated the beast," he agreed. "The tribes can return to our homeland." He pointed at Mescator, his huge finger shaking with accusation. "But I know you're not a god, Mescator the Celestian. You couldn't beat Gorgroth on your own, as you said you would. You needed help to beat Gorgroth." The ogre stared at the slab that marked where the beast was entombed. "Perhaps it was a god," he mused. "Sent to punish the tribes."

"It was no god," Mescator told the ogres.

"Neither are you," Lugbrug grumbled. "I will return and tell the tribes to come back to the steppes, as we agreed, but don't return to our lands, Mescator. We have our ways and no interest in changing them. Play at being a god among the humans and leave us to ourselves."

The ogres turned away from Mescator and walked toward the slab. He could sense their thoughts. The fierce battle had impressed them, but it was the strength of Gorgroth that had impressed them the most. Now they were wondering if their people might not be able to appease the monster in some way and spare themselves its wrath should it emerge again.

"Half a victory is better than none," Liliana said.

Mescator looked down at Oskan and the gravity of his wounds. "It was a high price to pay for half a victory."

Chapter XIII

-878, Time of Light

Karinna smiled as she watched her grove grow. The seeds of the Sahlirian Tree flourished in the fertile soil she'd found in which to plant them. Hundreds of them had already reached maturity and were ready to shed their own fruit and produce new seeds. Her magic added to the richness of the land, nurturing the trees and helping them thrive far better than her most hopeful aspirations. In a matter of decades, perhaps, the grove would be so fruitful that the Celestians could begin the great work of removing the shadow of death from the mortals of Pannithor, and with it, the savagery of war.

Kyron's impetuous gift to the dragon Draumdraak had delayed the crop and denied its boon to generations of humans. Karinna knew that for all the good his kindness to the dragon had brought to the world, he bore a sense of terrible guilt over what it had cost. It would only add to Kyron's regret to tell him how near he'd been to finding the land in which the Sahlirian Tree could flourish. Just beyond the Dragontooth Mountains, below its northern slopes, Karinna had discovered the great forest of Galahir.

In times past, the land of Galahir had been the homeland of the elves, and there remained a remnant of that people scattered across its expanse, living the simple lives their ancestors had long before most of their race migrated farther south and west to lay the foundations of the kingdom of Elvenholme. These sylvan elves had little contact with their kindred and even less with other races, keeping to the environs of Galahir and remaining content with their old traditions and ancestral ways.

For these reclusive and isolated elves, Karinna's arrival was the first major event to happen to them for thousands of years. It was her genuine love for all living things and deep respect for nature that had overcome their initial wariness of her. Once certain that the Celestian meant no harm to Galahir, the sylvan elves accepted her wisdom and guidance. In truth, there was much Karinna learned from them as well, about the ways of the forest and the intricacies of its workings. She learned the order of the forest and the niche even the smallest animal and the tiniest flower occupied. How the wolf kept the deer from becoming too numerous and consuming so much grass that the absence of living roots weakened the soil and caused it to be washed away in the spring rain. She discovered the secret places where the trees whispered to one another and spoke of days so remote no living elf could recall them. The elves showed her how to live in harmony with all things, how their simple existence was sustained without inflicting hurt upon the many organisms with which they shared Galahir.

It was these quiet ways that had caused the sylvan elves to become so distant from their kindred in Elvenholme. Zealously did they protect the forest from outsiders who might bring harm to Galahir, and this included any elves who might see in the forest's bounty only a thing to be utilized and exploited. Few were the visitors from Therennia Adar deemed pure in their intentions and allowed to see the ancient realm from which their race had emerged.

The establishment of the groves was a subject that Karinna had been afraid the sylvan elves would resist, but they'd been quite accepting even without being told the boon the Celestians hoped the fruit from the trees would bring. Galahir was a living entity, and as such wasn't something to be preserved exactly as it was. The forest was in a continual cycle of change. A copse would die and a meadow would grow where the trees had fallen. A stream would run dry or change its course, and thereby the animals would adjust their habits and travel new paths through the wilds. One year the bees might favor the yellow flowers and spread the pollen of the butterweed far and wide, causing it to flourish in the coming season. The next might find the purple nightwort favored instead. For the elves, it was Galahir itself that would deny Karinna if there was no place in the forest for her groves. They were convinced the forest had its own way of sustaining what was good and eliminating that which was harmful.

Karinna smiled when she recalled the amazement with which the elves had watched her establish the first grove. They'd been prepared to watch her cast down the trees that already grew there so as to clear the ground. Instead, she'd woven her spells so that the trees would uproot themselves. A kind of reverent awe held the elves as they watched the trees walk away, shambling across the forest as they sought places in which to replant themselves. The elves had magic of their own, but never had they seen anything so wondrous before.

Her recollections were interrupted by the sudden appearance of a silver-haired elf. Entheiwaan was no stranger to Karinna. Many times had the young ranger visited the expanding groves and spent long hours talking with the Celestian. Never before, however, had she worn such a dire expression or had such a turmoil to her thoughts. Before a word passed between them, Karinna knew that the tidings she bore were grave. The rangers were the wardens of Galahir, keeping watch over the forest's boundaries. Among the sylvan elves, they alone made regular excursions into the world beyond their borders.

"I sense the trouble you bear with you," Karinna told Entheiwaan. "Speak freely and don't bother about any restraint. Ask what your people would have of me."

The ranger bowed her head, relieved by Karinna's understanding. "Trouble does indeed sit upon my tongue. A great host of humans marches upon the forest." Entheiwaan pressed a hand to her heart to emphasize the importance she put on her report. "Var'Kyr have tried to enter Galahir before, but never in such a horde as this. All the sylvan enclaves have been alerted, but as you know, we are few. In the past, we've managed to drive off invaders by harrying them from the shadows of the forest, picking away at their numbers until fear of what awaits them in Galahir made them lose heart and turn back." She ran a lean hand through her silvery hair. "This time, there are so many it is doubtful we can frighten them off. There are too many of them."

Karinna felt a chill sweep through her. The far north was where the barbarians who followed Korgaan came from. It had been a long time since the Battle of Hepshet, but Mescator had warned all of the Celestians against placing too much faith that the fearsome God of the Air was vanquished. She saw in this unprecedented move against Galahir more than just a migration of nomads. It would be in keeping with Korgaan's earlier strikes against the Celestians to make his move while they were beset by other enemies. In the past, that had meant the humans of Chult and Ahmun, now it was the invasion of the ogres that had drawn the attention of the Celestians and their mortal allies.

If this was the hand of Korgaan, then Karinna knew something else. The barbarians were moving against Galahir because of her.

"I will help," Karinna declared, feeling a grim responsibility within herself. "Your people were gracious enough to accept me into your homeland. Galahir is my home too, now, and I will do everything in my power to defend it."

Entheiwaan smiled when she heard Karinna's reply. "None of us doubted you would protect the forest," she said. Then the ranger's expression became troubled again. "We only wonder if your powers are mighty enough to overcome so many enemies."

Karinna shared the elf's worry, for the same concern was on her mind.

***

At the Battle of Five Hills, Karinna had seen the armies of Primovantor and Ophidia, but neither had prepared her for the sight she saw when she reached the edge of the forest. The horde from the north was more vast than both those hosts put together, the plains beyond Galahir seemed a single writhing mass, so great were their numbers. The Var'Kyr were taller and more muscular than any humans she'd seen before, sporting wild beards and shaggy heads of hair. Most were arrayed in mantles of fur and cured animal hides, but some wore iron armor and helms adorned with gold. All carried massive axes and swords, some had wickedly barbed boar-spears or immense longbows. Karinna could only compare the latter weapons to those the sylvan elves bore. She knew the humans wouldn't be able to match the accuracy of any elf, nor the speed with which a ranger could draw and loose a shaft. But there was no denying the obvious strength with which the barbarians would be able to launch arrows at their foes. An elven shaft might deal only a glancing wound, but one shot from those longbows would penetrate deep into any target.

The horde included more than humans. There were hulking, hairy monsters that snarled and snapped at one another even as they advanced toward the forest, brutes with apelike skulls and clawed hands. These, Karinna was told, were ice trolls called down from the frozen wastes beyond even the plains where the Var'Kyr dwelt. Seldom were they seen so far south, and only the mightiest of the barbarians' warlocks could induce so many to leave their glacial caves. The elves spoke of the awful strength trolls possessed and the ferocity that made them fight long after any other creature would succumb to its wounds.

Amid the humans were packs of enormous wolves with snowy fur, larger than any that prowled Galahir or more southerly lands. The animals moved with a sense of purpose Karinna had never seen such beasts display before, and she was stunned to see humans loping along with the packs. These were feral-looking men and women who arrayed themselves only in wolf-pelts and shunned any manner of weaponry beyond the clawed gloves they wore. The elves said that the humans who ran with the wolves were a maddened breed, little more than beasts themselves. The Var'Kyr called them wolf-shirts and except in times of battle shunned them for good reason. The crazed wretches were cannibals who delighted in nothing so much as the flesh of other humans.

Some of the barbarians rode brutish horses with wiry coats and wide hooves, animals equal in size to the huge destriers of Pannithor's knights. These however lacked the elegance and refinement of those carefully bred in civilized lands. Their aspect was that of primitive savagery, a fierce and malicious strength. Most bore gray scars from past fights against both beast and man. Some of them wore crude barding fashioned from the bones of animals, others had no more defense than the ritualistic designs that were painted on them. Karinna could see no evidence of lances among the riders, but many of them had shortbows and quivers of arrows lashed to their saddles. It was easy enough to appreciate the role they were expected to serve in battle.

"How can we defend Galahir against such a horde?" Entheiwaan asked, despair in her tone. Rangers were poised in the trees all around them, bows at the ready. Other sylvan elves waited deeper in the forest. Only those too young or too old to answer the muster had remained behind in their villages. There was an awful fatalism in the eyes of every elf. They knew they were too few to carry the day. All they could do was make the invaders pay a dear price for what they conquered.

"We *will* defend Galahir," Karinna vowed. It was more than just guarding the Sahlirian trees, more even than protecting the sylvan elves. The forest itself was a vital thing, had become to her more important even than her own life. Across all the worlds she'd traveled, she had never found its like. The harmony of Galahir had to be preserved, whatever came to pass.

Karinna closed her eyes and opened herself to the voice of the forest, that subdued vibration that coursed through every living thing within Galahir. Insensate and unfocused, it had ever been nothing more than a feeling before, something even the elves but dimly sensed. Now she drew on that force, calling it into her, refining it into something wondrous. The Celestian's body pulsated with the gathering energies while she watched the barbarian horsemen draw ever closer.

"Pull your people back," Karinna told Entheiwaan.

The ranger looked at her in shock. "That would leave the forest unguarded," she protested.

Green light shone from Karinna's eyes. "The forest will guard itself." There was a commanding tone in her voice that couldn't be denied. Looking chastened, Entheiwaan sounded her horn and called the rangers away from their posts.

Onward came the brutish men. Karinna could feel the tremor from the hooves of their horses pulse through the earth. Already their malice was disrupting the peace of Galahir. The appreciation of that fact coursed through her and rippled away among the trees. She funneled that alarm into specific minds.

The horsemen were still half a mile away when from the green canopy of Galahir a storm arose. From every bough and branch, the birds of the forest took flight. Hawks soared beside sparrows, shrikes followed after crows. Great and small, the winged inhabitants of Galahir answered Karinna's call. A chirping, screeching cloud shot across the plain and dove down on the stunned barbarians. Shortbows remained idle on saddlehorns as the flying swarm engulfed the riders. Men strove to shield their eyes from sharp beaks, while horses reared in sudden pain as talons ripped into their flesh. The charge broke apart as the birds brought ruin upon the enemies of Galahir. The cohesion of the force shattered, and riders galloped away in every direction as they tried to escape their tormentors. The birds pursued their routed foes with all the vindictiveness of creatures protecting their nests.

Sight of the disintegration of their cavalry caused the rest of the horde to pause, but it wasn't long before the barbarians were on the move again. Savage pride spurred them on, refusing to be balked by swarming birds. Drums pounded out a brutal cadence, horns sounded a ferocious call. The Var'Kyr shouted their fury and their determination. Galahir would fall before them.

Now it was the great packs of snow wolves and the feral humans who they ran with that came rushing toward the forest. Faster than the infantry, more agile than the cavalry, the vicious rush intended to gain cover in the forest before any lurking elven archers could whittle away their numbers. Once loose among the trees, the wolves would make for tenacious foes, able to sniff out the most cunningly concealed ranger. Such, Karinna could draw from their savage minds. Such was the ploy she would thwart.

Again, the incredible power she drew from the forest was set loose. This time, she didn't seek to rally the animals. Instead, Karinna would rouse the very spirit of Galahir. She shaped portions of the forest's essence into motes of awareness, spirits with purpose and intent. These were sent speeding away like fistfuls of fireflies. The shimmering energies flew through the woods, seeking out places in which to invest themselves. Trees receptive to the spectral wisps drew them into themselves. The arcane lights evaporated as they were absorbed into the heartwood of oak and birch.

The howling packs sped onward, every yard they advanced without sylvan arrows striking them only inspired them to greater haste. The wolves and madmen were just a few paces away when they discovered that the very trees they thought should hide them were instead their doom. Out from Galahir shambled things never seen before. The trees themselves lumbered out from the forest to give battle. The spirits Karinna formed to oppose the Var'Kyr reshaped the trees that had accepted them into themselves. Their trunks split to assume the semblance of legs, their roots curled up into toes and feet, their branches fused into arms and fingers. Garish knots contorted into frightening faces that poured terror into the ravening wolves.

Many of the animals yelped and withdrew with their tails curled between their legs. Others, the most savage of their breed, charged onward with the pelt-covered wolf-shirts. They threw themselves upon the walking trees, but fangs and claws that could easily rip flesh could no more than scratch the tough bark of Galahir's guardians. The punishing strength in the wooden limbs, however, was more than capable of smashing bones. Of the enemies who reached Karinna's strange warriors, not a single one remained alive a minute later.

Again the horde faltered. This time, it was the presence of a huge and horrible-looking chieftain that spurred them on. Karinna could feel the terrible potency that exuded from the warlord. Was this another of Korgaan's avatars, or but one of the demigods sired by the malignant entity? Whatever his nature, she knew that here was an enemy to be feared.

Now it was the trolls that the barbarians sent charging toward Galahir. The vitalized trees stalked out to confront the hairy monsters, fearlessly marching straight into the onrushing brutes. Troll claws, however, were able to do more than merely scratch the bark of the forest guardians. Limbs were ripped away from trunks, trunks were split asunder by the mauling savagery of the invaders. Splintered scraps soon littered the ground, and the trolls howled their vicious victory for all to hear.

Anger flared within Karinna at the display. She sent more motes of energy sweeping among the trees, but now they didn't separate as they sped away. In fist-sized clutches, they were drawn into the oldest oaks and elms. The strength of the trolls had overcome the first trees she'd endowed with purpose, now she would stir trees of such strength that they would overwhelm the trolls.

The ice trolls were turning from the destruction of their opponents to resume their advance when the newly raised forest warriors strode forth to confront them. As the trolls towered over men, so did these ancient trees loom over the trolls. With the cold vindictiveness of the angry forest, the wooden giants set upon the invaders. Clawed hands gouged deep furrows into the trunks of their attackers, but none were able to tear deep enough to split the heartwood beneath the outer layers of bark. The enormous tree warriors crumpled the trolls into twisted wrecks and tossed their mangled remains toward the Var'Kyr.

Still the barbarians remained steadfast. Bowmen came forth and loosed volleys of arrows at the aroused trees. Fire rippled about the shafts, ignited by the fell power of Korgaan's priests. As they stabbed down into the guardians, their wooden bodies began to burn. Raucous cheers rose from the horde, and while the arboreal giants took flame, the bowmen shifted their target to the green canopy of Galahir itself.

Karinna's eyes blazed as fiercely as the fire that now descended upon the forest. The Var'Kyr weren't going to wait to conquer Galahir before destroying it! The fury that coursed through her spirit drew ever more of the forest's essence into her. She fixated on the orange flames that now menaced her home.

The Celestian's magic caused the flames to spin upward into the air. As she'd done with the trees, so too did she now infuse the fire itself with a semblance of awareness and obedience. Unlike the trees, there was no germ of life to be reshaped, only raw elemental power. This was enough to harness, to congeal into a transitory being. Out from the forest, this entity now flickered across the plain, returning the fire the barbarians had sent to consume Galahir. More and more of the searing elementals took shape as Karinna unleashed them against the Var'Kyr.

The invaders railed beneath the fiery assault. Scores of men were incinerated as the fire elementals swept through their ranks. Karinna's rage swelled, and she fixated her powers on the very ground the barbarians stood upon. As she had with the flames, so too did she now invest the very earth with hostile purpose. Drawing themselves up from the dirt of the plains, brutes formed of rock and soil now joined the attack. Beset by elementals of fire and earth, the horde's courage failed. By the hundreds, then by the thousands, they fled, scattering back across the plains.

Karinna spotted the warlord she knew was connected to Korgaan. The man's gaze seemed to stab through the forest and stare directly at her. In that moment, she knew her rage was as nothing beside the malignance of this being and the god he served. His wrath at being balked on the threshold of Galahir would be unmatched. His vengeance would be swift and brutal, but Karinna doubted it would fall upon the forest when it struck.

The sylvan elves were celebrating the incredible victory. As they came toward Karinna, there was a worshipful reverence on their faces. The elves of Elvenholme had accepted the Celestians as teachers and guides, but those of Galahir looked at her as the men of Primovantor looked on Mescator. She'd transcended their old relationship. Now they truly regarded her as a goddess.

"You've saved Galahir, great and holy one," Entheiwaan muttered, her voice shaking with awe.

Karinna waved her arms, indicating the trees around them. "The forest guarded itself. All I did was to focus the strength that was asleep." She saw that her humility only impressed the elves further, so she cut short her explanation. There were far graver matters to consider.

"Entheiwaan, you must send some of your rangers away from the forest. Further than they've ever gone before. Word must be sent to Primantor and Therennia Adar. They must be warned that the north is roused against them." Karinna tried to impress on the sylvan elves that they'd had but a small taste of a much greater conflict, that they could no longer think in terms of Galahir alone. "Those who serve Korgaan will bring war to the noble races in their own lands. Their god demands it of them. If Primovantor and Elvenholme fall, then the hordes will return here to avenge the defeat they've suffered this day." The last was conjecture, for Karinna couldn't be certain when the barbarians would try again. It was why she dared not leave the forest to bring warning to the other Celestians herself.

"They will be warned," Entheiwaan swore. She bowed her head and added, "My rangers won't fail the Green Lady."

***

-877, Time of Light

Vast swathes of Pannithor and Elvenholme had been despoiled by Korgaan's hordes by the time Mescator and his companions returned from the Mammoth Steppes. Nor was it men and elves alone who had been casualties of the fighting. Three Celestians who'd taken the field against the barbarians were dead, their immortal spark snuffed out by the war god's spawn. Bitterly, Mescator blamed himself for their losses, feeling that if he'd been present to repulse the Var'Kyr, things would have been different. Still, he knew Primovantor could never have fought war on two fronts. It had been essential to turn back the ogres. Now, the full might of the civilized nations could be turned against the invasion from the north.

An enormous force had been assembled upon Mescator's return. Ten thousand soldiers of Primovantor were in the army the Celestians now led. With them were twelve hundred elves and twice as many dwarfs from Abercarr. Nearly a hundred ogres had remained to offer their services to the humans in exchange for weapons of iron and steel. The Ophidians too had sent mercenaries to fight for Primovantor. Tothmenes was no friendlier than before, but the God-King understood if the Grand Republic fell, Ophidia would be the next to face the rampaging horde from the north.

One other asset was now being brought into play. Kyron had finally managed to convince Draumdraak's brood to enter the war. Seven dragons were awaiting his summons, ready to shower the barbarians with fiery death.

The battlefield was one the Var'Kyr had forced upon Primovantor. The city of Farhn had endured months of siege by the barbarians. The warlords who commanded the hordes knew they couldn't push deeper into the south while leaving this bastion intact at their rear. So they'd settled in and tried to break the city, either by battering down its walls or starving its populace. The Var'Kyr were careful to conserve their strength, not willing to expend too many of their fighters in the siege, but when word of Mescator's army marching forth to relieve Farhn reached them, the barbarians unleashed an assault without restraint.

"They've put the city to the torch," Oskan growled as they watched the city burn from a hilltop.

"They've left nothing here to save," Mescator agreed, vengeance in his voice. The fields and villages surrounding Farhn had been laid waste, demolished by the invaders. Barbarous totems littered the landscape, savage columns fashioned from the skulls of the dead. The slaughter had been almost beyond comprehension. The city itself was faring even worse. Clouds of smoke billowed from its burning streets, fingers of flame flashed from its towers and parapets.

"We're too late to rescue Farhn, but we can still avenge its people," Mescator continued. His eyes focused on the great horde that marched across the ruined farmland to meet the army that had come to end their rampage. It was a force even larger than that which had been sent against Galahir. Even from a distance, Mescator could sense the powerful magics that surrounded the barbarians.

"Their warlocks protect them," Valandor told Mescator, reading his leader's thoughts. He closed his eyes and made arcane passes with his hands. "I can sense strong wards to shield them from hostile spells. Illusions, too, to trick our eyes. Much of that horde could be naught but a phantasm." He shook his head and his tone deepened. "Or there might be thousands more hidden to us. We can't depend on what we see to deploy our soldiers."

Mescator digested Valandor's warning. "It isn't our soldiers who will bring retribution on Korgaan's slaves." He drew the sword sheathed at his side and held it aloft. The weapon crackled with energy as he sent a beam of dazzling light shooting from it into the smoke-choked sky. The other Celestians were silent. The signal had been given. Now they awaited what must follow.

Kyron's dragons descended through the clouds of smoke. Hidden behind that dark mantle, they'd waited only for Mescator's signal to strike. Now they swooped down upon the advancing barbarians. It was the invaders' turn to burn as dragonfire engulfed them by the score. Seven dragons ravaged the Var'Kyr, returning to them the flaming death they'd brought to Farhn. Leading the dragons from Draumdraak's back was Kyron himself, clad in armor fashioned from draconic scales and bearing a bow so mighty even an ogre struggled to draw it. He loosed arrows as big as javelins into the enemy, picking out Korgaan's savage priests and the robed warlocks for his targets.

The havoc wrought against the barbarians was incredible, but the Var'Kyr stubbornly held their ground. Mescator was stunned by their courage, but too late did he find there was strategy behind their bravery. "Illusions!" Valandor cursed when the change occurred. "That's what the vandals were hiding!"

Concealed by the spells of warlocks were four towering creatures. Mescator had seen giants marching along with the ogre tribes, but they were nothing like these. Forty feet tall with pale blue skin and beards that looked more like frost than hair, these giants wore breastplates of steel and metal helms. They carried quivers of enormous lances, each weapon twenty feet long and with a barbed tip as big as a man.

The giants had been tasked with a specific role for Korgaan's army. Only too well did the god remember his defeat at the Battle of Hepshet. The giants had been brought here as dragonslayers. The moment they were revealed, the giants cast their lances at the flying reptiles. Where the arrows and spears of mere men glanced off the armored scales, the missiles thrown by the giants struck deep. One dragon fell to earth, a lance deep in its chest and blood streaming from its wound. It was dead before it hit the ground. A second dragon crashed with its wing transfixed to its side. Even as the wounded beast struggled, the barbarians were swarming over it, hacking it apart with axes and swords.

The dragons swept away, then turned back to the assault. One giant collapsed with two of Kyron's arrows in its skull. Another was knocked flat by a diving dragon, the reptile's fangs and claws tearing at the brute's flesh. The other giants were surrounded by flames, but their icy bodies resisted even dragonfire. A third dragon fell when it opened its jaws to bathe a giant in its incinerating breath. The huge lance flew at it as it opened its jaws and punched through the back of its throat. Mortally stricken, the wyrm crushed dozens of barbarians under it as it dropped to earth.

"Attack!" Mescator bellowed. The command rang out across the fields as Primovantor and its allies hastened to support the embattled dragons. Valandor set his magic searing into one of the remaining giants, killing him before he could strike down another of Draumdraak's brood. The last of them collapsed when Draumdraak himself dove down to attack. Such was the ancient reptile's size and strength that he lifted the giant hundreds of feet into the sky before letting him hurtle earthward and shatter scores of barbarians beneath his bulk. A shaft from Kyron's bow settled the crippled brute before he could rise again.

The death of the last giants took the heart from the horde. Still faced with four dragons and now locked in combat with the Celestians and their army, the barbarians began to break away. There was, however, no escape for them. In their viciousness, they'd put to the torch the only place that might have provided them a haven. Mescator offered the enemy no quarter when he gave the order to Primovantor's army. "Drive them into the flames."

It was slaughter. Of the thousands that had decimated Farhn, only a few hundred slipped through the chaos to quit the field. The rest died by sword or fire. Mescator took no pleasure from the massacre, but there was satisfaction in knowing the people butchered by the Var'Kyr had been avenged.

As he emerged from the fighting, Mescator saw Kyron and Draumdraak swoop down and land in the bloodied field. The other dragons soared over the scene in ever widening circles. The leader of the Celestians made his way to the dragonrider. Coming closer, he saw a misshapen corpse clenched in the reptile's claws. Draumdraak let the carcass roll onto the ground. Though he'd never set eyes on the malformed body, Mescator felt a sickening familiarity.

"One of Korgaan's avatars," Mescator named the thing. He cast an anxious look toward Farhn, where Oskan was busy leading the troops against the barbarians' last holdouts.

"This was the leader... here," Kyron said. "Another horde, just as large, is moving south from the edge of the Dragontooth Mountains." He climbed down from Draumdraak's back. "Maybe when they learn what has happened to this army, they'll turn back."

Mescator shook his head. "It is Korgaan's malice that sends them to fight. They'll not defy a god who walks among them." He looked over the carnage that littered the fields. "We'll have to fight them. Just as we did here."

"That will be impossible," Kyron said, his voice subdued. He looked aside at Draumdraak. The great dragon closed his eyes and lifted his head. A hiss rasped from between his clenched jaws as he fanned his wings and rose into the sky to join the others. "Three of Draumdraak's brood died here today. Any obligation he feels to us has been repaid. The dragons won't risk themselves again to fight our battles. They're returning to their caves in the mountains."

Mescator watched as the three reptiles turned and flew off into the clouds of smoke. It wasn't long before they were lost to his sight. A great weight settled on his shoulders. A second horde, as large as the one that had destroyed Farhn. Only this time, they would have to fight it without the dragons to help them.

"We have no choice," Mescator declared. "We have to fight, or Korgaan will destroy us... and along with us, everything we've tried to build here. It isn't a question of victory or defeat, but a choice between triumph or annihilation."

Chapter XIV

-876, Time of Light

Valandor was sickened by the almost continuous slaughter that had raged across the land for over a year. The forces hurled against Elvenholme and Primovantor seemed inexhaustible. One barbaric horde would be broken only for another to appear in its place. Nor were the Var'Kyr alone, for they brought with them giants and ice trolls, even companies of ogre mercenaries, to throw against the civilized realms. Many strange and horrifying beasts were brought into battle by Korgaan's disciples, terrible creature of immense size that combined the most murderous aspects of bears, wolves, and lions. There were great black-feathered eagles and enormous serpents covered in fur, ghastly entities shaped from glacial ice that froze men solid with a blast of their breath. All the north seemed to have answered Korgaan's call to battle.

Reposing within the semi-material sphere he'd evoked for himself to fend off both the morning snow and the stink of yesterday's fighting, Valandor contemplated the toll this war with Korgaan had already claimed. Four Celestians had died in battles now, for the previous day had seen Neron crushed by one of the war god's avatars. It was difficult for him to accept that the vivacious Neron was gone, for among the Celestians, he'd been a unifying personality. Songster and poet, he'd less taste for war than even Karinna, but to protect the mortals he'd come to love, Neron marched out to challenge the invaders. Now he was no more, his immortal spark extinguished by Korgaan's savagery.

The mortals too had sustained grievous losses. King Yarinathar of Elvenholme was slain by a giant, snatched from the saddle of his steed and crushed in the monster's fist. The loss of their king filled the elves with a deadly sorrow. Even on campaign, the elves had exhibited culture and refinement, carrying themselves with a nobility even the dwarfs grudgingly admired. Where there had been before a certain grace and hope about the elves, there was now only a grim, unwavering determination. No longer did the elves show mercy to the defeated and offer quarter to the Var'Kyr. Wherever the elves now met the enemy, only death remained in their wake.

Primovantor too had suffered. Many nobles had sacrificed their lives fighting the barbarians, bringing to an end bloodlines that could be traced to the beginnings of the kingdom. The High Consul himself had been mortally injured at a place called Blood Creek, his position temporarily filled by his daughter Laria while mages and surgeons tried to nurse him back to health. Valandor didn't hold much hope that they could. High Consul Quinton had been stabbed by one of Korgaan's demigods with a blade steeped in such fell magics that even the Celestians were unable to help with his wounds.

Korgaan. How little they'd really understood about this enemy. All the conflicts with him in the past had been merely overtures, probes on the god's part to test their strength. Because those who served him were crude and barbarous, they'd made the mistake of thinking him to be likewise. Valandor knew he'd certainly underestimated their foe. It was in keeping with Korgaan's pose as a god of warfare that his dominion would include strategy as well as brutality. If the Celestians were going to win, they would have to decipher his plans before they could unfold. The barbarians were in retreat now, but Valandor wasn't convinced their god was even close to beaten.

The protective sphere Valandor had woven about his camp rippled as two Celestians stepped through the barrier. He looked away from the crystal in which he'd been gazing and greeted the arrivals. Oskan and Kyron, both carrying with them the stink of battle. In the fiercest of the day's fighting, they'd been in the thick of the fray. Each had overcome one of Korgaan's foul offspring in personal combat, but they took no cheer from the deed. All knew that there were more of the demigods out there. Like the Var'Kyr they dominated, it felt as though their numbers were endless.

"Have you been able to spy their line of retreat?" Oskan asked, pointing to the crystal.

Valandor laid his palm upon the scrying stone. It was a lesser light to the great Scrying Star in the Tower of Heaven, crafted under the exacting supervision of Reiliur, but still its power had its limits. Even in the hands of a Celestian. "Korgaan's priests and warlocks strive against me. I can only gain the most infrequent glimpses of their army."

"Do you still flee into the north?" Kyron wanted to know. "Mescator's great fear is that we're being drawn into a trap. While we chase after one horde, another slinks around us to attack the lands we've sworn to protect."

"Only Eoswain remains in Elvenholme," Oskan said. "In Primovantor, there are only Hermanas and the twins. Abercarr is guarded by Fulgria and Belkon. Karinna abides in Galahir." He pointed at the great encampment all around Valandor's refuge. "The rest of us are here."

"That is why I think the lands we guard are safe," Valandor stated. "Korgaan only strikes at these places so that he may hurt the Celestians. His war has ever been against us and what we represent. We offer Pannithor a new way, a vision to shake off the shackles of the old gods. He would draw the whole of the world back into chains. A barbarous place of ceaseless conflict over which he would reign supreme." He shook his head. "We are the enemies Korgaan needs to destroy to achieve his victory. I think by drawing so many of us together in one place, Mescator has offered a target that Korgaan can't resist."

Kyron's expression was doubtful. "We've beaten the Var'Kyr every time they turn to fight. Another day, and they will be past the Dragontooth Mountains. We'll be fighting the barbarians in their own lands."

"Remember that Korgaan cares for his followers only so far as they serve his interests," Valandor said. "That they must surrender their homes to us as they retreat is of no consequence to him."

"Then he wants us to pursue?" Oskan mused. "Mescator is right."

"Partly," Valandor replied. "I remain convinced that Korgaan wants us to follow deeper into the north. He won't risk having Mescator turn back by splitting his forces and sending some to ravage Primovantor and Elvenholme." He nodded to himself. "Yes, I think even Galahir is safe... at least until Korgaan has drawn us into whatever trap he's prepared." He waved his hands in a gesture of futility. "If he prevails, I don't think Karinna will be able to save the forest again. Nor do I think the others who've stayed behind will stand long if our campaign ends in disaster."

"You've told Mescator this?" Oskan wondered.

"He knows," Valandor answered. "He knows that there aren't enough Celestians to both defend the lands under our protection and to persecute a resolution to this war. Eoswain and the others stay behind for a more tactical reason. They stay behind to assure the mortals that their nations will be safe, that the families and homes they leave behind will be defended." He looked each of his visitors in the eye. "While we know our limitations, the mortals don't, and that is the difference. They'll fight better if their minds aren't burdened with worries over those they've left behind."

Oskan frowned. "The dragons returned to their caves in the mountains because they viewed their losses as counting for nothing. Mescator thinks the other mortals will behave the same way and withdraw from the fight if we don't reassure them."

"But if we fail, then there's no protection for them anyway," Kyron objected, caring little for the ploy and the necessary manipulation of those who looked to the Celestians for guidance. "It is a false hope that gives them heart."

Valandor laid his hand again upon the crystal ball. "Korgaan hides his intentions from us, but of one thing we can be sure. If he isn't stopped, he will vent his malevolence on the noble races again. It is us he wants, and by accepting his challenge, we may yet force his hand.

A bitter smile worked itself onto his face. "Korgaan seeks to trap us, but if we're careful, we might trap him instead."

***

The Dragontooth Mountains were but a memory on the distant horizon. The lands that Mescator now beheld were such that had never been seen before by any Celestian. They were a harsh tundra speckled with marshes and forests. Barbarian prisoners called this region the Ardovikian Plain. Somewhere to the east were the Mammoth Steppes and the homelands of the ogres. Away into the distant north were vast mountains of ice and a frozen sea. Savage, unforgiving realms where only savage and unforgiving creatures survived.

Mescator could tell that the mortal soldiers were uneasy. It was most pronounced among the humans, but even among the elves and dwarfs there was a sense of mounting anxiety. Only the ogre mercenaries were nonplussed venturing so far into the grim north in pursuit of the barbarians. For the rest, they were venturing into the unknown, and the uncertainty of what lay ahead wore upon their nerves.

The mere presence of the Celestians gave heart to many, but Mescator himself would have been much more at ease if he knew what lay ahead of them. Valandor's scrying spells were continually thwarted by the magic of Korgaan's mystics. Only the most fleeting of glimpses were afforded to him when he found a way to slip past the sorcerous veil that confounded his divinations. Those prisoners captured by the army could offer only the most fragmented report of these lands. Before the great hordes had been unleashed against the south, few among them had ventured more than a hundred miles from their villages and hunting grounds. Frustratingly, the nomadic horsemen who had once been a fixture of the barbarian hosts were seldom seen now, and none had been taken captive. Mescator would have dearly liked to interrogate one of these far-roving riders and gained better information about what lay ahead of them. Even the great mountains of ice and frozen sea the Var'Kyr spoke of was expressed in the vaguest terms. Some claimed them to be only a week's travel, others claimed it would be many months before the Celestians crossed the plains and reached the edge of the frigid domain.

Frustratingly, the barbarians also spoke of a holy place, a site to which their priests and shamans made pilgrimage each year to render to Korgaan their blood-vow. This place they called the Graveyard of Swords, but none had ever seen it or could even express in which direction it could be found. A few even whispered it didn't exist on Pannithor at all but in the ethereal world where the old gods dwelled.

Day after day the army marched, sometimes catching stragglers from the barbarian horde. Simple villages and crude strongholds were sometimes discovered, but always these were found to have been deserted. In their ferocity, the Var'Kyr slit the throats of those too young or too old to join the retreat. Mescator reflected that they must have expected the Celestians and their followers to treat them as the barbarians had treated those in Primovantor and Elvenholme who fell into their clutches. When he considered the grim vengeance the elves exacted for Yarinathar, he appreciated that such fears weren't entirely unfounded.

It was a week into their march across the plains before Mescator's worry over what lay ahead was alleviated. From out of the east, a large company appeared. Not an enemy closing in on them, but allies seeking to join them. The Celestians had to assure the mortals they led that the strange host bore them no malice, for it was a sight beyond their ken. Lumbering creatures with wooden bodies in only the roughest humanoid shape, it seemed as though an entire forest was marching across the plain. Some of the weird beings were little larger than a human, while others towered above even the ogres. Soaring above the bizarre army was a flock of enormous eagles. Not the black birds of Korgaan's north, but regal creatures with golden plumage. Upon the back of the greatest of these animals rode someone Mescator hadn't expected to see. Karinna, the Mistress of the Sahlirian Tree.

The giant eagle wheeled above the mortal army, coming to earth where Mescator sat astride his warhorse. Karinna bowed to him in salutation. "Hail and respect, great Mescator."

"And to you, Karinna," Mescator returned her greeting. Most of the other Celestians were assuring the mortals that the walking trees weren't adversaries, but Valandor divested himself from the task to speak with Karinna.

"I am surprised to see you here," Valandor said. He scowled as he considered that the forest battalions had also failed to appear in his crystal. "We had thought you would remain to defend Galahir and the Sahlirian groves."

Karinna smiled at his uneasiness. "Korgaan's warlocks aren't the only ones who can cloak themselves from prying magic. I regret it was necessary to deceive you, but to allow a friend to learn of our march would expose us to the enemy as well." She turned and regarded Mescator. "As to remaining in Galahir, I know there is no victory to be had there. To save the forest, Korgaan must be defeated. Whether I stay or leave, it makes no difference now. The forest will not suffer while I am away."

"It is a wonderful army you bring to bolster our forces," Mescator commented as the trees came nearer. "The rangers who brought word to Primovantor spoke of how you defended Galahir, but the tale is less fantastic than the reality."

"Galahir defended itself," Karinna corrected him. "All I did was to focus what was already there. Give it the urgency to act." She pointed at the shambling tree-warriors. "Though they have marched far from where they set their roots, they understand why they must fight." She stroked the neck feathers of the eagle she sat astride. "Were the trip not so far, I should have rallied the whole of the forest to move against Korgaan. As it stands, I have brought such as would have the stamina for both the journey and the battle ahead."

Valandor nodded to the north, at the low hills and tall pines into which the barbarians they pursued had fled. "We've chased them all the way from Primovantor, and they give no evidence they'll stop. It could be they intend to draw us all the way to the mountains of ice and the edge of the world."

"Not so very far," Karinna assured him. "There was purpose to joining you here. I've not been so isolated as you might think in Galahir. Messages have reached the forest. When first you drove the barbarians past the Dragontooth Mountains, I set the sylvan elves to watching them. Spells can confound divinations and scrying stones, but not the eyes of rangers."

"Then you know what lies ahead of us," Mescator said.

"Indeed." Karinna's visage was grim. "You've hounded the Var'Kyr through their own lands, but before you is a place they won't abandon to an enemy. To them it is holy ground, the place where their priests make offerings to Korgaan."

"The Graveyard of Swords," Mescator invoked the name the barbarians had spoken only in hushed whispers.

A haunted look came into Karinna's eyes. "Just so. Many of the rangers who followed the route of the barbarians never returned. Those who did report to me spoke of a terrible plateau where the earth is littered with bones and the soil is the color of blood. It is there that Korgaan has gathered his slaves... and his spawn."

"Were your scouts able to give an accounting of numbers?" Valandor asked, worry in his tone.

"Of the barbarians, simply a great multitude," Karinna replied, "but the rangers have seen Korgaan's offspring before. They reckoned not less than two score of them."

Mescator looked aside at Valandor. "Enough for each of us and to spare. It will be no easy battle."

"No, it will not," Valandor agreed, his voice still laced with concern.

"It will be no easier if we delay," Mescator declared. "To delay would only mean allowing Korgaan to grow his power until he feels ready to strike at us again."

Valandor shook his head. "You forget that in only a few decades the conjunction will occur once more. Eoswain and Reiliur will be able to bring more Celestians through the gates. We'll be stronger then."

"Korgaan too might know this," Mescator said. "You yourself know it is reckless to underestimate the limitations of his intelligence. We can't depend upon him allowing us the chance to bring more Celestians across. Besides, if we did turn back, there's no saying when the Var'Kyr would attack again, and how much suffering they would visit upon the mortals we would protect."

"This could be Korgaan's intention," Valandor persisted. "Force us here into a fight on his own ground." He turned to Karinna. "Your elves make it sound like the enemy is waiting for us. I don't think Korgaan would push for a fight he wasn't certain his slaves could win. If he defeats us here, then what is there to stop him from pushing on to Ileureleith and destroying the Tower of Heaven before any more Celestians are brought to Pannithor?"

Mescator curled his hand into a fist. He looked across the army that had marched so far. Most had done so because of their faith in the Celestians, their trust that Mescator would save their homes from ever again knowing the threat of barbarian invaders. "What you say might be true, old friend. But again, it could be that Korgaan depends upon us to quail before him at the last and turn back before we can break his dominion here." He shook his head and stared off into the unknown north. "Shadows lie to either side of us. If I must go into a place I cannot see, then I choose the path that offers the most promise.

"We'll march on to this Graveyard of Swords," Mescator declared. "We'll challenge the might of Korgaan just as we have that of Bhanek, Ohmpek, and Shobik. We'll free Pannithor from the last of its merciless old gods."

***

The Graveyard of Swords was aptly named, Oskan thought. The place could be sensed before it could be seen, an atmosphere of dread and malice that reached into the mind and darkened the spirit. Once it was in sight, the effect only became worse. A craggy plateau that rose from between two streams of sluggish, icy water. The sides of the plateau were littered with bones, and in the absence of skeletons, there showed through earth that looked like crusted blood. The flattened top of the plateau was marked by the thousands of sword that pierced its surface. Blades of every shape and size, some so aged that they were little more than knobs of rust, others so new that their hilts glistened in the sunlight. Amid the sprawl of swords, a massive stone had been raised, a great slab around which a parade of feral priests marched and chanted, striking their shaven heads with sharpened blades. Whenever one of the zealots collapsed from his wounds, the others kicked him aside and continued their crazed procession.

The ground below the plateau swarmed with Var'Kyr and their monstrous allies. Oskan had seen larger hordes of enemies over the course of the war, but as he gazed down on these from the crest of a rise overlooking the little valley, he felt an intensity of belligerence that surpassed those greater armies. He saw in the eyes of the barbarians a fearful resignation. Win or die, they intended to fight to the last. They would ask no quarter and show none to their foes. Beyond them, on the far side of the icy streams, he could see the members of their tribes unable to take arms in the coming battle. Children and crook-backed elders, maimed warriors and crippled champions. All of them looked ready to cast themselves into the icy waters at the first sign that defeat was upon them.

"They will fight to the last," Kyron commented. The dusky hunter and the fair Liliana sat upon magnificent elven steeds, animals bred for their courage and speed. Since the Siege of Farhn, Kyron bore a special enmity for giants, and the horses from Elvenholme were the only ones that didn't balk at the smell of the hulking monsters. Kyron had taken upon himself the mantle of giant-killer, so it followed course that Liliana would also appoint herself to the role.

"Here they fight not only for Korgaan, but for their families as well," Liliana said.

Oskan turned and looked at the soldiers of Primovantor arrayed around them. Hundreds of faces seeing the same sight that the Celestians saw. Some faces were pale with fear, others dark with hate, but on none did he spy the softness of sympathy. "Men in Primovantor and elves in Elvenholme fought for their families too," Oskan reminded Liliana. "How many of them lost everything they cared about to these barbarians? Pity not these Var'Kyr. They've brought judgment upon themselves."

There was a flicker of shock on Liliana's face when she heard Oskan speak. "Don't confuse justice and vengeance."

Oskan shook his head. "Even if you tried to spare them, they wouldn't let you. Korgaan has enslaved them for so long that it is all they know."

As if in answer to his words, the barbarians began to beat their shields and howl their defiance at the Celestians and their allies. Amid the throng moved the grotesques that Oskan knew had been touched with Korgaan's power. Whether demigods or avatars, the abominations served as rallying points for the Var'Kyr, whipping them into new heights of frenzy.

A trumpet blared, and Oskan turned his head to see Mescator on his mighty destrier. He pointed his sword into the sky, and a bright flash rose from it. Commands were relayed through the mortal formations. Archers fanned out to send volleys down into the enemy. The tree creatures summoned by Karinna gathered at the flanks of the host to act as bulwarks against the barbarians. Dwarfs surged forward, their broad axes and thick armor ready to meet the enemy.

Oskan looked away from the gathering conflict and back to the top of the plateau. Only two of the priests remained marching around the slab of stone, and as he watched, one of them fell, his forehead slashed by the sword he bore. The instant he was alone, the last of the priests leaped onto the stone. In a revolting display, he took the blade he held and drove it into his own body, spilling his entrails across the primitive altar. The stone glowed with a crimson light.

The atmosphere of malice that hovered over the Graveyard of Swords now became a miasma of raw, unremitting hate. Anguished howls rose from the barbarian horde. The misshapen champions that constituted demigods and avatars writhed in pain. Blood poured from their bodies as eyes ruptured in their sockets and teeth burst in their jaws. Up from the sudden carnage, Oskan could see tendrils of black energy streaming away, burrowing like spectral maggots into the bone-littered sides of the plateau.

A tremendous roar shook the earth, and close upon it came a bestial bellow. "Mescator spare us," Oskan heard the human soldiers around him gasp. He glanced aside and saw both Liliana and Kyron staring toward the Graveyard of Swords in horror. He knew that his own face must be as stricken as theirs.

The plateau pulsed and swelled, then seemed to rise up into the sky. Great slabs of rock and bone shifted and fell as they were sloughed away from a gigantic shape. Oskan had been awed by the sheer size of Gorgroth, but what he saw now rivaled the gargantuan lizard. It was a titanic frame of roughly human shape, two hundred feet tall with purplish flesh and nodules of calcification spattered across its enormity like warts on a toad. Everywhere its skin was pierced by swords, the weapons that had previously been stabbed into the plateau, and from each wound a trickle of black ichor seeped. The limbs were corded with tick ropes of muscle, and its chest swelled with strength. Rearing up from its shoulders was a massive head with curled horns and strips of scaly hair. The face was fiendish in its evil, with three close-set eyes that blazed with frozen fire. A mouth distorted by the great tusks that sprouted from its jaws leered obscenely at the Celestians, but in the curl of its lips there was a note of sadistic mirth.

"It is Korgaan!" Oskan exclaimed, sensing at once the nature of the titan. "Not an avatar, but the war god incarnate!"

"He's drawn his essence from all the beings that carried a portion of him within themselves," Liliana declared. "Slaughtered them all so he might reclaim his energies and bind them into a single manifestation."

"This was the trap," Kyron snarled. "To lead us here, where he could focus his full might against us." He tried to calm his elven steed, for even its brave heart quailed before the manifestation of Korgaan. "Bring us here where his power was strongest."

Oskan shook his head as the monstrosity used its four arms to raise itself from the plateau's rubble. He could see the ground crackle under the war god's touch. "Korgaan can't maintain this incarnation for long. That's why he worked through avatars and demigods. Pannithor can't sustain such a concentration of power."

"It will sustain him long enough for his purpose," Liliana said. Around them, soldiers were screaming in terror. The army that a moment before had seemed poised on the edge of victory now teetered at the precipice of utter collapse.

At Mescator's command, the archers shifted their aim and pelted Korgaan with waves of arrows. The missiles clattered harmlessly from the god's purple hide. Mages and wizards unleashed their magic against him, but their spells only crackled uselessly upon his skin. Oskan saw Valandor focus his energies into a sheet of lightning that surged across the landscape. The streams rippled with electricity as it swept over them, shocking the barbarians who stood in the water and leaving them blackened husks. But when the spell struck Korgaan, it was diverted into the swords piercing his colossal frame. Some of the blades exploded as the force overwhelmed them, but most successfully diffused the attack.

"Spear and sword! Axe and maul!" Mescator's voice thundered above the army, projected by the intensity of his power. At his direction, the templars charged down from the rise into the plain. The Gold Blades plowed into the Var'Kyr, smashing them beneath the hooves of their horses as they rushed toward Korgaan.

"Free peoples of Pannithor! With me!" Oskan shouted, drawing his blade of Ophidian copper and directing the soldiers at his back against the gigantic war god. Kyron and Liliana followed alongside him as they rushed into the horde below.

The valley echoed with the clash of battle. Dwarfs met the claws of trolls with axe and shield. Elves peppered giants with arrows until their brutish endurance was overcome and the ground shook with their falling bulk. Knights from Primantor rode down barbarians clad in the pelts of bears and lions. The tree creatures of Galahir tore into packs of white-furred wolves until their limbs were red from the slaughter.

Above it all, however, loomed Korgaan himself. Oskan thought the war god reveled in the havoc, drawing glee from the striking down of both follower and foe. His clawed hands tore into the enemies who came within his reach. He lifted screaming fistfuls of men and dwarfs and hurled them to their deaths against the slopes of the valley. His tramping feet crushed elves and tree-warriors alike into ruin. The great eagles that dove at his head were swatted down like flies. Oskan saw Karinna narrowly avoid being caught by Korgaan's clutching fingers, her flying mount wheeling away at the last instant to dodge the mighty grip.

The cavalry Oskan led to the attack fought their way through files of barbarian warriors to finally reach the hulking war god. Lances stabbed into Korgaan's legs, drawing out the foul ichor that coursed through his veins. The titan reacted with a vengeful sweep of his claws. Dozens of knights were felled by the savage assault. Oskan spurred his bucking steed away from the monster's reach.

Then he heard an anguished scream. Liliana! He spun about, nearly breaking his mount's neck as he jerked at the reins. He saw her jump down from her saddle. The cry wasn't an indicator of her own peril, but that of another. On the ground, strewn beside the mangled wreckage of his elven steed lay Kyron. The Celestian hunter's body was painted in his own blood.

Oskan spurred toward the scene, but as he did, a shadow fell across him. Korgaan had noticed Kyron's fall and was reaching down to seize the fallen Celestian. He turned his horse about and raised his enchanted blade, intent on giving Liliana time to drag Kyron to safety. He knew it was a gesture that even if successful could only mean his own destruction, but he would stand his ground before the sky god's malevolence.

Before Korgaan could close his fist around Oskan, the titan lurched back and pawed at his face. One of his eyes dripped from his head in a welter of torn jelly. Diving away from the enraged god was Karinna on her eagle, gore dripping from its talons. "Kyron! Quickly!" Oskan shouted to Liliana. She lifted the wounded Celestian from the ground and threw him across the back of Oskan's horse. The animal stumbled at the double weight, but regained its footing as he urged it away from the fighting. Liliana hastened after him, her retreat covered by the mortal soldiers who yet strove against Korgaan.

Oskan regained the rise and swiftly dismounted. He laid Kyron down on the ground, shaking his head when he saw the severity of the hunter's wounds. He regretted the gesture, for despite his hurt, Kyron was aware enough to know what it meant. "Another victim to add to Korgaan's sins," Kyron cursed, blood trickling from his mouth as he spoke. He glanced away when he noted Liliana rushing toward them, her face twisted with panic. "All great things are bought only through sacrifice," he tried to console her. "We must prevail against Korgaan."

"I won't leave you," Liliana vowed, kneeling beside him and cradling his ashen face in her hands. "Not while there's still breath in you. Not while your heart still beats."

Oskan thought neither of those things would last long but kept from saying as much to Liliana, unwilling to snuff out her fragile hope. The next instant, he swung around and raised his sword. A shadow had fallen across the three of them. He laughed in relief when he saw that it was cast not by Korgaan's hand, but by the great wings of Karinna's eagle. She turned the animal and landed beside them. Jumping down from the bird's back, she scrambled to Kyron's side. Her eyes glowed with jade fires as she laid her hands on his battered body.

"This will hurt," Karinna warned, "but it may keep your life from fading." Though she spoke to Kyron, her words seemed more intended for Liliana, advising her that whatever her lover suffered, it was necessary.

"Come, Liliana, we must help Mecsator," Oskan suggested, trying to lead her away from whatever would transpire. He pointed back at the battlefield where the other Celestians and their allies tried to whittle away Korgaan and his followers.

Liliana only shook her head. "I'll not leave him," she repeated. Bitterness overcame her face. "We can't defeat Korgaan, no matter how many of us there are." She clasped Kyron's hand as he snarled in pain. Karinna's energies were spreading into him, vine-like coils of magic that dug into his ravaged flesh, trying to weave him back together. "It would take a force mightier than we have here to overcome Korgaan."

Oskan's spirit surged with inspiration. "The dragons!" he hissed. He crouched down beside Kyron. "The dragons! If we could convince them to fight for us one last time..."

Through his pain, Kyron managed a weak smile. "They won't come," he protested.

"We have to try," Oskan insisted. "At least ask them!" His tone became imploring. "Tell me where they can be found. How I can speak with them."

Kyron struggled through his agony to focus on Oskan. "I know where Draumdraak's cave is," he said, and as he spoke, he placed the image in Oskan's mind. "To speak with the dragon, you must drink of his blood." He winced as pain closed around him. "But they won't come..."

"You can say that after I've failed," Oskan told him. He looked to Karinna. "I must borrow your eagle. I need it to fly me to Draumdraak's cave."

Karinna bowed her head. Though she kept her hands on Kyron, she gazed back at the eagle. For just an instant, its eyes took on the same green glow as hers. "Tell her where you wish to go, and she will take you there."

Oskan hurried to the giant bird and climbed onto its back. He stared again at the desperate battle that was consuming the Graveyard of Swords. He could see Mescator's blazing sword shining amid the melee. "I am going to our last hope of victory," he said as he urged the eagle into the air. Once it was high enough in the sky, he turned it south. Toward the Dragontooth Mountains where he would find Draumdraak's cave.

***

The wyrm's cave could be smelled from miles away. But for Karinna's magic, Oskan was certain the eagle would have turned away. The area around the cavern was utterly desolate, devoid of any manner of life. The mortals said that the presence of a dragon was poisonous, and where they made their lairs, nothing else could thrive. Oskan didn't know if there was always truth to such tales, but certainly the approach to Draumdraak's cave supported the legends.

He left the eagle on a rocky ledge outside the dank cavern. Oskan felt the hot exhalations of the dragon plucking at him as he ventured toward the opening. The musky, reptilian odor was almost overwhelming now. He could hear the low hiss of the dragon's breath as he marched into the darkness. A slight exertion of his powers enabled Oskan to see through the gloom without the need for light. What he saw was a magnificent sprawl of gold and jewels, a hoard of treasure to make any king of the noble races look like a beggar. Upon this heap of wealth reposed the red-scaled bulk of Draumdraak. The reptile opened his slitted eyes as Oskan approached.

Remembering what Kyron had said, Oskan gestured to his mouth and then to Draumdraak. The wyrm peered at him for a moment, then stabbed one of his toes with a long claw. He held the digit out toward the Celestian. Oskan nodded and carefully dipped his finger in the bead of blood that dripped from the cut. He wiped the hot gore on his tongue. Kyron hadn't warned him of the sudden pain the dragon's blood would inflict. His knees buckled as torment blazed through every particle of his being.

The pain was only for a moment, however, and when it passed, Oskan realized he could feel the dragon's thoughts inside his brain. A lesser connection than the telepathy among the Celestians, but a connection just the same.

Draumdraak was puzzled by Oskan's appearance at his cave, a note of annoyance at the disturbance. He was wise enough to know that the Celestians had need of the dragons again, and his rejection of that request was the first thing that he conveyed to Oskan.

"Kyron, the Celestian who healed you when you were dying," Oskan told the dragon. "Now it is he who is dying." It wasn't an untruth, for he wasn't sure if Karinna's magic could heal the hunter's wounds or how the battle may have turned in the hours since the eagle had borne him away from the Graveyard of Swords.

There was a fierce sense of honor and obligation in Draumdraak's heart. Not concern or sorrow as a mammal might know it, but still a regret that stirred the reptile's blood. Still, a dragon lacked the emotions necessary to deal in either hope or futility. His thoughts flashed through Oskan's mind. Only he was obligated to Kyron. Would his presence sway the fight? Would he alone be enough to tip the balance against Korgaan?

Oskan wouldn't lie to Draumdraak. It was true that the revived wyrm was the greatest of his kind yet seen in the skies of Pannithor, but even so, he couldn't say that Draumdraak alone would be enough to stop Korgaan. "We need all your kind," Oskan said. "As many broods of dragons as can be enticed from their lairs."

Draumdraak's thoughts had a note of apology about them. What Oskan asked for was impossible. After some of them had been killed at the Siege of Farhn, the rest of Draumdraak's brood had no taste for the Celestians' wars and no responsibility to fight in them. The other broods, those with no connection to Draumdraak at all, had even less cause to fight.

Oskan mulled over the information. Entwined into their conversation was always the obligation Draumdraak felt toward Kyron... and why.

"What Kyron did for you, the juice of the Sahlirian fruit," Oskan said, desperation's shadow closing upon his mind. "I can offer this to any dragon who will fight with us against Korgaan. The same vitality and power that you've enjoyed can be theirs as well. If only they will fight."

Draumdraak reared up, a loud hiss rippling through the cave. His claws dug at the treasure heaped around him. His eyes fixated upon Oskan. In that moment, Oskan knew his appeal had won. The dragons wouldn't fight for nothing, but what he promised them now was more precious than all the gold in Abercarr's holdfasts.

For the power of the Sahlirian tree, there wasn't a dragon in Pannithor that wouldn't stir from its cave.

Oskan knew there would be grave consequences. He would be endowing perhaps hundreds of dragons with the longevity Draumdraak enjoyed, reptiles less noble in heart than the ancient wyrm. It would mean the loss of Karinna's grove in Galahir and the undoing of all her work.

But was the threat of wicked dragons greater than that Korgaan posed to Pannithor? As to the Sahlirian fruit, another could be brought when Eoswain next opened the portals and brought Celestians across the void between worlds. Karinna could begin again. There could be recovery. If Korgaan prevailed, everything would be lost. Perhaps even now it was too late. Even now, Mescator might be lying dead at the war god's feet.

"It is a bargain," Oskan told Draumdraak. "Those who fight with us against Korgaan shall taste the nectar of the Sahlirian Tree." He shuddered as he spoke the words, for he knew they could never be taken back. Already Draumdraak was relaying the offer to those of his brood, the mental connection between dragons reaching across the miles. Those reptiles in turn would spread the news to their broods. From Oskan's mind, the wyrms discovered where Karinna's grove had been planted.

A flight of dragons was taking shape. A weapon to unleash against Korgaan.

Oskan's dread now was that it would come too late to turn the tide.

Chapter XV

-876, Time of Light

Death was all around Mescator. His sword was slick with the blood of Var'Kyr and ice trolls, his armor spattered with the lives of vanquished enemies. Yet the foe with which he needed to come to grips remained beyond his reach. Korgaan's minions formed a frenzied barrier between his templars and the war god's terrible incarnation. Gold Blades fell to barbarian axes and the clubs of giants, sacrificing themselves to try and bring Mescator to the arch-adversary.

"Courage!" Mescator shouted to his followers. "Today you help bring justice down upon an evil god!" As he inspired the templars, he drove his sword into the throat of a roaring troll. The shaggy brute tried to claw at him, its talons scraping against the barding that covered his steed. Then the monster's vitality fled from it as he ripped the weapon free and left its chilly blood spraying into the air. The hulk toppled backward, crushing a few barbarians under its tremendous weight.

All across the plain, carnage ruled. The icy streams were now crimson with the lives of the fallen. The rubble that marked where the Graveyard of Swords once stood was strewn with mangled bodies as well as old bones. The raucous cries of impatient crows rained down on the combatants as the scavengers waited for carrion to tear with their beaks.

It was a vision of slaughter that Mescator had never expected to find in Pannithor, far exceeding in ferocity the other battles the Celestians had taken part in. And nowhere was the fighting more intense than it was around the monstrous titan toward which he strove. Korgaan, with his many arms and many eyes, crushing brave men and defiant dwarfs, powerful ogres and nimble elves in his fingers. Even the mighty tree-creatures Karinna had shaped from the boughs of Galahir were no match for the war god's strength, smashed into splinters when they fell into his grip.

Mescator could sense the fading vitality of Kyron, first of the Celestians to be struck down at the Graveyard of Swords. He could sense the intense power Karinna was pouring into the hunter to drive back the shadow of death. That made two of their number removed from the fight. Three if Liliana was aware of Kyron's plight, for she was certain to remain with him while his survival was in question.

And still a fourth, for he saw Oskan fly away on Karinna's giant eagle. Mescator knew his protege wouldn't flee from the fight, that only an errand of great import could draw him away. But what that errand might be, he had no clue. Oskan had closed his mind to him... or rather had sealed his thoughts against the awareness of their enemy.

Mescator could feel Korgaan's mind brushing against his own, goading him with brutal mockery, trying to burden his spirit with despair. The war god exulted in the combat that raged all around him. Friend or foe, every speck of hate and violence glutted Korgaan's hunger. The very struggle to overcome him was only serving to magnify his awesome might. What were the upstart Celestians, those who would be the new gods of Pannithor? Naught but pretenders, bold enough against powers that had lost their vibrancy and allowed themselves to fade into mere shadows. But what were they beside a god who had retained his strength down through the ages? A god who hadn't diminished but only grown stronger? There was no victory for the Celestians, only annihilation!

"Justice stands with us," Mescator growled, trying to shake aside the despairing thoughts Korgaan tried to stir within him. "Whatever your power, however great your strength, you use it for evil, and evil will be scourged from Pannithor!"

Korgaan reached down and grabbed two handfuls of knights in his clawed hands. His eyes bore down upon Mescator as he brought both hands smashing together, crushing his captives against each other. The war god let the twisted, bleeding wreckage drop back to earth. In his mind, Mescator heard Korgaan's voice. "The Celestians will bring upon Pannithor far more evil than you can imagine. To keep the world as it is, all of your kind must die."

Mescator railed against the foul influence Korgaan tried to exert, the fiendish claim that in some way it was he and not the Celestians who strove to defend Pannithor. Furiously he forced his horse through the ranks of Var'Kyr, riding them down as he tried to close with the malignant titan.

All across the valley, the fighting intensified. Arrows continued to pelt Korgaan, desperate volleys that sought any vulnerable spot on that gargantuan body. Wizards from Primovantor and mages of Elvenholme unleashed their spells on the roaring god, while Valandor lent his arcane might to the fray. Whatever damage their craft managed to visit upon Korgaan, it couldn't exceed the energy he was deriving from the combat around him.

Mescator slashed the knee of a giant, leaving the crippled monster for the templars riding behind him to finish off. Urging his steed to greater effort, he pressed through the last of Korgaan's minions and found himself before the god himself. Korgaan's eyes glared down at him. The one that had been ruined by Karinna's eagle was whole again, though now with a hellish scarlet glow to it. The titan's fanged maw spread in a malicious grin and he reached down to seize the Celestian leader.

Korgaan's hand never closed around Mescator. As the crushing fingers started to close, the rider struck with his shining sword. He poured his power into the blow, lending it strength beyond the stroke that had crippled the giant. The war god flinched back and stared in shock at his maimed hand. Mescator's strike had severed two of the fingers and left a third dangling by a strip of ragged flesh. Korgaan howled in rage and tried to stomp on his defiant foe.

Now it was into his steed that Mescator focused his powers. The destrier displayed supernatural quickness as it dodged and darted between Korgaan's stamping feet. Each time he avoided the god's wrath only fed further into that wrath. All other foes were forgotten as Korgaan fixated upon Mescator.

Mescator sent his thoughts speeding to Valandor, hoping that Korgaan's rage was such that the god wouldn't think to spy upon them. "While he's busy, you must pull our soldiers away and drive off what's left of Korgaan's horde. The fighting must stop."

He knew it was a desperate plan, contradictory by its very demands. Yet so long as there was combat from which Korgaan could draw strength, Mescator saw no way by which they could defeat the monstrous god. Of all the Celestians, it was Valandor's magic that might find a way to accomplish both tasks.

While he continued to dodge Korgaan's stamping feet and grasping claws, Mescator heard the clamor of many trumpets. Valandor had sent word flying among the commanders of their forces. The mortals were disengaging, drawing back to the rise overlooking the valley.

The Var'Kyr started to pursue, jubilant in the belief that they'd broken their enemies and eager to take vengeance on the routed army. Even as they started their maddened charge, they faltered. Awed by the sight that reared up before them.

The arcane assault upon Korgaan had fallen to nothing. Mescator now saw why. Valandor had focused every wizard and mage in their army to lend themselves to a single purpose. They fed their magic into a colossal manifestation. A towering shape of almost blinding light stood between the barbarians and the civilized forces. A figure larger than even Korgaan's titanic incarnation, it was clad in ornate armor and bore a sword of rippling flame, great wings of dazzling brilliance unfolding from its back. Mescator felt a twinge of both pride and humility when he saw that the image bore his own features – stern and judgmental. In weaving this illusion to stun the Var'Kyr, Valandor had drawn on Mescator's likeness.

Shrieks of terror rose from the horde. The bloodlust of only a moment before fractured, and what had been a vengeful army now scattered in fright. Across the icy streams, the barbarians broke in disarray, fleeing out into the plains, all reasoning driven out of them by their fear.

Korgaan wasn't deceived by the illusion. Indeed, the ploy acted to sober the enraged god. His sneering voice thundered through Mescator's mind. "You think a trick will win this battle for you? I've already supped greatly from this carnage. The power invested in this incarnation is enough to destroy you and a dozen of your ilk, usurper!"

"Prove it!" Mescator shouted up at the monster. He rode around the titan's foot and chopped into his ankle. Korgaan bellowed in pain as the tendon was severed and he slammed down on his knee. Mescator charged in to attack again, but Korgaan's hand scraped across the ground, digging a great furrow in the earth. He flung the mass of dirt full at the Celestian. The destrier snorted in fright as the cloud of earth splashed across it and blinded it.

Mescator leaped from the saddle an instant before Korgaan snatched up his mount. The war god laughed as he flung the animal away and stared down at the Celestian. All four of his arms reached for his enemy, forming a cordon from which there could be no escape. Mescator tightened his grip on his sword, determined to claim some of the god's blood before he sold his life.

Even as the hands closed in around him, Mescator heard Korgaan snarl in pain. From every side, the titan was now beset by enemies. The mortal troops remained up on the rise, away from the battle, but the Celestians themselves had returned to the fight. Shakara's icy bolts seared into Korgaan's face. Lightning from Valandor's palm crackled down the colossal arms. Relief rushed through Mescator when he saw Kyron, his body framed in emerald light, leaping among the debris of war to loose deadly arrows into the monstrous god. Liliana kept pace with him, plying her own bow with equal ferocity. The shafts dug deep into Korgaan's flesh and spilled much of his ichor. Karinna, with her own brand of magic, set wispy tendrils coiling around the mighty arms, dragging them back even as he tried to swat at his enemies.

All, however, didn't favor the Celestians. Mescator shouted in agony when he saw the bold Arkira smashed beneath Korgaan's palm, her bright spear impaling the hand that killed her. He felt sickened when he saw the valiant Orso give his life to defend Valandor. Korgaan caught up the axe-wielding fighter, and with two hands pulled his body apart, reveling in the brutal display.

"He weakens," Karinna's voice echoed in Mescator's mind, "but far too slowly. We cannot beat him."

"We must beat him," Mescator swore. "If we don't, Korgaan will strike again, and all those who've sacrificed themselves to stop him will have done so for nothing."

"If we perish here, what hope is there for Pannithor?" Valandor's thoughts flowed into him.

Mescator watched the remains of Orso drip from Korgaan's gory fingers. "There will be none if we retreat. Vanquishing Korgaan is the only hope this world has."

It was then that a shape dove down at Korgaan from above. The god cried out in pain as lightning crackled across his face, and one of his great fangs was cut away by a sweeping sword. Oskan riding Karinna's eagle! The young Celestian swept back around and drove again at Korgaan's face. His Ophidian blade ripped into the god's cheek, splitting the flesh down to the bone and sending another surge of electricity across the bestial visage.

Oskan didn't have the chance to strike a third time. Ripping free from Karinna's tendrils, one of Korgaan's arms came up and struck the eagle. The giant bird was knocked from the sky as though it were an insect. It crashed amid the piled bodies in a tangle of blood and feathers. Mescator turned and raced to the scene, heedless now of all danger to himself.

Korgaan made no effort to attack Mescator as he ran. Instead, his sadistic thoughts pierced the Celestian's brain. "Yes, run to your pupil! Gaze on his destruction and despair. Before I send your spirit into oblivion, you will know the depths of agony, Mescator Godling!"

The sky god's mockery stabbed Mescator as keenly as knives, their poison wracking body and soul. When he reached the eagle's mangled carcass, he was afraid to go further, yet further he had to go. He had to see. He had to know. Forcing himself onward, he pulled aside one of the broken wings and gazed down on Oskan.

Oskan lay in a contorted position that told a sickening story. His face was drawn and pale, blood seeped from the corners of his mouth. One arm, horribly broken, lay pressed against his chest. One leg, disjointed in the fall, was lying across the dead eagle's neck. Oskan's eyes were open but had the glazed, unfocused appearance of death. His mind, Mescator found, was locked to his mentor's thoughts.

At least so it was until Mescator drew closer. Then Oskan stirred. Biting back his pain, he turned his head and looked up at him. The mind that had been closed now opened to Mescator, unconcerned that Korgaan might know what had happened... and what would happen.

"I succeeded," Oskan's thoughts told Mescator. "I met with Draumdraak. Korgaan is finished."

The sky grew dark. Mescator leaned over Oskan, intent on shielding him from the titan's grasping claws. But it wasn't Korgaan's descending hand that caused the shadows to fall across them.

"The dragons are coming," Oskan reported, and even in his pain, he managed to smile.

***

Kyron sent another arrow speeding into the towering war god. It joined five others, all clustered about Korgaan's throat. Shots that would have felled any lesser foe, but the titan scarcely noticed his injuries. It was too much to hope to bring down their enemy with mere arrows, but he had hoped to at least draw his attention. Anything to keep him away from where Oskan had fallen.

"Nothing works," Liliana cursed. "We may as well be throwing pebbles at him!" Though she saw it as futile, she sent one of her arrows slamming into the monster's chest, desperately trying to sink one deep enough to hit Korgaan's heart.

"If we must die, then let us die fighting," Kyron said. He felt Liliana's anguish at his words. His revival by Karinna's magic had been nothing shy of miraculous. To see that miracle squander so soon, to again face the specter of death, this was almost too much for her. "When he tries to take us, he'll have to take both of us," he added, his somber words filled with love. Liliana offered no comment, she simply nodded to him. There was nothing to say that their hearts hadn't already spoken.

Then Kyron was struck by a new impression. The arrow he loosed went astray, glancing from Korgaan's shoulder. The hunter cast his gaze upward, unable to believe the sensation that had reached out to him. It was Draumdraak, the reptile's mind brushing against his own with that connection that was both less than telepathy and so much more.

"Draumdraak!" he told Liliana when she turned to him in concern. Out from the cloudy sky he saw the enormous dragon appear, his red scales shining in the sun, his massive wings stretched to the full. Kyron felt a great sadness in him, but also a great joy that the mighty wyrm had chosen to come here and stand with him in his final fight.

"Kyron! Look!" Liliana entreated him. Look he did, and a tremendous awe filled him. Other dragons were dropping down from the clouds now. Four! Ten! A dozen! No, more! Many more! His eyes gaped in shock at the sight. This was far more than just

Draumdraak's brood, far more dragons than Kyron had dared imagine. Their scaly coats were in all manner of hues. He saw blacks and golds, whites and greens, all sorts of colors. There were beasts with horned heads and those with leathery frills. Reptiles with sleek fresh scales and those with old, tattered wings. A flight of dragons, as described in the oldest elven legends. But this was no legend from the mists of history. This was an army unlike any in Pannithor, flying to bring doom upon Korgaan!

"Oskan did it," Kyron gasped in disbelief. "Whatever he told them, he brought them here! Here to fight with us!"

Through the hunter's mind there now coursed a note of warning. Kyron drew Liliana back when she would have loosed another arrow into Korgaan. "We've fought as long as we dare," he said. "Now it is the dragons who will face him. If we don't want to be caught in the storm, we must withdraw now."

Liliana lowered her bow and followed Kyron away across the battlefield. They sent their thoughts racing to the other Celestians. One after another, they joined the retreat. It was an easy thing for them to disengage. Korgaan too had noted the new army come to challenge him.

The war god reached down and raised up slabs from the plateau that had been the Graveyard of Swords. With his four arms, he flung these boulders up at the dragons. Several of the great reptiles were knocked from the sky, for each of the stones carried with it a caustic enchantment that melted their scaly armor and burned the flesh within. Six of the dragons were slain in this way, but the flight sped onward. Soon they came within range to match Korgaan's attacks.

Orange fire spilled from the heavens as dozens of dragons expelled their flaming breath against Korgaan. Other wyrms unleashed bolts of lightning and sheets of frost, some spit acidic blobs that seared the titan's hide. Smoke billowed about the war god as the corpses piled about his feet were ignited. His enraged bellows were like the roar of a volcano as he struck at the tormenting reptiles. Another dragon fell, its body shattered by a boulder. A second was caught in grasping claws to have its neck wrenched and its carcass hurled back at the rest of the flight.

Still they came. Kyron gasped in wonder at how many of them there were. More swooped down to join the attack with every minute. Creatures that looked mighty enough to crack a castle with their claws and others so young and small that a bull might have matched them in a fight. Elder wyrm or fresh hatchling, each dragon persecuted Korgaan with a viciousness the war god's berserk followers would have strained to surpass.

The slaughter was terrible. Dragons fell at every turn, many of them incapable of rising from where they slammed into the earth. Korgaan suffered in equal part. His body was ripped and slashed by draconic claws, his flesh scorched and blasted by dragonfire. The vast store of power that had allowed him to ignore his wounds began to fade. When a great dragon with golden scales spat what looked to be a spray of boiling metal into the titan's arm, it seared into the muscles, and the limb fell limp.

As grievous as the toll inflicted upon the dragons was, Kyron exulted in the fact that Korgaan was doomed. Then a hideous thought occurred to him. "What if Korgaan can escape this incarnation?" he shuddered. "What if his essence escapes again as it did at the Battle of Hepshet?"

The dread that filled Kyron's mind echoed into that of Draumdraak. The ancient wyrm, greatest dragon in all Pannithor, made a grave assurance to the Celestian who had restored life to him. Korgaan wouldn't slip free this time.

"No!" Kyron shouted, for he understood Draumdraak's intention. Liliana gripped his hand, trying to ease his acceptance of what must happen, for neither of them had the power to keep it from happening.

Smaller dragons circled around Korgaan, holding the god's attention. From almost directly overhead, Draumdraak dove down upon the titan. At the last instant, he unfurled his wings and arrested his fall. Before Korgaan could react, his claws were digging into the incarnation's chest and his jaws were ripping into the arrow-pierced throat.

Kyron felt Draumdraak's torment when Korgaan's hands closed around the wyrm and tried to pull him free. The dragon's bones were crushed under the god's rip, but still he held fast, biting deeper into the throat, sinking his claws into the titan's flesh.

While Korgaan was trying to free himself from Draumdraak, the other dragons swarmed over him. Kyron had the image of a bee hive roused to fend off a marauding bear. Not an inch of the god's body was spared the hostility of his enemies. Fire licked across his flesh, blood gushed from torn veins. Muscles shredded by claws and dissolved by acid failed him as he tried to move. The ground trembled as the colossus fell.

"They won't relent," Liliana said as they watched the gory spectacle.

"No, they won't stop until Korgaan is destroyed," Kyron replied. Tears were in his eyes as he watched Draumdraak being torn to bits by the desperate god. But even as his body was ripped apart, the wyrm sank his fangs still deeper into the titan's neck. The red scales were utterly black from Korgaan's foul ichor, and still Draumdraak tightened his hold.

Finally a howl of abject agony rang out. The fires in Korgaan's eyes flared into greater brilliance. He mustered one last great pulse of power, trying to throw off the tormenting dragons. Kyron raised his bow, sighting for the left eye.

"He's trying to break free," Kyron warned as he let loose the arrow. The shaft struck true, embedding itself at the center of the pupil. The eye exploded, the energies it had been gathering expelled in a burst of cinders.

Liliana followed Kyron's lead and sent her own arrow into the right eye. It too burst apart in a cloud of embers. The last eye, that which had already suffered from Karinna's eagle, darkened and dripped out from its socket in a stream of sludge. The titan crashed back against the ground, his body trembling as the monstrous vitality drained away from it.

The flight of dragons persisted in attacking until the very last speck of life was gone. Flames crackled about the great carcass, consuming the gigantic manifestation of Korgaan. Kyron watched with a leaden heart, for he knew within that ghastly pyre lay Draumdraak. With the last of his own vitality, the wyrm bit through another vein and set ichor spurting into the air. Then there was nothing. The reptile's presence vanished from Kyron's mind. Draumdraak was dead.

"Victory!" Liliana shouted, tears streaming from her eyes. All that had been threatened by Korgaan and his hordes was safe now. The noble races, the civilizations the Celestians had fostered, would be free to grow and expand without the looming threat of the barbarians and their grim god.

Kyron nodded. "Yes, but at what cost?" His gaze was drawn skyward once more. The triumphant dragons didn't linger over their vanquished foe. Great and small, they rose into the air and turned to the southeast as they made their departure. Though he shared no connection with these as he had with Draumdraak, Kyron could sense enough intent from those of the old wyrm's brood who flew away to know that the impression of haste they gave him wasn't mere imagining. The dragons were in a hurry to be somewhere now that Korgaan had been vanquished.

"We won," Kyron whispered as he watched the flight recede into the distance. "But what did it cost?"

***

"Quickly." Valandor urged Mescator away from Oskan's side. Karinna and Shakara were tending to him now. If there was any consolation to be had, his injuries were less severe than what Kyron had endured in Korgaan's grasp.

Mescator looked as though he would hesitate, but Valandor grabbed his arm and pulled him away. He pointed to the sky as the dragons sped away from the Graveyard of Swords. "They brought down Korgaan, but we must make certain. We've seen how sly the war god is. His destruction must be confirmed."

The warning impressed Mescator. Though he wanted to attend Oskan, he knew his responsibility was to do what Valandor had told him. If Korgaan escaped them, it would mean they'd have to do all of this again. Many lives, both mortal and Celestian, would be lost if that happened.

Mortal troops were drifting down onto the battlefield now, searching among the dead for lost comrades. The crows, frightened off by the arrival of the dragons, now came cawing and croaking onto the piles of bodies. Lanky mongrels, abandoned by the Var'Kyr on their long retreat across the plains, came slinking along to steal morsels from the corpses.

The fires that crackled about Korgaan's body continued to blaze, a great pyre that sent a pillar of foul smoke into the sky. Drawing closer, Valandor closed his eyes and let his magic channel through him. When he opened his eyes again, he made a gesture with his hands. An ethereal wind whipped over the immense carcass and snuffed out the flames. For an instant, steam rose from the cooling bulk, but as the heat rapidly evaporated, even this effect faded.

"I... I don't sense him," Mescator said as he gazed upon Korgaan's body.

Valandor frowned. He raised his arms. Little slivers of energy rippled from his fingers and flowed across the carcass. They burrowed into the charred flesh, probing the gigantic carrion. "He's here," Valandor said. "Trying to hide from us. Hoping we'll leave so he can regain his strength."

Mescator flourished his sword. "I won't let that happen."

Valandor's frown intensified. "It may be beyond all our powers," he cautioned. "But of this I am certain. We can balk Korgaan. Slow the process by which he would replenish himself. That much we can do. We can keep the lands of Pannithor free of his malice for many centuries." The frown was replaced by a smile. "By then, the Circle of Heaven will have brought many more Celestians into this world. Korgaan's power will lessen while ours will only grow."

Mescator stood silent and watched while Valandor played his spells across the corpse. He sought that speck, that lingering flicker of the old god that could not die. It was absent from those places he sought for it most keenly. Heart and brain were only dead tissue, quickly corroding without Korgaan's presence. The liver, held by human mystics as the seat of the soul, was also devoid of the god's essence. Valandor's frustration mounted. He knew the god's spark was still here, but where?

A bitter laugh stirred from Valandor's lips when he realized the answer. Once again, the malicious Korgaan had tried to deceive them. The god couldn't send his spirit far, but he didn't need to. Draumdraak's jaws remained clenched in the titan's throat. It was into the dragon's carcass that the divine spark had retreated.

"There," Valandor pointed to the dead dragon. Mescator started forward, climbing onto the god's carcass.

As he did, loathsome vitality stirred Draumdraak's remains. The jaws loosened their hold on the throat. Before Mescator could react, the dragon's head whipped around, the neck ripping itself free from the rest of the body. Like some hideous serpent, the dead thing struck at the Celestian. In Draumdraak's eyes, there now burned the wrathful glow of Korgaan.

A bolt of magic from Valandor's hand slammed into the animated wyrm, deflecting its lunge so that it missed Mescator. Sweeping past him, it was slashed with the edge of his sword. Scales already mauled by the god's fingers and seared by the fires of other dragons split under the blade, exposing the flesh and bone beneath.

The deathly serpent reared and struck again, but this time, Mescator didn't need Valandor's spells to thwart its strike. He brought his sword cleaving through the dragon's snout, cutting away a five-foot length of its face and jaws. Seizing the advantage, he leaped onto the reptile's head and stabbed his enchanted blade deep into its skull.

Valandor saw the lights fade from the dragon's eyes. The animated wyrm was once again only a dead thing. He set his magic probing into it. He found that a legend spoken of by the elves had much truth in it. They claimed that the oldest dragons developed a gemstone in their brains, a thing of fabulous arcane power. Valandor couldn't speak for whatever properties the stone possessed, but it was certainly there, and it was into this that the final immortal ember of Korgaan had fled.

"We must remove the brain," Valandor told Mescator. They both turned when they heard movement behind them. They found Kyron and Liliana climbing up to join them. Valandor felt a pang of regret at the necessity of this butchery. "Draumdraak fought valiantly for us all," he said, "but if his sacrifice is to mean anything, this must be done." He gestured at the wyrm's head. "The spark of Korgaan is there. If we can imprison it, then Pannithor might never need to fear his return."

Anguish was on Kyron's face. Valandor knew how great was his love for the wild things of this world, and the dragons most of all. Still, the hunter knew the truth when he heard it. "Do what must be done," Kyron said. He kicked the dead flesh under his feet. "Never let Korgaan plague this world again."

Mescator waved aside the help of the other Celestians and began his grisly task. It was some minutes before he had a hole large enough to reach into the skull and feel for the gemstone. At last, however, he ripped it free. It was an amber-colored thing, like a yellow diamond as big as his fist. At the core of the stone, writhing like a trapped flame, was a dull crimson light.

"We have him," Mescator announced, triumph in his voice. He looked across the battlefield. "We will raise a fortress here to imprison the stone and task the most valiant and virtuous of our templars to guard it. The last of the Var'Kyr must be hunted down so they can never return to this place and seek their god. The Graveyard of Swords will be too remote to draw thieves from civilized lands."

Kyron nodded in agreement. "This is a fitting place to build a tower. This is where Korgaan's power was broken."

"The tower will be called Wyrmspire," Mescator decided. There was sadness in his eyes as he gazed down at Draumdraak. "That way no one will ever forget that it was a dragon who finally vanquished Korgaan."

Valandor gestured at the shattered plateau, then at the warriors who'd survived the battle. "We'll begin to build before we turn from this place. The sooner the gemstone is secured, the safer it will be."

A scream of fury rang out through the valley. Valandor could tell that it came from where they'd left Oskan. So did the others. Mescator fairly threw the draconic gemstone into his arms before jumping off the titanic corpse and sprinting to where his protege lay. Kyron and Liliana followed close behind him, equally concerned for what the scream meant. A shiver ran through Valandor. He had a feeling he knew who had screamed... and why.

When Valandor reached the spot, he found a tense scene. Shakara was gripping Karinna's waist, trying to hold her back as she snarled and cursed both Oskan and Mescator. "After all I've done, this is how I am repaid?" she accused them.

Kyron tried to act as an intercessor. He stepped between the arguing Celestians. "It is my fault. I should never..."

Karinna shot him a withering look. "Your mistake is past, and I have tried to fix it." She turned back and shook an accusing finger at Oskan. "How could you do this, knowing all that was lost?"

Oskan shook his head. Karinna's magic had restored him so that only his bloodied raiment told that he'd suffered any injury at all. "I told you, it was the only way they'd come. The only thing that would make them fight."

Mescator nodded. "Oskan overstepped his bounds, but his heart was in the right place. If Korgaan was victorious here, then everything would have been lost."

"Everything *is* lost," Karinna corrected him. "The dragons have been promised the Sahlirian fruit. Even now, they fly to claim the debt."

Valandor came beside Kyron and faced Karinna. "It would seem to me that you waste time arguing here." He clapped his hand on the hunter's shoulder. "The dragons are thinking beings. They can be reasoned with. You may be able to restrain their hunger, but not if you linger here trying to assign blame."

"Galahir!" Kyron exclaimed. "If we hurry, we might reach the Sahlirian grove before the dragons!"

"The juice from a single fruit will be enough to extend each dragon's lifespan," Mescator said. "If we make that clear to them, much of the grove will be left untouched."

Karinna cupped her hands, and four enormous eagles flew across the valley to join them. "We must make speed if we're to stop them."

"Kyron must go with you, for the dragons respect him," Valandor stated. "So too must Oskan, for he is the one who made the bargain."

"And the fourth?" Mescator wanted to know.

Valandor smiled. "That can only be you. As our leader, you're the one who has authority to mediate disputes among the Celestians." He tapped the gemstone. "Besides, there is work here that I must attend to."

Valandor watched as the eagles bore their riders away from the Graveyard of Swords. He wished them success, but in his mind there was a sense of dread.

Had they broken the bloodthirsty dreams of Korgaan only to destroy their own vision for a Pannithor beyond the reach of death?

Chapter XVI

-876, Time of Light

A black bloom of smoke spread over the greenery of Galahir. It could be seen from hundreds of miles away. Mescator felt his heart grow heavy at the sight. There could only be one reason. They were too late. The dragons had already descended upon the forest and attacked Karinna's grove.

Mescator could feel Karinna's agony at the sight, a psychic knife that whipped through his soul. Her powers exhausted from the battle and healing both Kyron and Oskan, her mind reeling from her fears for the grove, she was unable to perceive what lay beneath the smoke. None of the other Celestians who flew beside her had the heart to tell her what they would find.

The eagles had to be encouraged to pass through the smoke. Mescator thought their reluctance had less to do with the presence of fire as it did the musky reek of dragon in the air. The giant birds balked at the descent, trying to pull back and rise above the mephitic atmosphere. The Celestians had to force them to sink down toward what had been Karinna's grove.

His heart felt sour when Mescator saw what had been done. He could well imagine what it must have looked like before. He knew the care and compassion Karinna had for the things that grew from the earth. In many other worlds, he'd seen the beauty she'd coaxed from plants, the graceful arrangements of garden and grove, simultaneously artistic and orderly. To walk among things planted by Karinna, nurtured into maturity under her guiding hand, was an experience that brought joy to both mind and soul.

What lay below the smoke was but a smoldering shadow of what it must have been. The emotions that filled Mescator were sorrow and anguish, the fruits of tragedy. He could see hints of what Karinna's grove must have looked like before, but they were merely hints. Charred stumps that designated where lines of trees had taken root, dry pits where streams had flowed. Blackened logs lay strewn about in all directions, splintered and scorched, their branches stripped away. Fires still gnawed at their heartwood, glowing evilly in the smoky gloom wherever some crack in the burnt shells allowed them to show through. The soil was gray and withered, torn up by the clawed feet of the rampaging dragons, its vibrancy sucked away by the intensity of their fiery breath.

An ashy, blasted wasteland, this was all that remained of the grove Karinna had nurtured for so many years. The place in which the Celestians had invested their greatest hope to turn Pannithor into a paradise for its people. To take from them the shadow of death, and with it, the blight of war. Mescator's throat tightened at the magnitude of the loss.

"The dragons consumed it all," Kyron moaned as he dropped down from the back of his eagle. "They left nothing."

Oskan was struck dumb by the scope of the destruction. The fires had spread to the boughs of Galahir beyond where the grove had been. Even now, groups of sylvan elves and tree creatures fought the last of the flames. He started toward the nearest group, then fell to his knees in shock.

"They were overeager to claim the prize they'd been promised," Mescator stated. "They must have gone wild when they descended on the grove, glutting themselves on the fruit that would extend their longevity." He kicked the barren earth and glared at the clawed trunk of a charred tree. "One fruit each would have been enough to accomplish their purpose. The others they ingested did nothing for them."

Kyron turned to Mescator. "They didn't know. Draumdraak wasn't here to guide them, and there was no other to restrain them. They only understood what the Sahlirian fruit would do for them, not how its powers worked."

Karinna crouched down beside the withered stalk of a sapling, cradling the dead thing in her hands. "The wyrms wouldn't have cared," she said, bitterness in her voice. "They hoard treasure because it is valuable to other beings. So they came to take everything that was here, because it could benefit others besides themselves." She looked up at Kyron. "You blind yourself with an idealized vision. A dragon is a selfish creature. It doesn't share, it doesn't sacrifice. It does what it needs to satisfy its own desires."

"Draumdraak was a dragon," Mescator broke upon Karinna's diatribe. "He knew it would mean his death when he dove upon Korgaan and sank his fangs in the god's throat."

"It is difficult now to think fondly of any dragon," Karinna said, waving her hands at the destruction all about them. As she made the gesture, her eyes focused upon Oskan. The heat of anger froze into the chill of contempt. "Yet you are right. The wyrms did only what they thought was their due. Exacting the price a fool so recklessly promised them."

Oskan stumbled onto his feet. "Fool?" he snapped, his own anger now kindled. "I saved us all! Without the dragons, we would never have beaten Korgaan, or have you forgotten?" He kicked at the ashes under his feet. "All of this would have been lost anyway. Korgaan's hordes would've burned down all of Galahir, not just your grove."

"Easy, Oskan," Mescator cautioned his protege. It was easy to understand his anger. He sincerely regretted the destruction and felt responsible for it, but at the same time, he felt Karinna was forgetting why it had been done. That his own heroism was being ignored.

"You speak of what might have been," Karinna retorted. "Look upon what is," she challenged.

Oskan's eyes blazed and his face curled with outrage. "No," he told her. "I will speak some more about what might have been. What in fact *will* be." He thrust a finger upward and pointed at the smoke-filled sky. "In only a few decades, as the mortals reckon time, the conjunction will occur once more. Eoswain and Reiliur will bring more of our people through into this world. With them, they will bring another fruit from the Sahlirian Tree. More seeds with which to begin again."

"Tomorrow is not today," Karinna persisted. "See what has been lost to your recklessness."

"I see nothing that cannot be replaced," Oskan said.

Mescator rolled his eyes. It was the worst possible thing Oskan could have spoken at that moment.

"Replaced?" Karinna snarled. "Will you say those words to all the mortals who died fighting Korgaan? That their loss is easily replaced? Will those words be of comfort to the families that mourn for those who will never come home?" She waved her arms at the blasted grove. "This was life. Only a little time has passed since this place was alive. Do those lives count for nothing, simply because they don't applaud the great Oskan and sing his praises?"

"You know that isn't what Oskan meant," Mescator said. "It is unjust of you, Karinna, to accuse him this way. He only sought to ease your sorrow. To remind you that we can begin again."

Tears were in Karinna's eyes as she looked toward the edge of the forest. "Galahir trusted me to protect it. It permitted me to plant my grove and lent me its support to ensure success. I've failed the forest. I share the responsibility of wounding Galahir." She reached down and took up a fistful of the gray soil. "This ground will never recover, and what right have I to beg another place from the forest to do my work?"

Kyron bent down at Karinna's feet and looked up at her with imploring eyes. "When I gave the first Sahlirian fruit to Draumdraak, it wasn't the end of your work. It must be possible to go on. We can make this place live again. I know that we can. We must."

"All the resources from all the Celestians will be put to this work, Karinna," Mescator assured her. "Now that Korgaan is vanquished..."

Karinna shook her head. "How many generations of humans and dwarfs have now been denied the promise of immortality?" She held Mescator's gaze, trying to impress on him this aspect of the loss. "Even if the land can be restored or Galahir permits me to transform another part of its forest into a second grove, the time cannot be reclaimed. No new seeds can be brought into Pannithor until the next conjunction. Then they must be planted and cultivated. Hundreds of years. The elves can wait that long. The youngest of the dwarfs might see what their parents could have been given. But the humans?"

Mescator felt the anguish of what must happen to the humans. Except those like Tothmenes of Ophidia who employed the blackest sorcery to sustain themselves far beyond their natural span, entire generations of humans would die before even the possibility was available to them. In a way, Oskan's desperate bargain with the dragons had doomed even more lives than Korgaan's hordes.

"Maybe all is not lost here," Mescator said, looking about the desolation. "The destruction may not be as complete as it seems. There may be fruit the dragons missed, seeds that can be recovered and cultivated before the next conjunction."

Mescator's words inspired the others, but not Karinna. She stood silent as the rest of them prowled the wasteland, searching under blackened trunks and sifting through piles of ash. The claim that anything had escaped the dragons was proving a fool's dream. Certainly Mescator felt foolish for having suggested it.

Then Kyron cried out. Searching the dried-out pit of what had been a pond, the hunter emerged with a small object in his hand. His face was flush with triumph. As he wiped away the patina of ash, the bright husk of a Sahlirian fruit was visible. "I found one!" he shouted. "The dragons didn't take everything!"

The Celestians gathered around Kyron. Mescator could sense Oskan's relief that at least something had been salvaged. It lessened the grave responsibility that tormented him. Mescator could easily understand the sentiment, for it was the same that pressed upon his own mind.

Kyron handed the fruit over to Karinna. Her hands caressed it while she closed her eyes. The faint trace of joy that had started to show on her face collapsed, consumed by disappointment. "It is too young," she said, opening her eyes and sweeping her gaze across the others. "It was torn from the tree too soon. No seeds have grown within it, and there is no magic that can make it do so."

"Then we must wait until more are brought into Pannithor," Oskan said.

Karinna gave Oskan a look filled with enmity. She didn't speak to him but turned instead to Mescator. She placed the fruit in his hand, then folded the other on top of it. "I'm giving this to you. It is of no use to me. No seeds can be drawn from it, but it does possess enough juice within it to vitalize a single life. To turn one mortal into an immortal. Enough to be worth a single eternity."

Oskan bristled at Karinna's disdain. "Another fruit will be brought to Pannithor," he snarled. "Nothing has changed, merely delayed."

Mescator felt disgust at his pupil's callous words. "This 'delay' as you call it, means untold lives must be lost. Think on all those who will die because of this. Respect what they've lost."

"They've lost something they never knew would be theirs," Oskan countered. "What would never have been theirs but for our victory over Korgaan. Except for Reiliur and Calisor, no mortal has even heard of the Sahlirian fruit."

"You forget the dragons," Karinna said, acid in her tone.

Oskan scowled at her. "I think it unlikely any mortal will seek to converse with a dragon." He nodded to Kyron. "It is an experience to daunt even a Celestian." The brief laugh that punctuated his little speech felt like a hot knife pressed against Mescator's skin.

"I don't expect you to feel ashamed of what you had to do," Mescator told Oskan. "But it seems to me you should feel contrition for what it has cost. A moment ago, I thought I sensed that in you. I don't do so now."

Oskan glowered at Mescator. "Perhaps it is because I have a better perspective now. Karinna bemoans the loss of trees and a bargain made with a forest, while I think of all we've tried to build here in Pannithor. We're reshaping this world into a better place for all its inhabitants. The lives that are lost while we're constructing the world that can be are simply the cost of that construction. It is the long view we must see. The suffering of the moment can't outweigh the glory of the future."

"I see that my pupil thinks himself wiser than his teacher," Mescator said, pained by Oskan's thoughts and words. "Since you think you know better than I do, then I will no longer restrain you from following whatever path you choose."

The words stunned the other Celestians. Even Karinna's antagonism toward Oskan faltered when she heard Mescator dismiss his protege. Oskan was silent. For a moment, it seemed he would repent his boastful pride and seek to reconcile with his mentor. But whatever he would have said remained unspoken. Instead, he turned and walked away.

Mescator started to call after Oskan, but he too was held silent by pride. His protege's disregard of the mortals was too ugly a thing for him to easily forgive. Perhaps in time, but not now.

"I never thought to see a rift between you," Kyron said as they watched Oskan disappear into the forest. "You were always devoted to one another. If you think Oskan oversteps himself, it is because he wants to prove himself to you."

"Oskan isn't content to be my protege," Mescator said. "He wants to be my equal. But he hasn't earned that right, and he's too impatient to wait. He doesn't appreciate that wisdom can't be hurried."

Karinna pointed at the Sahlirian fruit in Mescator's hands. "Let's see if your wisdom is greater than Oskan's. There is the last of the Sahlirian fruit. Enough for one eternity. What life will you raise up to shine forever alongside us?"

Mescator nodded. "It is a magnificent gift."

"It isn't a gift, but a burden," Karinna corrected him. "On you lays the weight of judgment. To decide of all the mortals in Pannithor, which should be given immortality. It will need the gravest consideration to make that choice. I do not envy you this power."

Mescator stared down at the fruit. The promise it represented was now tinged with horror. The decision Karinna had given him could only be described as horror. To raise one life and condemn the others to the inevitability of death.

"When the conjunction occurs and the next Celestians bring another fruit from the Sahlirian Tree, the burden will grow lighter," Mescator said. "But it is a harsh lesson you would teach me, Karinna."

There was sympathy in her voice when Karinna replied to him. "The most important lessons are always harsh." She turned her head and looked to where Oskan had withdrawn into the forest. "It is the lessons we are forced to learn that shape the future. For good or evil."

-701, Time of Light

Calisor Fenulian had the fire of expectation coursing through his spirit. Much had been lost in the war against Korgaan, many lives had been taken by the brutal god's barbaric followers, but most keenly of all did the Circle of Heaven feel the deaths of the Celestians. Each who had been killed in the war acted as a diminishment of Pannithor itself. So much hope and promise was invested in each of the Celestians, that to lose even one was a tragedy that laid its pall across the whole world.

But tonight that shadow would be driven back! Calisor felt pride swell inside him that he was a part of this monumental process. The constellations were right once more. Tonight the Circle of Heaven would perform the rites that would throw open the gates and bring more Celestians from across the void and into

Pannithor.

Calisor rushed about the great laboratory, inspecting every detail. The gates had been exactingly restored after the previous transference, tended to by the greatest artisans in Elvenholme until they were more magnificent than before. The wizards of the Circle assumed their places, ready to perform their part in the ritual. Many were veterans of the very first transference, others were new faces that had joined their company later, but all had undergone the most exacting training over the previous six months to ensure they would be at peak performance. Their memories were fixated upon the arcane formulae of the ritual, their willpower sharpened to a razor focus. They would not stray so much as a second from the cadence of the rite.

Satisfied that all was in a state of absolute perfection, Calisor walked across the great hall to the raised dais at the center of the room. He glanced up at the opaque dome crafted by Belkon, that enchanted ceiling that would bring the stars into such shining clarity that it would seem possible to reach up and grab them. Soon, the dome would be filled with the image of the constellations, displaying them as they drifted into the auspicious conjunction. The kraken would flow into the laughing dog. The dragon would enter the house of the sword.

Upon the dais where the Scrying Star rested within its enchanted framework, Reiliur and Eoswain held a last consultation. Eoswain appeared to Calisor to be filled with confidence, but there was a trace of worry in Reiliur's eyes. Perhaps he was thinking of what had happened to him during the last conjunction, when he'd been struck down by a strange affliction. Something that was as mysterious and unexplained a century later as when it happened.

Calisor learned this indeed was the subject the wizard and the Celestian were discussing. When he approached the dais, Reiliur turned to him. "It has been decided. You will take my place, Calisor. Your skill with the arcane arts is a match for my own, and you know the ritual as well as I do. You're younger and hardier than I am."

"You have always been the guiding spirit in the Tower of Heaven," Calisor started to object.

"And you have always been prepared to take over in the event something happened to me," Reiliur reminded his former apprentice. "The ritual is more important than any one elf. My ego cannot be taken into consideration when it is a question of success or failure." He shook his head, his expression turning sad. "Let's face it. There has always been an ordeal involved when guiding the Celestians across the void. My... attack... one hundred years ago puts my fitness into question. I believe, and Eoswain concurs, that a more robust constitution is required." He smiled and laid his hand on Calisor's shoulder. "Don't be obstinate, my friend. You're the only one to take my place. It is your time to become master of the Tower of Heaven."

"Take your place on the dais," Eoswain said as Reiliur withdrew. "Lay your hands upon the Scrying Star. The moment draws near, Calisor, and it needs a spirit of Pannithor to call out to the sphere wherein the Celestians dwell."

The enormous responsibility that was now his felt as though it was smothering him, but Calisor came forward when Eoswain beckoned to him. The strangeness of occupying the place he'd always thought would belong to Reiliur only added to his discomfort. He glanced aside at the older wizard. The confident approval that showed on his face did much to reassure Calisor.

"I'm ready," Calisor told Eoswain. He laid his hands upon the Scrying Star and sent his thoughts hurtling across the void to that distant reality where the Celestian Carnesus was waiting. Now it was to this distant being that Calisor spoke, reciting the words he'd heard Reiliur speak before. "I am here. All is ready."

In the past century, Calisor had spoken with Carnesus several times. Eoswain's student, he'd always impressed him as a nigh emotionless and precise being. Now, however, he felt a wave of panic sweep across him when his mind connected with that of Carnesus. "They reach across the void." The same response the wizards had received before, but now the voice was one of haste and urgency.

Calisor glanced up from the Scrying Star and saw the constellations in alignment. No, there was something different now! There, among the stars that made up the kraken, there was a change. Not a new star, but rather a blot of supreme darkness. An un-star was the only label he could put upon it, a cosmic body that emanated not light, but darkness.

"Something's wrong," Calisor called to Eoswain. Even as he spoke, he heard a wail of terror shriek through his mind. He knew it was Carnesus. He was thankful he was ignorant of what could provoke such a scream from a Celestian.

Eoswain leaped onto the dais and gripped Calisor's hands. He felt her energy rush into him, seeking to bolster the connection. For a moment, the shriek was even more distinct in Calisor's brain. He had a fleeting impression of some nightmarish presence. Before it could become more substantial, Eoswain pulled him away from the Scrying Stone and broke the resonance he'd established with the Celestians' world.

Calisor crumpled against the dais, his body shaking from the abrupt severing of the link. He forgot his own agonies, however, when he looked toward the portals. Each was filled with a miasma, but far different from that which had accompanied the other rituals. This was a dark, cloying vapor, denser than smoke yet less than fog. The miasma sent streamers of itself pawing about the gates, transmuting their precious construction into a brown sludge that dripped to the floor in streams of feculent decay.

The wizards of the Circle screamed, and then the mantras they'd been reciting became distorted, dropping from an arcane harmony to a horrible, glottal noise. Calisor gasped in disgust when he saw yellow ooze spilling from their eyes, gushing from their mouths, dripping from their ears. One after another, they collapsed, choking on the filth surging up from within them.

"Eoswain!" Calisor cried out to the Celestian, as though she were unaware of the plight of the elven wizards. He saw now that she was far from idle, that she'd raised up an arcane shell around the dais. Only three people were within its reach, however. Calisor, Eoswain, and the sobbing huddle that was Reiliur. Calisor started to reach for his friend, but then he saw a sight that made him freeze in terror.

The gates were collapsing, disintegrating by the corruption that emerged from the portals. But something else emerged from one of them, ere it was destroyed completely. Calisor knew that he screamed when he saw that squamous bulk drag itself across the laboratory on slimy tendrils. Its entire substance was in flux, shifting and distorting as though it were groping about for some shape to call its own. Its ropy limbs plucked dying wizards from the ground and smashed them against the floor in an exhibition of mindless rage. Over and again it battered their bodies, brutalizing them until they were as shapeless as itself.

"What is it? In Ohmpek's name, what is *it*?" Calisor cried out, in his fright invoking the name of a god he hadn't called upon since childhood. The loathsome horror reared back and seemed to look at him, though he could see no semblance of eyes or any other features upon its shifting bulk.

Or did he? For now it seemed that a monstrous visage was oozing up from the depths of the entity. A ferocious face with rows of sharp fangs and a leonine mane. Calisor started when he realized what he was seeing. Another fragment from childhood, the legendary manticore his mother would tell him stories about when he was bad. The atrocity was trying to shape itself into a manticore, match itself to the monster of his oldest fears.

"Don't gaze upon it!" Eoswain commanded Calisor. Her hand slapped against his forehead, and instantly everything went black. He knew some spell of blindness had been cast upon him, but from the sounds around him, whatever was happening was nothing he wanted to see.

The monster from the gate howled and raged, at first with the thrumming roar Calisor imagined a manticore to sound like, but then it became a slopping sussuration like a mire trying to suck down a boot. He could hear the thing thrashing about, smashing dying elves and shattering arcane apparatus. Its oozing gait drew ever nearer the dais.

Calisor bit down on his hand to keep from screaming when he sensed that the protective barrier was gone. The taste of blood somehow steadied him. A sense of reality in a place that had swiftly been consumed by unreality.

"I abjure you, atrocity of the void!" Eoswain shouted. "Foulness without form! Malignance without mind! I abjure you!"

Calisor felt his skin prickle as Eoswain unleashed her arcane might against the intruder from beyond. He was staggered by the amount of power she focused against the thing. No creature could withstand such an onslaught. Yet in this, he was mistaken. A moment later, he heard her shout another invocation. "Relent! By the ten thousand virtues of Uhlrah and the seven judgments of Woe, forsake the flesh you've stolen!"

Again there was a tremendous surge of magic. The glottal howls of the entity persisted however. Calisor wondered how much more Eoswain could do to it. How much longer she could keep it away. He thought of the tentacles coiling about him, smashing him against the floor until he was only a bloody smear.

"The Prison of Darklight be upon you!" Eoswain cried out. Even in his blindness, Calisor sensed the darkness intensify. For a moment, he felt as though his heart would burst from the fear that gripped him. Then the moment passed.

Vision returned to Calisor as quickly as it had been taken away. He gazed across the shambles that had been the laboratory. The wizards were all dead, most of their bodies utterly destroyed. The portals were naught but steaming filth piled on the floor. The wonderful dome was cracked, its enchantments broken, its opaque surface now simply a charred gray. The Scrying Star was shattered, shards of it scattered all around the dais.

Calisor saw Reiliur sitting beside the broken sphere, his hands cradling several of the largest fragments. There was a dazed, distant expression on his face, and his eyes were as empty as those of a doll. Calisor shuddered to see his teacher in such a state. He took hold of his shoulders and tried to shake him into awareness. "Reiliur Ythriil!" he called to him, hoping he'd respond to his own name.

"We must leave him for now." Calisor turned when Eoswain spoke. He saw her down on the floor, cautiously circling a quivering mass of darkness. "We must take this away. Put it somewhere it can never break free."

"Isn't it trapped in your spell?" Calisor didn't so much ask a question as beg for confirmation.

Eoswain stared at the thing in disgust. "The darklight imprisons it only for the moment. It defied my other spells, so I resorted to this. Where it comes from, all is darklight. It is trapped because it is absorbing its own prison. When it is finished, it will be free." She shook her head. "Calisor, we can't let this evil escape into Pannithor."

"But what *is* it?" Calisor was at the very edge of the same madness he saw in Reiliur's eyes.

"Even I cannot say," Eoswain told him. "The Celestians have encountered these beings before, when we ventured into worlds where only such horrors can thrive. They have no shape or substance of their own. These they must consume from others. They shape themselves from the fears of those they set upon. They take substance from those they devour." She pointed at the pulsating mass of darklight. "This... the physicality it took over, was a Celestian. The only one who was so far along the transference that it could emerge into Pannithor."

Calisor shivered at the ghastly explanation. His mind reeled from the abomination that they'd brought into the world. "It must never get free," he agreed. His thoughts raced to a solution. "The Scarlet Sanctum!" he exclaimed. "Will the trap hold it long enough to take it there?"

"We must make it hold," Eoswain said. She frowned when she saw Calisor glance back at Reiliur. "We have to attend to this first before we can try to help him. This horror can't be allowed to go free."

Calisor nodded. He led the way while Eoswain followed, using her magic to levitate the trapped abomination. Down through the Tower of Heaven and into the depths beneath the structure they traveled. Calisor found it impossible to keep from looking back. Every step he took brought the same nagging dread. Would the magic hold it? Was now the moment when it would break free?

At last, they stood before the great gemstone that Thaieweil Avasharr discovered long ago. Calisor drew forth the crystal gauntlet that was the only key to the Scarlet Sanctum. Then a new terror filled him. "Eoswain! No magic can endure within the Sanctum! The moment the horror is sent in there, your trap will disappear!"

Eoswain looked at the quivering mass of darkness. "It will break anyway. We must send the thing into the Sanctum. Lock it away forever."

Calisor set upon himself the most potent spells he knew, incantations so potent that only the most desperate elf would ever draw upon them. He heightened his own speed, quickening his body so that every heartbeat consumed a day of his vitality. His entire being was charged with magic. When he tried to speak, his words were just a blur that ran together in an unintelligible squeak. He focused his mind and sent his thoughts to Eoswain instead. "After I open the door, you must send the thing inside."

The elf didn't hesitate, for with each moment, his speed was increasing, devouring more of his lifespan. Calisor let the crystal gauntlet stab into his flesh and contort itself into the key-shape. He pressed the lock and the Sanctum opened.

Immediately, the mass of darkness shot past Calisor as Eoswain used her arcane power to thrust it into the Sanctum. The trap vanished the moment it crossed the threshold, but the impetus of its momentum propelled the abomination onward. Even then, it spun about and tried to rush back through the door in all its shapeless horror. Only Calisor's quickened speed enabled him to rip off the crystal gauntlet and hurl it into the Sanctum as the entrance snapped shut again. He trembled as he thought of the nightmarish thing locked inside the gigantic gemstone along with the only key to its prison.

"No power in this world can ever release it," Calisor stated as he banished the spell that had quickened him.

Eoswain's visage was disturbed by his choice of words. "It isn't the powers of this world we must fear, but those from another."

They left the Scarlet Sanctum and climbed back into the Tower of Heaven. Calisor assured Eoswain that he would have the passageway leading down to the prison sealed and guarded by the strongest wards know to elves. No one would ever find the place. Except for some of the Celestians, himself, and Reiliur, the only others who even knew the place existed had been killed during the ritual.

"Then we should be safe," Eoswain said as they returned to the laboratory. She stopped and pointed at the dais. Calisor saw at once what had changed. Reiliur was gone.

Calisor rushed to the dais. He saw that the pieces of the Scrying Star were also gone. "Maybe he recovered his wits," he suggested to Eoswain. "He might have taken the fragments of the Scrying Star to repair it."

"The Scrying Star is beyond repair," Eoswain told him. "I was the one who destroyed it. When you broke the contact, Reiliur tried to take your place. The effort broke his mind. I'm sorry, Calisor, but I don't think anything could heal the madness he brought into himself." She gestured at the twisted wreckage of the Scrying Star's frame. "I had to destroy it so that no one else would be destroyed."

"But how will we reestablish contact with the Celestians?" Calisor asked. "How will we rebuild the Circle of Heaven?"

Eoswain stared at Calisor, and for the first time, he noted the emptiness, the awful loneliness that was in her eyes. "There is no one to contact. There is no reason to rebuild the Circle." She bowed her head. "Before I shattered the Scrying Star, I had a glimpse of what happened on the other side of the transference. Be thankful only one of the horrors came through here. The other side was not so fortunate."

Calisor felt numb when he heard her words. "Then you... the Celestians who already crossed to Pannithor..."

"We are the last," Eoswain said. "There are no others. None to be brought across into this world." He watched her as she slowly left the laboratory. He wondered if she was going to look for Reiliur. He wondered if she would find him. Perhaps it would be better if the mad elf were never seen again.

Calisor was silent for a long time. Dawn was shining down through the broken dome before he stirred and started from the room. In only a few hours, everything was changed. The future, so filled with hope and promise, had now become dark with tragedy.

As he made his way from the Tower of Heaven, Calisor clung to one fragment of grim reassurance.

Certainly nothing would ever occur in the life of Calisor Fenulian that could exceed the anguish of this night.